FALLEN RACE:
The Inheritance

FALLEN RACE:
The Inheritance

Melissa Saulnier

Northern Gate Publishing

2018

First Printing: 2018

ISBN-10: 1792971338

ISBN-13: 978-1792971334

Northern Gate Publishing
P.O. Box 141475
Anchorage, Alaska 99514

www.NorthernGatePublishing.com

www.JustWriteBusyPen.com

U.S. trade bookstores and wholesalers: Please contact Northern Gate Publishing at:

NorthernGatePublishing@gmail.com

Dedication

To my beautiful children, Veronica Lynn Bailey, and Ronald Coy Bailey Jr. To my amazing grandchildren, Treyton, Tyler, Kylie, and their parents, Veronica and Matt. To my amazing grandchildren Emma, and Preston and their parents, Buddy (Ronald Jr.) and Heather Christine Miller Bailey.

And, to my mother, Barbara Jean Smith, who instilled a love of reading. Thanks, mom.

Without your support and patience, I would have never achieved my dream. I love you. Thank you.

Contents

Prologue 2

Chapter One...5

Chapter Two 10

Chapter Three 13

Chapter Four..17

Chapter Five...22

Chapter Six 27

Chapter Seven 29

Chapter Eight...35

Chapter Nine..40

Chapter Ten 44

Chapter Eleven...47

Chapter Twelve...51

Chapter Thirteen..54

Chapter Fourteen 59

Chapter Fifteen 63

Chapter Sixteen..66

Chapter Seventeen...71

Chapter Eighteen...75

Chapter Nineteen 79

Chapter Twenty 83

Chapter Twenty One 90

Chapter Twenty Two...96

Chapter Twenty Three..100

Chapter Twenty Four 106

Chapter Twenty Five 112

Chapter Twenty Six..115

Chapter Twenty Seven 119

Chapter Twenty Eight 122

Chapter Twenty Nine...127

Chapter Thirty 132

Chapter Thirty One 138

Chapter Thirty Two 141

Chapter Thirty Three 147

Chapter Thirty Four..152

Chapter Thirty Five...155

Chapter Thirty Six 159

Chapter Thirty Seven 164

Chapter Thirty Eight..169

Chapter Thirty Nine...172

Chapter Forty..176

Chapter Forty One 180

Chapter Forty Two 185

Chapter Forty Three 187

Chapter Forty Four...193

Chapter Forty Five..196

Chapter Forty Six 198

Chapter Forty Seven 202

Chapter Forty Eight...207

Chapter Forty Nine...212

Chapter Fifty..219

Chapter Fifty One...222

Chapter Fifty Two...226

Chapter Fifty Three...231

Chapter Fifty Four...237

Chapter Fifty Five..241

Chapter Fifty Six...243

Chapter Fifty Seven...249

Chapter Fifty Eight..258

Chapter Fifty Nine..260

Chapter Sixty...266

Chapter Sixty One..268

Chapter Sixty Two..271

Chapter Sixty Three...277

Chapter Sixty Four..283

Chapter Sixty Five...289

Chapter Sixty Six..291

Prologue

Alex surveyed the white and red striped lighthouse on the bluff as the vessel made its way into the crystal-clear waters of Westonville Bay. In the distance, St. Francis Abbey built into the cliff rose high above the pine trees. Meadow Manor and the two-hundred-year-old vineyard sat in a unique southerly location facing the river between the foothills overlooking Westonville and the sun-drenched Bay.

Victoria wondered how Alex would react to the antediluvian proof she was prepared to show him. Traditionally, the Abbey always kept the Historical Society of Westonville at arm's length. The Westonville Historical Society would be livid if they knew Victoria was going to share something with Alex she hadn't shared with them. If that wasn't enough, she was about to shoot an arrow at the heart of a comprehensive belief system.

When the vessel reached the port, Alex was surprised to see a tiny solitary figure waiting for him at the end of the pier. Her small frame stood proud, wrapped in a black wool coat, and a red silk scarf billowed behind her in the wind. Alex recognized her as President of Westonville Historical Society from photos he'd seen in their journal. Unexpected excitement surged through him. She was going to reveal something incredible, and she'd chosen to share it with him.

She's greeting me personally.

Victoria Munroe was a dynamo persona in Westonville, not only as a trusted friend of the Historical Society but also as an influential family name in the community. The preservation of a way of life protecting the traditions of the Abbey and every family or business who had made the coastal town their home.

"Alex Mirabelli, I assume?" Victoria said as Alex approached her on the pier.

"Guilty as charged." Smiling, he took her fragile hand in his. "Victoria, I am intrigued and glad you called me."

"And I am grateful you came." Her voice was surprisingly strong for an eighty-two-year-old and reflected the confidence of a wizened woman. "It isn't often I've had the privilege to consult with an astronomer such as yourself. Follow me. We'll take my car."

Victoria guided him to a chauffeured Mercedes. Fresh air blew across the bay, whipping a stinging spray of salty mist through the air. Once inside the car, Victoria confided, "I must admit I expected you to look more like a priest. Your attire is very…fresh." Her eyes sparkled with wit and intelligence. She eyed his black slacks, Italian loafers, and turtleneck. "Worldly."

Alex smiled politely. "Thanks, I think."

A professor at the University of Arizona, he didn't wear his robes during the teaching season.

"I've been reading up on your accomplishments. What exactly does a Jesuit priest do at the observatory? I'm not sure I understand."

"My particular brand of science deals with celestial objects, space, and the physical universe as a whole."

"You study the stars."

"I can assure you I study far more than stars."

"Recently, I read that the Vatican has built one of the most powerful telescopes in the world."

"Vatican Advanced Technology Telescope (VATT). The telescope is affectionately titled LUCIFER, which is an acronym for 'Large Binocular Telescope Near-infrared Utility with Camera and Integral Field Unit for Extragalactic Research."

"Science is beginning to sound like a fantasy." Victoria looked out the window as the car drove through a large iron gate. "We have arrived."

Victoria led him past the manor and to the winery. Inside the dimly lit stone structure rows of enormous oak casks sat on their edge. The air was thick with the fragrance of oak and fermenting grapes. Alex followed Victoria through the winery and into the cellar where bottled wine aged on specially built shelves. Finally, they arrived at an arched wooden door. Victoria took a key from a silver chain around her neck and unlocked the door.

Hesitating, Alex walked through the door.

He found himself in a stone chamber whose walls were lined with bookshelves. Persian carpets covered wood floors. Leather books filled the shelves and gave the room a sense the guest might be going back a couple of centuries in time.

Alex raised his eyes and stared in wonder at the magnificent star-studded constellation painted on the curved ceiling. Ophiuchus, the Serpent Bearer.

"This is my private space, Alex. Very few have ever crossed the threshold."

"Thank you for inviting me. It is an honor."

He followed Victoria to a sitting area and took a seat. Alex felt amused that the tiny senior woman chose to stand. She did not want him to see her weakness. She studied Alex.

She had been looking forward to this moment. The time had arrived for her to reveal the secret to another human being.

"Alex," she began. "I have brought you here to show you something more astounding than anything you have ever seen. I believe you will find it stunning. I am requesting your secrecy. It must be kept in the strictest of confidence. I want your solemn vow of silence. Do you agree?"

Alex held his hand up and gave a nod of agreement. She locked the door.

"I have brought you here today to show you something I discovered long ago. It is something that will cause you to question everything you thought you understood. It is the substance of myths and fairy tales. Now that I am aging, I have come to you specifically because I believe you may have the key to understanding its origin. It is so astounding it could disrupt if the information and knowledge are placed in the wrong hands. Soon, I will no longer be the only person to carry this truth. You also will know."

Victoria stood and pushed a book on the shelf. The shelf slid sideways to reveal a spiral staircase leading down into the darkness. Alex glanced around the room. Things were becoming strange.

Victoria carefully led him down the tight winding stair and into a long stone passage. At the end of the tunnel, once again, she took the key from her chain and opened a door leading into a cavern. Alex ducked his head and walked through the narrow doorway.

Electric lights strung along the ceiling, emitted an eerie glow. It took a second for Alex's eyes to adjust. When the room came into focus, his breath sucked in sharply, and a small sound escaped his lips. Fear. The sound of fear.

Chapter One

Kaira Munroe gazed up at the manor. One of the most stunning estates in Westonville, built with over forty rooms, a winery, and a small horse stable overlooking the vineyard and the Bay, it was a sight to behold.

Grandmother, I love you, she thought. *Why didn't you contact me sooner?*

She sat at the entrance a minute longer then continued along the road leading to the circular courtyard and sprawling front entry. The great fountain in the center of the court jarred the visitors from their reality. Sensational, she decided, staring at the giant creatures rising from the basin. She parked her aqua blue VW and stumbled, climbing out of the car. If drama is what her grandmother intended, she'd accomplished her work.

On the other side of the fountain, Kaira jerked to a stop, staring at the creature that loomed out of the center of the basin.

Was it an angel? Or something more sinister?

Three towering winged creatures circled each other in different stages of flight, until the final being's wings fully extended, and arms lifted high with his sword in hand prepared to impale the enormous skeleton beneath his feet. Writing on a metal plate caught Kaira's attention. מִילְפָנ

"Nephilim." A voice spoke to her from behind. He had an Italian accent. "Shocking, aren't they?"

Kaira lowered her gaze and saw an older man with gray hair standing behind her. He wore a black suit and looked uncomfortable in it. "I've never heard of them."

"Most people haven't. My name is Umberto DiCecco," he continued, "I'm here to welcome you to Meadow Manor." He pulled a list from his pocket. "If you don't mind, what is your name?"

"Of course. Kaira Munroe."

Immediately, the man reached out, took her hand, and kissed it. "I am so sorry. I did not know who you were."

I hardly know who I am, Kaira thought, advancing up the stone steps leading inside. *I guess I am the last of the Munroe family, but I barely remember my grandmother*. Kaira wore a simple black dress and a string of pearls her mother had given her. One of the few things she possessed from her family who had died in a fatal car accident.

"The invitation said it was a Wake," Kaira said. "I hope I've dressed appropriately."

"You look just fine. Besides, your grandmother wouldn't have thought of this as a Wake." Umberto carefully crossed her name off the list and placed it back inside his jacket. "It is a great honor to meet Victoria's granddaughter." He said. "You've been here before as a child?"

Kaira gazed at the fountain. The only vaguely familiar thing she'd seen so far. It had haunted her dreams. "I am sad to say I've not spent much time with my grandmother. There was something about a family feud. I never quite understood."

"No? How sad." Umberto seemed genuine. "But, you are a fan of angels?"

Kaira had always enjoyed the stories her father had told her about angels and the stars. And, there were chronic nightmares. She'd continually been challenged by what her father seemed to believe so easily, angels and aliens, life from the stars. She thought of the art painted in all the churches across Europe - Michelangelo and Da Vinci. Kaira felt more comfortable discussing the science of stars and the power of the brain.

"I guess I'm more of a realist," Kaira replied. "I do better with science."

"But science is beginning to look like fantasy; you might be surprised."

Kaira smiled. "They say science is stranger than fiction."

"Well, I am glad you are here." Umberto looked out over the vineyard beyond the courtyard. "It is fabulous, isn't it? The best wine in the country. You will enjoy the countryside."

"I certainly intend to," she replied. "Do you know what my grandmother planned for this evening? The invitation said it was a celebration of life and a disclosure. I wonder what she meant?"

"Everyone has been asking me the same question." He shook his gray head. "Victoria was special, unique, clever, and sometimes very secretive. No one knows what is happening. Not even her priest.

She loved mystery and counted on the sensationalism to bring everyone together. There are probably over a hundred guests here at the Wake tonight. People from businesses in town, some from the Abbey, but most are from the Westonville Historical Society and St. Francis Abbey."

Victoria had handwritten the invitations before her death. She knew she was dying and intentionally invited every person that was present. It didn't take much to persuade people to attend her Wake. She had been very influential in America and Italy.

Kaira stood in the courtyard entrance, eagerly studying the creatures in the fountain. She wondered what her grandmother planned to give to the Westonville Historical Society during the Wake. She moved along the circular entrance and rounded the bend to a grassy pathway. She gazed at the massive stone manor in wonder. The structure was beautiful, with a suggestion of centuries past.

Meadow Manor resembled something out of an Italian wine magazine, with tiled roofs and multiple chimneys. Tall cypress trees lined the drive, a definitive Italian influence. In the distance, past the vineyard and across the river overlooking the Bay, rose St. Francis Abbey above the trees clinging to the cliffside. The entire scene was old world.

As Kaira approached the winery, the building offered its personality. Dramatic overlooking the vineyard, the structure was enormous and housed hundreds of casks six feet in diameter. Behind the winery, a thick veil of fog rose from the river in a slow-moving cloud. *Haunting,* Kaira thought. The effect was ethereal, and Kaira expected some creature like those in the fountain might rise from the fog at any moment.

Walking back to Meadow Manor and the entrance, Kaira prepared to walk through the large front doors and into the Wake. She had an uneasy sense as she neared the entrance that something extraordinary was about to take place.

***

Alex exuded the confidence of a well-educated Jesuit priest. Fifteen years earlier, he had been the top student at the Vatican Observatory, a scientific institute of the Holy See subject to the

Governorate of the Vatican City State. Alex spent the first five years of his classic study at the Observatory at the Papal Summer Residence at Castel Gandolfo in the Alban Hills 35 kilometers southeast of Rome. Later, he transferred to the Vatican Observatory Research Group in Tuscan, Arizona. An astronomer and mathematician, he studied scientific data and implications on the calendar.

Finally, the brilliant Jesuit had discovered a secret.

Unique in the world of Jesuit priests, Alex was a maverick of sorts. His studies had given him insight into the past and future revelation regarding stars, planets, constellations, and ancient meaning before the deluge. He was a brilliant gem in the astronomer's treasure trove of geniuses. His knowledge of classical texts regarding the universe and scientific breakthroughs had created intrigue among scholars.

Alex could read and absorb information with almost an eidetic memory and had an astounding knowledge of the world and universe. His passion for understanding surpassed that of men his age. For the past few years, he lived in Arizona, attributing his choice to the fact that LUCIFER was the most powerful telescope device in the world with the ability to see into black space like no other. Once a year, he returned to Italy and the Vatican to report his findings. During these times, Alex searched through the private archives in the Vatican library, which consisted of thousands and thousands of ancient texts.

Alex had found a connection between pre-deluge and post-deluge events. His curiosity to understand what had been going on in the universe during the time before the flood had become an obsession. It would be easy to imagine him as a robed priest who was somewhat of a geek. However, he was nothing of the sort. He chose instead to wear fashionable clothing and move in wealthy circles that would further his studies and passion.

A year ago, Alex had surprised some of his wealthy influential partners with the announcement that he was on the verge of a discovery that would turn the world on its head. He wanted to reveal a deeper understanding of what was going on before the deluge, what kind of beings were on the earth then, and how had they reached past antediluvian times and into our world. The question? Were there portals in the heavens, and had beings traveled these portals? The bible called the beings angels. Other ancient texts called them gods. Some called them aliens.

His curiosity into the past had created some friction with the Vatican and the Holy See. However, surrounded by influential, wealthy partners, he spoke freely. All the ancient texts were trying to tell a similar story. His open mind came from the desire to understand.

Alex threw himself into his studies and dropped out of contact for a while. It was then, Victoria had sent him the invitation to meet, and he'd surfaced just over a year before she died. Their meeting had not been in vain.

Chapter Two

The man eyed his reflection in the mirror behind the bar. He sat on a barstool inside Friar's Deck Tavern in the small coastal town of Westonville. He was tired from the journey, having sailed into town from the Dominican Republic. He took a sip of his beer and watched the bartender cleaning beer glasses.

The sailor was of average height, athletic, and muscular, but he looked older than his years. He had salt and pepper gray hair at forty-two and an air of confidence that came with a few life lessons under his belt. His skin was tanned and creased from working in the sun on a sailboat.

Tonight, he dressed in a black caterer's jacket with a logo on the pocket, tan pants, and running shoes built for comfort. Pirates weren't as fearsome and potent as in the past, but he could fit in anywhere, and no one would know the difference.

He rarely dressed up, but this would be a special evening.

"Can I get you something to eat?" asked the bartender. He was cleaning up after a group of men who had been talking about the dunes and bluffs along the edges of the Bay.

"I'm fine, but I would have another beer."

The tavern was empty, and the sailor could feel the curiosity of the bartender.

"So, what brings you to town, stranger?"

He must have seen the sailors tattoo beneath his long sleeve jacket.

"Just visiting friends."

"Didn't mean to seem nosy. Just that we've had a rash of bad luck lately. Modern treasure seekers are tearing up our bluffs and dunes."

"Ah. I overheard the men at the bar talking about that."

"The American Shore and Beach Preservation Association is finally taking note that we're losing shoreline due to tourists digging up our bluffs along the Bay arms. It's always worse after hurricane season."

"I read that a man and his wife found a hoard of Spanish pieces of eight waiting to be scratched out of the sand with bare fingers. The stuff of pirate legends." He said.

"Well, that is the problem. For many people, hurricane season is the time to board up windows and dread the worst. But, professional and amateur treasure seekers see it as the time to hit the beaches and hunt for lost riches. The treasure coast reaches from the east down to Florida and into the Caribbean. But, what am I saying? You're a sailor."

"I have to admit. I sailed north to escape the Irma and Jose hurricane season."

"I've heard that a good hurricane can bring a slice of shoreline back to where it was in the 1700s, pulling all the sand away and uncovering secrets. Of course, the high tide after the storm will dump several feet of sand back on the beach, so you have to be quick. Basic rules of treasure hunting on our beaches include finders keepers, but don't dig in the dunes and protected areas. Authorities are cracking down pretty hard on offenders."

"Who were the men at the bar earlier?" asked the sailor.

"That was the Treasure Coast Archeological Society, TCAS. Mitch and his buddies. Many marine archeologists call treasure seekers "plunderers," but professionals give more discoveries to museums and make more historical finds because their ventures pay for new searches they couldn't otherwise finance."

"Sounds like there might be conflict."

"Right. The Westonville Historical Society in our coastal town is very protective and secretive about what they know and what they've found over time. They're anti-treasure seekers, even with locals who don't follow their protocol."

He knew all about the ten commandments of the TCAS. "What is Westonville Historical Society protocol for locals then?"

"Never dig on the bluffs and dunes, hand over your find immediately, and expect nothing in return unless you've lived in this town for 50 years."

He smiled. That's why he was a pirate. He didn't follow the rules. Treasure and shipwrecks weren't the only things that surfaced after hurricanes. He was looking for something far more sinister. He looked at his watch. "Gotta jet."

He paid the bill and turned to go as a group of fishermen stumbled in wearing raingear that smelled like oil and gas.

"Bloody newcomers." One of the men said loud enough for everyone to hear. He stared at him as he passed and sat on a barstool.

Two other fishermen stood between the stranger and the door. "Another nosy tourist?"

The stranger attempted to step around the men, but one of the men put his arm up and blocked him across his chest. "Where do you think you're going? You one of those bloody treasure-seeking vermin tearing up our cliffs?"

The stranger looked at the man's dirty arm on his catering jacket.

"Take your arm off my shirt. I'm not your guy."

The fisherman shoved his arm, pushing him back onto the barstool.

"I saw you down by the lighthouse digging on the bluffs. You're wasting your time and ruining our bluffs."

He reminded himself he had something more important to do. The simple-minded fishermen had the wrong man.

"What's that on your neck?"

The stranger's muscles tensed. The Hebrew symbol on his neck was unfamiliar to most people, and he wasn't about to tell these men what it meant. The man at the bar spoke up, "Let him go, Joey. He's just a cook."

The fishermen squinted at the logo on the sailor's shirt and backed off. He seemed to be satisfied and turned his attention to the bartender.

Chapter Three

The house looked like something you might see in Europe. Kaira stepped inside, and her gaze shifted to the gilded iron staircase banister topped with rich oak curved railing to the left of the entrance. Nearby a long table covered with red tablecloth stood on a large silk rug in the center of the foyer. A young man dressed in a suit signed in guests. To the right, a hallway led to the banquet hall.

Guests entered Meadow Manor from the front driveway and fountain or the lobby on the riverside of the house. Guests arriving for the Wake gathered in the banquet hall for cocktails and hors d'oeuvres.

Kaira didn't remember visiting the manor often as a child. She had a vague memory of the fountain outside, but that was it. The taste of bitterness stung the back of her throat. Her family had never been a part of her grandmother's world of wealth and influence. Strangely, instead of the quiet, reverent hush of a funeral and mourners, the place was alive with voices echoing through the enormous rooms with high ceilings and tall glass windows.

She moved through the hall and series of rooms toward the reception area. The long banquet hall was two stories high. A colossal fireplace took up the entire wall on one end; it's decorative mantle carved with images of angels in battle. A caption above the fireplace read, "Men of renown, heroes of old." On the long wall, a tapestry hung, reaching to the floor, about ten feet high. A young David held up the severed head of the nine-foot giant, Goliath. On one side, an army of Philistines fled in one direction while behind him, the Hebrew Israelites cheered. Kaira wondered if it was an original tapestry copied from the French artist, Paul Gustave Christophe Doré.

Security guards stood at each end of the room as guests wandered past the buffet table full of appetizers and drinks. Kaira drank a bottle of Perrier and walked back out to the entryway, looking for the music room and salon where guests would assemble for the celebration of her grandmother's life.

Just outside the music room, a young lady was handing out small gift boxes and programs to each guest. Kaira smiled and introduced herself. The young woman looked at her list.

"You are Kaira Munroe, Victoria's granddaughter?"

"Yes. I am."

"You have a special gift. Father Murphy asked that you open the box right away."

"Oh. Of course, and thank you."

Kaira took the program, and the gift then glanced through the doors. At least fifty people were already seated with room for a hundred or more. She opened her box and was surprised to find a sleek new phone with something that looked like an earpiece. She looked puzzled. Seeing her expression, the greeter came out from behind the table to help.

"This phone was built especially for you." She said, pushing the power button. Then she looked in the box and found the earpiece. "This is wireless technology. It will allow you to listen to the app privately as you wander throughout Meadow Manor."

"How clever."

"Your grandmother was quite savvy for a woman her age. You have about an hour before the celebration of life begins. Your app works like a GPS. When you stand in certain locations, you will hear directions and information your grandmother pre-recorded for your advantage and pleasure. I hope you enjoy it."

Kaira turned and looked back at the entry, which was now in front of her. On the left, a glassed winter atrium allowed natural light to filter into the room. To the right was a long gallery that led to the library. She turned on the app, and blueprints of the manor popped up on the screen with an arrow indicating where she was standing. A woman's voice sounded in her earpiece. She realized it was her grandmother.

"Good evening, Kaira. Welcome to Meadow Manor. You have activated your app, and that means that I have passed on from this world, and you are at my celebration of life. I wanted to be your guide. I regret that we have missed spending time together. But, I'm not going to focus on that. Everywhere you go on the grounds, an arrow will follow like google map. I have recorded key information at certain points. My voice will activate when you stand at these locations."

Kaira was impressed that her grandmother had gone to so much trouble.

"As President of the Westonville Historical Society, it is my delight to share the secrets of Meadow Manor with you. Please do not lose your phone and earpiece. Guard it closely."

Kaira stepped from the entrance to the crossway at the gallery hall and watched the arrow. A sign on an easel announced that Alex Mirabelli, an astronomer from Tucson, Arizona, would be speaking on behalf of the late Victoria Munroe. Kaira looked on her program and read that Alex was a Jesuit priest who worked at the Thomas J. Bannan Astrophysics Facility, which housed the Vatican Advanced Technology Telescope.

She turned down the gallery hall and stood in front of a painting. Immediately her grandmother's voice began describing the piece where she stood.

"The Cantino World Map is showing Portuguese discoveries in the east and west is named after Alberto Cantino. He was an agent for the Duke of Ferrara, who successfully smuggled it from Portugal to Italy in 1502. It shows the islands of the Caribbean and Florida coastline, as well as Africa, Europe, and Asia. This is one of the earliest known maps.'

Kaira slowly drifted down the hall toward the library, intrigued by the ancient maps. Victoria's voice interrupted again in front of another framed piece.

"Johannes Ruysch, an explorer, cartographer, astronomer, and painter from the Low Countries, produced the second oldest known printed representation of the New World. The Ruysch map was published and widely distributed in 1507. This map documents Christopher Columbus' discoveries as well as that of John Cabot, including information from Portuguese sources and Marco Polo's account."

Kaira enjoyed listening to her grandmother's soothing voice but had to admit it was uncanny that she was no longer alive and present physically.

"As you know, I am an avid fan of history and astronomy. I have collected art, books, and ancient maps my entire life in hopes of bringing understanding and knowledge to Westonville and you. As you move to the library, look to the east wall, and you will see a large collection of books, I want to share specifically with you."

Kaira entered the library doors and stood stunned. Like the banquet hall, the library ceiling was two stories tall. A solid black oak mantle intricately carved graced the fireplace. Above the mantle, an intriguing tapestry depicting angels looked out over the library. Ornate iron railing lined a walkway around the second floor, and books filled the shelves floor to ceiling on both levels.

Four chairs and a couch upholstered in luxurious red velvet fabric gathered around a silk rug. Tall electric candelabras stood on each side of the fireplace as well as along the second floor, emanating a golden glow on the wood and glass-enclosed bookcases.

Kaira walked toward the shelves along the east wall. The symbol she had seen on the fountain repeated on a plaque above the shelves. Umberto had said it was the Hebrew name for Nephilim. Her grandmother's voice interrupted her thoughts.

"The books on these shelves are quickly becoming one of the fastest-growing interests in the world of religious and non-religious alike. Scholars who study Babylonian, Sumerian, Kabbalah, Torah, Bible, and other ancient texts are speaking out more forcefully than ever before regarding the deluge and other antediluvian activity, angels, and beings from other planets."

Extraterrestrials? My grandmother believed in aliens?

"Kaira, the Vatican has always held ancient texts and secrets that only a few select have had access to, until recently. The Vatican Secret Archives is the central repository in the Vatican City for all the acts promulgated by the Holy See. The Pope, as Sovereign of Vatican City, owns the archives until his death or resignation, with ownership passing to his successor. The Secret Archives became separated from the Vatican library in the 17th century. Scholars had limited access to them until 1881 when Pope Leo XIII opened them to exclusive researchers. There are an estimated 53 miles of shelving and 35000 volumes in the selective catalog alone. So, as you can see, many secrets are hidden from the public. Some of the books on the shelves in front of you are replicas of information smuggled out of the Vatican in the late 18th century." Her grandmother chuckled. *"Please don't ask how I've acquired them."*

Great. My grandmother is a thief who believes in extraterrestrials.

Chapter Four

The Local Steam Espresso was pleasantly full at 6 pm for a Friday. A newspaper sat on a table next to two leather chairs that filled a cozy corner. The front-page article was dedicated to Victoria Munroe and her service over 60 years at Westonville Historical Society.

The Westonville Historical Society's President, Victoria Munroe, is being celebrated and remembered as a leader and advocate for preserving the Westonville heritage by her family, friends, and colleagues, after her death. Victoria Munroe died Sunday, October 8, 2017, of an apparent aneurysm while working in the winery.

"It is with profound sadness mixed with gratefulness that we celebrate the long and full life of our friend and colleague, Victoria Munroe," said Father Murphy of St. Francis Abbey, chairman of the WHS Board of Trustees. "The entire Westonville Historical Society family mourns this loss, and our deepest sympathies are with the families and friends who treasured her life."

Her life is remembered and celebrated by her granddaughter, Kaira Munroe; St. Francis Abbey and priest, Father Murphy; friend and companion, Umberto DiCecco; Westonville Historical Society; Jesuit priest and Astronomer at the Vatican Observatory in Arizona, Alex Mirabelli; and a host of friends and colleagues throughout the state and country.

A Celebration of Life is to be held at Meadow Manor, her beloved home and sanctuary. Alex Mirabelli, Astronomer, and colleague will speak regarding her love of theoretical cosmology and the origin of the universe, among other issues. The foundation of Jesuits remembers her as "a real scholar who had a passion for talking about faith and science. Her gentle sense of humor was sometimes self-effacing, but not afraid of speaking difficult truths."

Speaker and friend Alex Mirabelli began his studies at the University of California Los Angeles and Cambridge University in England, where he worked with Stephan Hawking, the famed British theoretical physicist, and cosmologist and received his doctorate in astrophysics. After studies at the Jesuit School of Theology at Berkley, he was ordained as a Jesuit priest and now works as an Astronomer at the Vatican Observatory in Tucson, Arizona.

Also, Alex Mirabelli is known for his dedication to the study of antediluvian relics and ancient texts supporting activity before the deluge. He is sought after as a retreat presenter of antique maps, constellation studies, and pre-deluge theories.

The Celebration of Life is closed to the public.

***

Castel Gandolfo, Albano Laziale, Italy

For more than four decades, Giovanni Fiorelli, leader of archeological digs around Castel Gandolfo, had been the primary Jesuit archeologist and gatekeeper who, despite his years, remained an active member of the antiquities community in Italy, England and around the world.

The center of his work, 25 Kilometers Southeast of Rome in the Lazio region, occupied a height on the Alban Hills overlooking Lake Albano, in the town of Albano Laziale. Within the town's boundaries lay the Apostolic Palace of Castel Gandolfo, which had served as the summer residence and vacation retreat for the pope.

A beautiful resort area, the town stretched across almost the entire shoreline of Lake Albano, surrounded by villas and cottages built during the 17th century and before.

Castel Gandolfo, was the location of the Specola Vaticana, astronomical research and educational institution supported by the Holy See. The observatory also operated a telescope on Mt. Graham in Tucson, Arizona, USA.

Few were aware that the papal summer residence of almost 400 years had a curious history, serving as a hideout for Jews and other high-profile wards targeted by paparazzi. The place was prominent, and not just because of its long history.

It was here that Emperor Domitian (AD 81-96) once ordered the bloody persecution of early Christians. Roman emperors had come to appreciate the climate it offered at 426 meters (1,400 feet) above sea level, and Domitian had a palace erected here. Around 1200, the Gandolfi family from Genoa, which Castel Gandolfi would later be named after, built a villa here. Since 1596, the central part of what is now the papal summer residence was owned by the Vatican.

As the sun began to set across Lake Albano, Giovanni exited the observatory. He made his way down Via Appia Nuova to the heart of Albano Laziale past villas and cottages to his home. Usually, Giovanni enjoyed the time of year, holidays were approaching, and yet since his conversation with Alex about the recent discovery in a series of caves thought to be an antediluvian tomb full of extraordinary remains, he had been looking over his shoulder. The feeling of profound disquiet followed him day and night.

I wish I hadn't told him.

The extraordinary discovery had plagued Giovanni for the past four months. Now, as he arrived home, he went directly to his private study full of antiquities. He frowned down at the scattered books and maps on his desk. He had the Babylonian, Sumerian, and Kabbalah texts open to the account of the deluge and had marked other passages referring to pre-deluge Nephilim.

Some of the recently discovered caves were large tombs, so-called by the dimensions, a typical element of the megalithic period. In the middle of the tomb-like caves, an enormous granite stele for commemorative purposes carved with text and ornamentation held an opening which led to the center of the series of caves. The bones were found in the middle of the cavern. The walls revealed drawings oriented toward the Milky Way with references to the constellation Ophiuchus.

Giovanni was, of course, very familiar with Genesis, the story of creation, the fall of Adam, and the flood. But, he was particularly intrigued by Genesis chapter six. Typically, he was more likely to be reading academic commentary on cosmology theory. Today, his mind was distracted by the latest connection between earth and the heavens. He had bared his thoughts to Alex knowing that he ran the risk of being accused a lunatic.

Giovanni had started with the Book of Enoch, a story of Nephilim shared with other ancient texts. The book began with the story of the Watchers, then Enoch's journey's through the earth and Sheol, three parables, a book of Noah, a book of the courses of heavenly luminaries, dream-vision, and the conclusion.

One of the most important non-canonical apocryphal works written during the second century B.C.E. having a significant influence on early Christian and Gnostic beliefs, the book was filled with hallucinatory visions of heaven and hell, angels and demons. Giovanni focused on Enoch's concept of fallen angels.

After connecting with Alex and contemplating the recent discoveries along with his collection of information, there was no longer any doubt in his mind regarding the proof he had been searching to find. One contradiction after another had left him at a dead end until the recent discovery in the series of caves. He had made the connection, and now along with Alex, they wondered how best to present it to the world.

He had accepted a disturbing truth. Their work would cause repercussions that could be dangerous, even fatal. It was old news that the Catholic Church could hide historical evidence. But, the new astounding proof of the incredible antediluvian activity before Noah's flood would shift the most entrenched belief systems of the world.

Add to it the distressing discoveries of Alex and his covert work at the Vatican Observatory, Giovanni was no closer to a decision regarding what he should do. Then, Alex had visited with Victoria Munroe and made the surprising decision to bring her into the equation. A decision Giovanni didn't understand. He wondered how much Alex had shared with her before she died.

Alex and Giovanni had communicated by phone a few days ago, but they had come to no real conclusion regarding what to do next. Both Alex and Giovanni had a new respect for the legitimacy of ancient texts and the common thread of stories regarding the creation, the flood, and the reality of other beings the document referred to as angels, demons, Nephilim, demigods, and sons of God.

Alex believed they should be proactive. The world should hear what was coming within the next decades. We need to take the control out of the hands of the wealthiest in the world and make it accessible.

But, Giovanni knew there would be no way to soften the truth and make it palatable. The impact would be threatening.

And Alex had made a vow to keep a secret only he and Victoria knew. But, now with Victoria gone, he was ready to take action for the greater good of the world. All faiths will reconsider their beliefs when the new information surfaces.

Giovanni was aware of the challenge. He knew Alex to be a brilliant astronomer, and his disclosure had been incredible and horrifying. Giovanni reminded himself that every discovery ever made had a similar impact on those who made the discovery. But, none had been as terrifying as what he'd heard and seen when he'd met with Alex.

On a deeper level than the belief that humans were the only life in the universe, was the realization that there might be other life outside our solar system. *I wish I'd never made the discovery*, thought Giovanni. When he had first contacted Alex, his only goal had been to prove that creation was real, there was indeed a flood and humans before the flood were unique and different, living longer than modern man. He had been entirely unprepared when Alex disclosed his findings.

His muscles were tense, and anxiety kept him up at night. A knot of fear clenched in his gut when he thought of releasing the information. Attempting to defuse the tension, he took liberal walks. He meditated and tried to connect with God. His belief in God was more robust than ever. That had been a surprising turn after the recent events. He gathered his thoughts.

A few days from now, after Victoria Munroe's Wake, they planned to speak again. They would make a final decision. He felt the chill of fear still — a cold chill.

Chapter Five

Victoria's elderly voice continued to direct Kaira on her tour. *"The large French doors will lead you to the terrace. From there you can see the winery. Guests schedule wine tasting all year long."*

Kaira walked through the doors and onto the terrace. The stone winery she had seen earlier when she arrived was now directly in front of her.

"Our winery is unique. I hope you enjoy wine as we produce some of the very best along the east coast states."

Sorry, grandmother. I didn't grow up drinking the best wine, thought Kaira. The sprawling winery stretched out in the distance, and the vines made their way down to the river edge, which eventually flowed into the Bay. The building consisted of tan and brown colored stones, and terracotta tiles covered the roof in real Italian form.

"The winery is approximately 8,000 square feet, almost the size of the manor. It is affectionately known as Little Italy."

Kaira had to admit the stone, and decorative cypress trees lining walkways leading to the vineyard caused her to feel as though she was actually in Italy.

"Umberto produces our wine." continued Victoria. *"He is from Piedmont Italy, where he trained with the very best producers of Italian wine. Our climate is similar to hot, dry summers, cold winters, and temperate springs and autumns are common with occasional fog during harvest time. We have a long history of wine production, great respect for tradition, a wave of young, dynamic producers who recognize the potential of the local vineyards. I hope you will follow suit, Kaira."*

Kaira sensed an urgency in Victoria's voice.

"Umberto is best known for a boutique wine he has produced here at Meadow Manor called D&G. It has become one of the favored wines among collectors. We make only 5000 bottles per year and sell only 2000 per year. The price range is around $917 per bottle. Some of our cuttings are from the Nebbiolo, Dolcetto and Moscato Bianco grapes. The most exalted red wine variety of Piedmont is Nebbiolo. This wine is striking to experience because its delicate, pale, brick-red color and floral cherry and rose aromas contrast with somewhat

aggressive, chewy tannins, particularly in wines from Barolo. Because of its structure, you'll find that Nebbiolo wines are a favorite for wine collectors who will happily set aside wines to open them decades later to reveal a delightfully soft and delicate wine."

Kaira wondered if her grandmother just assumed she knew something about wine or if she was subtly trying to educate her. Either way, Kaira was learning about her grandmother and the life she had led. In truth, Kaira was anxious to try the wine produced by the brilliant Umberto.

"Also," Victoria said, *"Umberto produces a Dolcetto wine loved for its lower acidity and soft, fruity flavors of plums, blackberries, and raspberries. Dolcetto wine often has lifted floral aromas of violets and black peppercorn contrast with firm tannin texture that can come across as similar to chocolate."*

She'd never heard of it. It sounded good.

"And last, the highly perfumed Moscato Bianco variety delivers sweet notes of honeydew melon, fresh grape, ripe pear, and mandarin orange all wrapped up in floral winter daphne aromas. Moscato can be made in a range of styles, all with varying degrees of sweetness, from a delicate frizzante to creamy sparkling Asti Spumante, with a dried grape still wine called Passito. Moscato wines are often served and sold in featherweight portions to accentuate the importance of their aromas."

Kaira had devoted the better part of her career to journalism, but it troubled her that she'd never studied or learned how to appreciate fine wine. The appeal of wine for those who collected remained a mystery to her.

She meant no disrespect to her grandmother and the heritage she had built, but she couldn't picture herself buying a $917 bottle of wine. She was happy with a $25 to $30-dollar bottle from Napa Valley.

"Kaira, in the world of fine wine and collecting, wine is revered for the skill of the producer- that is how well a producer works the land from tradition and makes decisions filtered through thousands of hours among the vines. Umberto was born in San Giorgio Monferrato, close to Casale Piedmont, Italy, and he understands the vines. He produces 20,000 bottles of wine per year, and our wine is certified organic since 2004. Low sulfur, no enzymes,

added yeasts, no animal gelatin, and are harvested in 14kg baskets to eliminate bruising. He focuses on finesse, elegance, and authenticity."

She must be joking. Why did people take this all so seriously? In her grandmother's defense, the production was a big business, yet only 20,000 bottles were produced each year. With a cap like that, how could one grow the business?

"D&G stands for David and Goliath. It is a tribute to my love for the underdog."

Kaira thought of the massive tapestry she had seen hanging on the wall in the banquet hall. She felt a bit like David herself. Meadow Manor and everything about it was larger than life. Larger than her life.

"Kaira, I imagine that you of all our family would appreciate David and Goliath. You are a young, vibrant yet vulnerable girl who has had to radiate lethal determination to survive. I've always watched you from a distance. Though family quirks and feuds have separated us, we are very similar you and me. You are more powerful than you know in your fragility."

Her grandmother's thoughts stirred empty loneliness inside Kaira. She had dreamed of seeing her grandmother, but never that it would be a Wake bringing them together. Her grandmother guided her past the terrace to a garden below and a path she'd seen earlier, leading to the winery.

A small group stood in front of the winery, looking up at a phrase painted over the door.

"What does it mean?" asked a woman in a tight black dress with bright red lipstick. "It looks like something from a Runestone."

"It looks similar to the inscription on a metal plate at the fountain." Said Kaira.

The woman eyed Kaira with a look of disdain, snobbery. "That doesn't tell me what it says."

Umberto walked up just then. Perfect timing.

"Well, first of all, it's Hebrew Scripture."

The woman cocked her head. "I didn't know Victoria was religious."

"Oh, I don't think she was religious at all. However, she was deeply spiritual." Said Umberto patiently. "Hebrew reads from right to left, unlike the English language." He pointed to one of the first words beginning right to the left, מִיְלְפָּנ "This word refers to ancient beings. Nephilim."

Heads were nodding. "The entire verse reads, "There were Nephilim in the earth in those days; Mighty men of renown."

The woman in the black dress scowled. "Why in the world would Victoria put that over the winery door?"

She had verbalized Kaira's thoughts. Why in the world those words? What did they have to do with wine? It seemed like a riddle of sorts.

As the group walked away, Kaira could hear the woman muttering, and she chuckled. She had to appreciate her grandmother's eccentricity. Most wealthy people she'd encountered in life had been quirky and eccentric. She could see that Umberto was far more than a producer of wine. He had been his grandmother's friend and possibly her companion. Kaira wondered if that was the case.

Kaira noticed her grandmother was no longer speaking in her earpiece. Umberto stepped up to her side.

"Your grandmother asked me to show you something that none of the other guests are going to see. I believe we have just enough time before the Celebration of Life begins."

"Oh? What might that be?"

"Follow me."

Kaira followed him through the winery entrance, and after looking to see that no one had followed them inside, he slipped down the long hall surrounded by oak casks and into a small area in the back out of sight. He walked to an arched wooden door and pulled a metal key from a lanyard under his shirt. He gave the key to Kaira.

"Open the door."

Kaira pushed the old-fashioned skeleton key into the lock and turned. She stopped taking a moment, uncertain of what to expect. The space behind the door was dark.

Umberto walked in and flicked a light switch. "Please come in."

Kaira inched inside and closed the door. Gradually, soft gas lights began to glow in lovely sconces around the edges of the stone room, revealing a beautiful space. The central area was a library office of sorts, and other rooms branched off into a bedroom and kitchen — an apartment.

"This was your grandmother's private space. I am the only other besides your grandmother who has been in here. Now you are here as she would have wished."

Decorated tastefully with rich dark wood and leather furniture, it was a reflection of Victoria's taste. Shelves lining the walls were full of books, and a large silk rug covered the old floor. On the ceiling, a magnificent painting held her attention.

"What am I looking at?" she asked.

"It's called Ophiuchus, The Serpent Bearer. It is a constellation whose southern portion dips into the dense part of the Milky Way."

"And why was my grandmother interested in this constellation?"

"In time, that will be revealed, I am sure. As I said, Victoria wanted you to know about this room. She has given you the winery. It is separate from the estate, which she has asked the Westonville Historical Society to manage. She was in hopes that the two of you could work together."

The lights flooded the space with a soft glow. Kaira stood in bewilderment.

"She's given me the winery? I know nothing about wine!"

Chapter Six

The stranger arrived at Meadow Manor and checked in with the caterers. He glanced at his watch just as the first guests were arriving. Perfect, right on schedule. He presented his catering card to the chef and made his way toward the bartenders. He would be filling in for one of the servers who had suddenly taken ill.

He had been planning for a year. Tonight's guest list consisted of all the officials representing the Westonville Historical Society whom he despised, but oddly enough, they were not the reason he was at Meadow Manor. In an unusual belt around his waist, a long, flute-like object fit snug in a loop on one side and three vials on the other. With caution, he checked to see that the lids on each bottle were secure.

Guests picked up a cocktail at his station then wandered through the Manor looking at art and antiques Victoria had collected over the years. His heart pounded in his chest as he scanned the people walking through the doors.

Soon, he thought. I hope I'm ready for this.

***

At that moment in southeastern Arizona, Chris, a Jesuit priest, was looking through a new instrument with an evil-sounding name, LUCIFER. The chilled device attached to a telescope, named after the devil, whose name itself means "Morning Star," was helping scientists see how stars were born.

Chris turned pale, and a violent shudder shook him so hard he had to stop pacing and stand still for a moment. The device allowed observations of very distant galaxies that had been impossible to see only a few short years ago.

Now, gazing at the Milky Way about 8,000 light-years away from Earth through clouds that are typically opaque to visible light, could be penetrated. That wasn't all he saw. The unusual weather and recent hurricanes that had ripped through Florida and the Caribbean caused by the plasmatic electromagnetic connection from inbound planets we didn't know existed until now.

The Mayans had known and created a calendar. The Earth was full of warnings from the past. Up all night, Chris worked tirelessly on documenting his discoveries and secretly filing them. The last astronomer who tried to speak out disappeared. Alex and Chris had watched the planet for three years and worried about the substantial damage it could cause Earth during its passage. Alex had named it the "Great Star."

Chris worried his Jesuit friend Alessandro died at the hands of someone in a secret Order who did not want the information revealed. Before he disappeared, Chris asked Alex what Alessandro found, and he replied, "It is the third secret of Fatima, Wormwood." And, when Chris asked how bad the news might be, he had said, "Possibly millions will perish." Then he said, "It's much worse than that. It's worse than you can imagine."

Alessandro, an eminent theologian, and expert on the Catholic Church, Jesuit priest, and professor at the Vatican's Pontifical Biblical Institute, had authored a book, "Chained to the Morning Star." Trained in theology at Louvain, he had received his doctorate in Semitic languages. Was his disappearance the result of his open disclosure of the inbound planet known as Wormwood to the Catholic Church?

Suddenly the nation's oldest planetariums were undergoing significant renovations. Two included in the restoration were Adler Planetarium and Astronomy Museum in Chicago and the Rose Center for Earth and Space in New York.

Why the renovation? Were they updating technology to search for something?

Chapter Seven

Kaira's eyes were drawn to the painting on the ceiling. A towering image of the Serpent Bearer, Ophiuchus, filled the entire center of a light blue sky. In each of his hands, he clung to a serpent. His left hand held the neck close to the head of the snake. The other handheld his tail. His left foot stood on the head of Scorpio with Libra to his left and Sagittarius to his right.

Embellished with a blue background and yellow stars, the nine-foot ceiling curved elegantly along the corners of the room. "The Serpent Bearer." said Kaira, "The painter's brilliant use of his medium created the illusion that the stars are glowing." She stared up at the muscular figure. The paint had not faded with time, and the image held a raw organic strength.

"This particular constellation is associated with the figure of Asclepius. He was the famous healer in Greek mythology. It was one of the constellations first cataloged by the Greek astronomer Ptolemy in the 2nd century. Sometimes it is known as Serpentarius." Umberto said.

Kaira squinted up at the painting. "It is splendid, isn't it?"

"Yes, it is." He continued. "Ophiuchus belongs to the Hercules family of constellations, not the Zodiac. Because it crosses the ecliptic, there have been attempts to include it in our Zodiac."

Kaira saw that the head of the serpent made its way into the Hercules constellation.

"Ophiuchus and Orion have been called the *Star Gates of God and Man*." Said Umberto. "The intersection between Scorpio and Sagittarius where Ophiuchus sits is also known as the *Golden Gate of Heaven*."

Kaira had never made the connection with Orion though she had vaguely studied Ophiuchus and mistakenly thought it was the 13th Zodiac sign.

"The directions of Ophiuchus and Orion offer opposites as they lie 180 degrees across from each other." Umberto shifted and took a different tone. "We must be moving to be on time. "Look here, child. See where the bookshelves have marked the floor very slightly?

Behind the shelves is a passageway. It is something you will have time to explore soon enough."

Unless I'm scared out of my mind, thought Kaira, moving to look at the markings on the floor.

Umberto put his hand on a set of books. "You see these books with the label VM on the binding? They are attached to each other and to an electronic mechanism that opens the shelves. This passageway snakes beneath the winery. One passage leads to the manor, and the other leads to the vineyards."

"This is remarkable, Umberto. But, please explain why my grandmother needed passages beneath the winery?"

Umberto replied, "The passages were here before the winery was built and they've become useful. There is, however, a labyrinth you must avoid, or you could be trapped forever. But don't worry about that. The passages are marked."

A labyrinth?

Umberto pulled one of the books, and the shelves quietly swung open.

Kaira squinted into the dark space. A spiral staircase led down.

"Who built the passages and labyrinth?

"That is a good question and one your grandmother wished to answer for you. I would tell you if I knew, but I don't. You will understand everything soon enough. Alex is going to tell us more tonight."

Alex? The astronomer on the program for tonight?

"Shall we take a look?"

Tentative, Kaira glanced back at the door to the apartment. Then she made her way toward the spiral stairs where Umberto stood. He continued speaking.

"Your grandmother loved you very much. She read all your articles and was proud of your work to preserve the coastal areas. She was particularly proud of the connections you were making regarding the weather patterns along the coast and our alignment in the universe. You have much in common with your grandmother."

"Thank you." *I wish she had told me in person,* Kaira thought. "She had a leg up. I didn't know she was such an avid collector of ancient books and texts. She might have been insulted if she thought you were comparing the two of us."

"Well, she had a few years on you and a lot of friends who have influence. She did nothing on her own other than independently decide to make it her quest to understand. You have that same spirit in you. I see it."

"Why do you say that?" countered Kaira. "I hate to admit how vulnerable my life has been since my family died in the accident. I don't feel independent at all."

"I don't mean to debate or argue Kaira, but you choose your interest in similar subjects regarding the Earth and the heavens. No one forced you to think the way you think. Maybe you do not realize how much your grandmother influenced you as a young girl."

"I stand corrected. And you are right. I do not remember much regarding Meadow Manor, but I do remember the fountain. I've had dreams since I was very young regarding the fountain. Sometimes they are nightmares. I think I was seven years old that last time I saw my grandmother."

"I do hope you are enjoying our tour?" Umberto asked, changing the subject.

"Yes, it has been a dream of mine to come back and visit. I didn't expect it to be at a Wake."

"I'm sorry. In Victoria's last years, she became very busy with a specific project, and I must admit, I also didn't have much of her time to be entirely honest with you."

"Really? What project was she working on?"

"First of all, though we were companions, she didn't tell me everything. And second, whatever it was, it had something to do with astronomy. She recently met with Alex, and they worked day and night until she passed."

"I'm so sorry, that must have been difficult for you." Kaira imagined Umberto waiting patiently for his turn to visit her grandmother.

"There's no need to feel sorry for me. I had many years with Victoria. Wonderful years. And, as the producer of her wine, I stay busy."

Now that her grandmother had educated Kaira regarding the grapes and kind of wine produced at Meadow Manor, she had no doubt Umberto was an excellent producer and a very busy man.

"Many years ago, when I first met Victoria, my life was very different. You see, I was a priest."

Kaira looked uncertain. "What do you mean?"

"I am quite serious. Your grandmother spent a considerable amount of money to free me from the monastery where I lived. My life here is a gift."

"But, are you still a priest?"

Umberto chuckled awkwardly. "I think the answer is no. I loved your grandmother, and she loved me. My life was complicated when we met."

"I am amazed." Kaira declared. "My grandmother certainly had a colorful life full of interesting twists and turns."

"My apologies that you hear this all at once. It must be a lot to absorb." Umberto continued. "I learned about wine at the monastery in Italy. Like our Abbey here, we were self-sustaining, and our wine was the best in the Piedmont region of Italy. Our monastery had the advantage of hundreds of years of knowledge regarding the vines."

Kaira was barely paying attention now. She was slowly making her way behind Umberto down the winding stairwell. She stopped. "What did you mean when you said she freed you?"

"We were young and in love."

She felt him hesitate. She wondered if he had meant more than that, but regretted his choice of words. She had heard of a monastery that took in orphans and raised them as monks and sometimes used them as pawns for a higher, more diabolical scheme.

"I want to remind you that no one else knows about this apartment in the winery. Only you, Alex and me. It will be essential that you keep it secret."

"Secret?" Kaira asked. "Why?"

"You will learn in time. For now, I must ask you to trust me. Essentially, I need you to believe what I am telling you and give me the chance to earn your trust over time. Not a single one of our guests will know the things you've seen and heard tonight."

"You mean the rest of the group doesn't have an earpiece? They aren't following the GPS directions on their phones?"

"Oh, everyone received a lavish gift. But, nothing electronic."

Kaira had never been to a Wake where mourners received gifts. But, it seemed her grandmother wanted her friends and family to celebrate her passing.

"I realize this is happening quickly," Umberto said apologetically. Alex Mirabelli requested to speak with you, and he is waiting in the passageway. He asked that you continue with me to the cavern." Umberto looked at her.

She peered down the stone tunnel and felt her stomach tighten in knots. *Was her grandmother challenging her from the grave?* "I'm meeting Alex down here?"

"It's unusual, I know, but you are a brave girl, much like your grandmother." Umberto placed a comforting hand on her shoulder to steady her. "There's no need to be afraid. Alex is a wonderful man."

Umberto led them down the passageway disappearing into the darkness. Kaira took a deep breath and followed. The path curled on farther than she imagined curving this way and that. *Take a moment to breathe. Why am I doing this?* She was thinking of turning back when the tunnel ended, and a door opened into a cavern. The chamber was large and dimly lit by a candelabra on a table in the center. She followed Umberto exhaling as she surveyed the unusual scene in front of her. Footsteps approached out of a dark corner.

Kaira stood close to Umberto as the footsteps grew louder, then a man appeared in the glow of the candles. He was tall and thin, dressed in a dark jacket and turtleneck. He had brown hair and glasses. Alex smiled at Kaira.

"I apologize for the clandestine meeting. I would hope at least to make an impression on Victoria's granddaughter."

"You couldn't have chosen a more bizarre place to meet."

"You speak your mind as Victoria did."

"I hope that's a good thing."

Alex laughed. "It is one of the things that made her so dear to me."

Now in the dim light, Kaira could see that Alex wore expensive Italian clothing.

"It has been very unnerving to learn so much so quickly. Why are we meeting in this clandestine manner?" Alex must be in his early 40's thought Kaira, but she noticed deep lines on his face.

"Recently, I was working with Victoria on a project, a discovery," Alex said. "Your grandmother held the other half of the breakthrough. I wanted to speak with you in a secure area."

"What do you mean secure?"

"Victoria was concerned that the Manor might be bugged," Alex said.

Umberto pushed a button on his wrist, and his watch screen lit up. "We have to hurry, Alex."

Alex's face turned serious. "No one knows about Victoria's discovery nor what she has in her possession but me and our mutual connection in Italy. I want to pass this information on to you tonight after the Wake."

Kaira's brow furrowed, and questions flooded her mind.

"Not even Umberto has been told." He said, looking at Kaira. Then he spoke slowly. "I can no longer continue this project without help, and I fear it may put us all in danger."

Chapter Eight

Umberto stepped in close. "Alex, what is going on?"

Kaira felt the heaviness of his concern. The flame candles dimmed as if a ghost passed the candelabra.

"I have been working on a project with Victoria. She secretly funded me. I've discovered something remarkable, something threatening."

His whisper was rough with tension.

"It sounds fantastic." Said Kaira, but she shivered and held her arms together in the chill. The natural cavern was damp and chilly.

Alex shrugged, "It is fantastic and dreadful all at the same time. At first, I was excited to share it with the world. It will shift what we understand of the planets and the Earth forever. But, it seems there is a repercussion for those who know."

For a moment, Kaira thought he was overdramatic. But, Umberto's expression told her something different.

"Prophecies and myths regarding a planet which orbits the sun, Babylonian claimed every 3600 years, Sumerian, the Bible, Mayans, and even NASA confirms the existence of a hypothetical new planet deep in space in the solar system."

Prophecies? It had always been Kaira's belief that prophecies were dished out by people who were trying to make money on the vulnerable masses, or they are legitimately cracked in the head. Maybe her grandmother had been involved in a cult. That would explain the feud between their families.

"I see your skepticism. Tonight, I will show you, and then you will see." Alex said.

Kaira smiled and nodded quietly.

"Kaira, you know the Catholic Church is notorious for keeping secrets. When they began to allow a few researchers into their Secret Archives located in the Vatican City, potent information surfaced. I don't know that anyone is prepared for what has been discovered, not even the Pope."

"What is the mystery that lies at the heart of these "potent" discoveries?"

"Many believe events are happening on the Earth and in the Universe before the flood will happen again. My discovery answers a question of the pre-flood Universe, and your grandmother's discovery answers a question regarding the pre-flood Earth."

Kaira grappled with Alex's words. They seemed like a riddle with enormous ramifications. "I…don't know how to react. I am not religious, and I've never studied texts regarding the flood or the Earth before the flood if there even was a flood."

"Without a doubt, the question of the flood has been answered in every ancient text and now with modern Earth Science. But, in answering these questions, another set of questions arises. It is a much darker question and conflict."

"Interesting. And this is why you took up the mantle from your friend when he died?"

"It is. I will give you my guarantee that this breakthrough will cause a tsunami in the governments of the world. In truth, some in wealthy circles may already know, and we've all been the victim of their coverup."

"I've never given much thought to conspiracy theories. I've never really wondered if the Pope was upset about something nor cared that he might be hiding something from his fans. I expect it. Most governments and religious leaders are hiding something." Kaira wondered what purpose would be served in bringing the truth to the surface.

"My mentor, Alessandro, was a Jesuit priest and astronomer. He challenged me to speak openly to religious and science groups. He believed in talking through conflicting ideas and working intentionally to find common links. We know that ancient texts tell the same stories in separate languages. The same is often true of science and religion."

Umberto cleared his throat. "We have about ten minutes, Alex."

"When Alessandro went missing, I didn't believe he just left…ran away. There are many reasons he wouldn't do that. Mt. Graham is a mountaintop sanctuary for astronomers, and he was happy following his passion and discovery. He had been preparing to present his discovery to a community of astronomers and observatories at a conference in Tucson, Arizona, but he didn't show up."

"I remember Victoria discussing the conference," Umberto said

"I believe he might have been murdered. I immediately gathered his files and the work we had collaborated on and continued my research covertly. I did not want the information to get into the wrong hands. I scheduled a meeting with Giovanni Fiorelli, an archeologist in Castel Gandolfo, Italy. Giovanni had been in touch with Victoria regarding her discovery, and that is how I came to know your grandmother."

The story was fascinating.

"I cannot begin to tell you my excitement and trepidation when I met with Victoria. Our discoveries do not separate religion and science. Our discoveries bring them together. All the polarization we've experienced as a nation and internationally in the religious and scientific communities is dispelled considering this information. However, some do not wish to bring the two together. We should not be surprised at how the wealthy few would receive it. They have a different agenda." He continued. "Together, we contacted Giovanni, leader of archeological sites in the Lazio region of Italy. We told him of our discoveries, and he, in turn, told us something unbelievable he found at a new dig site."

"And this is what you will share with me later this evening?"

Alex shrugged. "We've touched the tip of the iceberg. I didn't want to take the chance that you would slip out before we could talk, so I set up this first meeting. I hope to explain later in detail the discoveries and how they change everything."

"My grandmother never mentioned anything to me, but we haven't been in touch since I was very young."

"She wanted to speak to you earlier, but we had so much to do. I have photos. When Giovanni saw them, he warned me to trust no one and keep the information covert. I will be speaking with him in a few days. But tonight, following the Wake, I will show you, and you will know the truth."

"Have you mentioned anything unusual to Father Murphy?" Umberto asked.

"No. He would not find it amusing that Victoria kept him in the dark." Alex looked at Kaira. "Do you know Father Murphy from St. Francis Abbey?"

"I know he was Victoria's priest. That is all I know."

Umberto nodded. "Yes, he was Victoria's priest for many years. She was faithful to the Abbey."

"Giovanni Fiorelli is a powerful figure in the Italian archeological community. I want to bring Father Murphy in on a conference with Giovanni. He is known for his strong influence on the Pope, who spends time at the summer residence in Castel Gandolfo. Giovanni is also known for his liberal views and study of antediluvian culture." Alex shifted uncomfortably in the candlelit chamber. "We will need these men and their influence locally and with the Vatican. Do you think Father Murphy poses any threat?"

"Threat in what way?" Umberto asked.

"Would he share this information outside the circle?"

"He is a faithful and loyal man. I do not think he would do that unless he thought we were in danger if he did not come forward." Umberto said.

"Yes, I worked with him to put the presentation together for Victoria's Celebration of Life. He has a good heart, but that is what has me worried. He might decide with the intentions of doing good, but the outcome could be devastating."

"Tell me about Giovanni," Kaira asked.

"He is a powerful archeologist living in Castel Gandolfo, Italy. His recent discoveries show that before the Romans existed, the fair land of Italy was inhabited by nations who have left permanent monuments as the only records of their history. What he found proves who built the massive advanced, prehistoric ruins."

"Did he speak with the Pope regarding his discovery?"

"No. But, we didn't expect him to. The church is notorious for hiding information they perceive as a threat. He wants to get this into the hands of the public when the time is right. There was an urgency in his tone when we talked."

"Did he mention the nature of his urgency?"

"Only that in curiosity, we study the past without considering the dangers. Giovanni also said the innocence of not knowing everything is where the best life is lived."

"Are you worried you're in danger here tonight?" Umberto asked.

"No. The guest list consists of Westonville Historical Society, friends, and you, Kaira, the last family member. I am more worried about what happens when we bring Father Murphy in on the truth. I guess I feel the weight of responsibility."

"None of Victoria's friends would ever be a threat, including Father Murphy. It's time to go Alex. The celebration begins soon." Umberto spoke quietly.

Alex looked at his watch. "Thank you. We'll meet back here after the guests have gone. Just in case something goes wrong, here is my card." He handed it to Kaira.

The simple card showed the address on Mt Graham in Arizona and his office number. On the back were two sets of numbers. The first looked like a number for the boat slip along the pier at the marina on the bay. The second set of 4 long strings of numbers looked like code. She slipped it into her pocket.

Chapter Nine

According to legend, two knights far superior in comeliness and gigantic stature compared to human nature were in the Roman army between the 7th and 4th centuries BC. They were the sons of Jupiter (Jove), Dionysius, and Halicarnassus, who led the Roman army to victory. A significant and famous temple to Jupiter was built near the volcanic crater of Monte Cavo.

Giovanni lived not far from the Appian Way in Albano Laziale, a lively community a few kilometers south of Rome whose palace and temples built around 81 – 96 AD and developed by the Roman emperor Domitian. Domitian's palace was later purchased by the Apostolic Camera in 1596 and is now Castel Gandolfo, the summer residence of the Pope.

Giovanni knew well the miles of old stone streets, temples, and ruins scattered across Lazio, so stunning and bizarre, they caused him to wonder how they were built. Very little was known about the prehistoric builders and their strange megalithic masterpieces that had survived the deluge.

He studied their building techniques, which resembled that of the Incas and pre-Incas of Peru. Sadly, most archeologists ignored them while an even more vast world remained oblivious to their existence.

Modern scholars were silent regarding stonework several thousand years old. They were built not only before the ancient Romans but before the Etruscans, who were the remote ancestors of the Romans. Their monuments still stood strong, bearing mute testimony to the power of the builders and their strange history.

University students weren't given a chance to soak in the glorious mystery of the ruins. Giovanni's passion for keeping the innovative monuments from being erased from existence caused friction among his community of priests and Archeologists.

Tonight, deep in thought and unaware of the time, the elderly archeologist sat in front of his computer entirely absorbed by the bizarre scene depicted on the screen. Who would believe him? Who could he tell?

For decades Victoria Munroe led the Historical Society in Westonville. Giovanni's heart had filled with hope when she contacted him. She'd become a good friend, a collaborator who was devout and private at times, but outspoken and incredibly sharp when necessary.

Between the two of them, they were on the way to building a case that would explain what Plato described as a type of futuristic race of humans living on an island continent called Atlantis. Plato spoke of it as a sophisticated, antediluvian city that flourished for ages on a now-submerged continent in the middle of the ocean, from which its name was derived.

Giovanni grieved Victoria's death. More than a collaborator, she'd brought him comfort that somehow their secrets would eventually make sense to the world. But, she passed before their day in the sun.

One of Giovanni's students had been trying to reach him for twenty minutes. Giovanni's phone was buzzing, but he didn't answer it. Only this could cause him to miss his class.

Sitting at his desk, staring at the blue glow from the computer screen, he pieced the puzzle together. Victoria's discovery, his discovery and now Alex would bring an extraordinary piece to the equation. Everything finally made sense. Bizarre, horrific, sense.

***

The server poured wine for the growing crowd in Meadow Manor, grateful that they would be the perfect distraction.

Tonight, he focused on the mission.

He looked at his watch and eyed the guests. They were beginning to head for the Music Salon, where the Celebration of Life would take place. He felt a knot tighten in his gut. The same tremor of unease he'd felt the night before. Would he be capable of pulling it off? The pompous soul who had ripped his opportunity away from him and given him so much grief would finally feel the repercussion.

As he reached the hall, his gaze was drawn to a man descending the staircase. SSRL's famous oceanographer, a treasure hunter in disguise, he thought bitterly eyeing the successful Oceanographer. The man wore a black suit and a classic white silk shirt. His tall form and curly dark hair were easy to admire, and the server noticed the women in the room were watching him too.

Also, Father Murphy and another man shadowed him closely. They moved with wary confidence toward the hallway where he stood. He was not surprised by the men, he had been preparing for this moment, but his pulse quickened as they passed him. At least his disguise was a success.

"Hello good looking." A woman's sultry voice spoke directly behind him.

He turned to see a woman in a tight dress with bright red lipstick smiling up at him. "You still serving wine?" she asked, holding out her empty glass with red smudges on the rim.

He clenched his fists. Patience, he thought. "The bar is closed," he said and shrugged. He slipped down the hall to the empty library. Alone, he felt the demon of anger trying to surface. He couldn't afford to allow his emotions to destroy all his hard work and planning. He touched the vials on his belt for comfort. His life was on the line tonight.

Two years and the frustration still threatened to overwhelm him. The newspaper read:

EAST COAST TRAVELER - A James Bond fantasy may be coming true on the small Caribbean island of Dominican Republic, writes Kaira Munroe. A powerful Mafia family is reported to have attempted to buy up much of the island in the Caribbean with the aim of turning it into an independent Mafia state. But, one thing is standing between them and their plan. Oceanographer Jonathan Bell and his team at Sub Sea Research Lab (SSRL) is an occasional shipwreck hunter. SSRL research permits are tying the hands of the mafia.

Angrily, he pushed the memories from his mind.

When vengeance was this necessary, the family had promised, compensation was guaranteed.

He glanced at the reminder on his arm, "morte prima di disonore," which means "death before dishonor" in Italian. The phrase is more commonly a military tattoo accompanied by images of a scroll and dagger.

They occupied the highest levels of the Italian mafia and guaranteed his deliverance from harm. He had first witnessed their

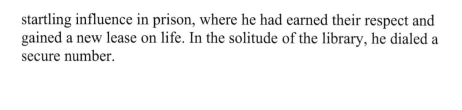

startling influence in prison, where he had earned their respect and gained a new lease on life. In the solitude of the library, he dialed a secure number.

Chapter Ten

Chris admitted astronomers were monitoring something that was approaching the earth. That wasn't a secret among the Jesuit astronomers who worked at Mount Graham International Observatory. They knew local Indians believed Mt Graham was the darkest place for observing the night sky.

Mount Graham, located in the beautiful Southeastern Pinaleno Mountains of Arizona, was a sacred mountain for the San Carlos Apache tribe, who named it Dzil Nchaa Si'An. They believed that the mountain should remain untouched. However, when the Vatican built the Gregorian Telescope on Mt Graham, those sacred spaces were not taken into account as known portals to the spirit world. The stories of the San Carlos Apache tribe were well known to the monks who had built Chapels over sacred places throughout Arizona.

Tonight, a group of four Apache leaders gathered in private to hold a sacred vigil. The son of one of their families had disappeared in the mountains. The young Apache was last seen near a gateway they believed could traverse time.

One of the elders spoke, "In this rugged terrain, my brother and I discovered a location where time was altered. We were in camp one evening and saw two large balls of blue-green lights. They slowly descended behind the mountain silhouette in front of our camp. There was no noise."

"There are some stories we must keep within our tribe." Said another elder after a long silence. "I have seen the archway made of stone. I have seen the geodes and felt the electricity in the air. We must be careful when we search for him."

"It is a doorway to the gods."

***

In the mountains where the observatory stood, a jeep bumped to the left and skidded to a stop, sending a cloud of dust billowing in front of the grill.

The young man behind the wheel stared ahead of him at the object in the middle of the narrow dirt trail. Tentatively, he climbed out of the vehicle and approached the object on the road. There in the headlights, a large rock lay embedded in the dirt.

"Meteor?" he called to his friend. "It wasn't here yesterday."

"Cool."

It sparkled with flecks that looked like grade school glitter. Uncertain, one of the boys nudged it with his shoe. The asteroid was solid. A half dozen other vehicles pulled in behind the jeep, buddies from the University of Arizona. A few of the boys reached down and grasped the rock and tried to heave it over, but it was too heavy.

They parked and gathered around to examine the object. One of the young men became excited as he recognized the meteor or asteroid might be valuable. They did what most guys with their kind of jeeps would do. They pulled out some chains and threw them around the massive rock in hopes of dislodging it from the road. Billy snapped a photo of it and sent it to his astronomer friend.

Suddenly in the distance, a green light hovered and disappeared behind the silhouette of the mountains.

***

Dizzy from confusing thoughts, Kaira emerged from the underground cave beneath the winery. Conversation with Umberto and Alex had been thrilling and alarming. Alex and Victoria had discovered something they believed would cause an impact in Westonville and possibly the world.

Kaira had heard the legends of pirate treasure for years. Illegal treasure hunters had been tearing away at the bluffs out at the lighthouse since she could remember. When they emerged from the passage, she felt relieved. Time was short, and they made their way quickly to the Music Salon, where the Celebration of Life was about to begin.

Past the fountain and up the entrance stairs, down the hall past the paintings of ancient Italy to the Music Salon. Kaira found herself staring at the gallery with fresh eyes and a much more profound intrigue than before. She thought of the Tapestry of David and

Goliath in the banquet hall and felt sure there was hidden meaning beneath the woven carpet of silk.

When she arrived, Umberto helped her find a seat at the front of the room. "The Celebration of Life is scheduled to begin in just a few minutes." Said Umberto. "Do you need anything before the event begins?"

"No, thank you. I'm fine."

"Excellent. One final point. Do you see the door to the right of the platform? Alex asked that you exit from that door. You will be able to find Father Murphy, Alex, and me from that place in case we need to avoid the crowd."

Kaira thought of the business card Alex had given her and the number for the Yacht slip. Did he think something was going to happen tonight?

"It's about to begin. I hope you enjoy the presentation your grandmother and Alex put together."

With that, Umberto was gone.

She slipped the earpiece from her ear and waited as the last of the guests were seated.

Once again, she felt alone.

Approximately two hundred guests cramped into the music salon, which held 150 comfortably. There was a podium at the front, and a large screen read:

Celebration of Life
Victoria Munroe
1935 – 2017

She was eighty-two years old when she passed. Kaira felt a surge of anticipation as her eyes watched the screen. What was the presentation about to share?

Chapter Eleven

Sitting with guests in the stillness of the Music Salon, Kaira Munroe watched the screen in anticipation of celebrating her grandmother. Tonight, she would see images of her she'd never seen before. A few guests whispered and chattered in the cramped space utterly full of chairs.

Father Murphy stepped to the front. "Thank you for coming. Please turn your phones on silent for the Celebration of Life."

The list of guests were people who loved and respected Victoria Munroe. Soon they would witness some of the most astounding photos of her life. In the back of the room, a cameraman from the local television moved into position.

The Board of Directors sat in the front row along with other officers and members of the Westonville Historical Society. Across the aisle, Father Murphy. The Abbot and a few priests sat in the front row. Kaira sat directly behind the priests.

They waited as the last of the guests wandered in and found their seats. It seemed to be taking forever. A small door opened to the right of the Music Salon. It was open for a few seconds, then Kaira's heart stopped. A man emerged, moving forward to the front. She'd expected Alex. The man was strikingly handsome, tall with dark curling hair a little long around the collar. Taking the stage, he adjusted the microphone. Kaira closed her eyes for a moment then opened them again. He was a portrait of strength.

"Good evening." He began, his voice rich and gracious. "My name is Jonathan Bell."

The crowd burst into applause, making it apparent that everyone who knew him watched the news and tabloids as she did.

"Glad to have you home." Someone said loud enough that everyone could hear.

He waited for a moment, and Kaira sensed she had missed something. She'd written one of the most recent articles regarding his exploits in the Dominican Republic, but she hadn't seen him since high school.

"Ladies and gentlemen," he said, quickly moving on, "for the past few years, I've been working in the Caribbean studying the ocean. As a director and member of the Westonville Historical Society, I am here tonight to welcome you to a special evening, a Celebration of Life for an incredible woman, Victoria Munroe. She would wish us all to enjoy this evening."

The crowd applauded, and Kaira joined them.

"Victoria Munroe was not only the President of the Historical Society here in Westonville, but she was also my trusted friend. It has been my honor to have worked so closely with her all these years, and planning this evening with Father Murphy has been a privilege. Many of you may not know that Victoria was also interested in Astronomy. Her friend Alex Mirabelli, from the Vatican Observatory in Tucson, Arizona, has joined us tonight to fill you in on a project they were working on this past year."

A murmur of excitement sifted through the room.

The lady with red lipstick spoke up. "We hope you'll tell us about your treasure too."

A round of agreement shot through the room as heads nodded.

This is no typical Wake, thought Kaira.

"Tonight's event is about Victoria Munroe and her eccentric and intriguing life. She did not want her Wake to be morbid. She wanted to celebrate life. Victoria hoped that none of you would mourn for her. She is in a better place." Jonathan continued, "Victoria had her fingers in a lot of pie, so to speak. Just as she loved history, she also loved astronomy and ancient texts from around the world. Victoria spoke three languages, Italian, English, and Spanish. She had her Masters in History from Harvard and studied International Relations, and Anthropology, and Archaeology. Tonight, we'll take a deeper look at her outstanding life, and all that Victoria brought to Westonville and the world."

So that's who my grandmother was. Kaira mused.

She turned her attention back to the front, where her high school sweetheart continued. She spotted someone at the side door. Alex. She wanted to crank her neck around and see what was going on in the back of the room, but from her front-row seat, it was too obvious. Father Murphy stood and walked to the side door. She wondered where Umberto was. It seemed likely that he was watching from a position where he could see everything in the room. He had been a constant, loyal companion to Victoria Munroe, and Kaira trusted him from the first moment she'd met him.

The well-known treasure hunter, Jonathan Bell, owner of SSRL, Sub Sea Research Lab, held enormous influence over the guests in the room. For many of the Westonville locals, the legends of treasure stood as a symbol of their traditions and their identity as a community.

Kaira had heard that: "Intellect rules but treasure reigns." For years, the treasure hunters who had landed in Westonville seeking the lost treasure of Captain Benjamin Munroe had become obsessed in their search. She had seen it throughout childhood. Her father had become obsessed. Her high school sweetheart was no exception, she thought, having read his latest tabloid revelations. She wondered if he read the articles she wrote about his quests in the Caribbean.

Now with the monarch of the Westonville Historical Society gone, she wondered who would be the gatekeeper for the treasure seekers who threatened to destroy the coastline in their search for Captain Benjamin Munroe's treasure.

According to the Westonville Historical Society, Jonathan Bell was the next in line to become the gatekeeper, but many wondered what kind of gatekeeper he would be with his conflict of interest.

Was Jonathan also searching for the treasure?

Kaira flashed to the information she had learned in the cavern with Alex and Umberto. Despite her concerns, she sensed the atmosphere in the room was light and amiable. Safe. She recalled Alex telling her there was nothing to be afraid of, the security was tight.

"For those of you who knew Victoria intimately, you would know of her passion for drama." Jonathan continued. "you know she would never plan to show us a boring presentation."

He motioned to the screen above the platform behind him. "So, if you would, ladies and gentlemen, please check your phones to silence them, and we will see what the amazing Victoria Munroe has in store for us."

On cue, the presentation began.

Kaira peered up at the screen, expecting to see ancient art and tapestries as she had seen throughout the manor. Instead, she found herself startled by photos and videos of Victoria and Umberto in Italy. They appeared to be in front of a megalithic structure.

A stranger sat in the back as the guests watched enthralled by the photos on the screen. As he attended the presentation, he was pleased to see the glass of water gone from the podium.

Darkness would create the confusion he needed.

Touching his heart, he gathered his wits, going over the details in his mind he realized timing was critical.

Chapter Twelve

"Megalithic ruins of strangely built polygonal stone walls so stunningly unique, bizarre, and futuristic are scattered throughout the ancient region in Italy where Rome was later founded. For thousands of years, it was believed they were constructed by an ancient race of giants, now forgotten."

The voice was Victoria Munro, and the picture on the screen showed her with Umberto in front of some ancient ruins.

"I'd like to ask you to forget being practical. For the next few minutes, go back to your childhood when you were able to dream; anything could be a reality. Please remove the tainted glasses of "truth" as you think you know it and walk with me."

Mentally, Kaira stepped out of her practical mode and allowed her mind to sink deep into the adventure on the screen. Her mind felt alive, and she heard pleased and surprised sounds around her.

As the presentation progressed, Kaira saw massive structures and giant statues lifted from the sea.

"As you will see in the pictures, the relics recovered from the excavations boldly reveal the cities' beauty and glory before it was buried by water and sediment," Victoria said.

In another photo, Umberto and Victoria stood with a colossal statue of red granite representing the god Jupiter sometimes called Jovi, which decorated the temple of Jupiter. The god of the Roman victory, symbol of strength, has never before been discovered on such a large scale. This points to the importance of the Lazio region.

Umberto began to speak.

"Ages before the Romans existed, the fair land of Italy was inhabited by nations who have left permanent monuments as the only records of their history. Those wonderful cities of early Italy which have been termed Cyclopean, are thickly scattered throughout certain districts, and are often perched like eagles' nests, on the very crests of mountains, at such an elevation as to strike amazement into the travelers who now visit them."

For the second time, Kaira was forced to stop and think. Although she knew her grandmother had researched antiquities, her mind could not have conjured the images she was now seeing on the screen along with two hundred others in the room.

Did he just say Cyclopean?

The next photo showed her grandmother standing with Umberto next to The Saracena Gate, a Cyclopean masterpiece. Massive stones fitted together using the polygonal technique, long before the Romans and the Etruscans. Her grandmother's voice continued.

"Speak with a scholar today and tell her to believe the Cyclopes were a group of giants who built these monuments—she'll laugh, and fairly sarcastically too. However, a Victorian-era scholar wouldn't have laughed. Yes, many Victorian scholars were women, and they would have been open-minded to the possibility."

"For one," Umberto said, *"Victorian scholars were smarter and more sophisticated than today's scholars. Anyone who reads academic books from the Victorian era can spot this fairly easily. The Victorian scholars were not distracted by mass media sensationalists like we are today. They were certainly more open-minded—a sign of intelligence—and why shouldn't they have been? The remains of cavemen were being discovered at the very start of the Victorian era, so the idea of a different reality was becoming widely accepted."*

Kaira looked out the side windows in the Music Salon. Dusk spread across the horizon, and in the distance, a slender crescent of the moon was rising behind the Cypress trees next to the winery. She longed for her family and the time they had lost. More photos flashed across the screen and captured her imagination.

It took a few moments to realize this was her grandmother's story, something her parents had kept from her. The flabbergasted guests were watching in rapt attention as more photos of Victoria and Umberto in Italy projected onto the screen.

Kaira felt uncomfortable, which was not unusual when it came to her family history, but she was grateful to be at the celebration. She had read about her grandmother's interests regarding antiquities, and yet the presentation had gone a step further and created food for the imagination, as though her grandmother wanted to give subtle messages to the guests.

Kaira recalled the first time she was introduced to her family quirks. At nine years old, she'd walked along the sandy bay in front of the lighthouse, daydreaming. Her young mind was incapable of understanding that she came from a family name with a history of pirates. She'd been exploring the underground caverns with Jonathan when he reminded her that her family name was associated with smugglers and pirates. That was the day he kissed her.

We used to be kids, but somehow, we stopped along the way.

She melted into the chair and forced her shoulders to relax. Overhead the screen continued to reveal amazing photos of Victoria's life as a historian and owner of the vineyard at Meadow Manor.

At the rear of the room, the stranger took a final survey and moved silently toward the exit. Alone in the hallway, he found the door leading to the terrace entrance where Alex and Father Murphy were waiting. Stealthily, he opened the door into a long hallway parallel to the terrace. He was no longer visible to the guests. The long hallway before him was surrounded on the east by the glass atrium and west by the wall separating him from the Music Salon.

He must remember why he was here. It was for survival and treasure. Carmelo cared deeply about wealth. He had an agenda to fund. He wondered if he had put enough of the vial in the glass of water. Sooner or later, he'd take a drink. The result would not harm and be the perfect distraction he needed to search the manor.

At that moment, from a speaker in the hallway, he overheard Jonathan's voice announcing Alex Mirabelli. A bit too early to announce Alex according to the program.

"Good evening, I hope you are enjoying the presentation. My name is Alex Mirabelli. Our presentation is divided into three sections, and I'll be explaining the next set of photos." He paused. "But excuse me. I'm thirsty."

Chapter Thirteen

In Albano Laziale, Giovanni Fiorelli sat restlessly in the dim light of his study. Watching the computer, he waited anxiously for word from Alex and news regarding the revelation.

Internet online networks in Italy were often interrupted during skype usage. He wondered if he would be lucky enough to get a skype feed. Speculation about Alex's upcoming revealing to Victoria's granddaughter and Father Murphy caused him to cringe.

I have a feeling I know what is coming.

Four weeks earlier, Giovanni had seen the relics. Now he worried that the world would see the same thing only prematurely. He knew everything would change.

His phone rang, and he jolted from his contemplation.

"I'm afraid I have some disturbing news." A somber voice gave him a bizarre report. "The bones are gone from the dig site." Giovanni put his hand over his eyes. "No," he moaned.

"I must admit, I am having difficulty accepting this news." Said the man on the phone. "Who else could it be?"

"Anyone who wanted to keep our discovery a secret," Giovanni replied. "Someone who believes as we do that this discovery will change everything as we know it."

"But who knows besides us? Antonio Calo? Even if we are the only ones who knew, do not forget, there are eyes everywhere in Italy. All discoveries are reported to the Holy See and the museum. Any undisclosed discovery can have dangerous repercussions."

"What are you trying to say?" asked the archeologist frustration evident in his voice. "The Catholic Church has gone to these lengths to keep it quiet?"

"I don't know what I'm saying." The voice said. "The truth is, I don't know who it is or how it happened."

Giovanni let his breath go out in a long exhale. "I'm sorry. I'm trying to absorb the news of Victoria's death plus the entrance of her granddaughter. There is much to consider. Do you believe we may be in danger?"

"The possibility is there. Anyone helping us may be in danger. I suspect Alex will have more to add to this tonight at the meeting.

We must stay focused and of the same mind. Without proof, we have nothing, and we are no more than old men looking for sensational stardom." Giovanni hesitated as if he wanted to say much more.

"What?" his friend pressed. "Tell me what you are thinking."

"Let's talk later after the meeting. I'll call you after I speak with Alex."

"Lock your doors, and for God's sake, don't talk to anyone but Alex."

"You are giving me a fright, my friend."

"I am sorry. I don't mean to frighten you. We must wait until you speak with Alex."

***

The guests grew quiet when Alex took the microphone.

"Like my professional colleagues at other observatories and research institutions, as astronomers and astrophysicists, we are trying to unlock the secrets of the universe and human knowledge and understanding. But, we have another urgent mission: to build a bridge of understanding between science and religious faith. Building this bridge is something Victoria Munroe was very interested in."

A photo of the Milky Way filled the screen behind Alex.

"As a Jesuit astronomer, my effort to understand the cosmos is a form of ministry. I am passionate about the farthest reaches of God's creation for many reasons. I am also passionate about the world we inhabit. I will continue to study and learn the deeper levels of our civilization. Evolution would have you believe you have developed from something simple over millions of years. I would present to you that the past is far too complex for that to be true."

He took another sip of water and loosened his shirt at the neck.

"Victoria wanted everyone to remember what it was like to be a child. To look up at the stars in wonder. To dream and realize we haven't come close to knowing the whole story. Not until now. We've made some recent discoveries at the Observatory in Arizona, in the Lazio region of Italy, and right here in Westonville, and these discoveries have brought astounding information to light."

A wave of excitement rippled through the crowd.

"The Vatican's interest in studying the heavens dates back at least to the late 16th century when the Catholic Church set out to fix problems in the old Western calendar, problems which jeopardized the accurate observance of holy days."

"It was Pope Leo XIII who, in 1891, founded the modern Vatican observatory, its telescope was located near St. Peter's Basilica. In the 1930s, the observatory was moved to the pope's summer residence at Castel Gandolfo. In 1981, the Vatican moved its astronomers to Arizona. That was followed by the installation of the Mount Graham telescope in 1993. The heavens are not the only thing the Vatican has an interest in."

"There is the issue of megalithic structures from before the flood. It would not be absurd to say that over the past century, in Italy and Europe, there appears to be a sophisticated cover-up of these lost archaeological sites. They've been ignored into obscurity. It goes on today as if the wealthy powers who rule the world don't want the mystery of the ruins to be studied or widely known. But, unlike gigantic skeletons, megalithic ruins are too massive to move or hide.

"Most people—even many Italians—are unaware of their true impact. Many Italians living next to megalithic ruins do not recognize the magic and mysticism the ancients associated with them. This lack of understanding is peculiar, considering how advanced these prehistoric ruins are."

Alex took another gulp of water and rubbed his throat. Sweat was beginning to trickle down his temple.

"Victoria wanted to not only look back through history but to look forward and explore. She realized there was a time when explorers had a relationship with the heavens and wonder of the phenomena they lived with and experienced. We think of early explorers in ships out in the ocean. For a moment, let's go back in time to ancient Egypt and their culture. They also built ships. They studied the stars. They didn't have the amazing telescopes we have today, like the one we use on Mt Graham."

Jonathan's eyebrow raised, and he spoke up. "I've wanted to ask, why did they name it LUCIFER?"

The guests burst into nervous laughter. Alex's face seemed pale, but he smiled and lifted his glass in salute.

"We'll get to that later," Alex said, smiling.

"Men have always wanted to know what is beneath the ocean, what is beyond the stars, what is buried in the ground. In all this searching, men have theorized and experimented. Men have read ancient texts and written their texts in an attempt to explain. But, we have bits and pieces of information here and there. The more we learn about the universe, the more we learn about the ocean, and the more we learn about the earth, we continue to be confounded by new pieces of the puzzle. What if there is more to mythology than myth?"

Kaira recalled the images of Victoria standing at Stonehenge and in Egypt next to the high Pyramids. It revealed her desire to find the truth and experience the wonder first hand.

"You see, Sumerians tell elaborate stories of flying discs and tales of trans-dimensional gods who flew in them through gateways. These stargates are represented in our solar system and our zodiac. Two of these Stargates are the Golden Gate and the Silver Gate, which are on opposite sides of our known Universe. Orion corresponds to the Golden Gate. The Silver Gate corresponds to Ophiuchus."

"What does it mean, and exactly how has it brought us all together tonight? I know you are a rational group of Historians and individuals. We continue to struggle to explain why all the cultures of the world include a similar story and host of mythical gods and magical claims."

"Tonight, as with all shifts in philosophy, it is critical to understand the historical context. We are fortunate to have Jonathan Bell with us. Board member and director of the Westonville Historical Society, he is a legend in the world of Sub Sea Research. His lab, SSRL, has been working along the east coast and the Caribbean for the past fifteen years. He was a dear friend of Victoria and a recent friend of mine. We are putting the pieces together. Welcome, Jonathan Bell, for the last part of our presentation."

Surprised, Jonathan hopped upfront as Alex picked up his glass of water and walked to the side door. His actions were unexpected. Why would Alex cut his presentation short? Had he changed his mind about what he had planned to say? Jonathan had to wing it. He glanced at Father Murphy, but he just shrugged his shoulders, confused at the change in plans.

Jonathan cleared his throat and began. "I've known for quite some time about Victoria's Secret." Everyone laughed at his joke. He continued. "She eluded to it on occasion, but never spoke of it fully. However, when our team at SSRL made a discovery, it became evident that Victoria wanted to speak with me. We talked extensively over the phone before her death. I'd like to connect some of the dots tonight as I believe she would have wanted."

"Let me preface this with a warning. What I am about to tell you will no longer be a secret. You can talk to anyone you want about what you hear tonight. However, the preservation of our town and its extraordinary legends may depend on your ability to know who to talk to and only when it is necessary. I am hoping that you are a discreet group of historians and friends."

"And it is an amazing story because it is so far-fetched, it is difficult to believe." He paused. "You see, SSRL discovered a shipwreck using a space treasure map created by a Jesuit priest and astronomer, who went missing a year ago. I am telling you, stick around, this is just the beginning of the intrigue. Captain Benjamin Munroe's ship wasn't all that we discovered."

"As you know, Westonville is full of legends about the famous Captain Benjamin Munroe. Victoria Munroe married into his bloodline."

The crowd was on the edge of their seats as images of the shipwreck beneath the blue waters of the Caribbean projected onto the screen.

Chapter Fourteen

The newsman usually picked up a few leftover newspapers at Local Steam Espresso. Today, there were no papers left on the stand. Inside the coffee shop, customers sat drinking coffee and reading their social media. There was plenty of local buzz surrounding the wealthy Victoria Munroe and rumors of the Southern Pacific discovery topped buzz feed:

Jonathan Bell Reveals the Legend

In a search for an unprecedented treasure worth millions, SSRL and owner Jonathan Bell appear poised to announce their discovery and hints more than wealth came with the package. Off the Caribbean coast, Jonathan Bell and his team from Sub Sea Research Lab launch their critique of the relics and artifacts which are being raised from the sunken ship.

So far, rumors are circulating that what he's found may prove more than local legends. Jonathan refuses to give us more information until professionals have studied the relics.

Oceanographer Jonathan Bell and Victoria Munroe were longtime friends. Initially, the search began with the desire to find proof of Captain Benjamin Munroe and his Galleon. You might recognize one of the oldest names along the Eastern Coast, Munroe. Captain Benjamin Munroe, one of the founders of Westonville in 1746, is direct lineage with Victoria Munroe's late husband, Benjamin Munroe.

***

Amused that the security hadn't thought of checking the caterers, it had been easy to slip in unnoticed, disguised. Gently Brian opened the plastic curtain a crack and peered down the hall. He kept himself hidden from view behind the curtain covering a niche in the wall where remodeling was taking place.

Silently he listened as Alex began to speak to the crowd. He had planned to sedate his brother, Jonathan, out of personal spite, but it didn't matter if it was Alex. He needed a distraction so that he could search for a particular item.

He had one vial left. He might need it in case things went south.

He could see that Father Murphy and Jonathan had taken up positions inside the doorway. A few minutes into the presentation, Alex called Jonathan up to the platform again. Father Murphy stood in rapt attention as Jonathan took the platform. Nearby, members of the Westonville Historical Society shifted nervously as they watched Jonathan.

Surprised that the schedule changed suddenly, Brian closed the crack in the plastic curtain and refocused his attention to finding the map. The sedative would take a few minutes to do the job. It was tasteless. Whoever ingested the knockout drug would seem as though they were dead.

The metal tube in his belt held darts in case he needed them. He had bought it from the black market in the Dominican Republic. He hadn't established the full nature of the vials' potency. He wasn't sure if one bottle would be enough.

All I need to do is get close to him.

If the plan worked, his current position would be perfect. But, why had Father Murphy switched the presenters on the program? Had he purposely swapped them? Brian was beginning to feel paranoid. Knowing that he had given the cocktail to the wrong man caused him to worry. He must complete the job and find a way to get to the map. He was in the Manor, and that was half the battle, but he couldn't afford to be caught by his brother, Jonathan.

***

Standing on the small platform and speaking, Jonathan hoped he didn't look as uncomfortable as he felt. Alex had left the presentation early and had seemed a little out of breath as he walked off the platform. He knew that Alex and Victoria were interested in science and history. Victoria had never been shy about her beliefs in religion, the bible, and all the quirky things that came with it.

Father Murphy had refused to allow anyone to see the presentation before tonight. There would probably be some fallout with the Westonville Historical Society and Board members. But, Jonathan's concerns were more personal. He hadn't realized how he would feel seeing Kaira for the first time in years.

Umberto confided in Jonathan a couple of weeks earlier that Victoria had written Kaira an invitation. Jonathan almost backed out as a participant, but Father Murphy begged him not to cancel. Now, as he stood in front of the crowd gathered in Victoria's Music Salon, he wondered if his brother was watching. The celebration was live streaming by the local news station from the back of the room.

Of course, my brother knows. *He's been following me for months.*

***

Albano Laziale, Italy

Inside the study, Giovanni sat rigidly at his desk, thinking about the call he had just received. He couldn't take his eyes off the laptop. He did not doubt that the Governing Board and the Curator of the local museum had been watching his every move. Though the purpose of the institution should be to collect, preserve, interpret, and display, it seemed enlightenment was elusive. As the manager of collections, the Curator was primarily responsible for the hands-on care, movement, and storage of objects.

Giovanni was about to explode with anger. *Or was it fear?*

He had been collaborating with a prominent American and Jesuit astronomer to eventually broadcast proof that at in our antediluvian past, gigantic beings had lived on the earth, and they were responsible for the unanswered questions surrounding the megalithic structures that still existed.

Now that he had fanned the flames of controversy, Giovanni was sure the Curator was having him tailed and possibly bugged. In the event of Victoria's Wake and the spectacular discovery Alex represented, he had chosen to take the risk by agreeing to meet and speak with them.

The Curator was irritated at being excluded.

His role as the head of the museum and all cultural discoveries in the Lazio region would be challenged if Giovanni declared his discovery without his approval or knowledge. But, it was a risk Giovanni hoped he was prepared to take.

Chapter Fifteen

Kaira Munroe was feeling unsettled and nervous about her earlier discussion with Umberto and Alex. Jonathan seemed focused on legends she'd heard her entire life, but Alex had said some things that skated dangerously close to what you might read in the tabloid section of the grocery store with headings like "Extraterrestrial."

What was the point of igniting the interest of the people in the room if you weren't going to tell them everything? She was deeply troubled by being drawn into the controversy and would have preferred to stay innocent of the truth she was about to hear, though she despised that quality in others.

Alex's expertise in astronomy had come through in his visual presentation, but for what purpose? Jonathan's voice filled the room, and her thoughts turned to the relics on the screen.

"This is one of the relics we found on Captain Benjamin Munroe's ship. It looks just like a metal rusted wheel. We believe the disc you are looking at on the screen is an ancient celestial map used to predict planetary positions and eclipses for calendar and astrological purposes." He paused. "I must admit at first I didn't understand what I was looking at."

"The relic was found housed in a 13 in × 7.1 in × 3.5 in a wooden box. It looks like a watch. It is a complex clockwork mechanism composed of at least 30 meshing bronze gears. A team from the University used modern computer x-ray tomography and high-resolution surface scanning to peer inside fragments of the crust-encased mechanism and read the faintest inscriptions that once covered the outer casing of the machine. What we discovered changed our perspective forever."

"Detailed imaging of the mechanism suggests that at one time it had more gear wheels enabling it to follow the movements of the moon and the sun through the zodiac, to predict eclipses, and even to model the irregular orbit of the moon. There are some missing pieces, and we hope to find them in the wreckage."

Hushed whispers echoed throughout the room.

"As you could expect, we reacted with astonishment when the team from the University told us what we had discovered. While the excitement of the discovery of this device is profound, so is the desire to understand its ancient uses fully. You see, it is far more ancient than we first thought."

"Based on the captain's ship log, the artifact was discovered in 1754 by Captain Benjamin Munroe among wreckage retrieved from a shipwreck off the coast of Italy. The instrument is believed to have been designed and constructed by ancient Greek astronomers and dated to approximately 70-60 BC."

A wave of whispers filtered through the room again. Kaira suspected this would have a significant role in the meeting later this evening with Alex and Father Murphy. She wondered what Jonathan knew.

"Many things have suppressed progress in understanding not only the legends of Westonville but how science and religion have become woven into our history. What we do know is that knowledge of this technology became lost at some point in antiquity and technological works approaching its complexity and artistry did not appear again until the development of astronomical mechanical clocks in Europe in the fourteenth century. Because of Captain Benjamin Munroe, and the Jesuit who invented Space Treasure Mapping, here we are today looking at this gap in history and asking ourselves how it became lost in the first place."

"Its construction relied on the very complex knowledge of astronomy and mathematics developed by Greek astronomers. The University created a replica of what this device would have looked like when it was created."

The visuals overhead dissolved into images of a watch with intricate gears and inscriptions within a glass case for viewing.

"Rings and scales represent the path of the ecliptic through the heavens and the 365-day civil calendar, which we believe is Egyptian. Also, we believe a partial second dial marks the Greek signs of the Zodiac. How could they have understood the position of the sun on the ecliptic corresponds to the current date in the year? Or the orbits of the moon and the five planets defining their positions?"

"Some single characters marking locations of longitudes on the ecliptic for specific stars are shown on the zodiac dial. The rear face of the device has inscriptions in Greek of the Moon, Sun, hour of the Day, and hour of the Night. Also, on the back, the twelve Corinthian months are represented."

A closeup of the image revealed the actual complexity of the dials with Greek letters engraved in the metal.

Challenging enough in the modern-day to create, thought Kaira.

"I know you are asking yourself the same questions we have been asking since this discovery. How did they have this knowledge in 60 BC? Why was it lost? How did Captain Benjamin discover this, and now that we have it, what will we learn?"

Chapter Sixteen

Jonathan had experienced many moments of wonder at a discovery site with the SSRL team. He'd felt the total exhilaration of bringing artifacts to the surface of the ocean many times and understood what the guests were experiencing. At this moment, he watched the faces of the crowd as they absorbed the information he had given them and wondered how they would react.

As the presentation ended and the lights came up, Jonathan resisted the urge to walk out the door and avoid the questions he knew were coming. The display created curiosity, and he was sure the influential wealthy who had gathered in the room would want time with Alex too.

He glanced at Kaira and saw an expression he couldn't read. Was it confusion or anger that caused her brow to furrow between her beautiful eyes. He wanted to take her far away and talk to her alone. He was longing to permit himself the pleasure and joy of his discovery, but with her only. Why was the emotion so strong?

He glanced toward the door to give Father Murphy a nod and bring him to the platform. To his surprise, however, Father Murphy was not looking in his direction. Instead, he was bending over something in the hallway outside the door, his face full of concern.

Kaira had been watching Father Murphy from her chair behind the priests. Something was wrong.

One of the servers from the catering company was walking toward Jonathan. He wore a black silk catering jacket and tan slacks. Where was the other caterer who had served her a glass of wine? Kaira sensed the alarm on Jonathan's face as the caterer approached the platform.

What's going on?

Kaira turned to look at the door where the guests were noticing the commotion as well, but Jonathan was not looking at Father Murphy. He was staring at her.

Something's wrong!

In that instant, the girl with the tight dress and red lipstick, utterly oblivious to the chaos unfolding in the room, jolted forward in an awkward attempt to get close to Jonathan and question him. Kaira watched in horror as a small trickle of blood ran down the stunned girl's bosom, and she fell in a heap at Jonathan's feet. The man in the black silk catering shirt was gone.

Before Kaira could comprehend what she had witnessed, Jonathan was at her side and dragging her away from the chaos.

In the hall, Father Murphy and some of the priests were moving Alex's body to a bench along the wall. A group of guests had formed around the scene blocking their attempt to help Alex.

"Call an ambulance." Father Murphy shouted.

As the chaos continued, Kaira felt paralyzed by shock. Alex lay on a bench with blood foaming at his mouth. His face was white and lifeless. The television crew had left the camera on and unattended.

Jonathan pulled her hand, and she felt as though it were a dream. She turned one last time and looked at the confused guests and knew for sure their lives were in danger.

"We've got to leave," Jonathan whispered.

Not far from Father Murphy and Alex's body, Kaira saw Umberto protectively overlooking the scene. A guest tried to push his way toward Alex, and Umberto acted on instinct. Putting his arms out, he blocked the crowd and guided them away from Alex and Father Murphy.

"Move back and make way for the gurney." He shouted.

The crowd formed a path, and Kaira could hear the ambulance pulling up at the front entrance.

A few yards away from the chaos, Jonathan and Kaira scrambled through a group of guests in the gallery and tried to reach the library. They were safe, Jonathan assured himself, but he'd seen Alex's face and knew he was dead. He felt confident there was nothing he could do for him.

Jonathan had noticed the caterer seemed to be out of place an instant before the girl hit the floor. He wondered if anyone thought to check on her. Then the second gurney came through the front entrance. At this moment, he had one task. Get Kaira to safety.

As they arrived in the library, he found an empty vial on the floor. Jonathan wrapped the bottle in a napkin and put it in his pocket. The door to the terrace had been left open. Carefully he glanced through the door looking out onto the lawn.

To his left, he caught a glimpse of one of the servers dressed in black silk caterers jacket and tan slacks sprinting toward the vineyard at the far side of the property. There was something very familiar in the way he ran. An instant later, the fleeing figure crashed through rows of vines and into a grove of trees along the river.

Not far behind Umberto gave pursuit weaving through the vines and bursting through the grove of trees he peered over the river ledge and saw the fugitive floating down the swift current. Racing back to the Manor, he reached for his cell phone, and Jonathan heard him talking to Police Chief Jackson.

Downriver, Brian pulled himself out of the water and into a rental car that now accelerated down the road. Something had gone terribly wrong. No one was supposed to die. And soon, they'll come for me, he thought.

As his car sped along the river and disappeared into town traffic, he allowed himself to breathe. A year wasted. His mission couldn't have gone worse. He could feel invisible chains tightening around his middle as fear tensed inside his gut.

He had grown into adulthood under the adventurous spirit of his profoundly eccentric father, who had believed he and his brother would both continue the tradition of seeking treasure through underhanded conventions, a network of investors, and above all, never allowing the Westonville Historical Society any knowledge of their findings.

For years, their father had built his contacts, but in recent years the network had seemed to be crumbling, and he found himself locked in a tug of war between lack of finances and respect from the investors.

A growing number of investors were now going into seclusion and suggesting they no longer needed him. Emerging from his father's shadow to become a bold leader in the underworld of those who seek treasure, stoked the fires in his soul.

His father had played an active role as a leader in the treasure hunting world and openly stated he wanted his sons to follow in his footsteps. He had believed they would eventually take his role and engage in matters of business. Despite his father's wishes, Jonathan had left the family and gone on to get his masters at a University. Over the years, he had done well.

He was wealthy, successful, and, most importantly, followed the rules of the American Shore and Beach Preservation Association. He was their pet. Now that he'd found a shipwreck, he would give its contents away to the Westonville Historical Society. Brian's blood boiled as he allowed his feelings of failure to turn to anger.

There was nothing conservative about him. He had never been discreet and cautious as a child. Willing to allow his sibling to be the noble and responsible brother, he had always hoped to be his father's successor. After their mother died, their father didn't remarry. He enjoyed not being tied down by matrimony.

A growing number of modern pirates were flooding the underworld, and rumors suggested that Brian would reveal his true self, a weak, insignificant leader unable to continue the work his father had so meticulously guarded and managed. Brian had no place to participate in the new market.

He wondered about Jonathan and Kaira. She was more than a pretty face. After high school, Kaira Munroe quickly revealed her fierce independence, who, despite being the only heir to Meadow Manor, had gone to University and become a leading New York journalist. She'd refused to permit the wealth of her grandmother to interfere with her daily life.

The local Westonville newspaper splashed a photo of Meadow Manor on the cover, "Kaira Munroe, a Vineyard's Youthful Future!". She refused to interview when they found out she was coming to her grandmother's Wake. Local journalists hailed her as independent and the new future of Westonville.

Brian knew he had been a selfish, power-hungry opportunist who was mostly trying to stay alive. He and his brother hadn't spoken since he'd left just out of high school. Tired of playing second fiddle, he'd gone off on his own and used his father's name to find a niche as a treasure hunter.

His blatant disregard for the investor's reputations landed him in an Italian prison. The investor's initial concern about him centered on his habit of addressing the leader of the covert group by a nickname. Their second concern, however, seemed more pressing. After being contracted for a specific job, he made himself entirely unavailable to the leader, yet he had repeatedly been seen diving off the Italian coast.

Despite his insistence that he was merely exploring beaches, his resources had quickly dried up, and the investors suggested to him that the leader's patience was beginning to wane. The truth of the matter was that he had decided to go rogue, only days after investors bankrolled his job, choosing to spend his time on his clandestine projects.

Chapter Seventeen

Jonathan remained focused on Kaira's safety. The weight of responsibility was heavy. Strangely, she looked serene. His emotions were shattered and numb woven with threads of fear and outrage. Alex, one of Astronomy's most genius minds, had just died a horrible death. He died before he could reveal Victoria's discovery to Kaira.

What if they would never know what Alex and Victoria had discovered?

His fear for Kaira's safety turned to anger, followed by bold determination. He would do anything to protect her and find out who was responsible for this tragedy.

"Did you know him?" Kaira's voice whispered, close to his shoulder. I thought I saw you look at him just before...." Her voice trailed off.

"I...I'm not sure." Jonathan barely managed. "I think he wore a disguise."

Jonathan could feel her staring at his face twisted in anger. "The caterer...I might have known him."

Kaira's head was close to his ear as he bent closer. Her voice was breathless and urgent.

"Was he after you?"

Jonathan shook his head.

"The truth, I don't know. I saw two servers at the wine bar. They dressed alike."

"The girl, she blocked the killer."

As the word "killer" was spoken, Jonathan stood straight and took a deep breath. One of the caterer's... *I know him*, realized Jonathan. Kaira's right. He pulled away and looked at the path where they were standing. Kaira stood in front of him, looking into his face for answers.

Jonathan's heart twisted painfully into a knot as he looked back into her face. She wanted answers, but his head was spinning, and he felt a deep ache in his soul.

"We have to find a safe place, Kaira."

From their position at the side of the Manor, they could see the ambulance loading the gurneys.

"Where's Father Murphy?"

Umberto was shouting across the yard toward the entrance, where a group of guests still stood stunned as they gave an account to Police Chief Jackson.

Jonathan reached out and put his arm around Kaira and led her toward Jackson.

"Jackson, we need to talk."

Jackson turned from the EMT's loading the gurney.

"Jonathan, I'm here. Let's go up onto the porch."

Seconds later, the ambulance slowly pulled out of the entrance, dissolving any illusion that Alex was alright.

Jackson was tall, almost as tall as Jonathan, with gray hair and a trim build that fit well in his officer's jacket. His face was somber, and his eyes focused on Kaira and Jonathan.

"You were here tonight speaking, weren't you?"

"Yes, that's right. Alex and I had just met a couple of weeks ago through Victoria."

"I've spoken briefly with Father Murphy." He said. "Can you tell me what happened tonight?" He asked Jonathan. "Tell me what you know about the caterer."

Jonathan glanced toward Kaira, who stood motionless beside him on the porch. Father Murphy was guiding people back inside to the banquet hall, where officers were taking statements. Kaira moved close to Jonathan and gently put her hand on his back. Alex and Victoria were gone forever. She found it challenging to comprehend.

Jonathan focused his eyes on Jackson.

"Did you know him?" he asked. "Had you ever seen him before?"

Jackson was a professional though they had been friends for years. His tone left no room for error.

Quickly Jonathan and Kaira relayed what had happened, that Alex had fallen ill in the hallway, and while the guests were distracted with him, the girl had fallen at Jonathan's feet. Then he had tried to get Kaira to safety, fearful that they might be next.

"Why would someone be after you?" Jackson asked his face intense.

"I don't know. I need to make sure Kaira is safe. We ran to the library and out onto the terrace where we saw a man running through the vines toward the river. Umberto chased him, but he must have jumped in the river."

"Umberto relayed to us that he was a last-minute replacement for one of the servers who had become ill." Said Jackson.

"He wasn't regular?" Jonathan looked disturbed.

"No," Jackson told them. "We found that he had no connection whatsoever to the catering company, nor to Alex Mirabelli, which bothered me. I contacted the catering company, but they argued they didn't want to ruin the Wake at the last minute knowing how hard Father Murphy had worked putting it together."

Jonathan found it unnerving that the killer seemed to have no direct connection or contact with Father Murphy. He glanced at Kaira and saw the confusion on her face.

Jackson continued to focus on Jonathan.

"Do you have a name for the caterer?" asked Jonathan

"Yes," he said, "but it's an alias. "He was registered under the name Dwain Watson."

As he spoke the name, Jonathan froze and looked down at Kaira, a look of anger in his eyes.

Jackson noted his reaction and immediately turned toward him. "Jonathan, do you know the name?"

Unable to reply, he lowered his gaze and shook his head, but his face paled.

"Jonathan," Jackson repeated. "Are you sure you haven't heard his name, Dwain Watson?"

After a second, he blinked, and his eyes began to clear. "No, I'm sure I don't know that name," he said firmly, stepping close to Kaira. "I was just surprised to hear you already had the name of the killer."

Kaira knew he was lying but was puzzled why he wouldn't tell Jackson the truth. He had recognized the name.

Jackson was interrupted by a sudden release of guests coming through the entrance. The officers had finished taking statements. The guests headed toward their cars talking on their cell phones, some shaking their heads as they still processed the shock of the evening.

Seeing one of the officers approaching, Jackson took a deep breath and stepped to the side. With Jackson distracted, Jonathan gazed at Kaira. She returned his gaze for a moment. He spoke in a quiet calm voice.

"Kaira," he whispered, "I don't know him personally, but a man with that name has been stalking SSRL for weeks."

Jonathan needed to process the information.

The killer followed Jonathan to the Wake? Why wouldn't he want Jackson to know?

Umberto spoke to Kaira before she had a chance to process.

"There's a call for you inside on the landline from East Coast Traveler."

Kaira immediately recoiled at the name. "No. I can't take the call."

"He says he's your boss."

"I don't care if he's the President of the United States," she fired back. "If he's going to get my work, he'll have to give me the freedom I need."

"Tell him she's just witnessed a tragedy, and she'll call him back." Said Jonathan.

Her eyes burned with fire, but she said nothing. That's the girl he remembered from high school, fiercely independent and beautiful when she was angry.

Umberto stared at her, then walked back inside his emotion, bordering on admiration. He walked down the hall and spoke into the phone then hung up.

Jonathan wondered if Kaira had a relationship with her boss. The last few minutes had solved one mystery. Her boss wanted a story. Then another thought struck Jonathan. She's connected with the tabloids, and that's why her boss is checking in. Of course, he's calling for the latest news. Maybe she just got her biggest tabloid story.

The revelation sent anger through him as he recalled the tabloids that had harassed him over the past few weeks.

Chapter Eighteen

Across the river along the rock cliffs, Father Murphy stood looking out of the Abbey window. He still wore his clothing from earlier at the Wake and was fixated on events from the evening. He knew everything. Victoria wasn't about to leave any room for error. Thank God for that, but the next few months would be dangerous.

He'd believed she was going to unveil the truth prematurely and tried to warn her. Now from what he had witnessed tonight, an undercurrent of predators might be on the way. Jackson and the officers seemed to agree that by all appearances, someone had a vendetta out for Alex, but had Alex been the only target? Was it his silence they sought, or something more sinister?

After a long moment overlooking the river below and Meadow Manor beyond, Father Murphy sat down at his desk and placed a call.

Giovanni Fiorelli answered on the second ring.

"I have some good news and some bad news. Which do you want to hear first?"

"Tell me the bad first."

"Alex is dead." Said Father Murphy flatly.

"Dio!" the archeologist's voice croaked. "How in God's name? Who did this?"

"Yes, it is the most horrifying event. They are coming after the relics, I'm sure of it."

"Who do you mean?"

"You know who I mean. But we need to think. We can go to the media now, but we must think this through carefully."

"What is there to think about? Either way, we are in danger." He shot back. "It is clear they want to snuff out the truth. They will stop at nothing to possess the relics."

"I am convinced there is more than one group looking for the relics." Said Father Murphy.

"What do you mean? More than one group will be coming for us?"

"Not exactly. Father Murphy said. "It is my belief a rogue may have committed the deed tonight. He wasn't a professional. But, that doesn't mean professionals won't be far behind."

"What was the point of killing Alex?"

"I've been asking myself the same question. Killing Alex would silence the publicity of his discovery. At first, I thought it was the Order of the Serpent sending an agent to silence the truth, but there may be more."

"Yes, Order of the Serpent was my first thought. I respect your thinking." Giovanni said in an even tone. "I am open to discussing what you think might have happened."

"I don't think anyone knew what Alex's discovery was other than Victoria. Alex's discovery may go to the grave with him."

Father Murphy could hear Giovanni's troubled breathing on the line.

"Are you saying we may never know?"

"I'm not sure. I must think this through in the light of day with all the evidence in front of me. We are familiar with the Order of the Serpent, and we are fully aware of their capability. They are heartless killers. However, someone may have inadvertently done them a favor tonight, but all parties are empty-handed."

"The murder has put us back in the spotlight." Said Giovanni.

"Exactly."

"And the Order of the Serpent will think we know where the relics are." Giovanni was beginning to see. "Do you know where the relics are hidden?"

"My friend," Father Murphy continued ignoring the question, "the most pressing issue at hand is our safety. We are dealing with an old society whose long arms reach from the time before the Vatican became a reality. We are suddenly, inadvertently, exposed. I am worried that if we come out with the truth, we will end up dead. You must find protection."

"I am surrounded by secrets and societies. I am buried in their nonsense. I'm not sure where to go for protection. It has been difficult here. The museum curator has halted our permits and blocked access to our discovery."

"I have resources there through Umberto. Do you remember Victoria's producer?"

"Yes, he is a good man."

"Stay where you are in Albano Laziale. I will speak with Umberto and request a safe home for you until we can speak again. Together we will find the best solution for our situation."

"And if Umberto cannot help?" Giovanni pressed.

Father Murphy felt his brow tighten with tension. He paused and exhaled. "Many years ago, Victoria rescued Umberto from the hands of the Order of the Serpent. He will help you, my friend. Stand firm."

"On your honor, I will stand," Giovanni replied. "On your word, I will have faith."

"Good. In the meantime, do not send any emails and do not speak about this on an unsecured line. Tell no one about this conversation. Hang in there, my friend. I hope to speak to you again very soon."

"What's the good news?" Giovanni asked.

"Victoria's granddaughter came to the Wake. She'll inherit."

Father Murphy hung up, knowing what he had to do. He suspected the request he was about to make of Umberto would require an enormous sacrifice.

The Order of the Serpent was panicking. They saw the bigger picture. Soon they would be on the doorstep.

Father Murphy tidied his desk and made his way toward the evening's ceremony in the chapel. Glancing once more from the window, he observed Meadow Manor in the glow of the moon. "Heroes of old, Men of Renown," he said out loud. Still wearing the same robes from earlier in the day, he exited his quarters and headed toward the chapel brightly lit in the cold moonlight.

The motto was becoming more and more relevant each day. His thoughts turned to Victoria.

I will miss her. So many owe her so much.

He had visited with her for months throughout her illness. Some days were better than others. Just before she died, she had summoned him and shown him things that had caused his blood to run cold.

"Please, make sure you contact my granddaughter." She had whispered through parched lips. "She is our hope."

Father Murphy had held her hand and smiled at her. "Yes, I will do all that you have said. I will make sure she receives the invitation."

"She is not aware of who she is. While she is well able to take care of herself, and she doesn't need my help, it is the fire in her that changes everything."

"I have seen it in her writing. I concur." Said Father Murphy.

Victoria reached out and took Father Murphy's hand. "You are a good friend. We are growing old. I want to thank you for all you have done for Umberto and me. You have given me great strength and courage throughout my life and counseled me wisely. I desire to give back."

"I will always treasure our friendship forever."

Victoria smiled. "Father, please do for Kaira what you have done for me."

Father Murphy smiled and shrugged. "That is my job. I am a shepherd. There is nothing I want more than to care for your granddaughter. It is an honor and a privilege."

"Your goodness to me has been a tremendous blessing." Said Victoria weakly.

"I will never forget what you did for our Abbey and me all those years ago."

Victoria closed her eyes, gripping Father Murphy's hand. "Please find Umberto. I need Umberto."

"I will find him."

Now in the cold November air, Father Murphy made his way to the chapel and raised his eyes toward the stars.

I will follow your wishes, Victoria.

Chapter Nineteen

There is no time to hesitate, Jonathan told himself, fighting back the sluggish feeling in his feet. I must act quickly.

Jonathan caught Umberto in the entryway and asked him to send any information regarding security feeds that might be helpful to his cell phone. Then quietly, he asked for help distracting Jackson.

Jackson was on the phone, and Jonathan could tell he was about to end the call. He watched as Jackson turned to Kaira.

"We must leave." He turned his full attention to Kaira, "Father Murphy has requested that we get you to safety at the Abbey."

Her body visibly tensed. "I will not be going to the Abbey." She motioned to Jonathan.

"Local authorities will be working in the manor, taking over this matter," Jackson replied. "It will be more comfortable at the Abbey."

"I will not be going to the Abbey!" Kaira declared and looked Jackson squarely in the face. "If someone wanted me dead, I would be dead. They did not."

"Kaira, how about New York? Mr. Mercer would like you to come back. You can safely continue your work there."

"No!" she shot back. "There's nothing safe about Mr. Mercer."

Jackson exhaled, lowering his voice. "Kaira, this has been a terrible blow. You've lost your grandmother for God's sake. We should have contacted you earlier. How could we have known this would happen?"

Suddenly Umberto was next to them. "Jackson? The forensic team has been analyzing the glass from the podium."

Jonathan listened as Umberto said, "One of your forensic team found something from the glass."

"Oh?" said Jackson, surprised.

Umberto relayed the information. "Looks like it's a kind of poison…the kind you find on the black market…kills within a minute, depending on the dose."

Jonathan was amazed at how quickly Umberto had been able to shift the attention.

"As you are aware, the poison will have to be analyzed."

"Are you saying my team already knows what killed Alex and the girl?" Jackson was surprised at the speed of their assessment. "Why would someone kill Alex with poison?"

They'd gone inside and were sitting in the banquet room. Jackson had set up a center of communication with his team on one of the tables. Sufficiently distracted from Jonathan and Kaira, Police Chief Jackson sat at a side table drinking coffee and wearing a look of frustration on his face. It seemed the killer had escaped downstream. He'd floated down the river to a turnout where he must have had a car waiting. Maybe he hired a taxi, Jackson thought.

They'd been working for a couple of hours, and it was getting dark.

"Sir," one of Jackson's team was on the line, "she was a nobody. I mean, she has no ties to Alex or Victoria."

The young woman who had been targeted with the poison dart was in the hospital.

"Looks like she wasn't poisoned, just sedated."

"The killer used a volatile poison on Alex knowing it would kill within seconds, but not on the woman," said Jackson. "It doesn't make sense."

"He was after Alex, sir." Said the officer. "But why not her?"

"Good question. Keep at it, Fred. Get to the bottom of this." He turned to Jonathan.

"He's made his getaway. We've notified authorities in Westonville and along the highways. They are preparing roadblocks." Jackson felt like he was playing catch up with the killer. "You two might still be in danger. I want you to stay at the Abbey until we find him."

Kaira's mouth fell open, and Jonathan sensed she was not accustomed to being told what to do. Jonathan thought she was going to ask Jackson to mind his own business.

Jackson was signaling for Umberto while Kaira shook her head.

"No, that isn't going to happen." She commanded.

Jonathan had to admit it seemed safe compared to the Manor. However, the likelihood of the killer coming back to the manor was slim.

"We've already made arrangements with Father Murphy. You'll be staying at the Abbey." Demanded Jackson.

Umberto dialed Father Murphy to let him know they were on the way, and Jonathan felt his confidence rising that Kaira would be safe. Protecting the innocent and vulnerable was the heart of St. Francis Abbey. All Jackson was asking is that they stay there until the killer was caught.

"Jonathan, I will transport the two of you to the Abbey."

"I don't plan to stay at the Abbey." Said Jonathan.

"Oh yes, you and Kaira will stay together until this is over."

"Jackson, I will not be staying at the Abbey."

"I find it odd that you do not wish to stay with Kaira." Jonathan was unaccustomed to the harsh tone Jackson had taken. With that, Jackson walked out of the room.

Jonathan watched him leave.

"Kaira," Jonathan moved in close to her and whispered. "I have to tell you something vital."

Kaira was startled to see the expression of fear on his face.

"My grandmother trusted you, and It's clear to see you have the respect of Father Murphy and Umberto." She said.

Jonathan faced her and placed his hands on her shoulders.

"I think this might be my fault." A frown pinched his brows.

"How could this possibly be your fault?"

He glanced nervously through the door where Jackson was talking to one of his officers.

"I think I'm the reason Alex was murdered." Now his eyes were filled with pain. "The killer followed me here."

"Wait a minute…don't jump to conclusions just yet." She took his hand. "Tell me what happened."

Jonathan shot another glance at the door where Jackson talked into his cell phone.

"He was following our team in the Caribbean. There are lots of pirates lurking about when someone finds treasure." He rubbed his forehead. "I received a threatening letter a few weeks ago that

someone was going to send a message very soon." She looked up at Jonathan. "How could I know he would do this?"

"Jonathan," Kaira was whispering. "Who knows about the threats?"

"My team at SSRL. No one else." He shook his head.

Kaira sat back in her chair in disbelief, trying to comprehend his words.

A stalker had just claimed responsibility for the life at Victoria's Wake. Alex, a well-known astronomer, and an attempt on a guest no one knew. It didn't make sense.

"No one here suspects I've had any contact with the killer or that I know his identity," he said. "But, I think it is true, and my greatest fear is that we are both in danger."

Jonathan took both her hands in his.

"Kaira, other things are going on here that you don't understand. We need to get out of here now."

"What will happen if we run?" Kaira countered.

"Listen to me," Jonathan urged. "I know what we need to do."

"What? You should tell Jackson you're in danger."

"No. Please listen to me Kaira," His tone was insistent. "First, we have to get away from here. We need to get out of Westonville for a while."

"What are you saying?"

"Listen, I know what Victoria would want us to do."

For the next few seconds, Jonathan whispered in her ear. As he talked, Kaira felt her heart begin to pound.

"My God, what are you saying?" She wasn't sure if he was right. But, nothing else made sense.

Jonathan found Umberto. "We are going to need your help."

Chapter Twenty

As they moved down the gallery hall toward the library, Jonathan kept an eye on Jackson, who was still talking on the cell with one of his officers. Kaira casually drifted toward her car and told Jackson she was moving it to a better location in the garage.

As Jonathan reached the library, he thought of the vial he'd found on the floor and touched his jacket pocket. It was still there. He looked at the library full of an extraordinary collection of unusual books and thought of Victoria's bright blue eyes. She was gone and now, Alex too. His heart was pumping with anger.

For a moment, he could see the brilliant astronomer and recent acquaintance. He had been full of hope and excitement, a man who had accomplished so much in his short life. Horrifically, tonight, someone had murdered him and most certainly by accident.

Jonathan positioned himself in the library next to the French doors and lifted his eyes to search quickly for a book. When he was sure Jackson hadn't spotted him, he discreetly slid the book out of its spot and slipped through the doors onto the terrace then sprinted toward the aqua blue Volkswagen.

Kaira winced as the motor roared to life. She pulled the car around to the riverside and hid behind the winery. Jonathan glanced back toward the entrance, where Jackson still seemed more interested in what the officer was telling him.

He turned his eyes to Kaira's blue VW and took a breath. Then he opened the door and folded his body into the passenger seat. He barely pulled it shut against his side.

"Do you have the card?"

She handed Jonathan the card Alex had passed to her in the chamber earlier that evening. They headed toward the pier.

"I have to tell you about a conversation I had with Victoria a few nights before she passed. But, I'm not sure how to begin."

"Begin at the beginning."

"There's a secret society who wants something your grandmother has."

"A secret society? I didn't know they existed any longer. Who are they?"

"Order of the Serpent." Jonathan looked at the book in his hands. "And they are the underbelly of all secret societies."

"What does my grandmother have that they want?" Kaira thought of the passages beneath the Manor, which sent a slight shiver up her spine.

"Alex was going to show you after the Celebration of Life." He paused. "Ironic isn't it….two deaths…Victoria and Alex. Both full of secrets."

They were quiet.

"They'll see us leaving through the entrance."

"We don't have to take the main road." He smiled grimly. "I used another trail when I was in high school."

Kaira looked confused. "Another trail?"

She saw a mask come over his features. "Go upstream. Everyone who looks downstream will see the roadblock. A quarter-mile upstream, there's a dirt road on the right. It crosses a rickety bridge, but it's strong enough for your VW.

"What were you doing up here when we were in high school?"

"Never mind."

Kaira threw up her hand and smiled playfully. "Okay, you're the boss."

Her focus turned back to the task as she spotted a faded dirt road up ahead.

In her rear-view mirror, she saw a vehicle pulling out of the gate at Meadow Manor. If she was lucky, they might not see her pulling off the road.

Quickly she turned right, and they bumped down the narrow, unmaintained road.

More alarming, she spotted the old covered bridge crossing the river.

"Oh, my God! You said we could cross. I don't think I can do this."

Wood slats had rotted, leaving a few beams. There was one place to cross, but she would have to keep the wheels straight.

We'll never make it!

Suddenly, Jonathan placed one hand on her shoulder and the other her hand on the wheel.

"You can do this!"

She shifted into first and pushed through some brush that had grown over the entrance to the bridge.

"They won't see us once we're inside the bridge." He said quietly. "Stay in first gear and take it slow."

Kaira felt Jonathan's hand firmly on the wheel, guiding them onto the old beams. The sound changed inside the bridge, and the rushing water below distracted her.

A whimper passed her lips.

"It's okay. You can do this. Kaira, where's your cell phone?"

"In my glove compartment."

Jonathan rolled down his window, then reached into her glove compartment and with his free hand-tossed her cell into the foaming water below.

Startled, she almost swerved off the rails. Good thing she hadn't told him about the cell her grandmother gave her safely tucked in her jacket.

"What are you doing?" she yelled over the noise of the rushing water.

"They'll track us."

"Who will track us?"

"Jackson, for one." He reminded her. "Even if he has good intentions."

Kaira tried not to look down at the rocks beneath the empty areas where the wood had rotted. Instead, she focused on the two rails she had to follow. They were more substantial than they seemed initially.

A moment later, they were on the other side.

***

Jackson sent officer Brody after Jonathan and Kaira. They weren't fugitives, but they were in danger. The police car pulled out of the entrance and headed downstream. A few yards down the road, he realized he should have seen the VW. How could it have disappeared?

Where did they go?

Officer Brody called Jackson.

"The car disappeared." Brody hated sounding stupid, but he didn't know what else to say.

"What do you mean it disappeared?" demanded Jackson. "There are only two directions they could go."

Up the hill a few yards, the road ended, so he hadn't looked in that direction. Jackson, a perfectionist who ran a tight ship, felt more than an obligation when it came to protecting the lives of his friends. Tonight, he'd given Brody a simple directive: "Don't let that girl out of your sight."

Jackson was glad the guests were finally gone. He made his way to the darkened banquet hall now empty of the group of wealthy elites with shell-shocked faces trying to make sense of what they'd witnessed.

Jackson's phone rang. It was an officer on the roadblock. "All the guests have left except two. There's no sight of Jonathan Bell and Kaira Munroe. They still up there?"

He didn't answer. Jackson didn't know how, but it appeared they had slipped past the roadblock.

"Stay on the lookout for the rental car. That's more important right now." They'd found a car rental with the name Dwain Watson on the rental agreement.

Jackson sat in the empty banquet hall. "Jonathan and Kaira just slipped past the roadblock? There has to be another road." He said to Brody. His heart was pounding in frustration. A new thought had been swirling in his mind. What if the killer was after Jonathan? His officers were having difficulty tracking the killer's rental. Could anything else go wrong?

He had never imagined that he'd see Kaira again, much less at her grandmother's Wake. Her family had stayed away from Meadow Manor since she was seven. After her family died in the accident, and she graduated, she'd become someone else in New York.

It seemed inconceivable that Victoria was gone, and another had died tonight in what was beginning to look like an assassination attempt. The expression on Jonathan's face when he had said the name Dwain Watson told him Jonathan knew the man. His unusual reaction had escalated when, by all appearances, he and Kaira had ditched security to run off together.

I'm missing something!

"Police Chief?" Brody's voice interrupted. "We've spotted a blue VW on the other side of the river climbing the mountain. The car was seen in the trees beneath St. Francis Abbey."

Maybe Jonathan was taking her to the Abbey after all.

"Thanks. Keep tracking them."

Several hundred yards up the hill, on the other side of the river, Jonathan and Kaira were making their way up the zig zags leading to the Abbey. Everything had happened so quickly with their decision to leave. They were running on instinct.

On Jonathan's cue, Umberto had distracted the officers, and they'd made their getaway. Jonathan recalled with gratefulness how Umberto had helped them.

"My promise to Victoria was to assist and protect Kaira in every way possible. I hope I have not failed." The words streamed from Umberto as though he were her grandfather, who cared deeply. "If I could protect Kaira, I would, but I believe you are aware we will have unwanted visitors soon. It appears I will be required to protect the secret Victoria has guarded so well for so long. Because Kaira has the only key to Victoria's apartment in the winery, she shouldn't be here when they arrive."

"I agree. Let's access Alex's information and files. I'm hoping he kept it on the Yacht. It seems probable that what he was going to release to Kaira tonight will be there."

"I do not think it would be wise to involve our local Police Chief any further. I will divert them while you make your getaway."

Incredibly, it appeared Umberto had found a way they could do just that.

They ascended through the tall pine trees at the foot of the mountain beneath St. Francis Abbey. Jonathan wondered if Alex had shared his discovery. Umberto said it seemed unlikely that anyone other than Alex, Victoria, and their friend in Italy, the archeologist Giovanni. However, was it possible Father Murphy knew? He had been a very close friend and advisor to Victoria. She trusted him. But, he was surrounded by those with questionable motives. Jonathan sensed Umberto understood.

"Jonathan, may I ask you something…" Kaira shifted into a lower gear, and they continued to climb. "Considering all that has happened this evening, it seems there are other forces behind what happened. I am not so sure this is just about your stalker."

Bearing in mind that all of it had started with her digging into the affairs of Jonathan and his shipwreck discovery in the Caribbean. "What if my articles inspired others besides the stalker?" Kaira continued.

Jonathan had considered the possibility and felt a flash of anger at the unsolicited publicity.

They reached the top of the mountain. The road separated up ahead. Left took them to the Abbey and right took them over the hill. Kara stopped and waited for his directions.

"Take a right over the mountain. Once we pass the old Nike missile site and go over the top, this road will lead us to the coast. From there, we can get to the port without roadblocks."

Kaira wondered if Alex had thought this moment might arise. She hoped the second set of numbers on the card would help them find Alex's files. If they could make it to the Yacht undetected, they'd have to hurry.

The VW topped the mountain, and they made their way down the backside now, hidden from view.

"Once we reach the road below," Jonathan said, "take a right and head to the backside of the port."

A few minutes later, the VW was on blacktop heading for the port.

***

On the outskirts of Westonville, parallel to the coastline, a motorcycle raced along the beach toward the port pier. He had removed the silk catering jacket and now wore a sweatshirt and knitted fisherman's cap.

After dumping the vehicle in an alley, he had confiscated the motorcycle from a young man. Brian had pulled a needle from his pocket and held it to the kid's neck. At his command, the terrified teen had handed over his sweatshirt, hat, and wallet. The kid had slid off the bike without question.

Soon I will be sailing out of town as quietly as I floated in, Brian thought. He could see the roadblock and police cars from the beach. They were looking for his rental. He sped up the beach wishing he was basking in the afterglow of the evening's events. Instead, he was thinking of the precautions he would have to take to protect himself and the misunderstandings that would surface.

As he rushed toward the pier, he gazed at the bay. He'd have to take his chances getting past the coast guard. His small sailboat rarely brought unwanted attention. He looked up the mountain and saw the Abbey rising from the tree line.

Their influence was everywhere. Two of Brian's investors were Catholics, but the Italian group he had aligned himself with were Order of the Serpent, a secret society that associated themselves as Catholics.

Brian realized Father Murphy was a devoted priest who would find no good in the Order. Father Murphy was appalled at how happy the masses were to believe everything they heard.

The only good to come of it was when he had been forced to join the Order of the Serpent, questions of all their secrets were open for discussion. A few secrets were revealed to the members. He remembered the legends of Westonville and his father's obsession, and now Brian knew something he wished he didn't. Jonathan was close. Too close. Brian hated what he was being forced to do.

Chapter Twenty One

Civico Museo Albano Laziale, Italy

Italy, one of the world's central hubs for discovering large bones and megalithic empires built during the time before the world flood, has been under the power of the Holy See from the beginning. Italy's oldest seat of world power, the Holy See, for centuries has sanctioned or taken under control the truth of antiquity, ancient civilizations, anything that did not fit the Catholic Biblical narrative. The golden empires of the Aztecs in Mexico, Mayans in Central America, the Incas empire, all have one thing in common, gold, antiquity, and cover-up.

He knew why they wanted to suppress the true origins of history.

Antonio Callo, Curator of the museums in Albano Laziale, Italy, was a small sixty-five-year-old man with a gray complexion, beady eyes, and receding hairline. His mousy features made him invisible. However, he had enormous influence within the Carabinieri Command for the Protection of Cultural Heritage.

His real power stemmed from controlling any new artifacts, ancient relics and antiquities surfacing from dig sites. His leverage gave him clout in the archeological communities, but it was his savvy that had established him as the primary connection among archeologists in the Lazio region.

Now, however, he faced uncertainty if Giovanni came forward with his discovery. Antonio had been a reliable keeper of secrets, loyal to his church, and never betrayed the confidence that would have placed the Catholic Church or the Holy See in a bad light. With intuitive discretion, he carefully documented and put under lock and key any artifact, relic, text, or discovery that would be a threat to the Holy See.

For years he had established this system for museums and curators all over Italy to manage ancient antiquities under the supervision of the privileged elite. His system had created security for the Archeologists and institutions in the Lazio region. If Giovanni came forward with this information, it would incite the anger of the elite group, and every thief in Italy and Greece would be prowling around the excavation site. Antonio worked closely with Carabinieri to cement the security around new digs. He picked up his phone.

"Ciao, This is Antonio."

"Buona sera, how can I help you?"

"It's Giovanni. He has done an admirable job with his students and their dig sites, deferring to me on matters of antiquities and never once overstepping the boundaries set in place. Tonight, however, secrecy might be lifted in light of the news Giovanni has received from his friend, Father Murphy, in America. I am anxious to weigh in on the conference call. I sense Giovanni is troubled."

"You've done the right thing to give me a warning." The Carabinieri officer was Antonio's friend and one of the Italian military force charged with police duties."Listen well and contact me afterward. We will watch Giovanni.

Antonio prepared himself to be the guidance Giovanni needed. He hurried toward his villa and took a long breath before stepping into the garden courtyard. Antonio tapped the heavy metal knocker on the tall wooden door. He heard scuffling, and a faint voice said, "Venire in è aperto."

Quickly Antonio opened the door and let himself in.

"Giovanni?"

"Nello studio."

It was dark in the villa except for the amber light flickering from the study door. He hurried in and found Giovanni sitting in front of the fireplace with maps and books scattered around his chair. His hair was unkempt, and he still wore his robe and slippers though it was midday.

"Sei malato?" The cluttered disarray unsettled Antonio.

"No, I am not ill." Giovanni cleared his throat. "Not sick in my body, only in my soul." He spoke without moving, and he continued to stare into the fireplace flames. "When I spoke to Alex last, we were going to meet tonight via conference call." Giovanni sounded perplexed. "I don't understand how this could have happened."

Antonio was unsure how to reply. Given the recent events, it seemed Giovanni should be willing to continue without rocking the boat. The thought of bringing more people in on the secrets they carried caused strain in all their relationships.

"I wonder if I've made a terrible mistake," Giovanni said quietly.

The elder man poised to retire was uncertain of the future and direction the new professor taking his place would lean toward. For decades Giovanni had performed his duties deferring to the higher authorities on matters that were kept secret.

"I imagine you are still shocked by the news as I am." Antonio offered. "Father Murphy will quiet your heart when he calls. It is a relief to know he is safe. And there was a young lady who died? Was it the granddaughter of Victoria?"

"No, just a guest at the Wake. No one knew her. I hear she is alive."

Antonio nodded.

"Alex spoke to miss Munroe before the Celebration of Life." Antonio listened carefully.

"She left with Jonathan Bell after the Wake. No one knows where they were headed. But, I wonder…" His gaze never lifted from the flames licking the wood in the fireplace.

Antonio clenched his jaw but swallowed his anger. Unfortunately, his influence and zeal for discreet diplomacy in handling and controlling sensitive information meant absolutely nothing in America.

Antonio had learned long ago that Giovanni's loyal exterior to the Curator and the Holy See concealed a deeper simple reality: Giovanni believed the truth should be exposed, but the price had been too high and involved hurting others. Until recently, it had been easy to ignore, but now with the network and ability to spread information quickly on the internet, there was a shift in the balance of power. The thought of him passing on information to Father Murphy or the heiress Kaira Munroe was cause for significant concern.

Giovanni had always considered Father Murphy to be a trusted friend. He would quickly become his closest confidant.

"Giovanni, I believe we should handle this situation on our own. I feel strongly about this."

"Do you?" Giovanni declared, his voice suddenly loud.

Surprised, Antonio quickly turned his gaze to the man in the chair.

"I must say, Antonio," Giovanni's voice was low but steady, "I would think you of all people should know how much we both need Father Murphy's help."

"But, this is more than a political situation," Antonio said with matching strength. "It is about ancient secrets and religious loyalties."

Giovanni's voice was bitter, "I have grossly underestimated my power and knowledge. It seems there is only one appropriate response to this crisis. We must immediately assure that others hold the secrets and carefully reveal them in time. The thought of continuing as we've done for decades and centuries is making me ill.

"I understand…but, there are consequences for every action we take."

"And when the news hits the press, no one will feel those consequences more than you, Antonio… I also understand." He imagined Antonio facing the public with the inability to explain why he had kept the secrets for so long.

Antonio bristled.

"Eventually, the world will witness the ancient truths that were hidden for so long, and you will need friends by your side." Giovanni laid his head back and closed his eyes.

***

St. Francis Abbey, a community of more than fifty contemplative monks located near the town of Westonville, New York, boasted the best view of the Bay. The Abbey was considered the most mysterious and beautiful place on the east coast.

What is going on in our community? Father Murphy peered into the valley and across the river at Meadow Manor. Why would the Abbot advise him to keep a low profile?

Whenever Father Murphy felt unsettled, something about the vineyard view had always calmed him. For years, the terrace at night had been a place to reflect and enjoy the salty breeze from the Bay.

Along the Northside of the mountain, he faced south to view Meadow Manor. To the east, the town of Westonville sparkled like colorful gems slung along the Bay shoreline. To the west, the pines in the mountains. But, the stone walls of Meadow Manor and the vineyard captured his gaze every time.

Between the Abbey and Meadow Manor, the river flowed from high on the mountain down to the Bay. Tonight, it wasn't the view that brought him to the terrace, but something else.

The mystery and the legends.

Captain Benjamin Munroe marked his land and founded the community of Westonville. He put aside pirating and became a gentleman. Legends about Captain Benjamin Munroe and the discovery of the Bay told of passages that were thousands of years old connecting caves from the coast to the mountains. Whoever the first settlers were, they were gone long before the captain found the Bay.

It seemed to be the simplest of legends, thought Father Murphy as he gazed at the manor below. But, a darker, more sinister truth lay beneath the legends. Tonight, as he stared at the scene below, it seemed the world was turning too quickly. What Victoria shared in confidence with him gripped his soul. Fiction becomes fact, and legends become a nightmare.

The threat of darkness revealed hung in the air like a cloud over the beautiful valley full of wonderful moments, community, festivals. A whisper in his mind told him it was coming to the surface, and he wouldn't be able to stop it.

Though he knew it was his dark thought, he turned to look back. The French doors to his rooms stood open, and a sudden gust of wind blew the curtains.

"What is trying to surface?" he asked out loud.

He walked toward the door to close it and heard a sound above him on the roof. A large stone shattered on the terrace where he had been standing seconds earlier. He gasped and slammed the door shut behind him. He looked through the window at the broken rock a shiver of premonition overcame him.

A knock on the door startled him, and he spun around, looking for a weapon. His heart pounded in his chest. Had someone just tried to kill him? Who was knocking on his door this time of the evening?

"Father Murphy?" a familiar voice inquired. "Are you in there?"

Quickly he answered the door. The Abbot stood in the hallway with a worried expression on his face.

"May I speak to you?"

"Please come in." Father Murphy was suddenly very alert.

The Abbot seemed tense but tried to mask his emotions.

"I apologize for interrupting your evening. I hope you will accommodate me."

"What is wrong?" Father Murphy instinctively knew to say nothing about the shattered rock on the terrace.

"I've received a call from the Curator in Albano Laziale. He is a man of discretion and loyalty. He is worried about the recent events here in Westonville."

"I don't understand?" said Father Murphy.

"He knows you spoke to Giovanni recently, and he's concerned."

How did he know?

"He is concerned that Victoria may have provided you with extensive information about Alex's discovery, and you are deeply involved in something you may not fully understand." Said the Abbot

"What do you mean deeply involved?"

"Listen carefully," the Abbot paused, then lowered his voice. "I am concerned that you may be in danger if the Order is involved.

Father Murphy was well aware of the danger he had just escaped.

Chapter Twenty Two

The Westonville port sits in the center of the Bay near Friar's Deck Tavern, recognizable by its unique stone foundation built in the 1700s. The tavern took its name from the monks who helped build it. Tales of pirates and priests abound in the inn believed to be over three centuries old.

After making their way down the mountain, Jonathan and Kaira quickly covered the distance between the road and the parking lot behind Friar's Deck Tavern. They waited in the car, making sure no one had followed them. It wasn't difficult to pick out the Italian built Benetti yacht sitting in the last slip at the end of the pier.

Jonathan could see Kaira shivering beneath her light jacket. He turned the heat up then placed his hand on her cold fingers. She turned toward him. For an instant, they were back in high school. Her expression was innocent and soft.

"I had no idea you would be at Meadow Manor this evening. I'm glad and grateful you are here now. With his eyes locked on hers, he reached out and pushed a lock of hair away from her cheek. Then he quickly removed his hand.

"I'm sorry. Memories." His voice was low and gentle. Kaira smiled, reassuring him. "The circumstances are quite extraordinary, wouldn't you agree?"

He smiled, but it was fleeting. "I'm worried, I must admit." He said, glancing out at the pier.

"Tonight, what happened to Alex…It might have been meant for me."

Appalled, Kaira was still in too much shock to express her emotions. She gazed out at the Bay. "Do you think Father Murphy is involved?"

Jonathan could hear the fear in her voice but wasn't sure how to reply. "I know how it appears," he said quietly, "but we'll need more information to make that judgment. Father Murphy is probably innocent. It seems the killer acted alone."

"It makes little sense that St. Francis Abbey would orchestrate an assassination of their own Jesuit astronomer, especially if it could be traced back to the Abbot."

Jonathan had to admit she had a point.

"The murder was messy. I don't believe the killer was a professional." He said in an attempt to comfort.

"Why did the speaker order change from our program?" Kaira asked, turning to him again. "Why would Father Murphy change the order? Alex drank a glass of water from the podium. It was laced with poison." Her eyes widened. "Oh God, it was meant for you?"

Jonathan studied her beautiful face for a moment. Her eyes were deep gray pools in the dark. He pulled her face to him and kissed her lips.

Kaira took a deep breath. "Where did that come from?"

"I can't apologize for kissing my high school sweetheart. Besides, I'm glad someone cares about my wellbeing." He said.

Before she could respond, he pointed to the pier. The fishermen who had been rumbling up and down the docks preparing their boats with lobster traps and bait buckets were finally silent. The dock was empty of activity.

Jonathan looked back and saw car lights speeding toward Friar's Deck Tavern. At that moment, he knew he had to place his faith in the safety of Alex's Yacht.

"We've got to get to the Yacht Kaira."

Kaira locked the doors, and they hurried toward the boat and quickly disappeared inside. Jonathan pulled the ramp up behind them and started the ignition.

Kaira laughed nervously, "This engine makes less noise than my Volkswagen." Jonathan grinned. Moments later, they were sailing eastward through the Bay entrance into the open sea.

Behind them, they could see the Abbey, eerily illuminated on the mountain behind Westonville. The spinning lights of the police cars at the roadblock were still in place along the coastal highway. Jonathan took Alex's card out of his pocket and looked at the code.

"What do you think this is?"

He held the card out to her, and she sat next to him at the helm.

"Maybe a computer password?" Kaira looked around for a computer. "How does a Jesuit astronomer afford the luxury of an Italian Benetti yacht?"

"Good question."

The yacht demonstrated the most exquisite Italian craftsmanship with the latest technology. Everything from the stairwells to the light fixtures reflected fanatical attention to detail and quality. The 95' Ophiuchus housed ten guests and five crew members. The deck in front of the helm was fitted with an unusual custom telescope.

"The Ophiuchus." Said Kaira. "He named his yacht after a constellation? I guess it fits. Why should anyone care if Alex studied constellations?"

Jonathan frowned at the memory of Father Murphy's voice in his mind. *Alex has been studying Ophiuchus and the 180-degree polar shift away from Orion.* Kaira was right. Why would the study of constellations threaten anyone?

"The numbers might be something as simple as a ten-digit phone number without the hyphens." She shrugged. "Maybe a cell phone."

"Let's call it."

Jonathan dialed the numbers on his cell phone and waited a moment.

The phone in Kaira's pocket began to ring. In astonishment, she pulled the phone out of her pocket and pushed the green button on the screen accepting the call. They watched as the phone became a computer monitor with information scrolling on the screen at light speed before ending with a login.

"What the devil?" Jonathan took the phone and looked at the login. "I thought we tossed your phone."

"No, you tossed my phone. This is a phone my grandmother gave me. She told me it was made, especially for me, and I must guard it carefully."

Jonathan looked at her with one eyebrow raised. "Your grandmother told you?"

"Oh, no, you see, a girl at the Celebration of Life gave me the phone and an earpiece. My grandmother pre-recorded information on the phone and connected the GPS to certain locations on the property. When I listen in the earpiece at certain locations, she talks to me."

"I see." Jonathan was quiet as he examined the phone. "This is a secure phone."

"Meaning?"

"It can't be tracked." He handed the phone back to Kaira. "I suggest you keep it very safe. We may have just downloaded a lot more than we realize.

Looking back in the direction of the port, Westonville was getting smaller in the distance behind the yacht.

"Why would Alex have the number to a cell your grandmother made just for you?"

"Maybe what he was going to share with us tonight is on here?"

Jonathan pointed the yacht out to sea. The moon was huge in the night sky. Kaira walked out onto the main deck in front of the helm, and the night air whipped her hair across her face. She looked up at the stars and tried to find the constellation Ophiuchus.

Grandmother, what are you trying to tell me?

Chapter Twenty Three

Albano Laziale, Italy

Curator Antonio Callo waited anxiously in the darkness with Giovanni. Antonio wanted to shout at Giovanni, *don't give away all our years of service.* But, it meant something entirely different to the older man. The archeologist would tear apart the delicate political relationship Antonio had built with the Holy See.

The phone rang, interrupting Antonio's inner monologue. On speakerphone, Father Murphy seemed to materialize like a light in the darkness. His graceful way with words and his intellect adorned the conversation, stealing Giovanni's attention away from Antonio's pleas.

Seething inside, Antonio sat in a chair and listened. Tonight, Giovanni and Father Murphy would decide how to proceed, and the last thing Antonio needed was to be distracted by their decision to bring others in on the secrets he had protected for so long.

"They were unable to capture the killer." Father Murphy spoke in Italian. "He managed to slip past the roadblocks."

Antonio swallowed and calmly tried to steady the anxiety in his voice. "I see." He said evenly. "And where is the heir to Meadow manor? I was hoping we might speak with her."

There was a long silence. Father Murphy did not like the question and wondered why the Curator needed to speak with Miss Munroe.

"Giovanni," Father Murphy spoke, ignoring Antonio's question. "It appears Miss Munroe and Jonathan Bell have left together. I'm not sure where they've gone. I didn't think it my business to ask."

"You have no idea where they've gone?" Antonio allowed some anxiety to escape in his words, and visibly reigned himself in again. He stared at Giovanni with apparent concern.

Giovanni sat forward, his facial features moving beneath his beard. "I see no reason to be concerned. They're probably escaping the prying cameras and paparazzi. Who can blame them."

Father Murphy didn't mention the attempt on his own life that very evening.

"What if Alex confided in Miss Munroe? And, she may tell Jonathan. The situation is becoming more difficult to control." Antonio could no longer control his anger.

"Ah…you are concerned for your own interests." Giovanni blurted suddenly. "How kind to always think of others."

Father Murphy agreed with Giovanni but stepped in, bringing focus. "There are details we need to sort out. One, who is the killer, and what did he want? Two, was he sent, or did he act alone? I am reluctant to leave this conversation until you can confirm that you will stay inside and hire security until this is over. You may be in danger."

"Why was Alex speaking at Victoria's Wake?"

Father Murphy relayed the story of how the two of them had met. However, Father Murphy hadn't been aware Alex would be speaking until days before the Celebration of Life.

"Alex died from poisoning. He drank from a tainted glass on the podium. There is a possibility it was not meant for him. The killer may not understand the Pandora's box he has opened."

"Was it meant for you, Father?" Asked Giovanni.

"I'm not sure."

"What do you mean, you aren't sure?" Demanded Antonio. "Have you been threatened?"

"What I mean is that everyone involved with the Wake may have reason to be a target. Kaira Munroe as the heiress, Jonathan Bell as the treasure hunter, Alex as the Jesuit astronomer, even Umberto does not escape the possibility as the producer of wine for Meadow Manor." Father Murphy sighed. "What the three of us are aware of is that Alex, and Victoria, had incredibly valuable information that some elite in the Holy See may wish to keep secret. They have eyes and ears everywhere. Giovanni, we are the last keepers of the secret."

Antonio snorted. "You sound like a crazy conspiracy theorist." It would be embarrassing both in his career and as an influential friend of the Holy See if he associated himself with conspiracy theories.

Father Murphy ignored Antonio's outburst. "Jonathan Bell may have something to do with it. It seems the unknown young lady took his hit, but she lived. We don't know why yet."

"I am acutely aware that Jonathan may be involved." Said Giovanni. "Victoria told me Jonathan was resistant to participating in the Celebration of Life. He made it clear he did not want to talk about his new find in the Caribbean. As you know, she planned the Wake months before her death."

"Are you saying he had reason to flee the murder scene?" Antonio sensed something else was going on. Giovanni hadn't shared everything with him. "Listen, I believe it is critical that you find both Kaira Munroe and Jonathan Bell before something worse happens."

"You expect me or Giovani to look for them?" Father Murphy was tired of the selfish Curator. "We could alert authorities to look for them. However, we would be alerting others as well. I do not wish to endanger them further."

"D'accordo." Said Giovanni in agreement.

"Father Murphy continued. "Giovanni, I will make some calls and find a security guard for you, my friend. Stay inside, and I'll contact you tomorrow." He hung up.

As Father Murphy stood from his desk, he noticed his computer monitor brighten. An article from the Westonville Historical Society popped up on the social media screen. Recent storms were uncovering relics on the sandy dunes along the coast. The American Shore and Beach Preservation Association scrambled to set up safeguards keeping treasure hunters from disturbing the eroding cliffs.

God help us. Father Murphy thought. We don't need any more treasure hunters.

Catalina Sanchez was the Westonville Historical Society's newest "public relations coordinator" her duties as media liaison and PR strategist and authority as communications director had given her an aura of importance and vigilant watchfulness.

Formerly from the Dominican Republic, Catalina held a communications degree from New York University and had done post-grad work at the Gulf Coast Preservation Society in Florida before taking her position at Westonville Historical Society.

Catalina attempted to connect with young friends in the Dominican Republic and keep up with the exploding influence on Twitter, Facebook, blogs, and online media. She owed everything to Father Murphy for his power with Victoria in appointing her to the

Westonville Historical Society staff as their strategist and communications director.

Considered one of the best in her business, Father Murphy found her energy and constant communication annoying. However, she kept him abreast of all that was going on.

"Legends and conspiracies are coming to the surface," Catalina announced in her email. "Social media is exploding with new relics and treasures from the coastline after the hurricane's Irma and Jose blew past."

Father Murphy read the email in disbelief. Did she need to clutter his mailbox with so much information? He was worried about more important things.

He typed his response, "Would you mind telling me if you are adding to the media frenzy with your PR concerning Westonville?" He worried about the rumor mill bringing more treasure-seekers who ignored posted no trespassing signs. They didn't just tear up the coastline; they also made their way up to the woods surrounding the Abbey.

"Are you in your office?" she asked

Father Murphy hesitated, "Yes. Why?" he typed.

"I just pinged your GPS."

He looked at the email, then closed his eyes and exhaled. There was no longer privacy with this generation.

"Before Victoria died, she had me implement new electronic security on your phone. I know it's generally used for data mining, but it comes in handy when we need to find someone. Yours is working."

"Who else are you tracking?"

"Kaira. My orders were to track her cell phone. Hers is special, you know. Fitted with all kinds of bells and whistles."

It felt unnerving to think that this girl who spent the majority of her day with an iPad was capable of digital surveillance from anywhere.

"There's been some rumor that the man who killed Alex may have been trying for someone else." She wrote.

"How can you vet information that comes through social media? Saying it doesn't make it true." Father Murphy countered.

"Yes, but the chatter can be damaging." replied Catalina, "and gossip is that the killer knows something about the treasure Jonathan found."

"That isn't surprising. Treasure hunters tend to follow each other." Father Murphy didn't like what he was reading.

"Yes, the killer was released from an Italian prison five years ago. He's been working in the Dominican Republic for the mafia. They are trying to buy an island, and Jonathan is standing in the way."

"Stop. This is crazy." Father Murphy was irritated. He looked at the screen and contemplated his next reply. "Suggesting Jonathan is still the target is serious, and we need more evidence regarding your supposed killer. These are not things that can be vetted online without a full investigation."

"There's something else I think you should know." He waited as an attachment popped up in the email. "This was taken a few months ago. Evidently, there's a recent discovery in Albano Laziala. A student on one of Giovanni's sites discreetly took this photo. When Alex was murdered last night, the picture popped up on social media and seemed to be going viral."

Archbishop Paolo Vincenzo, the Holy See's minister of foreign affairs and two other men, stood next to Curator Antonio Callo at one of the most ancient sites in the Lazio region.

"What does this have to do with Alex's death or Westonville for that matter?" wrote Father Murphy, angry, but fully engaged.

"Scroll in and look closely at the other men in the picture."

Father Murphy enlarged the photo on the screen then sucked his breath in sharply. It couldn't be right.

Next to the Archbishop stood the Abbot of St Francis Abbey, Petar Labini, and Alex Mirabelli.

Father Murphy was silent. The implications were tremendous. "Why wouldn't the Abbot have told me of this visit to Italy? Especially considering the murder tonight?" His hand was shaking.

"I wanted to tell you before you get blindsided."

Too late, thought Father Murphy. The Abbot and Alex had met with the Holy See. Father Murphy tried to wrap his mind around the information. Why had the Abbot neglected to mention this? Father Murphy worked to control the alarm he felt.

"Unfortunately, it's all over social media." Catalina typed.

"Father Murphy?" a voice called from outside his apartment door. "We need to speak."

Father Murphy's head snapped up from the computer screen.

"Do what you can to squash the media." He emailed. "I'll be in touch soon."

The voice outside the apartment door spoke urgently.

"I think I've come across something that will impact us deeply."

Father Murphy studied the screen for a moment before he put the monitor to sleep. "Let's meet in the study," he called out. "give me a minute."

Father Murphy poured a finger of whiskey from a flask and gulped it down then took a long breath. Calmly he strolled to the study down the hall from his apartment.

Catalina stared at the screen and realized Father Murphy had logged off.

"Is something wrong?" asked one of her colleagues.

"Yes," Catalina Sanchez replied. "I've been following unusual stories for years, and I know when something sinister is about to surface."

Chapter Twenty Four

The social media BuzzFeed read:

The Source of Westonville Legends

Questions swirl in the murky waters of the recent tragedy at Meadow Manor. Conspiracies were flooding the internet as theorists suggesting the killing was over secrets hidden in the Manor and something more sinister.

Why has the young heiress Kaira Munroe fled with Jonathan Bell, oceanographer, and treasure hunter? Are they in danger, or were they involved in a diabolical plan to kill Alex Mirabelli, Jesuit astronomer from VATT on Mt. Graham? We hope to have answers to these questions soon.

The next feed read:

Ancient Bones Found beneath a Temple dedicated to Jupiter

The Hellenic Ministry of Culture has announced that remnants of a city dating back 4500 years covers over twelve acres and consists of megalithic stone structures, paved surfaces, and artifacts. A team of students from Giovanni Fiorelli's School of Archeology at Albano Laziale, in Lazio region, made the discovery just south of Rome. The finding of this ancient city and mammoth bones is significant.

A picture of the Archbishop, the Abbot, Alex Mirabelli, and the Curator sat below the caption.

***

Kaira Munroe found a blanket inside a compartment beneath her seat and clutched it around her body. Earlier, Jonathan said he wouldn't apologize for kissing his high school sweetheart. She wondered if he meant it. He was at the top of the list of most wanted bachelors along the east coast.

Kaira had dated a few men in New York, but nothing to make her want to settle down. She'd never been engaged and wondered now if there was something wrong with her. She'd seen her friends who had become trapped in bad relationships. It wasn't something she wanted to feel.

Now, as she sat on the Ophiuchus, not sure where they were headed and wondering what her grandmother had left on her phone, an overwhelming sense of fear and loneliness engulfed her. She preferred to work than to give in to self-pity, but at the moment, she had no direction, no plan.

I'm sailing out into the ocean with a man I haven't seen since high school, and the murderer may be after him. Her fate was sealed when Umberto took her down into the cavern below the winery. Her heart had been giddy with the excitement of discovering more about her grandmother.

Since then, a man had died of poisoning, a woman was targeted, and she and Jonathan were high tailing it away from Meadow Manor on gut instinct. She looked at the phone in her hand. Victoria was speaking to her from the grave.

She touched the surface of the phone, and a PIN login came up. So much for accessing the data dump.

She closed her eyes and tried to visualize the man she had seen in the black silk catering jacket. He had been out of place at the Celebration of Life, but she hadn't questioned why he was in the room, he'd been pouring drinks all night.

Kaira walked through the entire evening, step by step in her mind. From the fountain where Umberto had first met her, he'd said one word, Nephilim.

She entered that in the PIN login, but it rejected the word.

She'd picked up a bottle of Perrier in the banquet hall before talking to the young lady in front of the music salon. After setting up her phone, she had wandered down the hall toward the library, enjoying her grandmother's voice explaining the maps.

The library. Why did Jonathan bring the book?

An oceanographer with a propensity to find shipwrecks. The women must adore him.

She wouldn't allow herself to think about his love life. It was none of her business. They hadn't seen each other in years, yet he seemed very comfortable with her. She could think of a couple of reasons someone might be after him. Maybe he had encroached on their permit area. Was he taking credit for someone else's discovery?

And Alex. What did he and her grandmother know that was such a threat to Westonville history and religion? Everyone seemed to have secrets in Westonville. Her desire to access the phone was growing strong.

Now Alex and her grandmother were gone, she reflected, returning her mind to the present. She harnassed her emotions to rid herself of the painful memories of the loss of family. Then a terrible thought occurred to her.

What if Jonathan is behind the murder of Alex and maybe her grandmother? Was it possible?

The notion caused her to shiver violently. She gathered the blanket around her and hurried into the cabin.

Jonathan was standing quietly at the wheel, staring into the night. She was startled to see that the lights of Westonville were so far behind she could hardly see them. The thought of being detached from all contact made her anxious, but Jonathan seemed confident and continued at top speed.

"Why did you think we should leave Meadow Manor?" she asked quietly as she stood next to him at the wheel.

"All I know is that Umberto, Father Murphy, and your grandmother wanted you safe. Something in my gut told me you wouldn't be safe at Meadow Manor. Technically, you haven't been declared Victoria's heir, but that *is* who you are."

Kaira nodded silently. "But, no one came after me. If I were in any danger, I would be dead."

"This is a delicate situation. Things are going on at the Abbey we don't understand, and with Alex taking center stage in the Wake, it's no wonder... well...I'm just glad you're safe."

"Let's hope whoever is behind this doesn't figure out I have this phone full of data," Kaira said,

As she spoke, Jonathan felt the weight of their challenge. Alex was murdered in his place. Someone wanted to know what he knew. They all had that in common. Each person carried a secret, and now Kaira held one on her phone. He was sure of it.

For an instant, Jonathan wondered if he had been hasty in his decision to take Alex's yacht from the port. It might have been simpler to take Kaira back to her apartment in New York. As soon as he had the thought, he realized there had been no option.

Jonathan didn't want her to know everything. It would breach the delicate balance of the trust to which they were clinging. But, he also had a sincere desire to learn what Alex and Victoria had so carefully guarded with their lives.

She was innocent. A woman who had entered into a crisis created by others. He sensed she was independent and strong, full of integrity and courage, but he'd seen her vulnerability tonight and now thrown together by circumstances, they both wanted to know what was on the phone.

He turned to her sensing her eyes on him.

"Where are we going, Jonathan?" she whispered.

He smiled, "Anywhere you want."

"Don't kid right now. I'm serious." Her eyes filled with tears of frustration. "Where are we going?"

Surprised, he reached out and put his arm around her pulling her in. "I'm not sure what we're facing. Your grandmother wanted you to know something important. I'm going to take us to a safe place where we can figure it out."

"I hate to admit it, but the more I think about what happened, the more afraid I am. I want to trust you, but I'm afraid."

Her flash of candor startled Jonathan. He wasn't used to women who were honest, but he found her utterly captivating.

"We owe it to your grandmother, to Alex and the community of astronomers, and to ourselves to find out what they wanted us to know. We'll do it together."

"Thanks." She said softly.

"By now, they will have realized we've left the docks. Alex is dead, so they'll assume we're in his yacht. Whatever Alex's breakthrough is, he spent a lot of time here, or he wouldn't have gone to the trouble of setting up such a complex telescope on the deck. It's clear to me that he was watching for something. Let's hope Umberto has found a way to divert the port police." Jonathan said.

Umberto had proven himself a faithful and useful ally.

"I'm sure we're fine," Kaira said. "I've been wondering why the port police aren't following us for stealing the yacht. Look at the license posted above your head."

"What?" Jonathan said, surprised, and looked up at the framed license. "The yacht belongs to Victoria?"

"Kaira laughed. "She must have been his financial support. But, what was he researching?" she paused then said, "I wondered why a Jesuit priest would own a Benetti yacht."

"If they were researching something together, it would be imperative that they stay in communication. I'm sure your phone is secure. Alex's probably was too. The information downloaded from their servers is likely to be secure. Can you get into any other apps on that phone, or are they all locked?"

Kaira looked at the phone screen and touched the phone app. There were only four contacts on the phone. No names, just numbers.

"When you say this phone is secure, do you mean you aren't worried about being tracked?" She asked.

He shook his head. "They'd need to be specialized FBI or CIA hacks to access this phone. I'm sure of it."

Jonathan glanced at the icon apps on the face of her screen. "What's that one?"

Uneasy Kaira pushed the icon and watched it come to life on the screen. She squinted at the screen and wondered if they were vulnerable to every satellite in space.

Suddenly, the phone pinged two locations. Two green dots illuminated a map on the screen: one from inside Italy and one was pinging from somewhere off the coastline of New York.

Jonathan wondered if they would be able to remain invisible. The news of Alex's murder and their disappearance would be all over Westonville by now. Both their faces would be exposed.

Kaira looked at her phone. The location marker was flashing. The Yacht must be a location her grandmother anticipated she'd be at some point. She dug into her jacket pocket and pulled out the earpiece.

She looked at Jonathan and smiled. "My grandmother."

"Yes, I see that," Jonathan replied, impressed that she was so calm and unruffled.

Kaira wondered if her grandmother had known how comforting her voice would be in Kaira's ear as if she was standing with her.

"Kaira, if you are on the Yacht, then you may have been chased out of town." She gave a throaty chuckle. *"I'm sorry dear girl. You've come back into this world of legends and tales for a reason,*

and you'll need to trust me. The yacht and your phone are secure. Your phone is more special than you realize. To access the code, you need to enter the word on the fountain. Do you remember?"

Jonathan frowned as he watched Kaira's expression. He gently reached over and pulled the earpiece from her ear and held it up to his own. Then gently handed it back.

"Jonathan," Kaira whispered, "She gave me the code. But, I don't know how to spell it."

"Excuse me?"

She smiled. "It's in Hebrew."

Chapter Twenty Five

Brian dreaded answering the phone, but it was a call from the Caribbean. He had no trouble blowing off the investors that had humiliated him and put him in jail. However, He couldn't ignore the Italian mafia.

"Did you complete the mission?" He spoke with a thick Italian accent.

Brian sat attentively in the small galley of his sailboat. He'd met with Carmelo in his luxurious compound on an island in the Caribbean. His rough voice did not match the luxurious life he led.

"I had an unexpected complication," Brian replied in broken Italian. "I'm tying up loose ends."

"I was told you'd be back within the week." Then in afterthought, "What loose ends?"

"I've stumbled onto something important. Give me a few days, and I'll bring it to you."

Carmelo stiffened. "I hope you are not bringing more trouble."

"Obviously, I do not want that. I believe I'll have the item soon. Give me enough time, and you will have your relic." Brian hoped the events of the evening would be hidden from Carmelo long enough to rectify the situation.

"Do this as fast as you can, but be discreet. Then contact me immediately. We'll be at the Arizona compound." With that, the connection terminated.

There were few vessels in the water, and no one paid much attention to his sailboat. Thankfully, the storms had subsided, and the horizon was pink with the hint of dawn.

Brian could barely believe the events that had led to the last evening. His feelings of despair escalated as he thought more about what he had done. Was he a murderer?. There was no turning back, no hope for his soul.

In an instant, his mind was in a dark cell, beat up and bloody. Three years in prison in a foreign country broke something inside him. His life was a living purgatory. Nothing prepared a man for the torments of a foreign jail, one outside the boundaries of government. Then out of the blue, a powerful man with significant influence bought his release — a man who expected lifelong servitude for the favor he'd given.

For weeks after his rescue, he lay trembling, ill, in and out of consciousness. When Brian closed his eyes, demons plagued him, suffocating him in fear. But, he grew healthier daily, and his life changed. Absolute loyalty to his new influential guide brought much-needed finances into his account.

The investors who had placed him in prison were on the top of his revenge list. His throat clenched as anger rose like bile. Forgiveness? Out of the question.

Brian thought of his father, who had spent his entire life addicted to the obsession of finding the lost treasure of Captain Benjamin Munroe. The carrot in front of the horse cart, ever dangling, yet elusive and unattainable. But, in the end, he'd found something impressive and kept his secret from the investors.

Jonathan, the pious brother who had chosen a different path, hid his desire to find the treasure. Brian read the articles and stayed updated on the activity of SSRL. The investors had turned from Brian to Jonathan and wanted to fund his ventures when Brian ended up in jail for theft in a foreign country. Jonathan turned them down.

The career of treasure hunting brought a little in here and there, just enough for him to stay in command of his boat, live by his own rules. But, he'd lost control. He was alive, and he could thank Carmelo for that.

It hadn't taken Brian long to learn to anesthetize himself with a potent blend of belonging to Carmelo's family and large deposits in his account. He gained influence by association and felt the heady power. It brought dark courage and the will to do what he needed to do. But, occasionally, he looked back and wished for younger days.

Brian spent weeks studying Italian and learning the history and motives behind Carmelo's choices. The new Pope Francis's campaign against corruption and the mafia association had brought some changes to Carmelo's organization.

Recently, at mass, the congregation was told that mobsters would be excommunicated from the church. The Bishop at Carmelo's church said, "We must all work together to combat this form of cancer that weighs on our community." He continued, "Mafia is like a woodworm that infiltrates the process of development and ruins the relationship between institutions and people."

Carmelo walked out with his family and bodyguards in the middle of Mass. Later at his home, he made a statement to his men. "We are no guiltier than they are. They've been happy to take our money over the years, and we've made them rich. If they think they no longer need us, we shall see."

Within weeks Carmelo moved his family to the Caribbean with the plan to buy land. An available island seemed a logical choice. However, a small company testing waters in the Caribbean had a ninety-nine-year lease on portions of the beachfront and permits in the surrounding waters.

Cruelly, the permits were under the name SSRL, Jonathan Bell. Years without speaking and now fate brought them together. It seemed the simplest of things couldn't go Brian's way. He felt the searing fear rip through him as desperation swept in devouring the last bits of courage.

Not long after the discovery, he'd found himself at Carmelo's attempting to propose his plan of ridding the island of Jonathan's presence, but nothing had prepared him for what took place at the Wake.

Chapter Twenty Six

At the Civico Museo, located on the ground floor, Antonio Callo sat in a spectacular office suite containing priceless art. He hurried not wanting to leave Giovanni alone too long for fear he might call Father Murphy again. He was trying to make sense of the news that the heiress Kaira Munroe and Jonathan Bell might have secret information that could be volatile if released publicly.

He moved quickly in his office, gathering information from his desk and locking it in the safe. He heard footsteps down the marble corridor and a knock on his door.

"I realize you are busy, sir, and it's very late." The young man was a student of Giovanni's and worked in communications and marketing for the Museum. "There's something you need to know. I've received an email that has me concerned."

"Da chi?"

"It is a woman in America, Catalina Sanchez. She is PR for the Westonville Historical Society. Her site is usually inferior, but on occasion, I find something interesting, so I've subscribed. She has thousands of followers and is well respected among other like-minded groups."

"Non interresato." Antonio shook his head and waved his hand, dismissing the young man.

"She's been talking about Giovanni's find all night." The student continued. "I'm not sure how she acquired the information, but it's spreading like wildfire, and some reputable news hubs are looking at her site."

"What are you getting at?"

"The information they are sharing relates to the Holy See," Luke said, hitching his backpack in place. "I thought you'd want to know before I leave. They're preparing to post another video within the hour."

Antonio stared at Luke. "The Holy See has no interest in conspiracy theorists."

"Maybe you should look," Luke said, holding out his iPhone.

Antonio took the cell phone and found himself squinting at a grainy photo of a few relics in a cave. He handed the phone back to Luke, impatient to make his way to Giovanni's villa.

"You don't understand, sir. Look at the next photo."

Irritated, Antonio snatched the phone from him. The second photo was clear and focused on an object in a fossilized rock on the cave wall. Frozen, Antonio stared at the image. He knew it well, as did the Holy See.

Gigantic fossilized bones.

Entombed in caves and rock, the bones were synonymous with the controversy surrounding antediluvian beings whose presence brought new understanding to scriptural context the Holy See wasn't ready to publicize.

Antonio stared at the image. This ancient fossil, he knew, when carbon dated, placed the human skeleton long before the flood. Antonio had seen several relics, artifacts, and bones whose size and carbon date astonished even the Vatican. The discoveries had quickly and quietly disappeared into the warehouses and archives.

Depicting himself as the protector of ancient artifacts and the enemy of those who would exploit, he accepted the Holy See's mentality of suppressing the knowledge that arises from archeological discoveries. Antonio embraced the controlling attitude, officially excluding archeologists and other Curators from positions of power, giving himself control over intake for all findings.

Unfortunately, everything changed with the invention of cell phones. Stunned at how quickly information spread across the world, Antonio had to strategize a new plan for suppressing the information highway. The Holy See's commitment to protecting everything found upon Italian soil and other parts of the world meant that some of the conspiracy theorists were correct.

A new poll in Italy revealed more young people would use the internet as a fact-gathering tool. Elderly generations weren't likely to use the internet at all. A certain amount of respect and intimidation lived in the hearts of those deep-rooted families.

Some wary, local communities, who made discoveries on their land, remembered the long reach of the Holy See. They harbored secret groups who were sworn to expose truth hidden for centuries and often fed conspiracy theorists with information. Antonio understood that when old-timers looked at the data spread by National Geographic, Smithsonian, and other Historical Societies, it barely scratched the surface. It was the force of the conspiracy theorists that was becoming powerful.

Recently a rising fear in the church had become the new progressive voice. Fueling their concern was the archeologists and astronomers among the outspoken Jesuits regarding their change in a worldview based on the discoveries they were making.

A vast chasm of lost knowledge bridging the ancient past and the presently created rifts. Also, the church forced a crossroads. How long can the Vatican retain its all-knowing power? Or, will the Vatican government be abolished by the anger of those who no longer hold respect for the church.

While elders were content to leave tradition alone, the young progressives rebelled against all secretive organizations, swearing to expose the truth.

"At first, I thought the image might be photoshopped," Luke said.

Antonio snapped back to the present as Luke continued.

"I took it to a friend who works at a news station. He doesn't think it was manipulated. Do you have a plan to counteract the conspiracy theorists?"

Antonio knew Luke was right. The entire world would clamor to see a photo like this. He needed to counteract.

"I'm not sure Luke." He said in an even tone.

"Over the past two months, I've read several articles concerning extraterrestrial theories and the involvement of the Roman Catholic Church. Comments made by Pope Francis and the former director of the Vatican Observatory, Father Jose Funes, there seems to be a resurgence of the idea that the Vatican's inner circle is aware of an extraterrestrial presence on earth."

Luke pulled up an article on his phone.

Antonio dreaded reading the article beneath a photo of the Pope. The heading read:

The Vatican Considers Possibility of Aliens

E.T. phone Rome. Four hundred years after it locked up Galileo for challenging the view that the Earth was the center of the universe, the Vatican has called in experts to study the possibility of extraterrestrial alien life and its implication for the Catholic Church.

"The questions of life's origins and of whether life exists elsewhere in the universe are very suitable and deserve serious consideration," said the Rev. Jose Gabriel Funes, an astronomer, and director of the Vatican Observatory.

It wasn't just philosophical and theological implications Antonio feared. When the world realized the Vatican had been sitting on the bones of ancient beings who may have come from another planet, people would revolt.

"Thirty scientists, including non-Catholics, from the U.S., France, Britain, Switzerland, Italy, and Chile attended a five-day conference hosted by the Vatican."

"I'm aware of what the Vatican is doing." Antonio looked at Luke, his anger apparent.

"An interesting group of astronomers, physicists, and biologists are studying the field of astrobiology. Is there something they know that they aren't sharing with the world?" asked Luke

"This is disrespectful." Antonio snapped. He'd read enough. "All this speculation means nothing.

"Sir," Luke continued, "Further in the article, they are trying to link the finds of gigantic bones with ancient aliens. I believe the church calls them Fallen Angels. Others call them gods."

Antonio knew about the Inkari Institute in Cuzco, Peru, where one of the strangest recent archeological discoveries surfaced. While researching in the Peruvian Amazonian jungle, looking for Incan Imperial presence and their central city, which appeared in 16th-century writing, they received a call. In October 2016, a person brought them a small mummified body and a crazy story. No stranger than what he'd seen in Italy and archived in the Holy See's secret warehouses.

"This new photo is from Giovanni's dig site. The allegations conspiracy theorists make that the Holy See has the Curator of Civico Museo Albano in their pocket is gaining traction."

Once again, Antonio found himself angry. He tried to speak calmly. "Luke, I will not waver to social media. I am not in the pocket of the Holy See. I have faithfully served our country and the Vatican by protecting our heritage with my life if necessary. The Holy See will have no comment."

Antonio turned to exit the museum.

"One last thing…You're going to hate this…" Luke said as they walked toward the door. "Disturbing photos were sent to Giovanni yesterday from a Jesuit astronomer and the wealthy American woman, Victoria Munroe before they died."

Chapter Twenty Seven

Mt. Graham, Arizona

Alex Mirabelli was murdered?

Jesuit astronomer Chris Gonzalez could feel his emotions trembling as he prepared to work on the latest project, picking up where Alex left off.

"The one aspect of the war on earth is the battle to become heir to all aspects of ancient knowledge of reality and keep others from finding out."

"Right," Mark answered. "And usually, those with the knowledge continue to make repeated conscious decisions to keep it for themselves.

I am in no condition to concentrate, he thought, knowing the other Jesuits were just as rattled. Chris and Mark had worked alongside Alex for three years, and the horrifying news that he had died came as a devastating shock to everyone at the observatory.

A few hours earlier, they had been talking to Alex on his cell phone discussing a meteor some college kids found on a desert trail.

"Full of knowledge," Chris joked, "Our very own walking encyclopedia." Who wasn't impressed by Alex's ability to access and define? Chris and his science partner had listened carefully to Alex's instructions as he gave them the next steps for filing information and storing the meteor.

Now, in the aftermath of the death of Alex, they were in a daze, wondering what would come of the project. But Chris's phone rang. He looked at Mark, "It's from the Abbey in Westonville." Furrows creased his brow. Why were they calling?

"Hello? Is this Chris?"

"Yes."

"I'm sure you must have heard the news." Father Murphy said, his voice full of empathy.

"We heard. The entire science community at the observatory is devastated as well as our Jesuit brothers."

"We hope you will continue his work." Father Murphy replied. His voice took a furtive tone as he contemplated the circumstances. "Prepare yourself for questions concerning his projects, but please, do not speak of them to anyone."

Chris knew Alex had been quiet about some of the projects. He hadn't shared the info with any of the others. But, at the moment, Chris saw no need to change protocol. He felt confident with guidance from Father Murphy they would finish the projects. They confirmed their commitment to secrecy and hung up.

A few minutes later, Father Murphy called back.

"Are you prepared to house two visitors?"

Mark held his hands up as if to say, what now.

"We can accommodate visitors."

"Good. They are headed your way. They'll dock in Washington DC tonight and arrive in Tuscan late tomorrow evening. They'll have a rental car."

"Who are they? I assume friends of Alex?" Chris found Father Murphy's tone slightly unnerving.

"Jonathan and Kaira. Please contact me and let me know they've arrived safely. Tell no one they are on the way and keep their visit and activity very low key. I prefer no one knows they are there."

"You mean you don't want anyone to see them while they're here?"

"That would be best for now. Don't forget to contact me when they've arrived." Mark and Chris stared at each other in surprise. Father Murphy's request was furtive and odd.

Maybe the killer is after them.

Nevertheless, Chris confirmed again that he would do as Father Murphy requested, preparing a room hidden from view and working out of sight during their stay. Chris wondered what Father Murphy was planning. It must have something to do with Alex's project. Fortunately, Chris had access to all the files, so at least he had some control. The only records were kept in the locked lab he and Mark accessed daily.

After he hung up a few quiet seconds passed, then Chris suddenly stood up from his chair.

"I've got something to take care of." His voice cracked with the tension. "I'm going to make sure all our files are secure."

Chris wanted nothing more than to continue the work they'd begun, but he was concerned Father Murphy's friends might take the only files he had.

"Sure," Mark said. "That's a good idea considering the conversation we just had. We should prepare for intruders."

Chapter Twenty Eight

Jonathan hoped Kaira didn't notice his hands tremble beneath the wheel of the Benetti. As the shock wore off, he realized he was rattled. Alex had been an acquaintance, but the Jesuit astronomer had established a genuine friendship with Victoria Munroe.

Alex was murdered instead of me, thought Jonathan.

Only hours earlier, he'd seen Alex alive and well. Jonathan had joked with Father Murphy about Victoria's ability to draw people into her network using dramatic antics. But, when Father Murphy asked him to swap places with Alex on the program, he'd thought nothing of it, until now. The evening flashed through his mind. Something was terribly off.

Was it possible that someone else had been planning to kill Alex? Had Father Murphy been protecting Alex from someone? Jonathan couldn't tell Kaira his brother Brian might have murdered Alex. Not yet. She'd find out eventually. The probability that she'd never speak to him again was high.

Jonathan wondered what to do next. He didn't want Kaira to sense his uncertainty. His phone rang.

"How close are you to DC?" asked Father Murphy. "I'll take care of your dock slip. Too bad you couldn't stay at the Abbey."

"I know. There was no time to warn you of our change of plans." Jonathan responded.

"I'm glad you didn't bring her here. I no longer believe it is safe. You should prepare for the worst. I believe some evil men have made their way to our town."

Thankful for the warning, Jonathan knew Father Murphy referred to something far more diabolical than his brother's heart of revenge.

***

"We're parking in a prime slip?" Surprised, Kaira wondered how much it cost.

"Father Murphy called ahead and scheduled it for us," Jonathan said. "I following his advice." He parked the Yacht in the wharf, which offered eight moorings on the northwest side of the channel with proximity to transportation.

"How much do we owe?" Jonathan asked the wharfmaster.

"Nothing. Your priest has paid for your slip."

Father Murphy already paid? Kaira was unsure how she felt regarding Father Murphy, but her grandmother had trusted him explicitly. Kaira knew, just because a man calls himself a priest or a preacher did not mean he was automatically worthy of the title.

His influence came as no surprise to Jonathan, considering the Abbey was part of the worldwide Roman Catholic Church. They had clout and credit in almost every country in the world.

Jonathan thanked the wharfmaster, and they gathered the few things they'd brought with them and hurried to find a taxi.

The yellow cab took them down Maine Avenue to Interstate Highway 395, which crossed the Potomac River and lead to the Ronald Reagan airport — pulling up to their Delta flight sign, they had plenty of time since they had no luggage to check. As usual, the airport was busy with business travelers and tourists.

Once the plane cleared the tarmac, Kaira laid her head back, took a deep breath, and closed her eyes. She had occasionally flown as a journalist, and each time her heart flipped as the plane left the tarmac. What am I doing, she thought? She felt Jonathan's warm hand cover hers. He gazed at her memorizing her face.

Kaira was struggling to process the unexpected circumstances. They hadn't seen each other in over twelve years. As if Jonathan read her mind, she heard his voice soft in her ear.

"Kaira, I realize we haven't seen each other in years, and you must have thought it crazy when Umberto told you to trust me. But, what I am going to suggest to you is what I think we need to do under the circumstances."

Kaira listened as Jonathan outlined his plan.

"What you are saying sounds crazy. Do you think we are being followed?"

"There is a good possibility. They won't be looking for a married couple."

"You haven't told me everything, have you?"

Jonathan didn't answer.

Kaira slept fitfully and was startled awake by the seatbelt sign signaling they were preparing to land.

When they arrived, Jonathan rented a car under Mr. and Mrs. Smith. Although she was curious, Kaira didn't ask how he had a card under the name Smith. With that taken care of, he bought a map and handed it to Kaira.

"According to the map, we are headed to the Mount Lemmon Sky Center owned by the University of Arizona. One of the Jesuits has booked us a cabin. It will probably be too dark when we pass Mt Graham and the VATT Observatory.

"I found it. I prefer to see it on my phone." Kaira pulled up directions from Google Maps on her cell. "The shortest route is 42 miles and says it will take an hour and fifteen minutes. It looks like the road winds up the mountain, and there are some switchbacks."

"Good. We should be there before 9 pm."

"Take El Valencia Rd to S Kolb, then right on East Catalina Highway. It turns into Mt Lemmon Highway."

A few minutes later, Jonathan and Kaira had left Tuscan and were winding along a deserted mountain road where nothing but white stone and cactus grew. As they wound further up the mountain, passing the Molino Basin Trailhead, Mercer Spring, and Willow Canyon, Kaira was beginning to feel very alone surrounded by the desert darkness.

After a while, they entered the tree line. Tall pine trees covered the mountain.

"There's no traffic up here past the camping area. Dark and lonely." Said Kaira.

"Maybe I didn't mention, Mt. Graham is off-limits to the general public," Jonathan said. "The development of observatories in the 1980s and environmental concerns about the spiritual significance of the peak prompted the forest service to declare all lands 9,800 feet surrounding Mt. Graham as a "refugium," meaning the general public is not allowed."

"According to Google map, we should be passing the University of Arizona's Observatory to the right." Kaira looked out her window at the darkness. "Oh, there's a dirt road with a serious iron gate. I bet that's it."

"The Mt. Lemmon Sky should be about seventeen more miles. A Jesuit astronomer is supposed to meet us at the general store in town and lead us to our cabin."

Chris wasn't difficult to find. Standing next to his jeep, he was the only car in the parking lot. He watched them pull in. Jonathan rolled his window down. Chris bent down and looked at Kaira.

"Hi, I'm Chris. You Jonathan?" He had a friendly tone.

"I am, and this is Kaira."

"Nice to meet you. I've set you up in the Antler Ridge Cabin. You'll be comfortable there. There's a queen bed, loft, full bathroom, and kitchen. Follow me."

He hopped back in his vehicle and headed further down the road.

"He doesn't look like a Jesuit priest," Kaira commented, then turned and looked out the window. "Looks like they had a fire out here a few years ago." Even in the dark, Kaira could see the trees had damage on some of them that time had not yet healed.

Chris led them to a spacious cabin and handed Jonathan the key.

"Welcome. If there's anything you need while you're here, just let me know." He looked at Kaira's dress, and she could feel his curiosity. She was too tired to explain.

Knotty pine covered the walls, and the floor was solid oak. A welcoming fire blazed in the fireplace across from the kitchen. A basket with water, protein bars, and muffins sat on the kitchen table.

"I had it cleaned this morning and made the bed for you." Chris thought they were married. Instinctively Kaira shoved her left hand into her coat pocket. She walked to the French doors that looked out over the deck and the view. Darkness accentuated the spectacular starry night.

Chris saw she was impressed. "Amazing, isn't it? That's why the Vatican moved their telescope and observatory out here. It's one of the darkest places for viewing the stars. Well, I'll see you two in the morning."

Standing in the middle of the cabin, Jonathan and Kaira gazed at each other for an uncomfortable moment. At Jonathan's urging, Kaira took the bathroom first and showered. She had no extra clothing, but thankfully, the cabin furnished large terry cloth robes.

Jonathan found eggs and bacon in the fridge and made breakfast while she showered.

"That smells heavenly," Kaira said as she opened the bathroom door and wandered into the kitchen where Jonathan had made himself at home.

"Looks like they stocked the fridge. Don't know how long we'll be here, but we won't go hungry."

Kaira gave him a tight smile.

As they ate their eggs and prepared for bed, Jonathan heard a sound outside in the dark. The Arizona Cougar average 2.5 feet tall but had a shoulder to tail length of up to eight feet and had been known to jump 18 feet vertically and 30 feet horizontally. Jonathan decided it wasn't a good idea to bring that to Kaira's attention.

At the kitchen bar opposite Kaira, Jonathan closed his eyes for a moment and exhaled. At that moment, Kaira realized how difficult the day had been for him. She put her hand out and squeezed his hand.

"Thanks for the eggs. Let's go to bed."

Neither of them had the energy to fuss over the bed or their situation. Jonathan gave Kaira the bed, and he bunked down in the loft with a pillow and some extra blankets.

Seconds after her head hit the pillow Kaira was asleep. Jonathan lay with his arms behind his head in the loft, looking out a large window. The stars were stunning. His mind ran through the events of the past few hours before a restless sleep finally came over him.

Chapter Twenty Nine

Albano Laziale, Italy

Giovanni Fiorelli slipped his arms into a warm jacket and placed a hat on his gray head and picked up a backpack. Through the back garden of the villa, he made his way to the iron gate and onto Via Miralago.

I no longer know who to trust, the archeologist told himself. His head pounded with a constant ache. *I must get to my storage area.*

Giovanni's villa, a sanctuary on the southern end of Lake Albano, was close enough to Museo Civico Albano. He often walked for exercise. The narrow street lined with trees and green shrub served as a beautiful respite. This morning, Giovanni was thankful he lived close to the museum. He needed to check on his relic.

The Museo Civico was a twenty-minute walk from the villa and usually cleared his head by the time he reached his destination, though this morning he felt apprehension as he scanned the empty street. Instantly, he heard something that placed his nerves on edge.

On the street behind him, a small black car sat parked a hundred yards past his gate. A dark figure sat hunched over the wheel, reading a map. The man looked down at his smartphone and punched something in the keypad.

Giovanni felt eyes on him as he slowly made his way down the narrow-shaded street. He pressed on and after turning a corner, stopped to listen. Surprised, he heard no sounds. Thankfully, the car wasn't following him. But, his feet moved a little faster, and his breath grew short. He hoped he hadn't made a mistake leaving the house. He'd thought Antonio was coming back last night, but when he hadn't returned, Giovanni slept fitfully, wondering, pondering.

The Brotherhood had warned him to trust no one. They'd urged Giovanni to lay low.

Giovanni had decided to wait for Father Murphy to decide on what to do with the incredible relic he'd found. But, Antonio made him nervous, and he wondered where he could hide the object to keep it from the prying eyes of the Curator.

Father Murphy had warned him that the Order of the Serpent would kill for the relic. Then, he'd presented persuasive evidence that had set him on edge. Giovanni prepared to move the relic from its place in the warehouse.

Now, as he hurried along Via Virgillio, he looked behind him and to his astonishment, saw the black car tailing sixty feet behind. Morning traffic picked up along the main road, and he hurried to reach the safety of the museum warehouse.

Giovanni wheezed as he stood in front of the stone building directly across from the Civico Museo. He stood inside the open museum gate, and his body went rigid as the black car passed slowly. He stood still behind the post for a few seconds before looking around. The black vehicle continued up the street and around the corner. Maybe he was just paranoid.

He chided himself for his fears. *He has no interest in your discoveries.*

He walked across the street, deciding he was probably worried about something that would never happen. *I need to see if it is still where I left it,* he thought. He wondered if the backpack he carried would hold the relic. Seeds of doubt grew in his mind as he tried to remember if the dimensions of his pack would hold the item.

When the Vatican had moved their observatory to Castel Gandolfo, the neighborhood had become the hub of Lake Albano's vibrant tourist scenes. A bus full of tourists pulled up in front of the Civico Museo Di Albano. Intuition told Giovanni to cross the street and enter the warehouse through the crowd of tourists.

The bus pulled away, and the tourists crossed the street to the museum. Giovanni entered the warehouse and turned to look down the road one more time. He felt his blood become cold as a black car slowly moved down the road where the bus had been. *I'm imagining things*, he told himself.

Ignoring the fear in his heart, he entered the warehouse and walked toward the stairwell leading to the basement. Below the first floor, there was nothing but silence, stone walls, and cold tile floors. Small locked rooms lined the hallway. Giovanni neared his locker door and had a chilling sense that someone was watching. He took a look before jamming a key into the lock.

Down the hall, a motionless figure crouched in a dark corner waiting a few seconds before leaving the shadows. The man pulled an empty pack around his shoulders and stepped from the shadows, careful that his footsteps made no sound, he hurried after Giovanni.

***

Museum Curator Antonio Callo sprinted to his car and headed to Giovanni's villa. Luke has sent him a photo of the relic, and he had it up on his iPhone. A conversation between Luke and Father Murphy's latest communications person meant the images were probably going viral.

Whether or not Father Murphy was behind the orchestration of Alex's murder, Antonio knew that when the image of the ancient relic went public, his clout with the Vatican might be in jeopardy of being destroyed. The shocking reality that the relic was antediluvian proof that beings before the flood understood the planets and stars more thoroughly than we do today would shape the worldview and bring the public to the Vatican's doorstep for answers.

Giovanni must be contained before the evidence leaked.

It was all about the perception of information. Antonio should prepare himself to disassociate with Giovanni if needed. Luke had advised Antonio to respond and make a statement regarding the post. He's right. I need to get Giovanni to make a statement regarding his discovery soon.

He sped down the narrow street toward Giovanni's villa, glancing at the iPhone on his dashboard. In addition to the image of the fossilized skeleton, the item buried with it would be most inflammatory of all.

The Constellation Ophiuchus, Giovanni called it. Once in a blue moon, the pole shifted from Orion to Ophiuchus. Conspiracy theorists analyzed and connected the dots that created havoc among the general public.

Zodiac experts predicted that when the pole shifted toward Ophiuchus, a star would be seen, and a planet would pass close to the sun affecting the earth. Unfortunately, that wasn't all. The Vatican also predicted the effect on earth would open what they were calling portals. Oddly, the Roman Catholic Church had built a chapel or monastery on many of the portal locations mentioned in ancient texts.

God help us if the Order of the Serpent learns of the device Giovanni found.

Antonio meant to return last evening, but it took much longer than he expected to confirm the warehouse was secure. He entered Giovanni's villa without knocking. "Giovanni?" he said as he hurried toward the study. "We must speak right away."

Antonio stopped short at the study door. A small ember was burning in the fireplace, but the room was empty. "Giovanni?" he called, turning toward the kitchen. A little espresso pot sat on the burner. His empty coffee mug sat in the sink with a platter dusted with pastry crumbs. Antonio searched the villa, but Giovanni was gone.

Antonio called his cell and heard the phone ringing. The faint sound came from the study. He called the phone again and listened this time, tracking the ringtone to the cushions of the leather chair in the study.

He must have gone out for a morning walk, but why would he leave his cell home?

Antonio could believe his friend didn't want to be bothered. He'd ignored Antonio's calls before. But, unease rose in Antonio as he walked out of the villa and headed for town. The next several minutes, he followed the trails Giovanni usually walked searching up and down the streets and around Lake Albano. No Giovanni.

Frustrated, Antonio made his way to the Civico Museo office. Anxiously, he sat in his room and looked at the dark computer screen.

***

Westonville Police Station

Jackson learned that Alex Mirabelli had shared his scientific discovery with Victoria Munroe, Giovanni Fiorelli, and Kaira Munroe. He knew Victoria died of natural causes, at least that was the report, but Alex died of poisoning, and Kaira Munroe was MIA along with Jonathan Bell. Giovanni was alive and seen in Albano Laziale, Italy entering a museum.

Adding to the complexity, Alex's murderer identified as Jonathan Bell's brother Brian had ties to the Italian mafia. Jackson wondered if Giovanni had ties to the mob as well. And then, there was Father Murphy. He had made last-minute changes to the program. Otherwise, it would have been Jonathan drinking the poisoned glass of water.

When Mafia Don, Carmelo, took his family out of Italy, he'd brought his followers with him. A group of angry men, a community of committed men who were devoted to the influence of Carmelo. The hit would seem like a vendetta, revenge against a brother.

Clever, thought Jackson. If Carmelo used Brian as a pawn, then the hit would appear to be less sinister. No one would suspect the Order.

There's nothing typical about the events of the evening, were Umberto's words. We may be at war with an invisible threat, he'd said. To make it worse, Jackson had no idea where Jonathan and Kaira had gone, and he couldn't reach Father Murphy.

Chapter Thirty

Staring at the knotty pine ceiling, Kaira tried to prepare her thoughts for the coming day. The past 24 hours had been a whirlwind of strange events and emotions she hadn't experienced since her family had died in the car crash. She had been thrilled at the invitation to be at her grandmother's wake, which was a Celebration of Life as Father Murphy had named it.

As the evening unfolded with the excitement of being guided by her grandmother's recorded voice, to the secret meeting with Alex, then the horrid shock of his murder and the realization it might have been meant for Jonathan. The mystery had deepened when Umberto told her she would inherit the winery, and the Westonville Historical Society would manage Meadow Manor. Was her life in danger too? Was someone after the discoveries Alex and Victoria had made, or was it a simple murder of revenge and jealousy for Jonathan's success as a treasure hunter?

Alex's words replayed in Kaira's mind. What project had he picked up from his friend at the observatory? He'd said it was remarkable and somehow threatening.

The questions about antediluvian humans and the mystery of their ancient depth of knowledge was answered. He had claimed to have solved who they were and where they came from, and yet, the news dangerously resembled conspiracy theory.

All Kaira knew for sure was that Alex and Victoria had worked closely on their projects. Whatever Victoria understood, it must have been closely tied to Alex's discoveries. He had seemed excited about the findings, and Victoria's celebration presentation had been beautiful, but confusing.

"Good morning." Jonathan knocked on her door. "Coffee's on."

"Morning," Kaira materialized at the bar in the kitchen. The fireplace was blazing, and the cabin was warm.

"You like it black? We have cream."

"Black. Thanks." Kaira cupped the hot mug in her hands and allowed the golden liquid to warm her insides. She brought the mug to her lips and gazed at Jonathan over the rim. Disarmed by his stare, she wondered what he was thinking.

"I couldn't sleep last night." He said. "Your grandmother and Alex were working closely together. Did she ever mention anything about the constellation Ophiuchus to you?"

"Not really, but I did see a large painting on the ceiling of her private room at the winery. It was the constellation of Ophiuchus."

"Maybe we can start there," Jonathan said.

"I don't see how it connects to anything."

"The legends of Ophiuchus are connected to mythical gods. The 13th, which didn't make the astrologer's cut, is the constellation Ophiuchus. It is called the Serpent-Bearer constellation, partially located along the ecliptic between the summer constellations of Scorpius and Sagittarius."

"I still don't see the connection."

"All American Indian cultures speak of giant gods coming out of the sky. We have proof of giant dinosaur bones, and until the early 1900's we had many discoveries of giant human bones over 10 feet tall."

"Are you saying giants from the constellation Ophiuchus came to earth?" She rolled her eyes.

"I don't know if that's what I'm saying, but I know your grandmother knew something significant, and she's been interested in astronomy for years. Her connection with Alex is no accident."

"What if grandmother discovered bones?" Kaira's thoughts wandered to the great underground chambers and passages beneath the winery. Umberto had said they were already there when the winery was built. "Old articles are referring to the uncovering of giant human fragmented bones all along the east coast and inland. I've read the stories out of curiosity but never given them any thought until now."

"Why wouldn't Victoria give them to the Westonville Historical Society? She was very loyal to that organization." Thoughtfully, Jonathan sipped his coffee.

"Good question. There must have been more to the discovery than finding large bones."

"What if their discoveries, when combined, reveal some incredible story that we would normally call fiction or fantasy? What if it corroborates all the ancient texts we've seen regarding giants and mythical gods?"

"It would debunk evolution and a lot of other theories. I'm not sure that would go over too well with some professors I know." Kaira grinned.

"Proving that there were huge humans and "gods" before the flood might debunk Darwin's theory of evolution." Said Jonathan. "The reason I've never believed in evolution is that the further back in time I look, the more complex it becomes. Darwin's theory is just the opposite."

The book Jonathan had taken from the library when they'd left Meadow Manor sat on the table between them. "If the information in this book is true, more than two hundred giants landed on a mountain in the Iraq desert a very long time ago. Only, they weren't called giants."

"Okay. Don't leave me hanging." Kaira sat facing him, her eyes intent.

"Based on the books in your grandmother's library, she believed they were fallen, angels. And their children, the Nephilim, were giants."

"What the devil?" Kaira sat stunned. Did her grandmother really believe in fallen angels?

"Jonathan, you've got to be kidding. That's crazy talk. It's just...too weird."

"I know. Hear me out. Many ancient texts talk about them, and though they call these beings something different, they seem to be referring to the same things. Gods, giants, aliens, they're all in the legends and myths of every culture."

Kaira's smiled politely. "Well, I don't know what my grandmother believed. I hadn't been around her since I was seven. I'm beginning to understand what my parents were protecting me from."

Jonathan frowned. "I'm sorry to hear you look at it that way. I don't want to sway your thinking. But, I think it's a good idea to keep your mind open. I think we will both be shocked when we discover what they wanted us to know."

"Okay, what does all of this have to do with the constellation Ophiuchus?"

"I'm hoping Alex's files will shed some light on that. Maybe Chris will help us."

"You think Alex was specifically studying Ophiuchus?"

"I think there was a lot more to his studies than that." Jonathan chuckled. "He was a Jesuit priest. He believed the ancient texts of the bible. He saw things through the scope of scripture."

"Meaning," Kaira replied, "he believed in the fallen angels and Nephilim as my grandmother did? Although it would explain so many things. I want the proof right in front of my eyes."

"Who doesn't. That's the thing about the bible. It asks you to have blind faith. That makes it difficult."

Kaira shook her head. "True. However, scientific research is beginning to collaborate with the Bible and ancient texts in an attempt to figure out cosmic riddles."

Jonathan nodded in agreement. "There's no question; the entire world experienced a devastating flood. Every culture has a creation story, and every culture speaks of giants and gods. I have to admit, no one talks about Nephilim in church. I find it odd that the most interesting parts of the biblical text are never mentioned."

"You went to church growing up?" Kaira teased him.

"You did too. I remember your pigtails. Your family sat in the pew ahead of us."

Kaira's mouth hung open in surprise. She said nothing and allowed him the pleasure of being one up.

"Alright," she continued ignoring the comment, "the question is not whether we believe there were enormous beings on the earth in our ancient past. The question is, where did they come from, and where did they go. Why don't we see them now?"

"That's right. And I have a theory. What if Alex discovered a planet we haven't seen until recently? What if the proximity of the planet causes something strange to happen to the earth's electromagnetic fields? We already know about Ley lines. What if they are the portals these other planetary beings travel through?"

"What in the world are Ley lines?" Kaira looked at him like he'd lost his mind.

Jonathan put his hands in the air. "I know, it's weird, but they are real. Ley lines are apparent alignments of landforms, places of ancient religious significance, or culture, often including human-made structures. They are ancient, straight 'paths' or routes in the landscape, which are believed to have special significance. It's like a grid on the earth."

"I don't think I've ever heard of Ley lines."

"The phrase was coined in 1921 by the amateur archaeologist Alfred Watkins, referring to supposed alignments of numerous places of geographical and historical interest, such as ancient monuments and megaliths, natural ridge-tops and water-fords."

"I don't quite understand. Why is it significant?"

"The best example I know of is Via Sancti Michaelis, going from the Mont Saint-Michel in France to Monte Sant'Angelo in Puglia, Italy. They are all located on the same axis. Even more surprising is that the Sacra di San Michele lies in perfect geographic alignment with three other Saint Michael monasteries. Built on a straight line, from Skellig Michael, Ireland, over Saint Michael's Mount, Cornwall, England, including the pilgrimage route previously mentioned, to the Monastery of Saint Michael in Greece. Finally, they come to an end in Jerusalem, at Mount Carmel."

"Why would the church build monasteries in a line across... how many countries did you say...five?"

"I have no idea why. But it gets even weirder." Jonathan took a sip of coffee. "The monastery in Italy, Sacre di San Michele, was constructed by the hermit Saint Giovanni Vincenzo at the request of the archangel Michael. Legends say the building materials which the hermit had collected were transported miraculously by angels to the top of the mountain when construction began sometime in 1000 AD. At the top of 243 steps is the stone Porta Dello Zodiaco, a portal to the stars."

"It seems that everywhere we look in antiquity, there are hints and suggestions of supernatural activity, but no real physical evidence or proof." Kaira held her mug between her hands with her elbows on the bar. "I'd say there's some connection between the stars and the ancients, but I'm not willing to say it's angels or giants. That's just too crazy."

"I get it. I feel the same way. However, there are extremist religious groups and secret Orders who will die for these beliefs. They can be dangerous."

"What do you believe?" Kaira asked, knowing it was an intimate question.

"I know what I'd like to believe." Jonathan got up and set his mug in the sink. The sun was barely peeking up over the horizon, and the view was incredible. Kaira swung her barstool around to enjoy the view.

Jonathan fell silent, and Kaira finished her coffee. As the sun ascended above the horizon, Kaira found herself wondering what it would feel like to be able to believe in a creator, to believe in angels and other beings. Why are we here?

Yet, that was only part of the question. Whatever the truth might be regarding the discoveries Kaira's grandmother and Alex had made, no one would know the truth unless they could find Alex's files and her grandmother's secrets.

Chapter Thirty One

Albano Laziale, Italy

Giovanni knew the Vatican, with its immense wealth and political influence had become a global force in politics. From its beginnings, the Holy See has been a rich source of intelligence. One of the world's greatest repositories of raw data, it is a spy's gold mine. Ecclesiastical, political, and economic information filters in every day from thousands of priests, bishops, and papal nuncios, who regularly report from every corner of the globe to the Office of the Papal Secretariat. So valuable was this source of data that shortly after the war, the CIA created a particular unit in its counterintelligence section to tap it and monitor developments within the Holy See.

But, Giovanni's interest wasn't in the Vatican or the Holy See. It was the legendary secret Order dating back to the Crusades when warrior monks served as military mercenaries. Its members were active in five continents forming the wealthy backbone related to the oldest and most influential families. The contemporary Order of the Serpent, perhaps the most exclusive club on earth, comprised of what he believed to be the very wealthy and some Italian mafia leaders, had an agenda.

Giovanni was disturbed by the role the Order had played with the CIA during war times. The CIA organized an elaborate spy network to obtain intelligence from behind enemy lines. Other secret Orders had risen over time and shaped their organizations, much like the Order of the Serpent. The mafia had become involved in some of these obscure Orders, and their influence had grown strong.

Distracted by his thoughts, he didn't see the man in a dark jacket moving stealthily down the stairwell, keeping a safe distance from Giovanni.

Jobs like this one had kept the PI well during war times, and now, back in the saddle, he worked for a new organization, men he'd never see. Stealing antiquities was a million-dollar industry. He didn't care who he took it from or why his employer wanted it. Most jobs involved some greenhorn who had gotten too thick into something they couldn't handle.

Don't ask questions, he mused. It was a rule that gave him clout with his employers.

The job he'd accepted several days ago offered him 20K to follow Giovanni and report his activities. They were looking for the whereabouts of antiquities taken from an excavation site managed by Giovanni but controlled by the Curator, who was employed by the Holy See.

Usually, Giovanni's routine would have taken him around the trails at Albano Lake. This morning he had unexpectedly taken a walk to the museum. Now, beneath the foundation in the belly of the warehouses, what had begun as a stakeout had taken a sinister turn.

Giovanni felt sweat trickle down the back of his neck as he quietly hurried to unlock the door. The dust made him want to cough. He placed his arm over his mouth and sneezed. The long room beneath the first floor lined with shelves housed a diverse mix of antiquities discovered in the Albano Laziale area. No one would have given a second look to some of the items stashed on the shelves. Giovanni headed towards the back of the room.

It will only take a moment and make sure it's safe, he decided, moving toward the back wall.

The town was known to hold secrets and ruins beneath almost every building. Long ago, the museum had been part of a palace in ancient Roman times. As Giovanni moved through the narrow, cluttered room, he passed a shelf with stones that held inscriptions. The message read נְפִילִים.

Giovanni knew Hebrew writing. He shivered as he read the word for Nephilim. It meant "giant." He looked around at the shelves realizing that the warehouse was completely overflowing with strange objects from all over the world. There were stones with ancient writing, bones, and pots for wine.

He walked to the back wall adorned with a tapestry that covered the wall floor to ceiling. The air smelled dead and dry. He had always found it ironic that as an archeologist, his job was to uncover and reveal the truth. The Curators job was to hide and shelf most of his findings in dark corners of the basement where he stood.

He had spent much of his time explaining to his students why it was essential to keep the artifacts safe from the public until further research. His students were young and impatient, but they were also intelligent and questioned everything.

The only thing he wanted right now was to make sure the latest find was still hidden safely in place. Without hesitating, he gingerly lifted the side of the tapestry and found the entrance. He moved through the cramped space and made his way down a dark stone-lined passage.

Once he was a few feet inside the passage, he turned on a small flashlight he kept inside his pocket. He moved quickly now, his hand guiding him along the cold stone wall. He peered inside the chamber, where a locked box sat next to some shelves.

Then he heard it.

He stopped short, his breath coming in small bursts.

There it was again. In the distance, Giovanni heard a door shut. For one brief instant, he panicked. Then, with the speed of a much younger man, he sprang into action and thrust his key into the lock, lifted the item carefully out of its hiding place, then put it in his bag.

He could hear footsteps in the warehouse. *Someone is trying to find the relic. He has followed me. God, help me.*

He would have no cell reception this deep beneath the museum. His only hope was to reach the other exit from the building next door. Giovanni picked up the backpack and made his way toward the backside of the chamber. He wasn't as familiar with this passage and had only been through it one other time many years ago. The back passage was damp and much cooler. He was panting and sweating profusely.

He wound his way through the passage and to a wooden door. He pushed one shoulder on the door as he turned the handle. It didn't budge. Carefully he placed the backpack at his feet and shoved hard. The door creaked as it gave under the force. He pitched headlong into dusty cobwebs. He picked his pack up and turned his flashlight toward the room.

Chapter Thirty Two

In the restroom, Kaira washed her face and hands then put on her evening dress. She'd talk to Jonathan about buying some clothes in the ski town of Mt Lemmon. Her wrinkled black dress was no longer appropriate.

What is happening, she thought.

She had to admit she didn't long for the lonely life she'd left a few days earlier. Single and engrossed in journalism, she'd been too busy for a relationship. Suddenly, everything had changed. She had inherited a winery. Whatever that meant, she wasn't sure.

In her heart, the change had begun when she'd heard her grandmother's voice speaking to her from the recording on the phone. Looking back, she realized she'd made up her mind then. Her old life had evaporated at that moment.

The horror of Alex's death had settled in as she weighed the implications of leaving her grandmother's estate.

She talked with Alex before the presentation, and he was anxious to share the discoveries he and Victoria had made.

Someone probably thinks I know what Alex and my grandmother discovered.

Security hadn't been that tight at Meadow Manor. Either no one expected it to happen or more horribly, they did expect it to happen. Kaira knew nothing about Umberto and the way he managed Meadow Manor. He seemed very loyal to Victoria, and Kaira wanted to trust him, but could she?

He knew more than he let on.

In the last few hours, Kaira had shared some things with Jonathan and now feared her openness might have been reckless. She tried to comb her hair with her fingers. In the mirror, she saw a woman who had lost that lonely, shy look. There was color in her cheeks and a fiery spark in her eyes that surprised her.

Returning to Westonville may have been the best choice she'd made in a while. What could she have done differently? It was her grandmother's Wake. And then there was Jonathan. A few months ago, she had written an article about him in the East Coast Traveler.

Though she didn't say it in the article, she assumed him to be the greedy, cocky treasure hunter, she remembered his father to be.

Most treasure hunters had one thing in common, obsession. Over the past few hours, she'd seen to a side of Jonathan that was kind and good. The thought of him being corrupt was too painful to address.

In high school, Kaira had been different than the other girls. She hadn't been interested in being popular, and if she was, she didn't know it. She treated everyone with the same respect and curiosity. Her friendships tended to be genuine.

She remembered standing alone, listening to the band at the school dance when she'd first met Jonathan.

"You look too beautiful to be standing all alone." A deep voice spoke to her.

Inside, her heart flipped, but she didn't turn. Instead, she continued to stare straight ahead at the band, but a small smile played around her lips. She felt awkward at events like this, where a girl was expected to arrive with a date.

He continued to press her. "Do you have a favorite song?"

She almost responded, "You're So Vain" by Carly Simon," but the sentence froze in her mouth as he reached around her and handed her a rose. Then she turned.

"Oh…" she stammered. "Ah…thank you."

"I know I'm a little clumsy. I was hoping for a dance." He smiled, and her heart skipped a beat for the second time. She felt her face blushing. She took the rose and allowed him to lead her onto the dance floor.

Later that evening, he asked her to go to dinner with him over the weekend. Surprised, she looked at him quizzically. He must have seen the question on her face.

"Kaira Munroe," he said, grinning, "you're the most intelligent woman in school. You love history, and your grandmother is the president of the Westonville Historical Society for God's sake. And…you're gorgeous."

"Does that usually work with the girls?"

"I don't know. I'm going to find out." He was still grinning down at her, and the butterflies in her belly fluttered. She accepted his invitation. Jonathan's buddies distracted him and began talking about their weekend plans. She didn't think he'd follow through, but Kaira held the promise of a date in her mind. She'd always thought of herself as too skinny and gangly. But, in reality, she had blossomed into a quiet beauty, unaware of the effect she had.

Two evenings later, when Jonathan collected her from her home in the heart of Westonville and took her to a beautiful restaurant up the coast, she'd found herself in the company of yacht club members whom she recognized as the wealthy east coast elite. That's when she discovered his family came from old money. Jonathan introduced her to some of his friends. He didn't behave like a spoiled rich kid.

As the evening came to an end, he pulled her close and kissed her gently. "I hope this evening was as wonderful for you as it was for me. I'd like to see you again."

"I've had such a lovely time, Jonathan. Thank you. My father has a business trip planned, and he wants to bring the family along. Maybe when we return?"

"Where are you going to be? I'll come to find you."

Kaira laughed. That he would follow her just to be with her endeared her to him. He walked her to the door and kissed her again.

That evening Kaira came down with a terrible cold, which turned into pneumonia. She stayed home with her aunt while the family went on a business trip. That's when her father, mother, and brother had died in the accident on the return home.

The next several months after the funeral, Kaira stayed with her aunt and graduated alone. She finished her senior year without fanfare. Soon after graduation, Jonathan left Westonville and went on to make a name for himself. She wasn't envious, just sad for time lost.

She reminded herself she hadn't seen Jonathan since. She should be careful and take things slow.

She heard voices outside the bathroom door. Chris arrived to take them to the observatory and Alex's office. She entered the room, slowly feeling uncomfortable in her evening clothes.

"Can you take us to a shop in town where we can buy a few things?" asked Jonathan.

"Of course. Have you had breakfast?" Chris rattled the keys in his hands, clicking the metal together. Kaira remembered her father jingling change in his pants pocket that way.

"Yes, we had coffee and muffins." Said Kaira eager to move on and buy new clothes.

"We have a ski shop."

"That sounds perfect," Jonathan said.

"You should ride with me this morning. When we go to the observatory, it would be best if we were together."

Skis, jackets, and a variety of hiking gear cluttered the little ski shop. Kaira found some black leggings, a long cream-colored sweater, and a pair of brown leather boots. Jonathan found cargo pants, a black pullover, and a jacket. Feeling much better, they made their way to the observatory.

Back in Chris's jeep, Jonathan asked, "What is happening on Mt Graham, and what was Alex working on?"

"You open a can of worms with those questions." Chris laughed. "First of all, In 1873, Mount Graham was removed from the boundaries of the San Carlos Reservation and placed in the public domain. The spiritual value of Mount Graham to the Apache was not considered. This action set the stage for the conflict we are having now." Chris continued. "In 1984, the University of Arizona and the Vatican selected Mount Graham as a site for a complex of 18 telescopes. To get around the legal barriers of the American Indian Religious Freedoms Act, the University hired a lobbying firm to put pressure on Congress to remove this and other roadblocks. The U.S. Forest Service administers the area in question."

"How do you feel about what happened?" Jonathan asked.

"I believe the goals of the Vatican will benefit all. However, that is not believed by some." Chris responded.

"Did the project Alex was working on cause problems with the Apache nation?" Kaira was trying to connect the observatory project with his murder.

"Interesting question Kaira. Just the opposite. His project confirms their legends."

"In what way?" Jonathan asked, surprised by the response.

Chris was beginning to look uncomfortable. They pulled into the central area and parked. "We've got to walk from here to see the Observatory. I thought we'd start there before we head to Alex's offices."

Kaira wondered if he was going to ignore the question. Up a dirt road, the green metal bottom of the building blended in with the trees. The white-domed top stood high above the trees. Inside, metal stairs next to a large round mirror led to a floor above.

Chris pointed at a particular part of the massive telescope. "L.U.C.I.F.E.R., which stands for "Large Binocular Telescope Near-infrared Utility with Camera and Integral Field Unit for Extragalactic Research," is a chilled instrument attached to the telescope. And yes, it's named for the Devil, whose name itself means "morning star" He grinned. "We get lots of questions about the name LUCIFER, so I just wanted to get that over with."

"What is the huge disk we passed on the way in?" Kaira asked.

"Its heart is a 1.8-m f/1.0 honeycombed construction, borosilicate primary mirror. The primary mirror is so deeply-dished that the focus of the telescope is only as far above the mirror as the mirror is wide, thus allowing a structure that is about three times as compact as the previous generation of telescope designs."

Pressing Chris, Kaira asked again, "What was Alex working on?"

"Over the last few years, he has focused so much of his time and effort in an attempt to reconcile science and religion in public forums specifically as it relates to the subject of extraterrestrial life and its potential impact on the future of faith." Chris continued but hid his discomfort at the pointed questions. "To illustrate the theological soundness of this possibility, many Jesuits argue that humans are not the only intelligent beings God created in the universe, and these non-human life forms are described in the Bible. We see this in scripture referring to angels and the Nephilim." Chris looked at Kaira to see if her interest had waned. He continued.

"Heavenly beings come up several times in the Psalms. For example, the passage in Psalm 89. "Let the heavens praise your wonders, 0 Lord, your faithfulness in the assembly of the holy ones. For who in the skies can be compared to the Lord? Who among the heavenly beings is like the Lord?... The heavens are yours; the earth also is yours; the world and all that is in it -you have founded them." Likewise, God asks Job (38:7) if any human can claim to have been around at the creation, "when the morning stars sang together, and all the heavenly beings shouted for joy."

"Not everyone believes in the bible." Said Jonathan.

"No, but the interesting thing is that all ancient texts refer to these beings. Also, all Indian legends tell of sky beings who came to earth."

"You mentioned Alex's project didn't cause problems with the Apache and that it confirmed their legends. What did you mean?" Kaira continued to press.

At first, she thought he would ignore her again.

"The Holy Scripture tells us that in times past, fallen angels made contact with humans."

"It says that in the bible? I mean fallen angels? I've never heard that."

"Most people haven't." He smiled at her. Apache legend speaks of giants coming through portals, and they had contact with humans." They were walking back to the jeep. "As a result of corruption, the scripture says God sent a flood. The deluge would have been during Noah's time. The flood would have killed the Nephilim."

"What exactly are Nephilim?" That was the word Umberto spoke to her at Meadow Manor.

"They are the offspring of angels and humans."

Chapter Thirty Three

Alex's apartment, located in an electronically secure building, had a windowless lab on the subterranean level. It seemed to Jonathan the room was intentionally isolated from the other activities of the Vatican's observatory.

Inside, the lab consisted of five computers, an old-fashioned black telephone, two large screens mounted on the wall, four tall lateral file cabinets and shelves. Heat filled the room from a stack of servers in the corner. The room was clean and smelled sterile. In the center of the room, a long table held some large meteorites.

This is where Alex's discovery is hidden? Jonathan thought.

Although "Assistant Data Scientist" wasn't technically the job of an astronomer, Chris had access to all the files and data Alex gave him. The computers were powerful enough to handle a tremendous amount of information.

For the past year, Chris had helped Alex focus on the project he'd inherited from Alessandro. It was terrible when Alessandro had disappeared, but losing Alex was devastating. According to Jesuit astronomers, Alex stood out among the rest as a brilliant astronomer and scientist. But, there had been something strange about Alessandro's disappearance. It marked the end of their open conversations regarding the project and their collaboration.

Although the Jesuits considered themselves to be unified, Chris knew the project they were working on would not bring unified support. Lately, Pope Francis spoke how he wanted to position the church and the Jesuit Order to be able to accept a significant shift in human consciousness as a result of extraterrestrial existence.

The Roman Catholic Church had known for centuries about the existence of life on other planets from ancient texts they housed in their archives. The increased discussion of life on other planets was becoming a problem among many Jesuit astronomers and scientists.

In the past month, Chris had tested large meteors recently found in Sedona at a site the Apache Indians believed to be a portal.

The Vatican, thought Chris, *intruding on Apache land where portals and legends were sacred.* Before Alessandro went missing, his relationship with the Apache had become a sore spot with some of the Jesuits.

And then, there was Alex. He had been very excited recently, and work became difficult as he stepped up the pace. A few weeks later, he made an incredible discovery, and the evidence was more astounding than anything Chris had ever witnessed.

Then he had received an invitation to Meadow Manor. On a day's notice, Alex packed his bags to visit Victoria in Westonville. It put Chris and Mark in a predicament, but they quietly managed their work.

Just hours after Alex's death, problems began to surface. The news and attention brought the curious to their door. Some were other Jesuits at the facility who asked about the project. The murderer hadn't been caught, and there was talk among the Jesuits that a secret Order might be involved. The rumors unnerved Mark. But the files were locked safely away, and Chris managed to create his secure drive for the project information.

I hope Mark doesn't lose it, Chris thought as he strode into the lab with Kaira and Jonathan.

"This is the lab Alessandro built. I worked with Alessandro before he disappeared. Then Alex took over."

"Disappeared?" asked Jonathan. "You mean he left and never returned?"

"Oh. I thought you knew. All of Alessandro's things are still here. He simply disappeared. The Jesuits put out a story that he'd died from an illness."

What an odd thing to do." Said Kaira. "Why would they do that?"

"We have all kinds of conspiracy theorists around these parts. They like to stir the pot. The head of the observatory is trying to keep them at bay. But now, with Alex's death, theories are popping up everywhere."

"Like what?" Jonathan gazed intently at Chris.

Chris hesitated, then spoke quietly, "There are some Jesuits here at the observatory who believe a secret Order may be involved."

"A secret Order? Involved in what way?" Kaira asked.

"They're looking for something." Said Mark nervously.

Jonathan wandered to the table and looked at the meteors. He could see the tension in Chris and wanted him to relax. "Did anyone look for Alessandro?"

"We all looked for him. We spent two weeks searching. After a while, most came to believe he left the Jesuits out of disillusion." Mark's voice was distraught.

"Why would he be disillusioned? Jonathan said calmly.

'I don't know. It's just a thought." Mark said. Feeling uncomfortable, he wandered to his desk and sat down in front of the screen and began to type.

"We've been told not to speak of the disappearance. I thought you knew since you were friends with Alex." Said Chris

"Why are you telling us?" Jonathan asked.

"I think Alex was working with Victoria to find Alessandro. They'd both made astounding discoveries. You know, Victoria funded this project." He looked at Kaira. "You're her granddaughter, aren't you? I've read your articles."

Kaira hesitated. "Yes…"

Jonathan gazed at Kaira perplexed. Realizing her unease, he stepped in. "I wonder if you would show us around the rest of the facility?"

"Sure." Chris seemed relieved, and Mark's shoulders visibly relaxed.

He proceeded to the show them all around the observatory— from the personal quarters of the Church's astronomers—where they ate, slept, relaxed, studied—to the control rooms, computer screens, and systems, and once again the telescope.

"What do the other astronomers study?" Jonathan asked

"Among the most important research occurring with the site's Vatican astronomers is the quest to pinpoint certain extrasolar planets and advanced alien intelligence."

"You're kidding?" Kaira was grinning, but Chris wore a serious expression. She tried to wrap her mind around his casual tone.

Chris didn't blink an eye, nor did the other scientists in the room who spoke casually of the redundancy of which UFO's are captured on screens darting through the heavens.

But, this was not the primary reason for being at Mt Graham. Jonathan had burning questions concerning high-level Vatican astronomers and what they had been gradually leaking to the media over recent days concerning planets and extraterrestrials.

***

"Everyone listen," Jackson stood in the small conference room at the Westonville police station. "We think we've located Jonathan and Kaira. Remember, they aren't suspects, but their safety is important." He watched the faces of the officers making sure they were listening. "Jonathan's credit card pinged from a ski resort in Tuscan, Arizona."

A couple of officers snickered. "Maybe they're on a ski trip." He joked.

"This is serious, men." Jackson kept his voice calm though he felt frustrated. "We haven't found the killer, and he may be after Jonathan. Someone bought clothes for a man and woman with a credit card we've traced to Jonathan. It sounds like they are there. Track them, and we might find the killer."

He strode into his office and motioned Brody inside. Quietly he updated Brody. When Jackson finished, he poured a cup of coffee. "Pull up the Mt Lemon Observatory, will you. I need to see it on a satellite map."

Brody pulled the map up on the screen. Jackson looked over his shoulder and looked at the information on the screen. "It looks like there are two observatories. What's that just south of the Mt Lemmon Observatory?"

Brody clicked a link and information popped up on the screen. *"Welcome to Mount Graham International Observatory. MGIO is a division of Steward Observatory, the research arm for the Department of Astronomy at the University of Arizona.*

"Look at the list of telescopes." One link said *Vatican Advanced Technology Telescope.* "Click on that link," Jackson said.

Suddenly the screen exploded with stars and constellations as the Vatican Observatory website popped up. The Vatican's logo read Specola Vaticana.

"Did you know the Vatican was working with Arizona State University in Tuscan?" Brody asked.

"No...no, I didn't know that. Why would I know that? This is rather disturbing. Listen to this." Jackson read further.

"L.U.C.I.F.E.R., which stands for "Large Binocular Telescope Near-infrared Utility with Camera and Integral Field Unit for Extragalactic Research," is a chilled instrument attached to a telescope in Arizona. And yes, it's named for the Devil, whose name itself means "morning star" and which happens to be housed at the Vatican Observatory on Mt. Graham in Tucson."

"Wow. That's creepy." Brody said.

"Brody, I don't know for sure why Jonathan and Kaira are at the Vatican Observatory, but someone may think they are a liability. We need to get them back here."

"What if they don't want to come back?"

Jackson was silent. "Do your best to get them back. I think we're in for more trouble. Call the Observatory and see if they're there."

Chapter Thirty Four

The newsstand in front of Local Steam Espresso had one paper left. Umberto picked it up and read:

WESTONVILLE NEWS

Alexander Gabriel Mirabelli, born in 1967, a Jesuit priest and astronomer at the Vatican Observatory, had his master's degree from Pontifical Academy of Sciences. A member of the Society of Jesus, he was ordained a priest in 1990. He joined the Vatican Observatory as a researcher in 2004.

In an interview in May 2008, he stated, *"the possible existence of intelligent extraterrestrials did not contradict church teaching. He also stated that ruling out the existence of aliens would be like "putting limits" on God's creative freedom."*

Alexander Gabriel Mirabelli died September 23, 2017.

American Shore and Beach Preservation Association

Living shorelines integrate structural and natural features to reduce erosion from the wave climate while keeping the connectivity between land and aquatic ecosystems. Our ongoing research aims to quantify storm wave dissipation and surge reduction effects of living shoreline designs to influence more sound design and practice when implementing such shoreline stabilization projects. The project is utilizing the non-hydrostatic NHWAVE model to examine wave dissipation over a marsh sill system during a storm event over a wide range of hydrodynamic and structural parameters, and vegetation characteristics. Over the course of the research, the model will calibrate with data from a field site in Westonville, New York. Preliminary results of the modeling project will be presented at the conference to highlight inroads in the research and to dialogue with other members of the coastal community to provide a better assessment of the level of protection offered by the living shoreline treatment as storm events and sea-level rise occur.

A Treasure Hunter Jailed until he Reveals Location of Treasure

Arthur G. Bell was once one of the greatest treasure hunters of his time: A dark-bearded diver who hauled a trove of gold from the Atlantic Ocean in 1988 — dubbed the richest find in East Coast waters.

Years later, his son accused of cheating his father's investors out of the fortune led federal agents on a great manhunt — pursued from an east coast mansion to a hotel room booked under a fake name in Italy.

Young Brian Bell's beard has grayed after a stint in an Italian monastery, held there until he supposedly gave up the location of the gold to a Mafia Don who had him released.

But for nearly two years, despite threats and fines and the best exertions of his captors, federal agents have not managed to learn whether he found his father's treasure.

The wreck of the Southern Pacific waited 400 years for Arthur G. Bell to come along. The ship went down in a hurricane in 1757, taking over 300 souls and at least three tons of gold to the seafloor off the Caribbean.

Many tried to find it, but none succeeded until a young, engineer, Arthur G. Bell, from New York, built an underwater robot to pinpoint the Galleon, then dive 6,000 feet under the sea and surface the loot.

"A man as personable as he was brilliant, Bell recruited more than 160 investors to fund his expedition," Westonville News noted in a profile. He "spent years studying the ship's fateful voyage ... and developing the technology to plunge deeper into the ocean than anyone had before to retrieve its treasure."

Bell's crew pulled up rare Spanish coins, the ship's bell and "gold bars ... Fifteen times bigger than the largest East Coast gold bar previously known to exist," the New York Tribune reported in 1995.

His son refuses to reveal the location of the wreck site still unexplored — potentially worth $400 million in gold alone, The New York Post reported a few years later. "The treasure trove is one of the richest in East Coast history."

The story recently captured the country's attention, as did the peculiarities of its leader — a young man whose father was a scientist-seafarer hybrid who worked on nuclear submarine systems before he hunted treasure.

"Brian Bell's father was not exactly the romantic, swashbuckling sort," Forbes wrote, resurfacing a fascinating story of the ship's treasure. "He was scientific and methodical, with none of the sensationalism of other salvors."

In his late 30s, during the height of his fame, Arthur G. Bell said little in public and tended to play down his role in the discovery.

"This gold is part of the largest treasure trove in American history," he told reporters in 1995. "But the history of the Southern Pacific is also a rich part of our nation's cultural treasury."

He added: "It's a celebration of American ideals: free enterprise and hard work."

But before long, some of Bell's bankrollers began painting a very different picture of the man.

Two of the expedition's most prominent investors took him to court in the 2000s, accusing him of selling nearly all the gold and keeping the profits to himself.

When a federal judge ordered Bell to appear in 2010, he didn't show. An arrest warrant was issued, but the man who found the long-lost shipwreck had disappeared.

Now there is a federal manhunt for Arthur G. Bell's son, Brian Bell, accused of following in his father's footsteps. It is believed he knows where the gold is hidden.

Chapter Thirty Five

Mt. Graham Observatory

After a unique tour of the Vatican Observatory and the offices and facilities, Chris dropped Jonathan and Kaira back at the cabin. As soon as they were inside, Jonathan pulled out a phone book and began looking for a restaurant.

"Are you as hungry as I am?"

"I'm famished. Does this ski town have a decent restaurant?"

"I think I saw something interesting when we arrived. Here it is." He ran his finger along the page. "It's called the Iron Door. A rustic mountain restaurant that serves comfort food."

"That sounds perfect."

They were quiet on the way to the restaurant, both trying to process the information the Jesuits had told them.

The restaurant was wonderful. The floor to ceiling fireplace of cut stone beneath massive wood beams created a rustic atmosphere. Small flakes of snow were beginning to fall outside, and the orange glow from the fire warmed the room.

Across the table, Kaira sipped a glass of wine and tried to relax. "I can't believe I'm saying this, but thank you for bringing me with you. I've never covered a story as interesting as this."

"You're welcome. I hope you're not planning to call the newspaper just yet?"

Kaira laughed and shook her head.

"I had my reasons for bringing you." He smiled.

"You were more prepared for this than I was. You've spoken with Alex before?"

"Only briefly, just before he arrived in Westonville to visit Victoria."

"He certainly seems to have information that someone thought worth killing him to contain."

Jonathan's face turned grim.

"Jonathan, what if there is more than one perpetrator?"

"What do you mean?"

"One man, a thief, the other a killer. A dead man can't tell anyone what he's discovered."

"I see your point."

"What if someone wanted him dead to hide information, someone else is trying to find. If they think we have the information, they will come for us."

Jonathan suspected she was right, and he may have brought her straight to the Hornets' nest. Maybe he should have left her at the Abbey, but he couldn't stand to have her out of his sight.

A young waitress took their orders and brought Kaira another glass of wine. Distracted by her ruminations about Alex and Victoria, she had another thought.

"What about Alessandro, the missing Jesuit? I hope you won't think ill of me. I took something from his room while you were talking to Chris."

"I'm surprised. You don't seem like the type to color outside the lines." Jonathan smiled. "What did you find?"

"A black book. It was inside a pillowcase."

Jonathan chuckled at the thought of Kaira riffling through the Jesuits room. "You're a real sleuth, young lady."

She opened the book. "Here's what I find interesting. There's an address a place in Sedona, AZ, and a group of numbers. It isn't a phone number. I already tried that. It's the only thing in the book. It looks like the rest has been torn out."

"Sedona isn't far from here. Maybe we should check it out."

Jonathan's phone buzzed. He read the text but hesitated to read it to Kaira.

"What?" she demanded.

A message from Umberto.

"I thought you should be aware that Westonville News just released a story about the killer. There is strong evidence suggesting a link between the killer and a seedy organization known as the Order of the Serpent."

Kaira was alarmed but tried not to show it on her face.

"There's more," continued Jonathan,

"Victoria wasn't the only person Alex met. He spoke with Giovanni Fiorelli, Archeologist, and professor in Albano Laziale,

Italy. A photo released on social media connects him with Alex and Victoria. It's what's in the photo that is so intriguing."

Jonathan sat stunned, looking at the image Umberto had sent to his phone.

Kaira reached for his phone and caught her breath as she saw the image.

***

The town of Sedona Arizona nestled along the side of a mountain was surrounded by green pine and red rock. Jonathan felt relieved to see it was more civilized than Mt Graham. According to the black book, Alessandro chose to spend weekends in Sedona to rejuvenate spiritually.

That wasn't the real reason, Jonathan realized.

In reality, Alessandro disliked crowds and admitted to keeping a place at Sedona only to have an excuse to research on his own. Supposedly, Alessandro had challenged the Jesuit Order to allow him time alone weekly for spiritual purposes, but they'd done it grudgingly.

I wonder if any family members miss him, he thought ruefully. Alessandro seemed to have been secretive, alone, but his brilliant work offered him privileges the other's might not have received so quickly. *I just wonder if he's still alive.*

After dinner, they'd packed everything in Kaira's bag and left Mt Graham. The three-hour drive seemed to go quickly. Sleepy from the second glass of wine, Kaira napped.

Jonathan's hand softly nudged her cheek. "We're here." He said quietly. Embarrassed she'd fallen asleep in his lap, Kaira sat up. "Thanks," she whispered, smiling at Jonathan. He looked wide awake.

"If you're up to it, we should try to find his place."

She nodded. She pulled the address up on her phone. "How will we get inside?"

"Well," Jonathan explained, "I'm hoping those numbers are a code for the door or entrance."

Kaira opened the map in satellite images. "Wow, it's all by itself out there in the middle of nowhere. Are you sure you want to look tonight?"

"I'm up for it if you are."

Kaira felt better after the nap. She shrugged her shoulders. "Fine with me. And, you think the numbers are the code?"

"For some reason, I doubt he would open his door with a key. He seems to be a tech geek."

"Must be the numbers then." Kaira cocked her head unnerved by the prospect of finding the home in the middle of the night. "It's dark out here."

Jonathan nodded in agreement and began winding his way up the side of the mountain behind the town of Sedona. "Only a quirky priest would build his home into the side of a mountain. It sounds like he loved his solitude. But, I think he was working on something else. I'd like to find out what that was."

Kaira eyed the satellite image again. She was thinking of snakes and spiders.

Chapter Thirty Six

Carmelo's Compound One Year Earlier

As they drove through the darkness, Brian recalled the last time he'd dived off the Italian coast. The life of freedom and safety was a world away now, having ended in an Italian prison. Experience was a wild gamble of risk. However, a new equilibrium had been introduced to him.

The same man who had left one of his men hanging from a bridge with a length of rope woven into a love knot around his neck had rescued him from the damp prison. In the same week, the mafia had been excommunicated from the Church and had gone underground.

"I want you to meet someone," Luigi said when he had healed enough to travel. "he works for the Holy See, well, indirectly."

He wondered if Luigi had lost his mind. "I thought your family was excommunicated from the Roman Catholic Church."

"There's always more to the story, trust me." Luigi laughed gruffly. "Unless you have something more important to do?"

Brian said nothing. His sides still ached from the beatings he'd received in prison.

"This will be worth your while," Luigi said. "I'm going to give you a nickname...*Robusto*. You like it?"

That afternoon they flew from Italy to Arizona. Brian wondered where they were headed, but he'd been too nervous to ask.

They drove for a few hours then turned off the main highway toward a cluster of mountains.

"Do you see it?" Luigi asked, looking at the mountains in the distance.

"I see red rock and a thousand potential homes for snakes." He had no interest in hiking the terrain ahead of them.

"It is incredible once you see it." Luigi declared. Brian could see he was serious.

He squinted and searched the mountains. As they drew close, his eyes widened. There it was, camouflaged in the rocky cliffs, invisible unless you knew where to look.

Brian grew up along the East Coast, and he'd spent a lot of time in Europe, but he'd never had any desire to be in the desert. The buildings were in the middle of nowhere on the rocky side of a mountain. The closer they came, the more impressive the structure seemed. The massive complex imitated Anasazi ruins, with a militant level of security.

Luigi drove along a switchback trail intentionally hidden from view. After the second switchback, they approached a metal gate, and Luigi punched some numbers into a box mounted on a pole next to the entrance. The gate swung open.

The road slipped behind a rock and into a tunnel. *Just like a James Bond movie*, thought Brian. The tunnel opened into a lot where two jeeps and a Humvee were parked. From this location, the buildings imitating Anasazi ruins were a few hundred feet above them.

A security guard approached the car. He wore black cargo pants and a black jacket. His right hand clutched the Uzi slung over his shoulder. He smiled when he saw Luigi and said something in Italian. They shook hands, and he introduced Brian as Robusto, and the two men laughed.

What are Italian mafia doing in the Arizona desert?

A set of steep stairs led toward the buildings above them. Stucco on the walls was the same color as the red rock creating a perfect camouflage. From above, Brian lowered his gaze to the access highway below. To his surprise, he couldn't see it. The entire road was hidden from above, as well as from below.

Luigi took the stairs slowly, his large frame reflecting his eating habits. Though Brian was sore and still recovering, overall, he was in better shape than Luigi.

"We're just in time," Luigi said. "He hurried through an iron gate at the top of the stairs through a precisely aligned wall, which runs north to south through the central plaza. That's when Brian saw the snake wound over the top of the gate. "Don't worry. It isn't poisonous."

A high round tower situated on either side of the wall created a symmetrical pattern. In addition to the large roundhouses, over twenty other round structures surrounded a central courtyard. The enormous complex covered two acres and incorporated many rooms.

A sign hung above the door of one of the more significant round buildings and read:

Serpentine Resources, Inc.

Brian had heard of the group in Italy. Again, he wondered what they were doing in the desert. Another snake slithered across the hard-packed dirt courtyard. He turned to Luigi, trying to control his shudder, feeling himself recoil. "Are you a part of the Order?" he asked Luigi.

Luigi just grinned. "There are some in the Catholic Church who still want us around. We have strategic places all over the world. Secret places."

Brian looked at the imitation ruins. "But, why out in the middle of the desert?"

"Have you ever heard of interdimensional portals?" Luigi asked.

Surprised, Brian wondered that Luigi could use the word in a sentence. "You mean wormholes?"

"Sure. It's becoming more feasible. The Vatican has been studying it for years. They have a telescope on Mt Graham, and they've been watching the Milky Way."

"Why is that?"

"It's believed that certain stars in the Milky Way galaxy could be close to a transport system."

Brian was beginning to see that the buildings were a giant science lab. "What are they doing here?"

"We are Serpentine Resources, Inc., a venture capital group that invests in scientific enterprises. We vet technology in this facility. The Vatican is instrumental in establishing our group for this research."

Brian remembered the strange comment Luigi had made earlier. *There's always more to the story.* According to legend, the Order of the Serpent has been present in the history of man for a very long time. It all started thousands of years ago with the "Brotherhood of the Snake," a secret society set up by a god named Ea or Enki. This story very carefully told in the Sumerian scriptures and dated back at least 6000 years.

A few years ago, a documentary had aired whose purpose was to reveal the idea of portals and Ley lines in some regions of the world and the power they held. Brian had been intrigued to learn that over the years, many unexplained disappearances were attributed to the opening and closing of these portals. Why would the documentary be suddenly removed?

As Brian gazed up, he couldn't help but view the complex as sinister. *Whoever Serpentine Resources, Inc. is, I have no interest in participating.*

In addition to the odd claims of portals in the Milky Way, the Order of the Serpent also believed alien activity was responsible for mysterious events happening in and around Sedona. Brian was in no condition to question Luigi, but he'd expected something entirely different from the trip. Most people wanted to know if Brian knew where his father hid his treasure.

"Luigi," he said carefully, "Why have you brought me here?"

"I wondered when you were going to ask me that question." Luigi didn't seem bothered by his question at all. "This place is hidden, secret, and we're in up to our neck with the Vatican. But, I assure you, the work here is incredibly revealing. You'll see."

"But what do I have that you want?" *Who could blame him for wondering? The leader of the Order released him from prison.*

"The Vatican had to excommunicate us publicly. For years we've been lining the Vatican's pocket with funds through our network. Brian assessed the ruins in the middle of the desert. Something wasn't right. "I guess I don't understand." He said. "If you have no ties to the Roman Catholic Church, how are you receiving funds for all this? Is your leader that powerful?"

"The boss has his fingers in a lot of the pie. But, when it comes to the church, the price for our silence is a few well-placed complexes operated by our leader. It's a good trade-off." He said smugly." "Finances are funneled through certain Jesuit groups."

Though the answer was unexpected, Brian knew that the Catholic Church throughout history had an insatiable obsession with the heavens. They'd been watching the galaxies since Galileo's time. The Church also had information no one else in the world could access. It wasn't unfathomable to imagine the church covertly associating with a seedy mafia group.

"Our leader is an amazing man," Luigi said. "He's willing to meet with you today after we get you settled in."

Brian wondered how long they planned to keep him at the complex.

"I think when you learn more about us, you will find it suits you well."

I hate snakes, thought Brian.

"Listen," Luigi said, "when you meet Carmelo, don't make the mistakes so many men have made before. He's a very personable guy. But, he won't hesitate to use his power if you force his hand. Understand?"

Brian listened then slowly responded. "I understand. I think everything will be fine."

"Fine? It's going to be fantastic. You'll see. Besides, a few weeks ago, you were sitting in a cold cell with your ribs busted. You would not be fine without Carmelo."

Thanks for the reminder, thought Brian. He was right. He had been rescued from possible death. Now he owed Carmelo. Brian had a terrible feeling he was about to pay the price.

"Why are you worried? You can't possibly be worried about meeting Carmelo."

Brian had been in control of his destiny since he'd graduated high school. The thought of following the orders of a mafia Don with a fetish for serpents rankled him. He hated how it made him feel, but he didn't show it. Instead, he turned to Luigi.

"Let's get settled then. I'm ready to meet the man."

Chapter Thirty Seven

Guiding the car along the mountain road, Jonathan was surprised to find Kaira still had an internet connection. The sky was dark but clear, and millions of stars twinkled above them.

In the seat beside him, Kaira was busy browsing google map and the internet on her iPhone. The web of intrigue was deepening with their visit to Mt. Graham and Jesuit priest Alessandro who had gone missing a year earlier. Chris had shared that Alex and Alessandro had been working on a secret project connecting the constellations, events on the earth, and ancient antediluvian secrets.

Kaira found an article and read aloud:

"What is going on at Mt Graham and in the Sedona desert of Arizona? The Vatican also owns most of the early books of antiquity on astronomy as well as owning the most patents on celestial observatories. Strange for an organization that was adamant about a geocentric universe."

Kaira looked up at Jonathan then continued to read.

"Two men interviewed a Jesuit priest, and it seems they've come to some interesting conclusions." She continued, *"They said, the idea of a traversable wormhole was considered too fantastic to be possible because the sheer force of the gravity would rip you apart. A scientist named Carr came up with something called a "Carr black hole," which means is it's spinning. The force of the spinning counteracts the gravity, and it wouldn't tear you apart. The idea is that if it was spinning at just the right speed, you could go through it and survive."*

"I can't imagine there is a stargate portal to other dimensions," Jonathan said. "But, I do know that CERN is trying to send particles back and forth through dimensions."

"It says here that the scientific community has done a lot of research on dimensions and they've established there are multiple dimensions existing in the same space. Why certain areas are portals hasn't been answered." Kaira stopped for a moment. "There are several documents about the Bradshaw Ranch here in Sedona."

"What is the Bradshaw Ranch?"

"A ranch in the Sedona desert that professes to have UFO activity. It says here that you can get a map from the government a geographical map of the magnetic anomaly."

"What exactly does that mean?" He asked.

"On a color map, it shows up pink where the magnetic anomaly is occurring. Sedona is covered in pink. People believe these are windows to other dimensions."

"This reminds me of the huge crystals found in Mexico by miners. The miners couldn't survive longer than 10 minutes in the cave. Some of the crystals were over 30 feet long. They had some kind of magnetic attraction with the ability to become an electrical conductor. Ancient Egyptians used crystals for protection and health and buried the dead with a piece of quartz on their forehead to help guide them to the afterlife. Why are you, smirking?" laughed Jonathan.

"I don't believe in all that mumbo-jumbo. But something is going on. I remember the first time I realized no one knows how the pyramids were built, and the first time I saw the Nazca Lines." Kaira smiled. "It is mysterious and wonderful, isn't it?"

"Ah yes, The Nazca Lines. A series of large ancient geoglyphs in the Nazca Desert in southern Peru, I believe. The largest figures are up to 1,200 ft. long."

"It seems you see the best from the air. Does that mean people could fly in ancient past?"

"Some believe so. The book of Enoch talks about flying." Jonathan had read the Book of Enoch and the more controversial Book of Giants.

"Really? Is that in the bible?"

"No. The bible speaks about Enoch, and much of the text is very confirming of the Book of Enoch."

"Tell me about it." Intrigued, Kaira wanted to hear more.

"Enoch describes a journey with the angels, where they are flying in some angelic ship moving toward the south of the earth and coming to a place where there are pillars of heavenly fire."

"Maybe they were over the South Pole?"

Jonathan laughed out loud. "So, you believe in angels, do you?"

"I'd rather believe in angels than in aliens. Continue your story." She commented, smiling.

"Enoch describes how he is passing several mountains, which fits in well with the mountains in the east and South Africa. He passes over where the "waters collect," which is where the oceans gather south of Africa. Then when he comes to a southern place, he sees a chasm or abyss, which would suggest that Antarctica might have been free of ice. And we know that there are ancient maps that seem to depict Antarctica as an ice-free landmass." Jonathan stopped to collect his thoughts. "Then, over this abyss, where the heavenly fire goes up and down like large pillars, there are seven stars. They are seen hovering over the South Pole horizon. A well-known formation of seven stars is the Pleiades. Then, the angels tell him that certain fallen angels were to be bound to those stars, because of their mingling with women on earth."

"Wow, that's quite a story. Odd how it matches mythology in Greece and Mesopotamia. In the Greek myth, seven women were placed in the starry heaven. They mingled with the Titans, and they were made pregnant. These Greek women were called the Pleiades." Something about connecting the two stories thrilled Kaira and caused a small shiver to tingle up her spine. "Then there is also a myth from Mesopotamia. Seven demons are bound as seven stars in the sky and identified as the Pleiades, which was known for its beautiful appearance and its role for agricultural dates."

Jonathan cocked his head, "I didn't know you knew so much about mythology."

"Well, I didn't know you knew so much about the Bible."

"What I am beginning to realize is that ancient mythology and texts, along with science, are beginning to come together. I think the answers we come up with in the future will blow us away."

"The interest in supernatural is growing at an incredible rate," Kaira said, glancing at the article on her phone screen. "The entire world is looking for answers to some of these questions."

The realization made Jonathan more committed to finding a way into Alessandro's retreat home. Maybe Alessandro was still alive.

"Have you heard from Umberto recently?" Jonathan said, looking puzzled. "I haven't heard from Father Murphy in a while, and it doesn't make sense. He's always been transparent and timely in sharing information with me."

"I can't imagine how Umberto is managing the winery and Meadow Manor after all that's happened. But, it seems he is a very competent person, seasoned in his experience and years. He's probably rushed. Besides, it's only been a few hours since he texted last."

Jonathan suspected Kaira was right. Life goes on in spite of all the tragedy. Considering the Westonville Historical Society would be managing Meadow Manor with Umberto, it seemed logical that investigation and transition would be ongoing for a while. Father Murphy wanted to avoid making any public statement that would bring the Abbey or Kaira and Meadow Manor under public scrutiny.

"Father Murphy would be relieved to know you are safe. There must be a good reason he hasn't tried to contact us."

"I don't know for sure." She said, looking out the window at the stars. "I'm not sure I trust him." She said matter-of-factly.

"Well, regardless, I'm glad you're safe. You're a trooper to come along."

"You make it sound like I had a choice." She said in a low fiery tone. He must not remember as clearly as she did.

Jonathan chuckled at her quiet outburst. "I believe your grandmother would have wanted us to stick together."

"Oh, now you bring my grandmother into this. She can no longer speak for herself." Her voice held a hint of humor.

Kaira had turned back to the iPhone to see the google navigation. A tiny blue dot indicated where they were on the mountain road. "There it is, just up ahead."

A dirt road, almost invisible, took off through the desert pine trees. Carefully Jonathan turned and slowly drove through the dark. The lights illuminated only a few feet in front of them. A hundred yards ahead, the dirt road came to an end. There was nothing but a red rock wall.

"The dot on my screen tells me we are at the door."

"Google map has been known to be wrong on occasion. We must have taken the wrong road." Jonathan said, putting the car in reverse and beginning to back out.

"Wait." Kaira spotted something unusual in the dark. "Shine the lights there." She said, pointing at the red rock wall.

Returning his eyes to the rock, he reached down and flipped the bright headlights. There it was, a slit in the wall and the glint of colored glass. "Let's just hope those numbers are the password to get inside."

Chapter Thirty Eight

Albano Laziale, Italy

Giovanni slowly put one foot in front of the other, keeping his eyes straight ahead, ignoring the dark shadows that cramped around him. Cobwebs and dust clung to his skin. He swatted to clear them from his face and hands.

I am taking control of the relic.

He made his way up some stone steps and arrived at a door that opened into a building next door to the museum. He pushed it open and looked into the hallway, startling a janitor who looked alarmed when he saw Giovanni, dust-covered with cobwebs in his hair.

"Mi Scuzi." Giovanni said. "Dove è l'uscita?"

Wordlessly the janitor pointed him toward the front door exit. Giovanni hitched the backpack up and pushed past the janitor and out the front doorway. He headed directly for the Poste Italiane eight minutes by car and about thirty minutes' walk on a clear day.

***

Across the world, in the Abbey at Westonville, Father Murphy stood in his apartment. Thanks to the Vatican and its new policy of revealing bits and pieces of news at a time, the deluge of conspiracy theories had become less ominous. The open revealing of Pope Francis's thoughts calmed the power of sensationalism. But, beneath the calm waters lurked an Order with a diabolical agenda.

As the news stations had settled back into their routine, coverage was already waning concerning the death of Alex. There was an occasional reminder that the murderer was still at large, a shameless cunning plan to ensure the channel didn't change. Father Murphy scanned his computer for his subscribed networks. Social media had become the breaking news hotline, and he watched as conspiracies filled the screen.

Jesuit Astronomer Murdered in Westonville
What is Meadow Manor hiding?

The Westonville Historical Society Inherits the Secrets

Angrily, Father Murphy read the headlines and shook his head. *It is too easy to look at the surface and think you understand, but the layers beneath this horrific event go deep*, he thought.

Father Murphy had always been responsible for running the Abbey with integrity. Broadcasting sensationalism created a depth of disappointment he couldn't avoid. Some of the monks were glomming onto the melodrama along with the crowd. News channels were continually questioning the Vatican. Occasionally, what they reported was true, and that caused Father Murphy to feel intense shame. But, not every story about the Vatican was true.

A flash on the screen caught his attention. The headline read: Vatican Planet X Disclosure

"Information is slowly being disclosed by the Vatican, which would strongly suggest the presence of an incoming planet anomaly and the presence of other beings who are presently visiting the earth. Those in power seem to know what is coming or what may already be present in our sky.

In late 2009 the Vatican hosted an astrobiology conference where the origins of future, extraterrestrial life in the universe, and life on earth were the main topics. French astrophysicist and member of the Pontifical Academy addressed the conference and warned the church that they must not be indifferent to the possibility that something extraordinary might happen to change the vision humanity has for itself.

The keynote speaker, a well-known professor at the University of Arizona, indicated that a profound discovery would be only a few years away."

Father Murphy clicked the sleep tab on his screen. Alex and Victoria were two people who loved astronomy and ancient history for all the right reasons. Victoria had an unusual ability to keep secrets yet disclose some things that caused people to ask themselves the right questions.

He remembered the presentation of Victoria and Umberto, healthy and robust, exploring the Lazio region of Italy. *"Today, I am with Umberto at the megalithic structure that predates the biblical flood."* Victoria had said on video footage. *"I have only a few years left to make sense of this incredible factual evidence. However, the advancement of truth in our history has been jeopardized, and I fear it will continue as many world leaders want control of new evidence rising from technology that allows us to make incredible discoveries at ancient dig sites."*

Father Murphy new that the intrigue would deepen as Kaira learned the secrets her grandmother had held. He wondered how she would handle the knowing.

Father Murphy's phone rang. It was one of the monks.

"What is it?" he said quietly.

"Giovanni just called." He sounded breathless.

Father Murphy frowned. "Why did he call you?"

"He didn't say that much. Just that we should expect a significant package to come in the mail addressed to you. His instructions were to get it to you immediately." The young monk worked in the administrative offices of the Abbey.

"Is he sending it from Italy?"

"Yes. Albano Laziale. It will take a while to arrive, but he wanted you to expect the package."

"Thank you. Have you told anyone else?"

"No. Giovanni said not to tell anyone but you. He wanted me to keep my eyes open for the package."

Intrigued, Father Murphy wondered if it had something to do with the recent death of Alex. According to Umberto, Alex knew Giovanni well. Father Murphy studied the young monk. "Who else has access to the mailroom?"

"Just me."

"I want no one to enter the mailroom, but you until the package arrives."

"What do you think it is?" asked the monk, his eyes shining with interest.

"What it is will not be your business." Father Murphy said firmly. "Our job is to protect the package once it arrives and bring it straight to me. Understood?"

"Yes, of course, Father." The monk's eyes went blank, and he dismissed himself.

Had his friend Giovanni sent him the key to unlocking the equation? Father Murphy wasn't sure. Whatever the package was, it was of utmost importance that no one saw it. The connection between

Alex and Victoria was a puzzle Father Murphy wanted to answer discreetly.

Chapter Thirty Nine

Facing the red rock at the end of the road, Jonathan pointed the car headlights in the direction of the wall. The glint of colored glass came from a cleft in the rock.

"Wait here," Jonathan said and opened the car door. "Let me see what it is first." He said, leaning his head down and looking across at her. Then he carefully strode up to the wall and examined it. The rock wall was about fifty feet tall and reflected the red and cream sandy layers that were prevalent in Arizona and New Mexico.

Jonathan waved at her to follow him. She grabbed the keys from the ignition and switched on her iPhone flashlight. The ground where they had parked the car was sandstone. Closer now, she could see the hidden entrance and the stained-glass window in the door behind Jonathan's shoulders.

There was no indication of any building material other than a door embedded behind a slit in the sandstone. A door, in a red rock wall. Odd.

Jonathan knocked on the door. There was no sound. He hit harder the second time.

"Do you have the black book?"

She pulled it out of her pocket and shined her flashlight on the paper.

The door shaped like a chapel window and had an electronic lockbox had been attached just above the door handle. Kaira read the numbers to Jonathan, and he punched them in. The door clicked heavily and swung inward.

Jonathan pushed it further into the darkened hallway and called out. "Anyone home?" There was no answer. He called again louder this time — still no response. He shut the door behind them and heard it lock automatically.

Kaira flipped a light switch and gasped in stunned amazement. Inside the walls were smooth, artistic, and breathtakingly beautiful.

"My God, the walls look as though they've been hand tooled." Jonathan's voice was low, almost a whisper.

The entrance hall curved gracefully to the right. The walls were smooth yet decorated with swirls and sculpture. The hall emerged into a living room with a large skylight window overhead where millions of stars twinkled above them. Two more smooth arched passages branched out from the center room.

"The room must be twenty feet high," Kaira exclaimed.

Jonathan led them toward one of the passages, still walking carefully. "We are breaking and entering." Kaira reminded him.

"Not exactly. We had a key and the code." He responded.

At the end of one passage, a beautiful set of stairs carved into the sandstone wound toward a second level. A chair had been cut into the wall just left of the stairs. "A resting place if you get tired of climbing." Kaira laughed. Occasional moonlight filtered in through skylights in the ceiling.

"The modern design doesn't seem fitting for a Jesuit priest, does it?" Kaira questioned.

"But it suits an astronomer perfectly," Jonathan said, looking through an arched doorway. Kaira stopped short behind him. Another circular room full of electronic equipment surrounded a telescope pointed at the skylight in the ceiling.

Jonathan turned to Kaira. "Chris said Alessandro and Alex worked at this retreat for three years before Alessandro disappeared. That means this is the birthplace of the discoveries Alex made, not Mt Graham."

Then Jonathan saw it. The room was set apart from the rest of the place.

"I was afraid of this," Jonathan said, pointing at the room. Kaira peeked over his shoulder. At least a hundred tiny pinpoints crisscrossed the room in a dense plaid pattern. Jonathan scanned the arch and surrounding walls for an electronic code box but found nothing.

"Maybe it's just for show. We could take our chances." Kaira said

"No, it's the real thing. If we trigger the lasers, we will be breaking and entering."

***

Billy gazed up at the house, still wondering where Alessandro had gone. The past few years, Billy had brought his meteors and geodes to Alessandro for extra cash, a collaboration that supported his schooling. Having the Jesuit as a friend had been a miracle.

Billy met Alessandro four years ago when the astronomer stopped at his booth and looked at his stash of strange rocks. His buddies thought his collection was ridiculous until Alessandro had agreed to buy them all and anything else Billy found.

Over time, a friendship grew between them, and eventually, Alessandro admitted to Billy he was working on something unusual. The lab was lined with shelves full of meteors and quartz from the geodes.

Alessandro told Billy he'd found a way to store trillions of terabytes of information in the crystals. But then he disappeared.

Billy's heart had been heavy when he returned to sell Alessandro some rocks and found he was gone. Finally, Billy realized he wasn't coming back. He had searched for other places to sell his rocks, but no one seemed interested.

Tonight, while he was out on his four-wheeler, a car driving through the dark towards Alessandro's retreat surprised him. Only one other person had visited the sanctuary beside Billy.

He moved slowly through the woods and parked his four-wheeler behind some brush. Turning toward the red rock, his eyes wide, he looked through the darkness. The car was empty.

The sight of the car parked in the driveway gave him hope that his friend had returned.

***

Inside the Civico Museo, in Albano Laziale, Italy, Antonio was listening to the man he had hired to follow Giovanni give him an update.

"Giovanni left his home for a walk. He didn't take the normal route. I looked for him after realizing he'd gone a different direction and finally spotted him entering the museum."

"You're right. That is unusual for him."

"I followed him inside and into the basement, but I lost him there."

"What? Antonio declared. "How can you lose an old man in the basement of a museum? His whereabouts are our number one concern."

"I understand." The private eye sounded uneasy. "There's something else you should know. He was carrying a backpack."

"Just a moment," Antonio was distracted by visitors at his office door. Two men in long black robes walked through the door.

"Antonio Callo?" One of the men said.

"Yes?"

"The Prefecture for the Economic Affairs of the Holy See requests your presence at once."

Antonio hung up on the PI.

Chapter Forty

From where they sat on the alcove bench, there were two paths. One led back down the stairs and the other through the arch into the secured room. Just inside the arc, the sandstone floor was level and smooth. A large telescope pointed toward the skylight glinted from moonlight reflecting off metal. A supercluster of computers, large mounted monitors, and equipment surrounded the room in customized compartments built into the walls. Shelves full of geodes and meteors lined the floor.

"The best man cave I've ever seen." Jonathan mused. His eyes climbed higher along the walls noticing a shimmer like a coat of glitter on the sandstone.

"The numbers," Kaira whispered, nudging his arm. "Should we punch them in?"

Jonathan shifted uncomfortably and tried to picture all the things that could go wrong. He made a mental note of the exit.

"What could go wrong?" Kaira said, reading his mind.

"Looks like he was working instead of resting in his retreat."

Jonathan punched in the first seven numbers onto the phone's code pad.

A third of the lasers disappeared. Encouraged and excited, Jonathan punched in the second set of seven numbers. More lasers faded, and the telescope made noise as it began to move

"Alessandro was eccentric. What a strange retreat." Kaira said as the telescope positioned itself higher toward the skylight making a series of clicking noises

Jonathan punched in the last code, and the lasers disappeared. The computers came to life, and a rock version of Gregorian Chant began to play.

"This is it. Let's go in." Jonathan said. Suddenly, Kaira felt nervous. What if someone showed up and found them here.

Jonathan stepped into the dimly lit room whose walls now glowed beneath the yellow light. A thin layer of dust covered everything. As he moved into the open space beyond the arch, he could see the ceiling more clearly and stopped dead in his tracks.

"My God,....this is incredible," Jonathan exclaimed.

Kaira gazed up, speechless. The ceiling painted with the constellation of Ophiuchus, and the serpent circled the whole room. Ophiuchus looked down at them from above, his head at the skylight and his feet touching the floor.

Kaira moved to the wall where the painting extended floor to ceiling.

"I first saw this in my grandmother's apartment," Kaira said. "Have you seen it?"

"No, but if it's anything like this, I'm impressed."

Kaira nodded incredulously.

"Ophiuchus means "Serpent Bearer" in Greek. Why would my grandmother and Alessandro want a painting of a man wrangling a serpent displayed on the ceiling?"

As Jonathan observed the ceiling mural, it suddenly struck him that Victoria had named the yacht Ophiuchus. Despite the intriguing serpent writhing in Ophiuchus' hands, his gaze moved to the stars. "Evidently, something about this constellation motivated them."

"Yes, hard to miss, isn't it. It must have something to do with their research, but what?"

Jonathan eyed the other elements of the painting, noticing the stars and their alignment. For a moment, he wondered if the constellation might relate directly to finding Alex's secret. The moment passed.

"We are looking for information data. We need to access the computers."

The equipment room wasn't the most comfortable part of the cave retreat. Alessandro lived in a cave. Kaira still had difficulty wrapping her mind around it. The hollowed-out rock was a fortress, and there were just enough windows and skylights in the ceiling to keep the darkness at bay. Carved out of stone, the passages wandered from room to room with the glide and flow of a river in nature.

Kaira moved to the computer sitting inside a rock niche. A bank of motion-sensitive lights lit the inside of the grotto when she sat in the chair. The computer screen lit up, and a message scrolled beneath the login field.

"Heroes of old, men of renown." Jonathan stood behind Kaira as she read the verse. Her mind went back to the sign above the winery.

"Jonathan, this saying is above the winery door at Meadow Manor."

Nephilim, he thought having remembered something Father Murphy had once said. "Nephilim" was a term that referred to the offspring of fallen angels spoken of in the bible. None of it made any sense.

"Try the word Nephilim."

Kaira typed the word into the login field. An error message told her she had three more tries before the computer locked up. She pulled her cell phone out of her pocket and hoping Alessandro had good internet reception inside the cave.

"Remember the word carved on the stone beneath the fountain? Umberto said it means Nephilim."

"Right. But it's in Hebrew.

That would require a keyboard with Hebrew letters, Jonathan thought, moving toward the shelves. As anticipated, three keyboards sat among some hardware next to the computer. He peered at the keys and pulled out a board that had odd images on the keypads.

"It might not match the American standard QWERTY. Hebrew writes right to left." He plugged the keyboard into the USB port.

"We'll match the image," Kaira said, holding up the image on her phone. She punched the letters מִיְלְפָּנ, and the screen went blank for a few seconds, then the desktop opened, and icons flooded the screen space.

"Good grief, where do we start?" Kaira said as she began reading through the icons, "Python computer environment, Matplotlib, ALMA telescope scripting, C/C++/Fortran code execution, IDL Interactive data language, Mathematica for math applications, IRAF infrared data processing…the list goes on."

"What's that one at the bottom?" Jonathan said, pointing to the skull and crossbones.

"Looks like a game." She smiled, "Even monks need to have fun occasionally."

She clicked on the icon. Data began scrolling on the monitor. It stopped, and a moving image of outer space suddenly played across the screen. The view of the earth was breathtaking. "It looks like a movie taken from the space shuttle."

Suddenly, three red lines pinpointed spots on the earth and zoomed in on them one at a time. The first was on the East coast, New York. A voice began speaking.

"Who wouldn't be captivated by the idea of fortune and glory? With the help of a friend of mine, I've been able to pinpoint an incredible discovery. Not just one or two anomalies, but hundreds of them. I've created a space map."

Jonathan listened intently.

"While I was researching unusual activity in the Arizona desert, I stumbled onto an incredible find. As I was looking at the photos of the earth taken from a satellite, I noticed some very unusual anomalies. I've deduced that some of them are shipwrecks, but it turns out some of them are more bizarre than I could have imagined. I've spent almost a decade researching this with the help of private funding. Some of the anomalies are too large to be shipwrecked. Each time I investigate these unusual sites, I have found something extraordinary."

Jonathan was familiar with space mapping. He had a friend at NASA who had helped him pinpoint the shipwreck in the Caribbean. The voice continued.

"I can render images of the earth from space, and now I've charted a space treasure map. There are a ton of files that come with this project, and I've had to create a retreat to get the work done. The map is huge. It covers the east coast, the Atlantic, the Caribbean, and Central and South America and Europe. It will take decades before the information I have will be exhausted. Potentially, this information will open Pandora's box regarding antediluvian earth and ancient world. Unfortunately, I think someone is looking for my map. I've hidden my files in an attempt to save years of work in case something happens to me."

The recording went fuzzy with static and ended abruptly.

As Jonathan pondered the recording, he was struck by a second realization. *Alessandro wasn't just a Jesuit astronomer. He was a treasure hunter!*

Chapter Forty One

Kaira Munroe sat in the blue glow of the computer equipment and ran her eyes across shelves full of books and hardware. His lab was extensive for a Jesuit astronomer.

Alessandro had transformed this side of the room into a display of three mounted monitors and stocked a sizeable library with a mixture of books and equipment. Eyeing the place, Kaira realized finding his files would be like finding a needle in the haystack and far more time consuming than she had realized.

The books on his shelves reflected the icons on his computer desktop. A wide array of topics included Greek Astronomy, The History, and Practice of Ancient Astronomy, Searching for the Oldest Stars, Celestial Geometry, and Cosmology. Nothing unusual for an astronomer. Jonathan had been quiet for some time and had wandered out of the room.

"Jonathan?" she called. "Where are you?"

"I'm in here." He called from the next room behind the lab.

"Do you think Alessandro funded this lab with his finances?"

"I'm not sure," Jonathan replied. "I don't think he would have wanted anyone other than Alex to know about this."

"His telescope isn't as powerful as the one on Mt Graham. Is there a chance he was doing something else?"

"I did find something interesting in here. It looks like a battery created from geode crystals. I think Alessandro found a way to run his equipment through the crystals. Unfortunately, I don't understand it well enough to say that for sure."

"I see," Kaira said thoughtfully. "He must have been planning to work out here for a while. Who do you think the man is in the video?"

"Alessandro. I think he was onto something more than astronomy."

"What do you mean?" Kaira asked.

"Have you seen anything about treasure or searching for treasure?"

"Only astronomy and cosmology. He obviously had an interest in ancient Greek astronomers."

"While you continue searching, I thought you might be interested to know Umberto texted me regarding Meadow Manor."

"What's happening?" Kaira demanded, her attention suddenly focused on Jonathan's voice. Her emotions still stirred over the death of her grandmother and the recent events. *The killer hasn't been arrested,* she reminded herself.

"He just reported that the Westonville Historical Society is setting up an office in Meadow Manor. They are suggesting that the situation is more complex than it seems. They believe the manor is in jeopardy of intruders."

Umberto sent Jonathan images of looters on the beach digging in the cliff where the recent storms had caused erosion. In town, protesters carried signs that read: Keep treasure hunters off our shore. Some protesters carried signs with a skull and bones and a red circle with a diagonal line through it.

No pirates allowed had become a widespread protest for Westonville's group of old-timers and fishermen whose families went back a few generations.

"Has anyone found anything yet?" Kaira asked.

"That seems to be one of the problems," Jonathan replied. "There's no way to know unless someone is caught red-handed. But, it seems someone has spread a rumor at Friar's Deck Tavern that a large human bone was discovered along the beach. Conspiracy theories regarding the legends of Meadow Manor and Westonville are running rampant. Umberto says the spreading rumor is that you know the secrets, and that's why you're hiding."

"They think I'm hiding something?" Kaira was horrified.

Jonathan was back in the room, standing next to her. "We were at the Wake when the murder happened, you are the granddaughter of Victoria and will inherit her estate. People are beginning to wonder if you are somehow involved."

Jonathan knew Kaira could not have possibly known the murder would happen. He recalled the sweet tenderness and sincerity he'd seen on her face when they'd arrived at the pier. She was somewhat naïve and romantic. She was no schemer.

"Umberto says questions are coming up about the two of us running off together. Westonville news media is asking why we left with no comment. A few town folks are suggesting we may be involved in the murder together."

"That's ridiculous!"

"It may gain traction. The rumor stems from my past research of shipwrecks and my connection with Victoria. Apparently, Meadow Manor's historical ties to the Abbey and Alex's murder…"

"Please stop." Kaira interrupted. "I can't take this. It's crazy."

"We have to think about this. Others are saying I was the target, and that's why I disappeared. Frankly, that might not be too far off. It seems everyone in town is collaborating to solve this mystery. I want to know who wanted him silenced."

Drawn to his words, Kaira asked, "You're beginning to think the murderer was after Alex, not you?"

"Umberto says the other woman is alive. She's in the hospital with a minor injury to her neck where the dart hit."

"She's alive?" Kaira said, startled. "You're sure?"

Jonathan pulled the vial from his pocket and told her where he'd found it. "I think the dart was meant to put me to sleep as a distraction while the intruder looked for something. Maybe he was searching for a map. The vial had no smell. It must have been a powerful knockout drug."

Kaira was thunderstruck.

That means the intruder who escaped didn't kill Alex.

Jonathan hadn't said a word about the vial. Now Kaira understood his maniacal desire to discover what happened.

"When did you know the intruder wasn't the murderer?"

"Not right away," Jonathan replied without hesitating. "I learned a few months ago that someone was following SSRL movements. It often happens in the Caribbean. Bottom feeders come out when they hear we've found something. But this is different. I investigated on my own and had reason to believe my brother was following me." Jonathan paused. "Based on the information we gathered, he's working for a man named Carmelo who is buying up land in the Caribbean. I have a 99-year lease and diving permits on an island he wants."

Overcome with guilt, Kaira realized the articles she'd written hadn't helped. The man was a legitimate oceanographer tirelessly working towards a pollution-free world. Her thoughts fueled a fresh determination to locate the files and complete what Alex and Victoria had been working on together.

"I haven't found any special files on the computer. Only cosmology and astronomy."

"The files we are looking for might be on your phone," Jonathan said. "Victoria most likely created a secure private share for those she's authorized. She built a cloud that can be accessed from anywhere."

"I've never grasped the cloud concept," Kaira admitted.

"I understand," Jonathan replied. "Even NASA uses secure cloud access. It is amazing, isn't it?"

Kaira hesitated. Holding secrets in a cloud didn't seem secure to her.

"To access the information on your phone," Jonathan prompted, "we'll need to type in the Hebrew symbols just like Alessandro's computer."

"Kaira nodded.

Kaira searched the icons on her phone.

"The icon probably won't tell you it's Hebrew."

"There are four screens of icons!"

"Look for something that reflects language."

"I'm sorry. I see nothing that suggests language. It's going to take a bit to go through each App."

"We'd better hurry," Jonathan said.

"Why do you say that?

"Umberto just texted that a private plane owned by Order of the Serpent landed at the Tuscan airport. Our presence here may no longer be a secret."

How did Umberto know the Order of the Serpent had landed in Arizona? Kaira wondered.

***

On the outskirts of Albano Laziale, Giovanni Fiorelli was thankful to have made it to the post office in time. In the backseat of a taxi, Giovanni hoped the desperate measures enacted would help him regain control of archeological discoveries he'd made.

"Via Miralago" Giovanni ordered as the taxi drove away from the post office toward his villa situated in a secluded area next to Lake Albano. He hoped to retire to his villa and lock himself inside. It would be best not to wander in the village for a while.

The taxi driver glanced in the mirror at Giovanni.

Giovanni knew he had been naïve. He no longer trusted anyone, and that included the taxi driver.

Chapter Forty Two

Civico Museo, Albano Laziale, Italy

The shirt collar around Antonio's neck felt uncomfortably tight. The Pontifical Commission sent the two men standing at his desk for the Cultural Heritage of the Church. They answered to the Roman Curia. Although Pope Francis had launched a new initiative and in spite of all the reforms, there was still something wrong with the communications strategy of the Holy See.

These men are dangerous, he thought, frustrated by his inability to follow Giovanni effectively. He wanted to ask them what the hell was going on, but no one talked to the men who governed the Church with disrespect. These men performed duties in the pope's name and with his authority.

As they moved into his office and stood at his desk, Antonio realized two black SUVs with tinted windows sat outside the museum at the steps.

"I am Cardinal Archbishop Edward Vigano. Do you know why we are here?" he asked.

Antonio shook his head.

"Do you know Giovanni Fiorelli?"

"Yes."

"Have you seen him recently?"

"No. I've been looking for him. I haven't seen him since early yesterday."

The cardinal was silent for a moment. "Did Giovanni tell you what he has found?"

Antonio sat quietly, a bead of sweat began to trickle down the side of his temple. The Cardinal reframed his question.

"Had you heard of his recent discovery?"

"I…yes. At least I've heard he found something though I haven't seen it."

"Will you describe to me what he has discovered?"

"As I said, I cannot describe it as I have not seen it."

"What did Giovanni tell you about this discovery?"

Antonio forced himself to assume a calm expression. He held his head up and looked directly into Cardinal Edward Vigano's eyes.

"Respectfully, why are you asking me these questions?"

The Cardinal ignored his question. "Were you involved with the recent discovery Giovanni made?"

"No."

"But, he stores artifacts here in the basement?"

"Yes. Every item is accounted for and has a permit."

"We believe he has something which belongs to the Holy See. We will be arresting Giovanni Fiorelli for his role in the theft of ancient cultural antiquities which belong to the Church. Anyone who is collaborating with him will also be implicated in his crimes."

Before Antonio could process the accusation, the men stood.

"Antonio, a scientist or an archeologist promoting evidence that developed civilizations may have existed long before ancient Egypt, will likely result in damage." With no other discussion, the two men walked out the door.

Giovanni had an abundance of interesting evidence from reliable sources, both in forbidden archeology and suppressed history. There was a huge chronological problem in his discovery. The entire model of the origin of civilization would have to be re-created from scratch.

Chapter Forty Three

Jonathan ran his eyes along the shelves and walls with increasing urgency. *There must be a map or a file somewhere.*

The unexpected arrival of the Order of the Serpent had changed everything. Jonathan hoped time would not run out. If they located the files, it would take only seconds to download. Victoria would have wanted them to find Alessandro's retreat. He was sure of it.

He glanced at Kaira, who was on the opposite side of the room just beneath the large mounted screens. She continued her search for the Hebrew app.

"Have you found anything?"

She shook her head. "I have a few more apps to go."

"Keep looking," Jonathan said as he scanned for maps and files.

He thought of Alessandro's disappearance as he searched through the books and titles. A thick brown leather-bound book lay beneath a stack of books and papers. Jonathan pulled it out and opened the journal noticing the handwritten ink.

"Listen to this." Jonathan began to read out loud to Kaira.

"My name is Alessandro. My mother was an archeologist from Italy and a devout Catholic." The writing was honest and forthright. *"The two do not mix, Archeologist and Catholic."*

My mother was the daughter of a wealthy family from the Lazio region of Italy. She fell in love with an American professor who had come to Italy to work at a dig site. She became pregnant and accepted the professors offer to marry. After her first son was born, they were happy. Then they had me. But, her family in Italy was not pleased that she eloped to America and married a professor.

After a while, she became convinced that someone was watching her activity. Then, my mother and my father were killed not long after in an accident on a dig site in Italy. I am sure it was the Order who murdered them.

"My God, what a tragic story." Kaira felt empathy, having had her own family abruptly taken from her.

Jonathan wondered at Kaira's ability to move forward in spite of all she'd endured. She wasn't the type to complain about her childhood. Instead, she learned how to live and thrive. It was a motivation for Jonathan first to be thankful for what he had and second, to be grateful for Kaira.

"How do you suppose he became interested in becoming a priest?" Jonathan asked.

"I don't know," Kaira said as she scanned through the apps. "Maybe, he felt as though archeology had taken his father from him. That might be one reason."

"Yes, but then later, he may have realized he enjoyed archeology."

"Why do you say that?"

"We saw the video of the space map. I keep running across references to his mother and archeological dig locations. He seemed to be trying to keep a record of her life. He must have had a moment of epiphany that changed his thinking."

"Then he met Alex and Victoria. It makes sense."

"Listen to this." Jonathan read from the journal.

"My mother and father found the remains of a massive lost city. They described it as 120 feet beneath the waters off the coast between Roma and Napoli. They believed the vast city to predate the oldest known remains in the subcontinent by more than 5,000 years. Substantial human bones, pottery, and sculptures were carbon dated and found to be nearly 9,500 years old. This city is believed to be even older than the ancient Harappan civilization, which dates back to 4,000 years. Though dozens of complexes were found under the ocean, most archeologists in Italy have ignored these finds. Some would suppress this information as it proves there was advanced civilization before the flood.

During our visits to the sites where my parents worked, I became familiar with the function of the Roman Curia. An Archbishop would visit every site they worked. No photos were allowed."

"This would explain his interest in religion and archeology. Do you think he became a Jesuit priest to access information he couldn't get any other way?" Kira asked.

"Maybe." Jonathan mused. The question of antediluvian civilization is at the bottom of this. I think it ties the discoveries of Alex, Victoria, and Alessandro with a common thread."

"And this notion stands in direct opposition to religion and science?" Kaira asked.

"I think it opens Pandora's box."

Jonathan saw that Kaira was shaking her head. "I don't understand."

"It seems there is a forgotten episode in human history — a lost civilization that cultures call by different names. It would have been a global civilization narrowed down to the end of the last ice age. That would be 12,000 years ago. That would have been the time of the destruction of that civilization. But, some believe it pre-existed that for many thousands of years."

"Wow, so it was caught up in the dramatic earth changes at the end of the last ice age?"

"Yes, you know there are questions concerning old world maps, something your grandmother shared an interest in." Jonathan continued. "Certain maps that were copied in the middle ages from older maps in 1400 to 1600s were based on hundreds of source maps that we no longer have. They are lost, but they tell us that information somehow crossed the ice age and made it into the hands of the new world. How this happened is a mystery."

"I wonder how all of this ties in with the Constellation Ophiuchus?"

"I'm not entirely sure. Have you heard of the precession of the equinoxes?"

"You mean as in the dawn of the age of Aquarius? My mom used to sing a song about that."

"Right," Jonathan smiled at Kaira. "What that means is that if you stand at any point on the earth on the 21st of March an hour before dawn and look east, you will see a constellation on the horizon in the place where the sun will shortly rise."

"Okay. Why is that important?"

"Because this is not easy. It requires a genuine understanding of astronomy and solar orbits. For some reason, this movement of the sun through the equinox moves one degree every seventy-two years, and there are thirty degrees to the house of the zodiac, so that means each age is 2,160 years and since there are twelve houses of the zodiac that brings you to 25,920 years."

Astonished, Kaira stared at Jonathan.

"What I'm trying to say is, this is complicated, yet these types of zodiac calendars were founded in myths that go back to the dawn of time."

"Is that what all the buzz was in 2012?" Her left eyebrow arched with skepticism.

"I believe so. These myths are all using the same system of numbers. It filters to us through the mists of history from lost civilizations."

"But, that still doesn't answer why Ophiuchus."

"You're right. I don't understand it yet. I think it will point to the antediluvian truth when we discover why Ophiuchus was important to your grandmother, Alex, and Alessandro. I believe it will take us back over 12,000 years ago to lost technology."

"You believe that?"

"I do."

As Kaira listened, Jonathan's phone pinged. He looked at his text. "It's Umberto. He says Archeologist Giovanni Fiorelli was arrested." Jonathan moved beside Kaira standing close, so she could read his screen. *"He is accused of stealing ancient artifacts from the museum in Albano Laziale."* Umberto sent a link to live news feed. Jonathan pulled it up on the phone screen. A uniformed man stood at the villa gate and took their prisoner to a black SUV. The camera showed the Museum Curator preparing to read a statement to the news team.

"I am Antonio Callo, Curator in Albano Laziale and Castel Gandolfo. The Pontifical Commission for the Cultural Heritage of the Church is pressing charges against Giovanni Fiorelli for his role in stolen antiquities as well as his attempt to accuse the museum of that crime."

Jonathan could feel Kaira stiffen slightly beside him as the Curator continued reading.

"Regarding his connection with American, FatherMurphy and the St. Francis Abbey", the Curator said in a dark tone, "We have received confirmation that they may have been working together. The

Roman Curia is now on full alert, and we will be watching for any other connections in this crime."

Jonathan was speechless.

"The public is urged to come forward with any information relating to stolen antiquities."

A young man stepped forward as the Curator left. The news reporter turned to him and shoved the microphone at him.

"This is crazy. I've known Giovanni for three years. He's my Archeology professor. There's no way he could have done this." The distraught young man shook his head. "This isn't right."

Kaira looked up at Jonathan.

"Someone's coming after his relics." She said.

Kaira's eyes were dark with concern.

Jonathan's voice was firm. "Umberto knows you haven't been kidnapped, nor have we run because of guilt. Unfortunately, we are caught in the middle of a war that isn't ours."

Kaira took a breath, "You mean the Order?"

"I've concluded," Jonathan said. "Father Murphy must know something vital that could threaten the Holy See. Victoria and Alex must have shared information with him."

Kaira closed her eyes. Jonathan sensed a wave of disappointment and fear washing over her. She wanted Father Murphy to be innocent. There was no incontrovertible proof that Father Murphy was not involved with the Order.

"Kaira, this is what I believe, your grandmother and Alex knew what Giovanni discovered, and they all have a common thread. Someone wants to stop us before the pieces are in place.

"They must have thought their plan worked when they killed Alex," Kaira said. "They had no idea he had spoken to me until later. We are the loose ends."

A distressing silence hung between them.

"Kaira," Jonathan said quietly, "I have known Umberto and Father Murphy as long or longer than I've known you. I suspect they are working together on this matter. Umberto knows Giovanni too. Giovanni and the Curator have been at odds for a while. It isn't a surprise for Father Murphy. I believe we can trust him."

Kaira nodded, but her eyes were dark, uncertain. "Either way, we are both in danger."

"We have to find the files now." Jonathan's pulse had quickened. He resumed his search with a renewed urgency. "We have to find out what they knew for our safety. If we go public with the information, then those who are hunting us will realize they are too late. We may have to beat the Order at their own game."

"I have an idea," Kaira said.

Jonathan listened while Kaira outlined a simple plan to pivot the focus from Father Murphy and onto Victoria. "The great thing about social media is that the knife cuts both ways."

"I don't want you to do that," Jonathan said warily. "You will also be dragged into this, and the focus will be on you as well. There will be no turning back."

"Jonathan, this is about my grandmother," she said, "she got us both into this, and now we are in danger. Someone is willing to kill anyone who threatens to make the secrets public." She paused, " But first, I have to recharge the phone, and my charger is in the car."

Before Jonathan could protest, Kaira was moving down the stairs toward the front of the cave retreat with her grandmother's phone in her hand. "Keep looking. I'll be right back."

"Watch out for snakes." He called.

"Thanks a lot!" Kaira shot back.

Alone in the room, Jonathan tried to make sense of the journal and the shelves full of books and geodes. He reread the quote, "Men of renown, heroes of old." So far, he had been unable to connect the dots between Nephilim and the discoveries made by Victoria and Alex. He thought of the megalithic stone structures from the presentation at Victoria's Celebration of Life.

I'm not much help, he thought as the silence grew menacing.

Chapter Forty Four

Carmelo's Compound

I am not the same as these men, Brian reminded himself as he took a break inside his room. He was trembling slightly, either from nervous energy or hunger. Carmelo brought him back to the complex, assuring him that no harm would come to his brother. He stared at himself in the bathroom mirror. He used to be a man who knew what he wanted. He had been angry with his brother and wanted to steal the map from him, but it had not occurred to him that others were after the same thing. They had murdered Alex. It could just as easily have been Jonathan. In all his anger and jealousy toward his brother, Brian was no murderer.

He checked the thin knife tucked inside his belt. It was his only weapon. He wondered if he'd have to use it. He looked in the mirror again and ran water into his hands and splashed his face. The tattoo he'd received on his neck while in prison mocked him. Odd choice, a Hebrew word for Nephilim.

He still wore the clothes he'd taken from the young man with the motorcycle. Ironically, the man in the mirror reminded him of his father and the way he'd appeared during his obsessive bottomless pit, the endless treasure hunt. The turning point had been the day he'd decided to hide what he'd found. He'd duped the investors and fled the country. Brian had been so close to finding his father's treasure before he'd been caught and jailed in Italy.

He would never forget the eerie monastery where he was held prisoner. When he'd been caught diving off the coast illegally, he was surprised that men from the Roman Curia had taken him to the monastery. Passing through the gates where monks were in their morning Mass, he noticed the Zodiac carvings over the arch.

Inside the sanctuary, it smelled of incense, and the dim candlelight revealed a painting on the ceiling of Ophiuchus. Standing in the back of the chapel waiting for the Archbishop, Brian wondered why he'd been brought here instead of an ordinary town prison. Apparently, the Roman Curia was involved in more than Church administration.

He had been miserable and vulnerable that day. A few monks glanced at him curiously then lowered their eyes. *He hadn't known then what he knew now.* He raised his eyes as a door behind the altar opened, and the figure of the Archbishop appeared, causing the men who held him captive to straighten.

The Archbishop was in his sixties and had an intense gaze. He wore a white cassock, a golden tippet, and an embroidered sash. He moved toward them, stepping down from the platform so that he was on the same level as Brian. There was something evil in his face.

"Good morning." He said in a hoarse whisper.

The men responded with a good morning. Brian said nothing.

Brian closed his eyes and tried to forget the memories of that time. The misery that came upon him for the next three years had been almost unbearable. These despicable men were not part of the church or the Roman Curia, yet they masqueraded as such. They brainwashed and tortured men into submission and dressed them in monks' clothing. Brian had witnessed firsthand the militant monastery and what he now knew as the Order of the Serpent.

"I believe," the Archbishop said, "we are looking for a man like you. We can permit you to do as you please in the world. That is what you want, isn't it? To do as you wish?"

Brian tried to turn the thoughts off in his head, but they flooded over him.

"There comes a time when you cross the line, as you have done here in our country. We can turn you over to the police or keep you here for our purpose and a greater cause. And so, we allow and encourage you to make a decision. Join us or suffer greatly for the crimes you have committed."

He thought of the evil he had seen on the Archbishop's face. Brian was asked to do unspeakable things, and when he refused, the pain had come. He struggled to stop the vivid memories from running through his head. They had asked what he was searching for in the waters. It hadn't taken long for them to piece together the story of his father's discovery.

Just before his release, the Archbishop assembled the monks and told them God had saved Brian for a higher purpose. The tragic crime he had committed was beyond forgiveness unless he turned and brought value to the order of the Serpent. The pain had been the catalyst that finally caused him to join. As soon as he'd committed, Carmelo was on the doorstep there to support him in health and with finances.

Brian wondered if his eyes looked as lifeless as those of the monks he'd seen at the monastery in Italy. Not so with the Archbishop. His eyes burned with the fire of evil.

"You are not finished." He had said to Brian in his hoarse whispery voice. "You will finish your mission and turn it over to the Order. In this way, you will serve."

From that day forward, with the help of Luigi, Brian began his slow climb back to health. Eventually, he was able to exercise, and the food provided by Carmelo was nutritious. Most importantly, his mind was beginning to clear.

"Remember," the Archbishop had said as he left the monastery, "When you think of becoming independent, God works to exert his will on earth through our Order. Pain can be your path to salvation. It's up to you."

Chapter Forty Five

Inside the Local Steam Espresso, people drank their coffee and looked at their social media. BuzzFeed read:

Watchdog: Westonville Historical Society
  The East Coast watchdog has submitted information to the newspaper. The Westonville Historical Society is now managing Meadow Manor and wishes the public to know that Meadow Manor is off-limits to trespassers who would wander onto the property looking for treasure. There is no treasure hidden at Meadow Manor, and those who stray unannounced onto the property will be prosecuted severely.
  The Westonville Historical Society is working closely with the American Shore and Beach Preservation Association to curb illegal hunting along the coast after our recent storms. Anyone found in areas designated off-limits or no trespassing will be immediately prosecuted and fined $5,000.

***

As Jonathan searched the last section of shelves, he wondered what he should do next. Outside it was dark, and there were no neighbors. Soon the Order of the Serpent would show up looking for the same thing. He glanced through a small portal window and saw Kaira below in the car looking for her phone charger.
  We'll be trapped in the middle of nowhere, he realized. *We've got to find it soon, or they will find us here.*
  Unfortunately, the only exciting book he'd found was the journal. The shelves on the ground were full of nothing but geodes. As he hurried to scan the shelves he'd already searched for the first time, he realized he might fail.
  His eyes moved to the collection of geodes. On one shelf, they had been categorized by color and placed inside of boxes. As he searched along the shelves, he wondered if there was some reason

Alessandro wanted the crystals other than to use as experimental batteries.

The last shelf held a metal box with a lock on it. Why was the box locked? More than likely, it held geodes. He had to open the box.

He looked for a key on the desk. Nothing. Jonathan picked up a meteor the size of his fist. He crouched down in front of the box and slammed the lock hard. The lock fell from the metal latch and clinked on the tile floor.

Jonathan opened the box looked inside.

A bright crystal sat inside a metal device that looked like future technology. *How does that help?*

He was about to close the box when he noticed a switch along the bottom of the metal base. He pulled out the object and flipped the switch. He stared in disbelief as a 3D hologram filled the room.

***

At that moment in Albano Laziale, Giovanni's student was tiptoeing through the dark in the villa. After locating the secret hiding place beneath the floor tiles, he found a note with instructions and an envelope. He looked inside and realized why Antonio had betrayed Giovanni.

He pictured Giovanni being taken into custody and felt the anger run through him. He could do this. He had to do it for Giovanni. He burned the note at the fireplace.

With the revealing of the recent dig site, the Roman Curia had shut down excavation and confiscated all the relics. Maybe they hadn't gotten all of it. The note he had just burned indicated Giovanni sent a package to America.

He found Giovanni's phone, and as the professor instructed, he deleted everything on the phone. The professor's phone was empty except for one photo. Luke opened the picture and enlarged it. At first, he wasn't sure what he saw. Then suddenly, he understood. Stunned that the professor had left it on his phone, he realized he had to keep the photo. Quickly he sent it to his phone, then deleted it off the professor's phone.

Placing the phone in his pocket, he wondered what to do and shuddered at the possibility of something happening to the professor.

As Giovanni had instructed, he wiped his fingerprints and left the villa as he had found it.

Chapter Forty Six

Just as he had feared, the Roman Curia had sent the Pontifical Commission for the Cultural Heritage of the Church to oversee the search and investigation of the Civico Museo.

Giovanni has the timepiece. The Holy See needs my help in finding it. The accusation that Giovanni had stolen from them was a cover-up to find the relic Giovani had found on his dig site. While this was a useful ploy, it was also a dangerous game. The Order of the Serpent was not to be toyed with, and the Holy See knew this. Creating a public outcry was a way to organize the hunt in a way the Holy See could control.

Antonio Callo stared out the museum window into the darkened street below. Despite the late hour, he could see the flicker of a few faint lights in apartments above the city street. The Order was always watching. It made him nervous. He could feel his fears spiraling out of control and wondered if the latest activity would end up in a deadly conclusion.

Thinking of the future, he wondered how he would keep from becoming the next target. He thought of the humiliation Giovanni must have felt when he was put into the car with spinning lights. He had called the news ahead of time to give himself the clear opportunity to perpetuate his innocence.

I should have taken care of this long ago and never permitted it to escalate this far.

Giovanni's arrest was no mystery to Antonio. He knew Giovanni had a good heart and didn't deserve what was going to happen. Nonetheless, Antonio took his orders from those above his head.

He made a call.

"Where are you?"

"Landing at the Tuscan airport now." Three men on the plane dressed in black khakis and black turtleneck looked at the empty hangar that the church covertly provided the Order of the Serpent. In addition to the aircraft, a convoy of black SUVs sat waiting in front of the hangar.

"Listen, she may seem small and helpless, but she is dangerous. We cannot allow her to take up her grandmother's mantle."

"Understood."

***

Kaira Munroe could see nothing in the darkness, but she knew time was running out. Desperately, she opened the car door and thrust the keys into the car, then plugged her phone into the jack and watched the battery power light come up on the screen.

Then her thoughts jolted in shock as she heard the sound of motorized vehicles on the road below. She stood up next to the car, continuing to allow her phone to charge. Directing her gaze toward the sound, she spotted three sets of headlights.

Oh my God, we have to get out of here. She wondered who it was, someone Jackson had sent for them or someone more sinister, the Order of the Serpent?

Her thoughts were distracted by a different sound. She turned to see a four-wheeler speeding through the woods to the right. Her phone had less than 20 percent charge. Just another 30 seconds would help. She knew she couldn't hide the car. The vehicles coming up the road were only a mile away. They'd be here in seconds.

The sound of the four-wheeler stopped. Billy sat in the darkness and watched the vehicles in the distance. He'd never seen the woman in the car before. She wouldn't trust him. He knew he needed to get inside the retreat with her.

"My name is Billy." He yelled into the darkness. "I was a friend of Alessandro."

The quiet was pierced by the sound of the vehicles which had now turned on the dirt road and were heading straight for Kaira. "How do I know that's true?" She yelled back in the direction of the voice.

"He was my friend. I collected geodes for him." Billy paused, "You're in danger, and I can help you. Let me come inside with you."

Come inside with me? Why would the stranger want to come inside? Suddenly the road erupted in light, and Kaira recoiled then grabbed her phone off the charger. The vehicles halted abruptly a few feet behind the rental car. The passenger door opened, and a face stared intently at her.

"Are you Kaira Munroe?" asked the man in a black turtleneck. Kaira said nothing.

Strange thoughts raced through her mind. Had Jackson sent them? Why would he send an entourage of SUV vehicles? She staggered back towards the front entrance of the cave. She felt rather than saw Billy behind her.

He asked again. "Are you Kaira Munroe?" This time to her horror, the man raised a gun and leveled it at her head. Without thinking, she stepped back again into the entryway, almost stumbling over a rock. She felt a strong arm grab her around the waist, pulling her toward the door. She heard shots. "Oh my God, he's shooting."

She tripped backward and twisted to the right, scraping her knee on rough rock. The stranger opened the door and pulled her inside.

"Hi, sorry to meet like this, I'm Billy."

He pulled her away from the door and into the living area. "We are temporarily safe. Are you Kaira Munroe?"

She nodded.

"Why are they after you?" Billy asked.

Bounding down the stairs, Jonathan burst into the living area. He found himself staring at a young college-age young man and Kaira. Dazed Kaira ran to him, and he held her. She whispered in his ear, "The man says he's Billy, and he knew Alessandro."

As he stared at Billy, a volley of bullets hit the front door.

"My God!"

They want to kill us, he realized. They think we know Alessandro's secrets.

"We've got to get back into the room upstairs and lock ourselves in." Jonathan pushed Kaira in front of him, and he and Billy followed.

"I know a better way." Said Billy. Another deafening roar of bullets hit the front door.

"Lead the way." Said Jonathan.

In the computer room, Billy typed some words on the screen, and a large shelf slid sideways. *Déjà vu,* Kaira thought of her grandmother's apartment in the winery.

"Hurry." Billy said, "Get inside."

Kaira recoiled, still wondering if Billy could be trusted. What if he killed Alessandro. "Now!" he yelled as the door downstairs slammed open.

Billy pushed something in the narrow passage, and the door shut behind them. Urging them to follow him, he turned his phone flashlight ahead of them.

Chapter Forty Seven

In the darkness, Kaira felt Jonathan's hands guiding her down the narrow passage toward Billy, a stranger. Kaira was unable to protest.

"You're bleeding!" Jonathan said as he clambered down the passage behind her. Billy heaved a metal door open and moved out into a large cavern.

Jonathan slid close beside her and examined her shoulder. "It doesn't hurt." She said softly.

Billy had jumped inside a Hummer and searched for the keys. "I bet there's a first aid kit in here." He said as he started the vehicle. Get in."

Kaira replied with a weak nod, and Jonathan helped her up into the seat. Once inside with Kaira next to him, Jonathan took her hand. "Everything is going to be okay."

Billy handed a first aid kit from the glovebox to Jonathan. As he leaned forward to bandage the scrape on her shoulder, he whispered excitedly in her ear.

"I found something unusual. A crystal hologram." He exclaimed. "I think it's a map."

In the front seat, Billy pushed a button on a square black box that looked like a garage door opener. A metal door at one end of the cavern began to lift.

"Alessandro was a genius," Billy said, looking in the rear-view mirror. "He ran this entire retreat, computers, and observatory with geode batteries he created. That's how we met. I sold him all the geodes I could find."

"What happened to Alessandro?" Kaira asked.

"I don't know. I showed up one day, and he was gone." Said Billy shaking his head. "This is going to be a bumpy ride. You better buckle up."

The headlights revealed high red and tan walls formed by the erosion of sandstone. Rainwater from the monsoon season ran into the slot canyon sections rushing through the narrow passageways. Over time the sandstone walls eroded, leaving deep, smooth corridors that flowed through the mountain.

The ground was flat and sandy. Occasional beams of moonlight barely radiated down through openings at the top of the canyon.

"You know your way around in the cave retreat. How long did you know Alessandro?" Jonathan asked as Billy sped through the curves in the mountain corridor.

"I've known him for four years. After a while, he began to show me what he was building. We became good friends."

"What was Alessandro building?"

"A massive battery and a data storage device. It probably doesn't sound that interesting, but the battery can operate all the equipment housed in the cave for many months. A year ago, Alessandro went missing."

"Missing?" Kaira asked

"The story in the paper said he disappeared as if he didn't want to be found. But, I think he went missing. Kidnapped or worse."

"Why do you think that?" Jonathan asked

"Because of the project. He was obsessed with it. A man with his ability doesn't just leave it and never look back."

"That makes sense. Did you ever meet a Jesuit priest named Alex?" Jonathan asked.

"No, but Alessandro spoke of him. Alex put him in touch with a private funder who believed in his mapping system." Billy said.

"What did you say?" Jonathan asked.

"A mapping system. Funding came from a person who has a satellite in orbit. He built three-D imaging software that could capture shapes from the surface of the earth and up to a few thousand feet deep in the ocean. He could create three-dimensional images from shapes underwater, giving him the ability to locate everything from underwater missile sites to lost cities and wrecked ships." Billy paused. "They were both geniuses."

"Did anyone else know you and Alessandro were friends?"

"I don't think so. My friends at college were jealous that I'd found a buyer for my geodes. I never told them who."

"Listen to me carefully," Jonathan said, his tone intensifying. "Alex was murdered a few nights ago. We think the men who murdered him are looking for something he discovered. They are trying to keep it from going public. Possibly, Alessandro was kidnapped or killed for the same reason. Whoever silenced them will stop at nothing to get to us."

"With the genius gone, there is nothing left!" Billy scoffed.

"But, his discovery is only part of the puzzle, and we may have the missing pieces to make sense of all this."

"And you came here to find it? Did you find what you were looking for?"

"Maybe," Jonathan replied. "I'm not sure. We need more time here at the retreat."

"Someone knows you are here. How did they find out?" Billy asked.

"Probably the Jesuits at Mt Graham. If you don't want to be a part of this, we should probably let you off in town, and we'll continue as if we've never met you."

Kaira looked at Jonathan, wondering what he was thinking.

"However, you say you were friends with Alessandro," Jonathan continued, "if you want to find out what happened, maybe you can help us."

"In that case, we need to turn around and go back where we just came from," Billy said. "Those goons will follow us, and when they do, we can loop back set the security fence up around the property."

"Security fence?"

"It's electronic. It circles the entire property. If unauthorized persons come close, they get zapped with invisible currents that leave them on the ground in a puddle. It's harmless. It just disables them for a bit."

Kaira looked at the two men. "Are you saying we have to go back?"

"We can circle back and set the security before they know what has happened," Jonathan said. "It will buy us time to finish what we came for."

Jonathan's expression never wavered.

Kaira's mind was racing. What was the hologram Jonathan had found? His intensity implied there was more at stake than safety. She heard the renewed passion in his voice and sensed he'd found something that would answer their questions.

Jonathan retrieved an odd metal device from his pocket. "I found this in the computer room."

Kaira studied the round metal object that held a crystal in its center.

"It creates the hologram. Somehow, Alessandro figured out how to store maps inside the crystals. When the light shines through the crystal, it projects a 3D hologram."

It sounded like a school science project.

"Alessandro spent hours on those crystals. That isn't the only crystal with information. There are hundreds of them." Billy looked in the rear-view mirror at the stunned passengers. "According to Alessandro, he stored satellite images and anomalies on them."

"I don't understand," Kaira said. "Why would a Jesuit astronomer want to store maps on a crystal?"

"Not just any map," Jonathan countered. "The locations of Victoria, Giovanni and Alex's discoveries are probably on them. Quickly becoming the hot commodity, I might add."

Billy turned the headlights off as the Hummer had exited the crevasse. He backtracked, climbing the rock overlooking the entrance to the retreat. They looked out the front window, peering at the driveway below. In the distance, the SUV headlights shone in the darkness as the men backed down the dirt drive and headed north in search of the three escaping in a vehicle.

For more than two decades, Jonathan's controversial father had been a legend of sorts in Westonville. Criticized for his obsession and unconventional methods, authorities hailed him as a rebel. But, he had discovered a treasure and kept it secret all these years. Something about Alessandro reminded Jonathan of his father. He was a rebel among the Jesuit priests. Unconventional and extremely intelligent.

I know him, Jonathan thought. He's hiding the maps in plain sight. Since they first stepped into the cave retreat, theories had been swirling in Jonathan's mind. He wondered how many of the crystals they'd found were encoded.

It hadn't occurred to him to equate Jesuit priests with treasure hunting until now. It didn't surprise him that Victoria had become involved, and the team had found a way to hide their secrets. Jonathan felt a growing belief that there was so much more than treasure hidden on the crystals.

Alex was going to tell Kaira something important the night he was murdered. With the help of Father Murphy, Umberto, and sheer luck, they had followed their gut instincts and made their way to Alessandro's cave retreat. They were supposed to find this.

"Even if we have a map on the crystal," Kaira said, "how will we know it's the right map? We'll have to go through hundreds of crystals."

"Kaira," Jonathan replied with an excited smile, "Watch this."

She glanced down as he flipped a switch on the metal circle in his hand. She sucked her breath in sharply and stared in disbelief. A detailed 3D image glowed green inside the Hummer.

Her eyes snapped to Jonathan's face.

"As I was saying," Jonathan said, flipping the switch off, "we've got to get back down there and look through those crystals."

"There's still a problem." Kaira's expression changed. "I still can't get into my grandmother's phone."

"We think the passcode is in Hebrew," Jonathan said, looking at Billy in the mirror.

"You need a language keyboard."

"Exactly, but it has to work with her phone."

"I believe I can solve that problem."

Kaira eyed Billy. "You are surprising."

"We need to get back inside. Those goons have gone further up the mountain, but they'll be back." Billy said.

"This is going to sound odd, but just now, I think I figured something out." Jonathan's voice trailed off.

"Are you going to make us guess?" Kaira asked expectantly.

"I should have realized earlier. It's something Father Murphy told me a while ago. It's beginning to make sense."

Jonathan shot a glance at Billy. "I want you to trust me on this. Right now, we need to focus on getting that password to Kaira's phone and setting the security fence in place."

Kaira studied Jonathan's face for a long moment. Then with a nod, she turned to Billy.

"Get us back inside Billy. And thank you for all your help. You've been amazing."

Chapter Forty Eight

Customers sat at tables in the Local Steam Espresso and read the BuzzFeed:

Gigantic Iron Age Skeleton Remains Discovered on East Coast Shoreline

The remains, found at Forlorn Point near Westonville, are believed to be over 4,500 years old, according to the State Pathologist. The discovery of a human skeleton was made just one day after the effects of Hurricane Jose.

The remains were found shortly before 5 pm on the beach by people out walking on Tuesday evening, according to East Coast Traveler, and photographed at the scene by photographer Tim Campbell.

Following the examination, it is believed that the bones are an enigma, and possibly dating to the beginning of the Bronze Age, between about 2500 BC and 3000 BC. The skeleton is now in the custody of the Westonville Historical Society.

***

Impressed with her courage, Jonathan put his arm around Kaira and hugged. She winced. "Sorry. I forgot. How's your shoulder?"

"Just a dull ache now." She put her hand up and felt the shoulder. It was tight from swelling. "I'll look for some aspirin when we get back inside. I'm hungry too."

As the Hummer began its journey back into the chasm, Kaira asked if she could look at Jonathan's phone. She prompted the phone and started searching the Westonville news.

"Looks like a can of worms has been opened." She whispered. "Listen to this." She read Father Murphy's article to Jonathan. "Sounds like he's protecting the reputation of the Church."

'You can't blame him for not wanting to be associated with the psychopaths that are after us?" Jonathan replied.

"That's not all." She said with a trace of excitement in her voice, "It appears a large skeleton washed up on the beach after the last storm blew through. They say it's from the Bronze Age." Kaira thought about what Umberto had told her. The passages were there before the winery was built.

She handed the phone back to Jonathan, and he scrolled through his social media.

Unfortunately, Alex's death and the publicity surrounding their disappearance had inspired local sleuths and gossip. Most theorized that Jonathan and Kaira were merely two high school sweethearts reconnecting after all the years.

The top conspiracy was that they'd been kidnapped and were prisoners. Another plot said that they'd found his father's treasure, and they were hiding out until everything settled. Town locals must be going crazy.

Jonathan continued scanning his phone until he found what seemed to be a common CNN Live link titled, "The Arizona Sky."

He clicked on the link and held his phone for Kaira to see. He turned up the volume and listened to the sound of the Hummer. A Reporter appeared.

"I am being joined by Paolo Vincenzo. Paolo, the Church has no objection to scientific research, is that correct?"

"Far from it." He replied. "It is a surprise to many Catholics and everyone else that the Church owns a professional, scientific Observatory. We call it Vatican Observatory Research Group, (VORG)."

"What exactly are the staff of 12 priest-astronomers focusing on?"

"Like many other observatories and research institutions, Vatican astronomers and astrophysicists want to reveal the secrets of the universe and push back the curtains hiding human knowledge and understanding. But we have another important mission: to build a bridge of understanding between science and religious faith."

"Do you believe there's life out there in the universe?"

"I would argue that humans are not the only intelligent beings God created in the universe, and this other lifeform\ described in the Bible are Angels who are referenced over and over."

"And you believe in them?"

"The Bible calls them "holy ones, heavenly beings, and there are many negative references to the Nephilim. But whether you believe these creatures as angels or aliens doesn't really matter for the sake of our argument here. The point is that the ancient writers of the Bible, like all ancient peoples, were perfectly happy with the possibility that other intelligent beings could exist."

Jonathan glanced at Kaira. "He didn't mention anything about UFO's."

Kaira nodded.

"He certainly isn't giving the full story we heard and the videos we saw at Mt Graham."

They listened to the ending statement:

"When it comes to the notion of Angels and Aliens, there exists a confusing array of conspiracy theories mixed with ancient text and fantasy. We have the responsibility to discover fact and separate it from fiction when possible. The truth is, the more we look into the past, and the more we look into the universe, we realize something incredibly complex was happening in our past that the ancients understood. This is what we are trying to grasp."

"And, what are your thoughts on the disappearance of one of your Jesuit astronomers?"

Looking annoyed, he shifted in his chair. *"Any Jesuit willing to learn would have nothing to fear at Mt. Graham. It is a sanctuary. But, one must be mentally prepared for the rigorous research."*

"Well, that's discouraging." The Reporter said. *"Are you saying he left the Observatory because the work was too rigorous for him?"*

Paolo Vincenzo signed heavily. *"It is my opinion that he was going to be exposed, and that is why he disappeared."*

Jonathan saw Billy's eyes. He'd been listening. "I am completely skeptical because I know how Alessandro felt about being a Jesuit priest." He was shaking his head.

"Why do you say he was an imposter?" the Reporter pressed.

"I have heard stories about the late Alessandro, which make me rather suspicious of his projects. I tried to talk to him, but he wouldn't open up nor have anything to do with me."

"You think he had something to hide?"

Paolo Vincenzo shrugged his shoulders. *"I have no idea."*

"I'd say Paolo Vincenzo has something to hide," Kaira said.

"I agree." Jonathan suspected Paolo Vincenzo was miffed he hadn't been let in on Alessandro's brilliant projects. Jonathan flipped his phone off to save battery. "With this in mind, I think Alessandro discovered a way to locate and mark sites that confirm complex life before the ice age. That would be 12,000 years ago. Just think what that would do to our understanding of world development?"

"My perception of the Vatican is that they want to know the truth as long as they are in total control of the truth." Kaira stared ahead thoughtfully. "They have the largest ancient text library archived at the Vatican. Anyone who has control of the information they want is considered a threat."

"But, is it the Vatican who threatened Alessandro and killed Alex, or was it a sect of the Church?"

"Is it possible the Church uses the sect to find what they want and then takes it from the sect?"

"You mean mercenaries? Hired by the church to do the dirty work?"

Kaira looked bewildered. Was it possible that the Church could stoop so low?

They crevasse ended, and they were pulling into the garage. "Jonathan, if Alessandro, Alex, and my grandmother discovered relics or items that prove the existence of civilization over 12,000 years ago, where did they hide it?"

"Right, "Jonathan said. "Let me rephrase that…How are we going to find it?"

They had come full circle. Billy hopped out of the vehicle and motioned them to stay put for a moment. He went inside while Kaira and Jonathan sat uncomfortably, feeling vulnerable.

Two minutes later, Billy was back motioning them inside. In the computer room, he pulled up the monitors and punched in the password. Once the screens were live, he went into a security icon that looked like a game.

"Alessandro liked to hide important apps like games." Quickly he pulled up surveillance, and the screen lit up with live images from cameras hidden in the retreat.

Jonathan watched as Billy set the perimeter security fence.

"We'll have a few hours of peace while you look for your maps," Billy said.

"What are you getting for this?" Kaira asked. "I mean, why are you so willing to help us?"

Billy looked surprised. "Well, at first, I was in it for the money. I needed extra funds for school. But, after a while, I became intrigued and helpful to Alessandro. He was alone out here, you know." He motioned them to stand next to him. He turned off the lights. "Now, turn on your hologram." He said to Jonathan.

Chapter Forty Nine

Albano Laziale, Italy

Grateful he hadn't been cuffed, Giovanni stole a glance at the officer who was staring ahead as the car sped down the street. He wondered what the man was thinking. He had been silent since Giovanni's sudden arrest. He wondered if Luke would find the note. Hopefully, he would know what to do.

Time is what he needed, but evidently, time had run out. The officer was still driving toward the police headquarters. Suddenly the officer turned and looked at Giovanni over the seat. "Please don't worry," he said. "I need to talk to you."

Before Giovanni could reply, the officer began to speak.

"I am sorry for your discomfort." He said, seeing the distrust in the older man's eyes. "You have good friends who want to help you."

Giovanni listened quietly.

"I am taking you to an isolated place. I hope you will trust me." He turned his head back to the road. "Tonight's troubling activity was not very tactful. Everyone in the Lazio region is discussing the archeologist who found the ancient relic. Your life is in danger. Fortunately, you are safe until the piece can be protected."

"Many will want to be my friend if I survive. Where are you taking me?"

"I am taking you to a Villa on the coast. You have a friend Umberto?"

Giovanni smiled. "Ah, Umberto. He is more than a friend. He is a brother."

The officer nodded his approval.

Giovanni was now pleased as he realized the car had passed the police station and headed for the main Strada leading out of town.

"I am part of a group who is fighting to bring the truth alive in Italy. We are fortunate to have received funds from a private group that has provided us with advanced technology. It is disconcerting that our culture has completely lost interest in the megalithic structures which surround us. Certain sects covertly affiliated with the Vatican have successfully hidden and controlled the ebb and flow of truth."

Giovanni nodded and listened.

"In America," he continued, "our private funder has recently passed, leaving a hole in our armor. But, there is a potential leader who we hope will soon step forward and take the mantle."

"It is dangerous," Giovanni said quietly.

"I agree, it is dangerous, but I assure you, our organization is great and loyal to freedom and truth. Many of the people who are coming into our group are brilliant astronomers, scientists, and even doctors. They are educated people aspiring to become agents of change by taking the highest offices in Italy, ultimately replacing secret societies." He paused.

"More troubling is the latest information coming from the Vatican." His voice grew somber. "They are telling us bits and pieces of truth, feeding the public what they want a little at a time. We are being prepared for a future paradigm shift."

"And how will this shift affect us?" Giovanni asked quietly.

"We are on the brink of a new enlightened era — a world where the word alien no longer sounds outrageous and where the parallel universe is normal. Your relic is the key to the ancient clock in the heavens. It predicts the orbits of planets we cannot see. It is the 25,000-year cycle of a planet that came close to the earth before. But, you know this, don't you?"

Giovanni said nothing, and the men drove on in silence.

***

Miles away at Mt. Graham, Chris stood next to Mark breathless from his dash through the facility.

"You have to look at this," Mark said. "Do you see what I see?"

"What?" Chris bent down to look at the screen. "How did you…"

"Just look at it."

Alarmed, Chris directed his eyes to the screen, watching the video. "My God, they found Alessandro's place…"

"Right, but they aren't the worry. Look who else was there."

"God, this can't be possible. Is it who I think it is?"

"I don't know for sure, but it might be. We have to clean out our computer before they get to us. Everything. It's going to take some doing." Mark said.

"The only other hope is to go public with our information." Responded Chris.

"We can't. That's what killed Alessandro."

"Don't say that. We don't know that for sure."

"Someone killed Alex too. The only way to save ourselves now is to go public."

Chris closed his eyes, trying to picture the reaction of the Jesuit astronomers when they realized that the Order of the Serpent was directly involved in the murder of Alex.

"Mark," Chris whispered, "We have to figure out how to erase everything from the computers. Will you help me?"

"I can try." He sounded discouraged. Their computers held massive amounts of data that continuously streamed from satellites and the telescope. Sifting through it to erase certain portions would take time. "Have you copied everything?" Chris didn't answer.

***

Carmelo's complex hovered above the Arizona desert evening. Intricate carvings and towers glowed in the dusk, giving it an air of an Anasazi temple shrine. Inside, Carmelo prepared for the next mission.

For the Order of the Serpent to meet the goal of the covert partnership with those who had global control, Carmelo strove to include visual, auditory, physical, cognitive, and neurological platforms to facilitate the mission. The technology and complex were built to CIA standards.

Brian sat inside Carmelo's office.

"Are you aware your brother is in Arizona?"

"Now, how would I know that Carmelo? I'm here in this facility with you constantly. You know when I go to the bathroom and brush my teeth at night. How would I know?"

"I want you to help us flush him out. He is in Sedona."

"And you know this how?"

Carmelo flipped a switch, and a panel slowly slid sideways, revealing a monitor screen. He pushed another button, and Brian watched heat signatures of what he assumed were his brother and Kaira inside the cave retreat.

"Why does the Vatican want my brother?" Brian was tired of the games.

"Now, now. No need to make unnecessary accusations. It has nothing to do with the Vatican. I want you to flush him out." He reached into a cabinet and poured himself a bourbon. "Have a drink with me, Brian."

"No, thanks." Keeping the separation between the two of them was necessary for Brian. He had to remember where his true identity lay.

"What's going to happen is this, you're going to call your brother, and I want you to find out what he's looking for."

Brian wanted to know what his brother was looking for too. But, he hadn't called him in years. He didn't know if he had the right number.

"You know your brother has caused me a lot of grief. I can't buy the island in the Caribbean because of his permits. I want to know what he's doing in Arizona. He keeps popping up, causing problems."

"What makes you think my brother will talk to me? I'm sure he knows I was at the Wake, and he probably thinks I tried to kill him."

"Look, there's a lot more at stake here than your father's treasure. I think your brother knows that. I want to find out what he knows and what he has." Carmelo studied him. "Remember, I'm the guy who rescued you. I feed you and take care of you. You're alive because of me."

How could he forget? Carmelo reminded him every chance he could.

"You lied to me about the poison. You said it was a knockout drug. How do I know you aren't going to have me kill my brother? Why should I trust you?"

"Well, it's Tuesday. I don't lie on Tuesdays."

Brian hated he was partnering with the devil. He found himself searching Carmelo's face for the motive. Behind the bigger than life façade, there churned something desperate. Was he in trouble? Had his funds been cut?

One thing Brian was sure of, there were bigger fish putting pressure on Carmelo. He looked at the screen and wondered who the men were in the SUV.

"This was a couple of hours ago."

Brian watched feeling troubled by what he was being asked to do. The second he drew his brother out, they would question him and kill him. Someone had already tried to kill them both. Feeling overwhelmed, he sat quietly in his chair and tried to clear his thoughts. But, the questions in his mind kept recurring.

What does my brother know? What did Alex tell them?

"We're just treasure hunters." Brian declared. "That's all we'll ever be."

The words resonated in the cavernous office. Suddenly the room began to shake as a deafening windstorm caused by a massive helicopter descended on an open area. Brian watched as the aircraft touched down on the dirt pad.

Two men descended from the craft and hurried toward the compound.

"You'll be riding along with them."

"But, I thought I was going to call…"

"You see, your brother has set the security fence, and we can no longer get inside from the perimeter. We'll land on top."

Brian glanced up at the two men. Mercenaries. Working for the highest bid. Carmelo motioned him to go with the men. They tied his hands with plastic zip ties. Bewildered Brian followed them to the helicopter.

Thirty minutes North of Alessandro's cave retreat, Brian gazed through a small window in the helicopter at the pitch-black below. *It's the reason Observatories were built in Arizona,* he thought, *it's pitch black at night.*

His phone rang. It was Carmelo checking in.

"Where are you?"

"Thirty minutes away," Brian said, feeling his gut churn at what came next.

"The timing is good. But, I have troubling news. We can no longer see inside the cave. There is some electronic shield in place."

Brian knew they wanted to kill Jonathan and Kaira, but wanted to extract information first.

"You successfully rid us of Alex, the leader. However, as we feared, loose ends are very dangerous."

When Carmelo had shared his plan, Brian was anxious. He did not imagine that the evening would entail more loss. He didn't want to question Carmelo. He acted as if he was a willing soldier, but Brian knew he was no more than a pawn, and he didn't kill Alex.

This mission would be dangerous. Once the Order took Jonathan and Kaira down, Brian would probably be next. The promise of freedom and influence had waned over the last few months, and reality had set in. Somewhere along the line, Brian grew up.

I don't intend on allowing anyone to die tonight, he thought.

He glanced at his hands. They shook slightly. He felt numb inside. That was good. If it went according to his plan, the two men in the copter would be dead, and this would be over.

The phone connection was spotty. He didn't care.

He raised his eyes to the highest line of rock spires, a silhouette on the horizon. He was repulsed knowing who was inside and what he was asked to do. Carmelo's adoration of the Order of the Serpent was his weakness. He may receive help from specific individuals in the Order, but if there were ever a public outcry of what was going on, the Order might drop him without batting an eye.

Hundreds of years of sects and cults that had formed from Secret Societies and Orders, not to mention the influence of the mafia on the church, had twisted and distorted faith into something else.

The Order hired Carmelo to steal and murder for them.

The inability to know who to trust terrified Brian. It appeared a new group of world leaders was rising in power — men who were willing to band together with the likes of Carmelo to accomplish their goals. They would do whatever it took to keep their agenda hidden.

We are merely casualties of a war we don't comprehend.

He remembered months ago when he'd received his first deposit from Carmelo. He had been high with excitement at the large deposit in his account. It didn't take long for the enthusiasm to wane and disillusion to set in as he began to understand his role as a pawn in the more excellent chess game.

Brian's blood quickened, and his palms were sweating. Carmelo had said that if he carried out the mission successfully and proved himself to the Order, he would be placed in the higher ranks, the invisible and dominant hierarchy. Brian loathed being part of anything Carmelo orchestrated.

Wary, he had wondered why Carmelo chose him? Carmelo said he liked him and wanted to help him. But why? Carmelo was using him to get to his brother and had been from the beginning. He should have seen it. Jonathan had something they wanted.

Shivering, he realized the target was his brother. He could never murder his brother.

Chapter Fifty

The Local Steam Espresso was full of patrons reading the latest news. The headlines read:

Gigantic Bones

A local Police investigation has confirmed that the massive bones found on the Westonville cliffs are much older than first anticipated. The discovery raises more questions, and further research is needed.

Meadow Manor Heiress Found

It is believed that Kaira Munroe, heiress to Meadow Manor, has been located in Arizona with Jonathan Bell. A recent visit to the Mt Graham Observatory confirms they are following up on the recent death of Alex Mirabelli.

Interesting Facts about St. Francis Abbey

The Abbey is one of the oldest structures in Westonville, along with Meadow Manor and the Winery. Built in the middle 1700s and steeped in legend, mystery surrounds both structures, including secret passages and pirate treasure.

Though many have tried to find the legendary Captain Benjamin Munroe treasure, it remains hidden. Other recent rumors have risen to the surface, suggesting that there is much more than wealth to be found beneath two of Westonville's oldest structures.

***

Castel Gandolfo, Italy

Located in an elegant waiting room of Castel Gandolfo, the high walls adorned with pictures of the pope and a ceiling of magnificent murals, Antonio sat waiting. A collection of many busts of Popes circled the room.

How long will they keep me waiting? Antonio wondered, looking at the images surrounding him. Castel Gandolfo was one of the most beautiful places, but also intimidating. Every room in the building was ornate and full of reminders that this was the pope's summer retreat.

Twenty years ago, Antonio was ushered into a similar room, where he had interviewed for the position of Curator in affiliation with the Commission for Cultural Heritage of the Church. Presiding over the guardianship of the historical and artistic works of art, historical documents, books, and everything kept in museums, libraries, and archives, he was assigned the esteemed task.

Antonio's bold move to clear his reputation by arresting Giovanni had apparently landed him here. The archeological investigation performed by the Civic Museum of Albano Laziale started ten years earlier when Giovanni was hired. Only a small part of the archeological site was excavated revealing rooms with ancient mosaic and polychrome marble floors dating it during the 3rd Century A.D. However, it was what lay beneath those ruins that caught the attention of Giovanni.

The original aim was to define the presence and position of some ancient structures that could be investigated through planned archeological excavation. If Giovanni would join forces with Antonio, they could accomplish so much under the guidance and protection of the Roman Curia.

Then again, the Roman Curia would never help Antonio if doing so meant forbidden secrets might be revealed.

He had watched the news and realized things had taken a sudden turn when the reporter mentioned the Curator might be withholding secrets from the public. "We're tired of forbidden secrets held by the Holy See." Said one of the bystanders talking to the reporter. "The Church owns images from the sky, and the Holy See controls all the archeological sites. The young generation coming up has little tolerance for such secrets. We long for truth."

Condemning the oppression of the Church, Italy's young generation was calling for change. They were ready to abolish the perceived monarchy of the Vatican. However, the power of the Vatican is unmatched.

Just what I need, Antonio thought, *upheaval as I prepare for my retirement.*

The door at the end of the ornate waiting area opened, and a Jesuit priest peered in.

"Antonio, why did you partner with the Americans to hide Giovanni?"

Antonio stared at him in disbelief. His mind spinning, he tried to make sense of what the priest told him.

"We know you are working with Giovanni and an American group to steal artifacts from the Church!" the priest declared as he strode toward him. "Where have they taken him?"

Stunned, Antonio had no reply.

"I am here for your full confession that you've been colluding with Giovanni all along to steal ancient artifacts that belong to Italy and the Church."

The Jesuit priest arrived directly in front of Antonio's chair.

"You'll have no confession from me," Antonio said. "This isn't true. I don't know what you are talking about."

Chapter Fifty One

As Billy led them back inside the cave retreat, Kaira found herself marveling again at the incredible details carved into the passages and curving walls. A retreat full of mysteries, she mused, eyeing the delicate carvings on the sandstone.

Inside the computer room, Billy punched something into the keyboard, and a security message came up on the screen. Entering a code, he set the electronic fence and turned to Kaira.

"I think I know how to help you with your phone." He held his hand out, and Kaira placed her phone in his hand reluctantly.

"I bet this has the same port Alessandro's phone had." He said, looking at the end of her phone. He rummaged through a box and found a USB cable then plugged her phone into the computer.

"What's the Hebrew word?"

"Nephilim," Kaira said. Although she knew the text was a description of a fallen angel, it's appearance was closer to that of encrypted art.

This place inspires mythological delusions.

Her gaze moved upward to the looming Ophiuchus overhead, dominated by the herculean figure holding a snake by the head and tail.

"Billy, what is the hidden tribute of this great painting of Ophiuchus?" she asked.

"Ah, I asked the same question when I first met Alessandro. It is a reference to the great deity whose secrets are allegedly revealed every 25,000 years."

"That's a good story, but what does it mean now? Why did Alessandro paint it on his ceiling?" And, why had her grandmother painted it on the ceiling of her apartment in the winery?

"It has something to do with an elliptical cycle through the zodiac. Ancient astronomers used the sky to create time maps."

"What do you mean?"

"They built their structures based on where the stars were in the sky at that time."

Billy entered the login, and the phone screen opened up. First, there was silence, then sound and video flooded the room through the mounted displays. Without introduction, Victoria Munroe's voice began sharing an astounding story.

"When I had first come to discover the unusually large bones beneath the winery, I realized immediately they were prehistoric, and I contacted the Smithsonian.

Kaira placed her hand over her mouth as a visual of the bones came up on the screen.

"They offered to make a considerable donation in return for allowing them to take the bones and study them. When men who looked very much like secret service came snooping around, we changed our minds. As an influential member of the Westonville Historical Society, I have been protecting them since that time.

Meadow Manor is at the heart of this, thought Kaira.

Victoria continued,

"The church built an Abbey here the same time Meadow Manor was built. This isn't unusual. They've built churches near unusual and supernatural sites like this all over the world. You see, the treasure of Captain Benjamin Munroe isn't just about gold, but about the truth of pre-flood civilization and a celestial gateway."

"Since I moved into the manor with my husband and made the discovery, my passion has been to prove that we came from something far more complicated than historians would have us believe. It didn't take long for the Church to become involved.

When I met Alex and heard about his discovery of a planet headed toward our solar system and how this particular planet orbits close to the earth after so many years, I became intrigued. I learned from Alex that the fixed star constellations shift in relation to the Earth's equinoctial points by 1° every 72 years, called Ptolemy. The movement and shift of constellations from or into view is a result of the Precession of Equinoxes. This cosmic clockwork is a set of cycles that take 25,920 years to complete and is known as the Great or Platonic Year. In current space-time, we are at the end of a Platonic Year. The Precessional cycles of Earth on its Axis cause a wobble at the North and South poles resulting in a shift of the axis by degree over time and a magnetic re-orientation of the poles along equatorial and ecliptic planes. The current alignment of our equatorial planes toward the Northern Hemisphere reveals the constellation of Ophiuchus along the Sun's path. This is the result of a shift of the

Earth's axis toward the galactic center caused by the Precession of Equinoxes."

"The Sun's annual path across Ophiuchus, the Serpent Bearer was not observable from our prior angular orientation yet has always been there. This constellation was known to our ancestors and was recorded in the Sumerian and Mayan astronomical records and texts. The Sumerians calculated that the current Precessional Season of the Bull began 6,444 years ago; this is concurrent with the Mayan calculation of 6500 years."

"The Mayans called Ophiuchus "The Hidden Sign." The Mayans predict the arrival of Ophiuchus at the end of the Baktun cycle and prophecy the return of an enlightened being, perhaps Quetzequatl, with a serpent rope arriving from the center of the galaxy."

Kaira wondered if she had misheard. "Did she say an enlightened being would be returning?"

Jonathan nodded.

"Oh, my God. She believes in Aliens."

"Or fallen angels," Jonathan said. Victoria continued.

"You see, the more I studied what I had beneath the winery and the more I studied the past, I began to make a connection with these bones and a long-lost civilization that would have been at least 12,000 or more years ago — pre-ice age. I poured my heart and soul into this, along with my husband, Benjamin. It led us to Italy, where we met Umberto. My husband died in an accident in Italy."

Victoria paused.

"That was many years ago. Umberto has become my comrade, and we've managed to make Meadow Manor and the winery into what it is today. I couldn't have done it without him. However, we continue to be challenged by those that would take from us our secrets. When a cult called the Order of the Serpent caught word that we had a secret, our work intensified."

Seeing the bones again, Jonathan was beginning to understand the controversy. Victoria had proof of pre-flood civilization over 12,000 years ago.

"We've marked the locations where these bones were found on a map. An archeologist in Italy has confirmed his discovery of similar bones, and he has found an ancient timepiece that predicts the *orbit of an unusual and bizarre planet that we believe is inhabited. The timepiece is made of metal yet pre-dates our timeline of the discovery of this particular metal."*

Suddenly, Jonathan's phone rang. He looked at Kaira in surprise. "It's Brian."

***

Father Murphy was grateful for a moment alone as he watched for the package. The growing tension of wondering what was inside had become worrisome. He felt baffled by Giovanni's arrest. Odd, Antonio had declined to share with him how the arrest had been made and by whom.

"This is a complicated situation." Antonio had said. "It is best that you know nothing."

Who was issuing orders? Father Murphy wondered. Was it Antonio or the Roman Curia? It seemed unlikely that Antonio would risk his neck by spreading a lie that Giovanni had stolen from the Church. However, he seemed to be working with someone who had that kind of leverage.

Now, Father Murphy awaited hourly for the arrival of the package Giovanni had sent.

Chapter Fifty Two

At the same moment, he checked the caller ID, the sound directly overhead thundered with the beating of helicopter blades.

"They're back," Jonathan said.

Billy jumped up from his chair and ran to a box. He began stuffing crystals in his pockets. Motioning to Kaira, he pulled the last of the crystals out and put them in her pockets.

"You'll thank me later." He said.

The three stood in the computer room, waiting. From inside the cave retreat, Jonathan answered the call.

"Hello, this is Jonathan."

"Jonathan," said an Italian accent. "I have someone here who needs to speak with you."

A moment later, a familiar voice came on the line.

"Jonathan? This is Brian. I'm sorry...I didn't mean..." There was a loud sound as a fist decked Brian in the jaw.

Brian...Brian...." Jonathan blurted, feeling a jolt of adrenalin. After a long moment, Brian's voice spoke again.

"Jonathan, you have something they want." Brian slurred. "They're going to kill us if you don't give it to them."

One of the men in the helicopter smirked at Brian. It was the first time he had acknowledged his predicament. Now it was out in the open.

In a split-second, Jonathan realized that the only way he could save Kaira was to hang up, but he couldn't do it.

"We don't have time. The Order of the Serpent is holding me. Listen carefully, run....run," he screamed, and then Brian kicked his foot hard against the steering shaft and felt searing heat explode inside his skull as his head hit a metal bar behind his seat, then everything went black.

***

Albano Laziale, Italy

News of Giovanni's escape was on the radio.

*"Roman Curia and Curator for Civica Museo in Albano
Laziale made an official statement earlier claiming that
Archeologist Giovanni Fiorelli has escaped and is being harbored
by Americans. The Roman Curia urged local villagers and
authorities to become involved and find the Archeologist. We
believe he has stolen a relic that belongs to the Italian
Government."* said the broadcaster.

Giovanni stared out of the window at the passing countryside
and tried to make sense of the strange rescue. *Was Antonio on his
side, or had Umberto orchestrated everything?*

It had been a couple of hours since the officer had placed
Giovanni under arrest. Giovanni had no choice but to trust. Umberto
had been a good friend to him, and he was confident that his proposal
to help was in play.

Now, as the vehicle bumped along the country road, he gazed
at the cypress-lined road ahead of them. At the end, loomed a
farmhouse retreat. Giovanni stared at the deserted residence and felt a
twinge of caution.

"Who is here with us?" he asked low and quiet.

"I know this has been tumultuous, but you must trust me that
you will be safe here. There is one other resident. She is the
farmhouse cook."

The driver reached back and patted Giovanni's knee.

"You will see. Everything will work out fine."

In the moonlight, the driver looked kind. "Do not be afraid,"
he said in a voice, gentle and kind. Giovanni pulled back, stunned by
his inability to know whether he should trust.

"I am a professor and archeologist. Tonight, I have been taken
from my home, arrested, and kidnapped all at the same time. I do not
know who to trust."

"I really am sorry."

"I need to understand."

The driver drew a long breath and turned to face Giovanni in
the darkened car. "The relic you found has opened a Pandora's box.
The Holy See is upset only because they have lost control of the
artifact. Now you must worry about the Order of the Serpent.
Unfortunately, they are a long and powerful arm working against us."

Giovanni felt the tension between his shoulders. "It is my fault for allowing the news to get out too soon. I should have kept control of the site."

"As you can imagine," the man continued, "the concerns of the Holy See are that forbidden secrets may be released to the public. However, many have longed for this day when the ultimate truth would surface."

"Why am I here?" asked Giovanni.

"We must keep you alive until the relic is made public. Only then will you be safe."

As he spoke the words, Giovanni turned to gaze at the farmhouse. Through the courtyard, he could make out the illumined kitchen windows.

He was in the middle of nowhere. He grasped the car door handle and let himself out. They ascended the stairs, one stair at a time in the darkness. Trembling, he stepped over the threshold and found himself in a splendid room. It smelled of bread and soup, and the warmth of golden light flickered from the fireplace.

In the quiet, Giovanni felt the weight of his burden fall away, although the gravity of the situation stayed with him. Without a word, the man-made his way into the kitchen and brought back a bowl of hot soup and a thick slice of bread. Giovanni hadn't realized how hungry he was until that moment.

"Grazie." He whispered hoarsely.

"My name is Guido. This farm belongs to my family." Guido sat in a leather chair opposite Giovanni. "I want to tell you my story."

Giovanni nodded. "I am listening."

"My father and my uncle, who also owns land nearby, have dug up many bones and human artifacts."

"This is unusual, how?" Giovanni asked. Many farmers in Italy had found large bones on their land.

"Traditional archeology does not accept my father's discoveries, and our family has been threatened. My father journaled about beings. He called them children of the stars."

"Are you speaking of aliens, then?"

"No. Something quite different." He was silent for a moment. "The reality is that we need to keep the stories safe until we can deal with them carefully. The discoveries are also the history of all of humanity."

"Slowly, media is picking up stories here and there. Enormous bones have been found in many countries and documented by archeologists." Giovanni replied.

"Knowledge is power, and no other organization in the world has more knowledge than the Vatican." Guido looked at Giovanni. "Isn't it interesting that the Roman Catholic Church has so many scholars devoted to astronomy, archeology, paleontology, studies that on the surface have nothing to do with the mission of the Church."

Giovanni replied thoughtfully, "Those who control the past, often determine the future. The greatest cover-up of history is the coverup of history. There is a truth concerning the pre-history of this planet that is far more remarkable and unbelievable anyone could ever conceive of."

"I believe you know my uncle, Umberto."

"Ah, Umberto is your uncle. Yes, he is a good man."

"When he was a little boy, he was kidnapped by men who wanted relics Umberto's father found. Umberto was kept in a monastery to control my family and keep my father and his brother from coming forward with the truth."

"I believe you speak of a monastery in the Piedmont region?"

"Yes, that is the one." Guido shook his head. "It was a terrible time. An American woman rescued him."

"Victoria Munroe?"

"Yes." Guido sat back in his chair and looked Giovanni in the eyes. "This is when my family became part of a Brotherhood. You see, our power comes from the fact that we own land, and everything that is buried beneath our farm belongs to us. This is where the threat is birthed."

Giovanni was beginning to grasp what Guido was trying to say. It was well-known that the Roman Church had built on top of ruins to control what lay beneath.

"Those in power have always worked hard to conceal the truth for many reasons." The discovery that would turn the world upside down was stolen from him within days of its uncovering. Giovanni stared blankly at his hands, overcome by the senseless loss. He turned his gaze to Guido. "How much time do we have here?"

Guido's voice trembled. "I do not wish to worry you, but probably not as much time as you need. For now, you should rest."

"Thank you for your generosity and your help."

"I have no choice. We must keep you safe."

Chapter Fifty Three

Standing in the computer room with the sound of the helicopter above them, Jonathan and Kaira peered at the crystal in Billy's hand.

"Give me the metal piece." He said. Jonathan handed him the round base and watched as he fitted the crystal in place. Jonathan glanced at his phone, waiting for a text. The helicopter continued to circle above the retreat.

The 3D image of a complex clockwork mechanism composed of 30 meshing gears popped up. The detailed model suggested the wheels enabled it to follow the movements of the moon and the sun through the zodiac.

"This was found in a shipwreck. It was believed to be constructed between 70 – 60 BC. Knowledge of this technology became lost at some point." Billy said. "Is this what they are looking for?"

Seeing the working wheels and the complexity of the clock, Jonathan felt hope that it was the discovery that Alex had brought to Alessandro. He scanned the front face of the machine where a fixed dial represented the ecliptic twelve zodiacal signs marked off equal thirty-degree sectors.

"This ring is the Babylonian assignment of ecliptic even though the constellation boundaries are variable," Jonathan stated.

"I'm impressed," Kaira said.

"This outside ring marks the months and days of the Sothic Egyptian calendar. And there…the names for the months were transcribed into the Greek alphabet."

"Why do they want it?" Billy asked

"If this is what I think it is, it is a detailed clock that gives the owner power to predict a 25,000-year cycle, which is called the elliptical year or elliptical precession."

The most considerable antiquity that we have is many ancient texts. One old text is the apocryphal Book of Enoch, which talks about Watchers who came to earth and bred with humans. Alessandro studied it often." Billy was looking at Jonathan.

"I am confused. I thought he was looking for treasure."
Jonathan felt anxious.

"I think he was trying to predict the return of the Watchers,"
Billy said.

"What are the Watchers?" Kaira asked

"Fallen angels." Said Billy.

Were they aliens or angels? The three stared at each other.
"Well, there's no longer any question that my grandmother believed
in extraterrestrials. Now, I realize she believed that the fallen angels
or Watchers would return. But, what made her so sure?"

"The bones are hidden beneath Meadow Manor."

As Kaira visualized the cavern beneath her grandmother's
apartment, a jarring sound pierced the cavern thundering and shaking
the ground as it crashed through the living room roof.

The helicopter.

Jonathan bounded down the stairs and rushed into the living
area, but was immediately lost in the debris. As he inched forward in
the darkness, his eyes strained to see signs of life. "Over here!" Brian
shouted in desperation.

Jonathan moved toward the sound, finally spotting his brother
through the murky fringes of dust clouding the air. Brian sat buckled
in his seat, hands tied with plastic ties. Jonathan recoiled at the sight
of the pilot's body lying on the floor his body grotesquely twisted his
head was almost entirely severed by one of the blades. Jonathan
cringed in horror, but reached for his pocket knife and quickly broke
through the plastic ties around his brother's wrists.

"How many of you were there?" Jonathan asked.

"Three," Brian answered.

A rush of fear surged through him, and he searched the dusty
air for any sign of the other man.

"He's gone," Brian whispered, pointing to the empty
passenger seat.

"Come on." Jonathan urged. "Can you walk?"

"I'm okay."

In the blackness, there was a shuffling of footsteps on the tile
floor and the sound of a foot stumbling over a metal blade. Then a
deafening gunshot rang out and echoed through the cavern.

Where was Kaira?

Jonathan's eyes probed the darkness as he tried to make sense of what was going on.

Suddenly, a bright flashlight pierced the dust in the middle of the room now invaded by a helicopter, its blades broken and slicing through the red sandstone.

"This way," Billy said, motioning them through a hole in the wall. Jonathan and Brian plunged ahead, stumbling through debris. Jonathan could hear Kaira and Billy ascending stairs above them. He turned to make sure the copter passenger was not behind them. Pressing a hand against the wall, he stumbled past a section where a portion of the staircase had been sliced away in the crash.

Raising his eyes, he saw a faint glow through the dust illuminating the others entering a passage. Somewhere behind him, Jonathan could hear the man reach the stairs. He backed around a curve in the wall, waiting until the man reached the broken stairs. Jonathan acted instinctively, crouching down and launching himself at the man's knees.

Jonathan fell, landing on the narrow ledge and grabbed for a handhold. The attacker fell backward through the darkness onto the crumpled metal of the smoking helicopter below. Catching his breath, Jonathan sat up and watched in horror as the man pointed his gun, staring defiantly at him. Suddenly, the last of the glass skylight fell from above and sliced through his body. There was no scream, only a violent shudder and then silence.

Jonathan closed his eyes and took a moment to catch his breath.

"I think my arm is broken," Brian said through clenched teeth. Sharp stabs of pain coursed through his arm. Jonathan stared at him now as they made their way past the computer room and out into the garage where Kaira and Billy waited.

Jonathan's anger kicked in as he assessed his brother.

"You have a lot of explaining to do," Jonathan said, pointing to the backseat signaling him to get inside. "You're lucky I have no intention of killing you with my bare hands."

"Brother, you have no idea how glad I am to see you." He laid his head back on the seat and closed his eyes. "You're in control. But, I guarantee you Carmelo will be sending more goons to finish the job."

"Who is Carmelo?" Kaira asked.

"You should know. He's the man you prevented from buying the Caribbean island. Something about your lease and permits."

Jonathan thought for a moment. "Do you work for him?"

"Not on purpose, but yes. It's a long story."

"Tell us while we drive," Jonathan demanded

"I'll try to make a long story short." Brian began. Five years ago, I was scuba diving along the Italian coast. I ended up in a monastery prison, nothing like you've ever seen. Like I said, long story short." He looked nervously at the natural crevasse Billy navigated the Hummer through.

"Carmelo got me out of prison. I was messed up after three years inside." He was silent for a moment. "After a few months of healing, I slowly learned about Carmelo."

"He's mafia." Said Jonathan angrily.

"Oh, he's so much more than that. He's head of a group that calls themselves the Serpentine Resources, Inc. At first, I thought he wanted me because of dad, you know?"

Jonathan said nothing. He just looked at his hands.

"He wanted you out of the picture because your permits and lease are giving him grief. I was supposed to give you a knock out drug as a distraction, so I could steal a map he wanted. But, as you know…" His voice trailed off. Saying it out loud sounded lame.

"Anyway, I realized he was looking for something else. He took me to his compound, and I learned some things. Did you know a secret branch of the Vatican is funding a group out in the middle of the Arizona desert?"

"You mean VATT? The Vatican telescope on Mt. Graham?"

Brian snickered, but his eyes were serious. "No, I mean, after the Vatican excommunicated the mafia from the Roman Catholic Church, they went underground. A secret sect of the Church still funds Carmelo's projects. Covert."

"What does the Sect want from Carmelo?" Jonathan asked

"His mission is to eliminate anyone who comes too close to the real reason they're out there in the desert."

"Who do you mean?"

"The Jesuits. The Observatory. The portals."

"Okay. You lost me on portals." Jonathan was staring at Brian.

"I know, I know. It's some weird stuff. Did you know some Jesuits believe fallen angels used to live on earth? They believe they're coming back. Supposedly, they're responsible for the pyramids and megalithic structures on the earth. It sounds crazy. It is crazy, but these guys believe this stuff."

"Does Carmelo believe it?"

"I don't know. I don't think so. He's in it for the treasure and the intrigue. The maps they're building show the Sect where to find ancient ruins, but they're also instrumental in finding treasure."

"Do you know anything about Alex?"

"Not really. Just that he knew a lot about satellite mapping."

"Why did Carmelo send you here to the retreat?"

"He thinks you have something he's looking for."

Jonathan was silent. Kaira looked over the back seat.

"And, he thought you could get it from me?"

Brian shrugged. "His goons didn't trust me. They tied my hands, but they weren't expecting me to jeopardize myself too. I kicked the steering shaft. I figured if I survived, it was fate. If not…well…I've already been through hell."

Kaira watched Jonathan intently.

"I don't have the map," Jonathan stated.

"Jonathan," Brian's face looked miserable. "I'm sorry for everything."

Jonathan's first reaction was distrust. Brian had been with Carmelo for the past two years. Apparently, he had been targeted by Carmelo. Jonathan's thoughts swirled as he pictured Alex dead at Victoria's Celebration of Life.

Kaira broke in forcefully, glaring at Brian over the seat. "You came to my grandmother's Wake to hurt Jonathan, and Alex ended up dying. Who killed him?"

The dark truth about Alex was a secret. Brian had only recently learned when he overheard a phone call that Alex had been part of the Order of the Serpent.

"You might not be ready to hear," Brian said quietly and winced as a stab of pain shot through his arm.

"Try me," Kaira demanded.

"The Order has been targeting what they call "loose ends" lately. But, I swear, I knew nothing of their plan to kill Alex. I was supposed to create a diversion and steal a map. When I saw Alex laying there with blood coming out of his mouth, I knew they'd made me the fall guy."

"What I hear you saying is that Alex was part of the Order of the Serpent?"

"That's right." He whispered hoarsely. "They have pawns everywhere, doing the work of powerful men, political and religious. Some have been enslaved, like me, while others have become convinced that their cause is worthy and true. Alex was targeted because he told Victoria the truth. And, now, you are targeted because they think you know."

Kaira thought of Alex in the cavern just before the Celebration of Life. It made sense. He had said the information would possibly put them all in danger.

"The most vicious mafia is not the goons who do their dirty work, but the influential leaders who cling desperately to power, inspiring their pawns to commit acts in the name of the Order. It took only one man to wreak this chaos. The Church secretly funds the Order and uses them to keep control."

Kaira's brow furrowed. "I still don't understand the goal of the church or this secret Sect you are referring to."

"The reality of what they believe is much more than a stretch of the truth. It will sound crazy. Have you ever wondered what they're looking at through that telescope device called LUCIFER?"

"I admit, I hadn't heard of that until a few days ago when we visited Mt Graham. The Jesuits said they are trying to bring science and religion together."

Brian snickered then winced again at the dart of pain in his arm. "They're watching for new moons and planets entering our solar system, and that sounds pretty normal, doesn't it? But, what they aren't telling you is that our world is ancient, and there is an ancient cycle of events that happen like clockwork. The Mayans understood this ancient 25,000-year calendar. I wish I could stop there, but there is so much more."

"We have from here to the airport. Spill it." Demanded Jonathan.

Chapter Fifty Four

As the monk approached the area where the Abbey received packages and letters, he saw the familiar postal vehicle.

Hopefully, the package had finally arrived.

From the looks of the cart, the Abbey had received more than the usual amount of mail. That wasn't unusual during harvest season and through the holidays. As he came to a stop, he strode to the vehicle and jumped back in surprise to see the Abbot.

"Father!" he exclaimed, jumping to attention. "I wasn't expecting you." He eyed the Abbot, who stood inside the mail vehicle rummaging through packages and mail. "Can I help you find something?"

"I believe you are needed in the apartments." He replied coolly.

Surprised by the brush-off, the monk said, "Of course. Right away, Father."

Then on second thought, the Abbot asked, "Have you seen Father Murphy?"

"Yes, he picked up a package from me earlier."

The Abbot looked horrified, and an icy chill ran up the monk's spine. "Is everything okay? Father Murphy left an hour ago to deliver something in Westonville." The monk stammered.

"That doesn't make sense." The Abbot said. "He was to meet me here."

The postman walked up behind the Abbot and exchanged a puzzled look with the monk who regularly picked up the mail. "What's going on?" he asked.

"Just looking for today's mail." Said the Abbot.

"Father Murphy advised me he would be picking up the packages a few days ago."

The Abbot turned on his heel and stormed inside the Abbey. The monk shrugged his shoulders, and the postman sped off down the road without a word, relieved the Abbot hadn't said anything else.

As the monk entered the Abbey, the Abbot stood inside, waiting. "I want you to find Father Murphy." He demanded. "Why has he been picking up the mail in your place?"

"I was following his orders, Father." Said the monk. "He was waiting for a package."

Behind my back? The Abbott Thought. *What is he hiding?*

Earlier, Father Murphy had picked up a package stamped Albano Laziale, Italy. Anxiously, he broke open the seal, opened the package, and extracted a note along with a wooden box and envelope. Giovanni's penmanship was shaky, but he could read it. Father Murphy's bewilderment grew as he read the letter. When he finished, he slipped the card back into the box and sat quietly, considering his options. There was only one thing he could do.

"Take me to the Westonville Police Station, please." He said to the driver.

As the taxi driver pulled away from the Abbey, Father Murphy could feel the driver's eyes staring at him.

***

"Brian?" Jonathan said.

Brian tried to respond, but sudden dizziness overcame him. "Brian…?"

Jonathan touched Brian's shoulder and slowly helped him sit upright in the Hummer. Disoriented, Brian thought he was back in prison. His captor was hovering next to him.

When he recognized Jonathan's face, relief flooded him, and he managed a smile.

"Thank God," he said, breathing a huge gulp of air. Jonathan held him in place. "Stay upright, or you're going to put a lot of pressure on that broken arm."

As Brian's awareness returned, he felt a rush of adrenalin. "Carmelo will send more guys…"

"For now, we're safe," Jonathan said, his voice calm. "The pilot and the other passenger are dead."

Brian continued struggling to clear the fog from his mind, his attention moving to the deep throbbing in his arm.

"How long is this crevasse?"

"We're almost to the end of it now."

Brian carefully pulled himself upright and leaned against the solid metal door of the Hummer groaning as the tires hit a bump.

"It's the Order. They killed Alex…" he said, looking at Jonathan miserably. "I didn't do it." He moaned.

"I know, Brian. We'll talk about it later."

Kaira turned and studied Jonathan. "We have it, Jonathan. We have proof of the clock."

Her words electrified his brain.

"We've made it this far," Kaira said, "But it's going to become more dangerous from here out. I'm not sure what we should do next?"

Jonathan's blood pumped through him in a rush. "I know what we need to do."

"Tell us."

"We need to get back to Meadow Manor."

"Where is that?" asked Billy.

"Just get us to the airport," Jonathan said quietly. "You going to be okay?" He said, looking at his brother.

"I'm fine." Brian lied. He was feeling woozy, but this was nothing compared to what he'd felt in prison. The makeshift sling made from rolls of gauze he'd found in the first aid kit held his arm close to his body.

"Pheonix airport is an hour and a half minutes from here." Said Billy, as he turned onto the main stretch of highway outside Sedona, Arizona.

"By the way, Billy," Kaira said with a weak smile, "You saved our lives."

"The least I could do."

"I just want you to know I won't forget it." Looking out the window at the sunrise, the macabre scene of the helicopter crashed through the cave retreat roof seemed far away.

Billy pulled the metal projection mechanism out of his pocket and handed it to Kaira. With one hand on the wheel, he emptied his pockets with the other hand, placing a pile of crystals on the seat between them. "As I said, you'll thank me later."

Kaira dumped the first aid box on the seat and placed the crystals inside. A sudden thought struck Billy. "These images are from multiple places. They are maps of some kind. I assumed they were treasure maps, but they might be more than that based on what your brother said." He was looking at Jonathan in the rear-view mirror.

Jonathan gazed back. "Billy, could you please relay a message to someone for us?"

"Sure." He said, looking puzzled.

Jonathan explained the plan to put Carmelo's men off their trail.

"I believe what we are about to do is going to change the dynamics of common world history belief systems. That's what Kaira's grandmother was working toward. It is a delicate situation." Jonathan paused. "I am requesting that you do one more thing, Billy. I want you to broadcast to the news station that the truth will be revealed very soon publicly."

Billy dropped the three of them off at the airport.

***

Albano Laziale, Italy

Inside, waiting at the Albano Laziale Police Station, the agent watched with rising concern as the clock ticked. He had not heard from the officers who had picked up Giovanni earlier. They were at least two hours past the scheduled time of arrival. Outside, a man in black robes emerged from a car and approached the station door.

The agent knew the Bishop of Castel Gandolfo. Both men had been taken off guard by the shocking kidnapping of Giovanni right from under their nose.

"I believe they have taken him to a farm on the outskirts of Albano Laziale, but there is a network of men working against the Order. They will most likely be moving him around." The Bishop paused. "We have a small window, you know what you must do when you find him."

Chapter Fifty Five

Local steam was buzzing with the news. The media read:

A credible informant has stepped forward with information concerning verified documents proving that a secret Sect has been functioning in Westonville since the founders established the town in the 1700s. This group is born from an older Sect in Italy known for its close and mysterious collaboration with the translator of ancient Sumerian text.

An Italian entrepreneur who worked with the translator says new information may cause people to have to rethink everything they have known and believed. He says the informant from the Vatican was in touch with the secret group by phone and writing.

While specific authorized individuals can access the Vatican archives, there is no access to the artifacts in a separate location, an underground basement. Some of these objects would help explain the confusion of what we have heard from the Vatican if they were made public.

***

Civico Museo, Italy

"He's been kidnapped," Antonio muttered, his voice resonating in the empty museum hallway. "I still can't fathom how the Brotherhood knew our every move. After all these years of service together, why did he turn to them?"

The PI placed a finger to his lips and looked through the room for bugs as they entered Antonio's office. He wanted to make sure the Holy See and Roman Curia were not listening. I will end up being the fall guy, Antonio realized, always suspecting that if he were up against the Bishop, might be forced to choose, would disassociate with Antonio.

Even so, Antonio could not help feeling wary about the PI's explanation. Something didn't fit.

"Are you saying someone in America orchestrated the kidnapping?"

"It seems the call came through to his phone from an American number. It is a different number from that of the Abbey."

Antonio gave the PI an annoyed look. "Did you find out who the number belongs to?"

"I did call the number from a local phone, but I cannot believe it was that of the Brotherhood."

Antonio stared in silence, waiting for him to explain.

"Well," the PI continued, "It was the office of the Westonville Chief of Police."

"Either Giovanni is a very lucky man, or he is brilliant." Antonio offered. "Brilliant or not, he is hidden somewhere in the farmlands outside Albano Laziale and will be moving through their network."

"Exactly." Said the PI. He eyed Antonio carefully. "Something else is bothering you."

"The relic he stole," Antonio said. "I admit it makes me angry that Giovanni jeopardized all the years of peaceful collaboration with the Roman Curia and the Historical-Cultural Commission. But, there is something else he hasn't told me about the relic that he has risked his own life to protect."

"He's a thief. He realized retiring he had nothing to show for all the years." His tone was bland. "In my opinion, he's an extremely secretive self-ambitious opportunist."

Antonio was startled to find himself wanting to defend Giovanni. "I find it difficult to believe a man who spent his entire life exploring, discovering, and protecting the culture and artifacts of Italy selfishly ambitious enough to do this out of financial gain."

The PI sighed. He pulled out a slip of paper from his jacket pocket. "I have no intention of undermining your faith in Giovanni, but you need to see this." He pushed the article across the desk.

It was a postal receipt for a package.

"This is a package he sent to St. Francis Abbey in Westonville."

Chapter Fifty Six

The three rested on the flight to Washington, D.C. Despite the pain coursing through his arm, Brian felt strangely happy, almost ecstatic, as the airplane left the tarmac and rose into the clouds.

I'm alive, and I'm with my brother, Brian thought.

The adrenaline in his bloodstream had kept him going for the past three hours. Suddenly, he was tired. Very tired. Slowly he turned his head and looked out the plane window. For the next two hours, he could sleep without fear.

The earth dropped away, dissolving beneath the fluffy white clouds, and Kaira leaned her head on Jonathan's shoulder. It seemed like only five minutes had passed, and suddenly, they were descending on the Ronald Reagan Washington National Airport.

Freemasons, Jonathan thought. *Most people didn't understand the architecture of Washington, D.C.*

An incredibly unique and definitively Masonic "pattern of three" could be seen in the architecture of critical federal buildings throughout Washington, DC, from an airplane. The Pattern was visible on the Capitol Building, Washington Monument, Jefferson Memorial, Library of Congress, and dozens of other federal buildings and notable landmarks.

Kaira was awake. He pointed out the window. "Quite a view of the Pentagon, Smithsonian, and all the buildings surrounding the Capitol."

"Where is the yacht?"

"It was there." Jonathan pointed down at the Southwest Waterfront close to the East Potomac Park. "Father Murphy arranged for it to be moved. We'll take a taxi."

The pilot banked toward the airport, and the seatbelt lights came on. Brain sat up straight in his seat and winced.

"A taxi? How far?"

"Yacht Haven at Reeds Point. A three-hour drive."

"Once we get to the Yacht, where will we go?" Kaira's expression reflected weariness from the travel.

"I think we should take my brother to a clinic where no one knows us. Once we're on the Yacht, we'll make sure we weren't followed before we leave port."

"And Alex's computer is there. We can probably access it now." Kaira said.

"That's what I'm hoping." Jonathan looked at Kaira. "Remember what Chris told us at the Observatory?"

Kaira smiled. "Which part?" she laughed. "The fact that they are working on an advanced project or the part involving little green men?"

Jonathan's face brightened at her humor. "My thoughts exactly."

"Do you think it's military?"

"Probably. What better way to appease the public than with disinformation."

Before they could speak further, the pilot announced their arrival. Within minutes they were in a Taxi and headed towards Reeds Point. Three hours later, Jonathan glanced out the window looking for the Reedville Fishermen's Museum, where Interstate 360 ended, and Main Street began.

The taxi followed Main street to the end and stopped in a dirt parking lot between a small marina and a restaurant called The Crazy Crab.

"Jonathan, are you sure this is the place?" Kaira was tired and sounded frustrated. There was no way they could miss the Yacht. The Marina was a tall two-story building with three small fishing boats tied to slips along the pier.

"Not there! Over there!" he said, pointing at the Marina. Kaira and Brian looked confused and stared intently at the source of Jonathan's finger-pointing. Antennae poked above the roofline behind the marina.

"It's directly behind the building. It's too big to park at the pier. It's sideways up against the backside of the building."

My God, it's the size of the marina." Said Brian.

Kaira's exasperation seemed to disappear. Jonathan paid the taxi driver, and the three of them walked toward the marina.

"Thank God for the far-reaching influence of Father Murphy. For the second time, he'd come through for Jonathan.

"Guys, I'm going to get lunch. Want a crab roll or something?" Kaira asked. Now that she saw the Crab shack, she realized she was starving.

Kaira ordered the food, and by the time she'd paid for it, the guys were ready to board. In less than ten minutes, the Yacht was in the Chesapeake Bay, and soon they were over the Bay Bridge-Tunnel and out into the ocean.

After they ate, and Brian was comfortably resting in his cabin, Jonathan pulled out the metal projection mechanism. The bizarre crystals with maps embedded in them had puzzled Jonathan from the beginning.

Kaira turned to Jonathan. "The crystal we looked at was a clock, not a map."

"Exactly," Jonathan said. "Since Alex and Alessandro were both astronomers, it is related to the stars somehow."

"The gears," Kaira said. "They're a celestial timepiece. Maybe they mark a location in the sky?"

"I was thinking the same thing." Jonathan flipped the switch on the metal projector and placed the crystal inside the slot.

"My God," Kaira blurted. "I think I know where this is pointing. Ophiuchus!"

"Ophiuchus?" Jonathan asked. "You mean the constellation…"

"Yes, the one in my grandmother's apartment and the one in Alessandro's retreat. Look, turn the crystal, and the image changes." Kaira assessed the 3D image of the elliptical path.

Jonathan smiled. "I am amazed at the knowledge the ancients possessed. However, the sun spends more time traversing through Ophiuchus than nearby Scorpius. The Serpent Bearer is not considered a member of the Zodiac."

"It must have something to do with the earth's wobble," Kaira replied.

Brian's voice spoke from the stairwell, "Ophiuchus may not be the 13th sign of the zodiac today, but the Mayan and Sumerian calendars and al alchemical manuscripts are based on the lunar cycle of 13 months of 28 days each."

"Okay. And you know this how?" Kaira asked.

"I studied navigational charts a while back." He glanced at Jonathan and wondered what their father would say to see the two of them together on a boat. "The Mayan Zodiac has 13 signs, one of which is Ophiuchus and is called, "The Hidden Sign.""

"The ability of the Sumerian to predict planetary alignments required substantial mathematical understanding. Their amazing skill of precessional tracking is astonishing."

"I still don't understand why they went to all the trouble." Said Kaira.

"In the ancient cultures, the rise of Ophiuchus is coupled with the return of a planetoid to our solar system. The Mayans called it Tzoltze Ek, and the Sumerians called it Nibiru, the Judeans called it Wormwood and modern-day astronomers call it Planet X." Brian answered.

"It's just cosmic clockwork."

"Listen," Brian leaned against the door jamb leading onto the Helm. "What if you don't like the answer at the end of this adventure?"

"What do you mean?" Jonathan asked.

"What if it doesn't lead to treasure, but disaster?"

"I haven't been looking for treasure." Replied Jonathan.

"That's not what you're doing in the Caribbean with your SSRL team? Looking for treasure?"

Jonathan was silent. His brother's ideas about life had changed considerably since they'd last seen each other.

"When I was in prison, I wanted to die. I've never been in such a desperate and dark place. And when I was allowed to live, then just a few hours ago, I was again given a second chance of redemption.... I don't know…It changes what is important to a man."

"I'm glad, Brian. But, we are still trying to stay alive. No one here is looking for treasure."

He's right, Kaira knew, *and in a few hours, they would be back in Westonville in the middle of the fray.*

"I'm not sure what to be afraid of," Kaira said, "But it is odd to me that for hundreds of years, a secret sect of the church has been trying to gain certain information. What does it mean? Is this crystal what the Sect has been looking for?"

"It is a replica of an ancient celestial clock," Brian said quietly. "It can predict."

***

"One year, I was hired to work at an archeological site. Our job was to dig up the skeletons of giants." Guido glanced at Giovanni. They sat at the table drinking coffee. Guido's wife, Lydia, placed a plate of pastries between them.

"The bones were buried beneath the church. It seemed the church had built over ancient ruins. I measured the larger skeleton. It was over nine feet tall. From that time on, whenever we would find the bones of giants, we would take them to the church."

"Did you find artifacts?" Giovanni asked.

"Yes, artifacts, everything went to the church." He hesitated. "Everything would disappear overnight, and we would begin the next day again. I spent an entire summer doing this when I was a young man."

"Did you know where it went?"

"No. We never found out where it went."

"It would seem that legends are often the shadows of truth," Giovanni said quietly. "When we follow a dry creek, it often leads us to the source. This concept is true in archeology."

"There is something I want to show you today before we leave." He drank the rest of his coffee and stood to get his coat. "This will help you understand."

They walked outside. The sun was just coming up, and a pink glow reflected off the stone walls of the farmhouse. Olive groves and vines filled the surrounding land. In the distance, stones on top of a knoll caught Giovanni's attention.

"Ah, you see the ruins. That is a megalithic tomb." They walked toward the knoll. "When my father got caught in the rain, he found shelter in these ruins. When he crawled through a small door, he found giant bones inside. The bones were huge, more than ten feet long."

Giovanni said nothing as they walked toward the ruins. Winded by the time they reached the scattered stones on top of the hill, he stopped and looked back at the farmland below before continuing.

Guido took him through a small door and into a human-made chamber. The massive stones were tightly fit together like those found in ancient antediluvian ruins. A sculpted arch loomed inside, a portal door into another entrance. The real miracle was not the ruins on top of the mound, but what lay beneath the dark space inside it.

Hollowed out on the knoll was a cavern of incredible proportions. A hand-hewn tunnel opened into a gaping cavern with smooth stone floors and a stone table.

I am inside an actual megalithic cavern, thought Giovanni, *an archeologist's dream.*

As they neared the table, Giovanni saw that it was hollow inside like a solid rectangular stone box with a lid. The lid was cracked, and a small portion of the corner had fallen sideways and was now leaning partially on the stone box. Giovanni gazed inside then crossed his chest with the sign of the cross.

Chapter Fifty Seven

Every seat in the Local Steam Espresso was full. Two minutes after the newspaper hit the stand, it was sold out.

What's Happening on Mt Graham?

An informant surfaced with information regarding the missing Jesuit priest from Mt Graham, Arizona. Alessandro worked with a group of Jesuit astronomers who are searching the skies through a telescope named LUCIFER.

Who is the Order of the Serpent?

Evidence has surfaced that a secret Sect has been functioning out of a compound in Arizona. The identity of the leader remains a mystery. According to a recent investigation, the person appointed to oversee the organization is a known Mafia Don. Rumor has it the secret society is performing scientific DNA testing in their multimillion-dollar lab. Where did this group receive its funding?

Archeologist Kidnapped from Albano Laziale

Giovanni Fiorelli, arrested for his part in stealing a relic from a recent archeological dig, was kidnapped while en route to jail. Carabinieri believes a Brotherhood has orchestrated the kidnapping. Anyone Caught harboring this man will be arrested.

***

Glossy burlwood paneled every inch of the interior walls below deck. The tidy cabins were minimally elegant. A narrow hall held a desk and phone for communications. But, it was the main bedroom of the Ophiuchus that Kaira wanted to explore. If there were a computer, it would probably be in the privacy of the main cabin.

The luxury yacht had been fitted with every amenity, giving the traveler access to anything he or she might need. A large screen TV housed in a burl hutch sat in the middle wall. Two large floor to ceiling bookshelves sat on either side of the television. A sliding paneled door on one side of the hutch hid the spacious bathroom behind.

Jonathan and Kaira searched the elegant stateroom and found a remote.

"How does a Jesuit astronomer live in such luxury?"

"Borrowed luxury. Remember, your grandmother owned the yacht."

Odd, Kaira had forgotten. *Do I own the yacht now,* she wondered?

Kaira pressed the button, and the television came to life. She pressed another button, and a large desk on the side of the room began to lift from the floor, revealing a computer center inside.

"Voila," she said.

"The best internet service has been installed on this boat."

"How do you know?" Kaira asked.

"I saw the dish and modems. There's a stabilized antenna for picking up the signal. Probably cost around $100K."

"Are you serious?"

"As a heart attack." Jonathan grinned. "Nothing but the best on this yacht."

Jonathan and Kaira quickly accessed the computer and found the boat command for monitoring everything from batteries to temperature and GPS routes. Jonathan expected to see an icon describing a security locked program, but saw nothing on the desktop.

Kaira looked at the television and realized it was synced with the computer. Jonathan hit an icon on the desktop, and the soft strains of classical music began to play. A video of nature illuminated the massive plasma screen. The presence of Mozart in the luxury yacht seemed fitting.

Jonathan selected an icon that read SpaceX Falcon, and the screen immediately projected a 3D CAD of a rocket.

"What the devil?" Jonathan exclaimed. "Look at this."

"I'm looking! What is it?"

"It's one of the most powerful rockets in the world. It has over 5.1 million pounds of thrust at sea level."

"Explain," Kaira stated.

"A company called SpaceX has flown a rocket called the Falcon 9 for several years. This rocket looks like the next step. I bet it has enough power to take payloads to the moon, Mars, and beyond."

"Alex seems to have had his fingers in more than astronomy and celestial charts. He doesn't strike me as non-intentional." Kaira said quietly, staring at the image on the screen. Kaira felt a chill. *What if he was working with the military.*

"Catapulting the very rich into space isn't new." Said Jonathan. "They're always spinning their crass ego gratification as selfless philanthropy."

"All done in the name of science, religion, and exploration." Kaira agreed. "I need to connect the dots. Why was an astronomer dabbling in space rockets?"

"Maybe the question is, who was he doing it for?" Jonathan said. "He was murdered even though I realize now he was probably connected with Order of the Serpent."

Something about that name made Kaira want to laugh hysterically or run as fast and as far away as possible. "Victoria made a discovery. One she kept secret for many years. It probably proves antediluvian theories." Kaira said. "I'm guessing that based on her presentation at the Celebration of Life."

"And, Alex was going to tell you or show you her discovery. If he thought he was losing Victoria's backing, he might have wanted to get you on board with his projects."

"But, I have nothing."

"Not yet. You will."

Kaira rubbed her forehead. She couldn't conceive what it would be like to have money, to never worry if she could pay her bills. "What about Alessandro and your brother?"

"We have only a few clues on what their agenda might be. Alessandro may have been hiding his work from the organization. My brother was caught up in something he couldn't manage."

"Jonathan," Kaira said, pointing at the television. "Look."

On the screen, the CAD image of the rocket moved into position and launched. The display burst into activity as celestial planets in orbit played in slow motion. A single planet blinked on the screen, its orbit far more elongated than Pluto, Saturn, Mars, and the other planets.

Kaira felt a premonition. The rocket was a moving dot on the screen headed toward the blinking planet in orbit.

"A recent trend is billionaires making fleets of rocket ships for private space exploration."

"But are they professionals?" Kaira asked.

"Probably not. The word exploration implies an attempt to discover something new and interesting about the universe." Jonathan paused. "I would think it is a goal of the Vatican. They have a well-funded interest in the universe. They've accumulated more knowledge and wealth than any other entity. Maybe they are behind it after all."

"What is the name of that planet in the elongated orbit. It seems out of place." Kaira asked.

"If I didn't know better, I'd say the one NASA calls Planet X," Jonathan said. "better known in the Sumerian text as Nibiru, or Judean text as Wormwood. It's considered a doomsday planet."

"I remember watching a documentary from NASA a few years back. They seemed to have recanted their earlier statements." Whispered Kaira. "Crazy."

"Exactly the kind of craziness the rich and powerful love to investigate," Jonathan said. "Covertly, of course." He added.

"I can't imagine my grandmother funding a project to send a rocket to Planet X," Kaira said, shaking her head.

"Not knowingly. Victoria probably thought she was funding a project to further our knowledge of the antediluvian past." Jonathan replied.

"What does the clock tell us?" Kaira asked suddenly, struck with a thought. "Is NASA or the Vatican expecting something to come from that planet?" Kaira stared up at Jonathan. "Okay, that was the craziest thought I've ever had. Sorry for letting that pass my lips."

"Maybe not so crazy," Jonathan said thoughtfully. "I've always wondered how the ancients had such advanced knowledge of celestial bodies. How could the Sumerians have known about Planet X or Nibiru?"

A motion on the plasma screen caught their attention. The rocket landed on the planet. "For a moment, I thought it would blow up the planet."

Jonathan laughed. "It would take more rockets than we can build and send to blow that planet up."

Kaira blushed. "So, what is it doing?"

"Maybe it's shuttling people."

"For what purpose?"

"I don't know." He resigned. "It certainly is bizarre."

"They must believe that planet can sustain life."

"UFO's and Extraterrestrials," Kaira said. "I'm struggling to realize that my grandmother believed in these things."

Jonathan paused for a moment. "Why not? You heard the Jesuits at Mt. Graham talking about UFOs. Even Jesuit priests from the Vatican speak as if it might be true." He paused and pulled an article up on his phone. "Pontifical Academy of Science in Rome asked whether aliens would present a challenge to church teaching."

"You've got to be kidding!"

Kaira stood next to Jonathan while he sat at the helm. Jonathan continued reading. "Questions about extraterrestrial life are fascinating and deserve serious consideration," a Vatican official stated yesterday at its first conference on astrobiology.

Kaira stood, shaking her head.

"What do they know we don't know?" a voice said from the doorway.

"Brian. I didn't see you come up the stairs. How is your arm?" Kaira asked.

"Dull, but manageable ache. I found some painkillers in one of the bathroom cabinets. It's helping for now." He replied. "Didn't mean to bust in, but that's what I've been trying to tell you. Carmelo works for a covert group from the Vatican. They're looking for something or someone."

"What do you mean by someone?"

"I saw some of the tests they were doing back at the compound. DNA testing from bones and mummified tissue."

"Where did the bones and tissue come from?" Jonathan asked

"Probably from Victoria's discovery," Brian said.

Surprised, Kaira turned abruptly toward him. "Why didn't you say something about this before?" she demanded.

"Because it sounds crazy, and I didn't think you'd believe me."

Jonathan and Kaira turned to each other, Brian's statement catching them off guard. With everything they'd endured the past two days, the ultimate moment of truth had arrived through an unlikely messenger.

"Jonathan," Kaira whispered. "The Nephilim, the bones, they're beneath the winery."

"Mighty men of renown, Heroes of old," Brian said.

"What?" Kaira looked at Brian. "Where did you hear that?"

"I saw it over the winery door when I was escaping from Meadow Manor." He was silent for a moment. "Carmelo talked about it too. He said they were going to build a weapon using the DNA of the bones and tissue."

"A weapon?" Jonathan looked surprised. That hadn't occurred to him.

"A super race of giant humanoids, practically indestructible and with supernatural powers. They believe these beings are from another planet, and they came to earth thousands of years ago. Antediluvian."

"Are you serious?"

"They are testing in the desert," Jonathan stated.

"Why don't we just call the press and release a statement saying we know where a Sect is building weapons in the desert?" Kaira asked.

"It's an interesting thought," Brian replied. "But, they will have already cleaned up the mess in Sedona. The Vatican and Carmelo have bottomless pockets. I have a feeling the government already knows. They always come out on top."

"But, we could broadcast that we are alive, and we have a significant discovery to share with the world," Jonathan said.

Kaira strained to keep up with Jonathan and Brian.

"More importantly," Jonathan said, "we have something to show the world."

"We don't have all the pieces until we look beneath the winery," Kaira said. "We'll have the clock images, the crystals, and whatever is lying in the cavern beneath grandmother's apartment."

Jonathan hesitated, suddenly feeling uncertain.

Kaira sensed his hesitation. "What's wrong?"

"We will continue to be in danger unless we handle this with precision. And, we can't talk about this to anyone until all the pieces are in our hands."

"Are we looking for tangible evidence of antediluvian life, or are we looking for ET's?" Kaira asked, still feeling confused about the mission.

"The clock proves a complex civilization existed much further back in our history than we first realized. How could they have known the movements of planets in such detail 12,000 years ago? Additionally, what were they watching for?"

"Some believe they were watching for the arrival of the gods," Brian said.

"We can't prove that."

"Right. But, someone murdered Alex to keep him silent. That means we are in danger until we come forward and make the information public."

"I agree," Kaira said. "From a practical standpoint, everyone in Westonville and the entire east coast is probably reading about our disappearance. Bringing attention to ourselves might keep us safe."

"I am just worried that for your sake, all the intrigue will somehow overshadow what your grandmother wanted for you," Jonathan said, looking at Kaira. She saw something in his eyes she hadn't seen before. His expression reflected a depth of care and empathy. She suddenly realized she hadn't felt lonely for the past two chaotic days.

"That's a valid point, brother," Brian interjected. "You may be overlooking an important fact. All that intrigue is the very reason folks in Westonville are reading the paper right now." Brian paused. "You may not read the tabloids, but the rest of the world has been secretly peeking at UFO magazines and tabloids for years. And, they love any gossip about the Vatican, especially if it's tied to the mafia somehow."

"I suppose the problem is I've been trying to avoid media all these years. They follow SSRL, and the team looking for any crumb of information. It's such a nuisance I haven't had warm thoughts regarding the press."

"You're right," Kaira said, looking at Jonathan. "I hate to admit it, but you're right."

"When Father Murphy and I planned the Wake, he was careful about keeping the Celebration a private event. Now I wonder if he had been expecting something like this to happen."

Kaira wondered that too. She still struggled with trusting Father Murphy.

"What are the obstacles we will face when we reach Westonville Bay?" Brian asked.

"You will immediately turn yourself into Jackson and let us handle it from there," Jonathan said.

"No way. You're going to need me." Brian exclaimed.

"Trust me when I say everything will go much better for you if you turn yourself in."

Always doing the right thing. Kaira smiled, recalling in high school how he kids berated him for turning in a hundred-dollar bill he'd found in the parking lot.

Brian said nothing, but Kaira saw a determined look on his face and knew he wouldn't listen to Jonathan.

An hour later, they were parking in the slip designated for the Ophiuchus. No one seemed to be paying attention. There were two other yachts parked on either side. They made their way down the pier and hailed a taxi in front of the Friar's Deck. Brian didn't like it much when his brother called Jackson and dropped Brian off at the front door of the Police Station.

"We've got something to take care of at Meadow Manor. We'll come in and talk after that." Jonathan told Jackson. He seemed satisfied. After all, they weren't under arrest for stealing Victoria's yacht and taking a trip.

Meadow Manor seemed deserted except for a vehicle with the words Westonville Historical Society painted on the side. Jonathan had the taxi driver drop them just behind the winery out of sight.

When they reached the winery apartment, Kaira reached inside her shirt and pulled out the chain which held her skeleton key. With an admittedly irrational twinge of trepidation, she unlocked the door, and they walked inside. Nothing had changed. It looked exactly as she'd seen it two days earlier.

Jonathan looked up at the ceiling painting of the constellation Ophiuchus. *Just like the one at Alessandro's retreat,* he thought.

Grabbing flashlights from the desk drawer, she looked at the shelf where the set of books were in place. She smiled when she read the titles on the four books, all referencing mythical Greek gods and angels.

"This is the entrance to the passages beneath the winery," Kaira said. "Only Umberto, Victoria, and Alex knew about it. I am the only one with access. Umberto said this is the only key to the apartment."

With that, Kaira pulled the books, and the shelves moved sideways, revealing the metal winding stairs. She stepped into the threshold and turned to make sure the door stayed open behind them.

"Umberto said some passages turn into a maze or labyrinth. We have to be careful and remember which way we've come."

"Great. You've only been down here once. Do you remember."

She turned and took his hand. "Trust me."

Chapter Fifty Eight

Billy made it to the local news station and did what Jonathan asked him to do.

Jonathan Bell to Reveal His Latest Discovery
Jonathan Bell and Kaira Munroe are returning from a visit to Mt Graham, where the Vatican owns an observatory and telescope. There is a connection between the information they've received from the Jesuit priests and the discovery made by SSRL in the Caribbean, where Jonathan and his team have worked for the past several months testing the waters. Anticipation is building as we await the news.

***

The tomb of a giant. Giovanni felt uneasy. The cold dark air smelled of damp stone. His new friend stood next to him, holding a flashlight that trembled in his hands. Giovanni was surprised that after living with a tomb in his backyard, he still seemed anxious.

Giovanni spoke in a quiet low voice. "Aside from cutting and lifting the massive stones in place, these master builders from ancient past configured their houses and tombs in circular patterns indicating an advanced mathematical understanding."

Guido nodded.

"There are many ancient tunnels beneath these tombs," Guido said.

"There is no way the Roman civilization could have constructed these tombs and passages," Giovanni replied.

"I know this is true, but how can you tell?" Guido asked.

"The walls were built with single huge blocks joined together with such precision. There are obvious indications that the Romans came in later and used the megalithic ruins for their purposes. Whoever the builders of the megaliths were, they suddenly disappeared."

"We have also found large blocks of stone in the ocean indicating large cities," Guido said. "My father wanted to keep these things secret. To be honest, I expected these findings to surface years ago." He exchanged an uncertain glance at Giovanni. "Follow me to the end of this tunnel. He motioned them through a narrow door, which stood partially ajar.

Giovanni thought as he and Guido began their walk through the dark tunnel that stretched out before them pointing to another chamber. The theory forming in Giovanni's mind was that the Romans found a highly advanced construction, and they decided to build on top of it or add to it. But, what happened to the race of beings that initially created the megalithic structures. It puzzled Giovanni.

The men entered a room with high human-made walls. The seams between the large rectangular stones were so perfect there was no mortar between the blocks. With reflections of the flashlight dancing on the glossy rock, the massive cavern had a supernatural ambiance. Giovanni could feel the spiritual presence of the gigantic beings who had carved the stones and built the caverns and tombs.

"Think of this," Guido said. "There are layers above us now, but at one time, these buildings would have been out in the open."

"Yes. Something catastrophic happened that buried them under sediment and rubble. Maybe an earthquake and a tsunami. The walls are built on a slant to withstand the earthquakes." Giovanni looked carefully at the smooth, glossy finish on the rock walls. "How did they vitrify these walls? The rock has a glassy finish as if they were heated somehow."

"That is another mystery, my friend. I do not have the answers." Guido said, shaking his head.

"Just as we do not have the power to build this kind of structure, we do not have the power to destroy it. That is why this place still stands." Giovanni declared, his voice full of wonder. I have seen many things as an archeologist, but I have never seen vitrified walls like these."

"I just hope our farm is never exploited by the greedy and powerful. That is what my father wished to avoid." Guido said with surprising passion.

Chapter Fifty Nine

Kaira turned her flashlight on and held it in front of them. Continuing down the winding stair and the passageway, they arrived at an unexpected split in the path. Kaira thought she knew which way they had gone. It had all happened so quickly that evening. They took the left passage.

Finding the cavern was easy. The table sat precisely where it had a few nights earlier. Even with the flashlight on, shadows clung to the edges of the chamber. Kaira pressed on walking around the chamber walls to where she had seen Alex enter from the darkness.

A narrow crack in the wall hid a dark entrance into another passage.

"Over there is where I saw Alex enter," Kaira said, pointing in the darkness. "Other than Victoria, who knew her way around, we are the only ones who have accessed this room."

With that, Kaira wasted no time stepping through the slit in the wall. At the end of the passage, she stopped short and placed her hand over her mouth to stifle the gasp. When Jonathan reached her and looked over her head into the second chamber, he understood.

The chamber's high walls dominated by a macabre scene sent a shudder down his spine. Skeletons scattered along the edges of the wall pressed between the strata of the rock like a layer of fossilized bones had to be ancient.

This is it, Kaira thought. *The Nephilim.*

The skeletons wore no clothing. If they had, it had disintegrated long ago. Mind-bogglingly large skulls pushed out from the rock layer, some stared through black eye sockets as large as a coffee cup saucers, creating a hideous scene.

Sudden death.

"In the layer," Jonathan whispered, "they are crushed together on top of each other as if some catastrophe happened so quickly it buried them all at once. Erosion in the middle of the cavern has left fragments of bones lying on the rock floor."

Stifling insane fear, Kaira allowed her eyes to examine the cave wall and saw that the bones were pressed together. As her gaze scanned the enormous room, something caught her attention, and she shined her flashlight toward one end of the chamber. There at the end of the long room, on a raised platform, stood a massive stone box.

Kaira now knew why her grandmother had thought so much about fallen angels and celestial beings because Meadow Manor was built over a crypt full of giant antediluvian bones. Fusing the two worlds of legend and visible reality created a robust platform for a pre-flood ancient civilization.

"Oh my God, Jonathan," Kaira whispered. "the legends passed down through Indian cultures are true!"

Inside the main chamber of the considerable crypt, Kaira followed Jonathan around the perimeter of the cave toward the stone coffin-shaped box.

"It's freezing," Kaira said. Jonathan took his jacket off and put it around her shoulders.

"Thank you." She said, her teeth chattering. "I have an eerie sense that we are about to peer into the crypt of a beast."

The gruesome array of bones and skulls protruding from the layers of rock created a nightmarish atmosphere. On Kaira's prompt, they climbed the steps and found themselves standing on a platform before the large stone box.

To Kaira's surprise, the stone lid to the rectangular box decorated with a zodiac star chart showed four of the brightest stars carved on each corner.

"It looks like Taurus, Leo, Aquarius, but what is this fourth sign?" Kaira whispered. "What does it mean?"

"I think it is the ancient symbol for Scorpio. Scorpio is only part of the full sign that is most corrupted of the ancient symbols."

Kaira gazed at him, not understanding.

"In ancient times, Scorpio was a composite of both an eagle and a serpent. For some reason, it has been suppressed on purpose." Jonathan said.

"See the carving in the center? It looks like an ecliptic crossing." Kaira whispered.

"I'm impressed," Jonathan said quietly.

"I'm learning as I go." Kaira pulled the jacket tighter around her shivering frame.

"I think you are correct." Jonathan agreed. "Only two of these four signs, Taurus and Scorpio, occupy the places where the Milky

Way crosses the ecliptic. At Scorpio, the ecliptic crosses the Milky Way at the galactic center."

"But what could this mean?" Kaira said quietly. Suddenly she twitched and slapped her leg. Something was crawling on her. Jonathan shined his flashlight on her leg but saw nothing.

"I don't see anything, Kaira."

She slapped her leg again, hoping with all her might a spider hadn't crawled up her pants. Then with a sigh of relief, she reached into her pant pocket and pulled out her phone. It was vibrating. The location GPS recordings her grandmother had installed was pinging in front of the stone coffin.

Astonished, Kaira held her phone up for Jonathan to see. She found the earpiece and jammed it in her ear then stood directly in front of the coffin. She pushed the speaker button, and they both listened to Victoria's recording.

"You are standing in front of Goliath's tomb. That's what I've affectionately nicknamed my mummified giant. I'm going to assume that if you've made it this far, you realize how this find impacts us not only on the earth but also from space."

"Every 6,480 years Taurus and Ophiuchus, you might know it as Scorpio, align with the cardinal points of the year known as the solstices and the equinoxes. The precession of the equinoxes is divided into four distinct ages of 6480 years. The entire zodiac cycle is 25,920 years. Try not to be overwhelmed by this information. It is a little much to absorb at first."

Kaira paused the recording. "Did she say Scorpio and Ophiuchus were the same?"

"Scorpio is a partial sign and has been corrupted since ancient times," Jonathan replied.

Kaira hit play, and Victoria continued.

"The symbols of the eagle and the serpent were both assigned to the Jewish tribe of Dan. The four fixed signs, Aquarius, Taurus, Leo, and Scorpio, are separated by 6480 years. These four signs have different names in the Bible, and we see it as a cherubim angel with four faces – Lion, Bull, Man, and Eagle. The faces of the cherubim align with the divisions of the year that an old age dies, and a new age begins. You would have seen this in 2012 when the Mayan

calendar spoke of an end to the precession of the elliptical and the beginning of a new age."

"Particularly with the sign of Dan at the galactic center, the end of the age is most dramatic. When the sun rises in this sign, also at the galactic center, the Milky Way surrounds the horizon of the earth. Ophiuchus was perched atop the galactic bulge with the sun rising at its feet."

Kaira pressed pause again and closed her eyes in thought. Shaking her head, she looked at Jonathan and pressed play.

"The new age will come "out of chaos" from the old. This sign was at its peak on December 21, 2012, exactly when the Mayan calendar ends, and their heavenly serpent god returns. Do not be fooled by what you cannot see."

With that, the recording ended.

"I'm so confused." Whispered Kaira. Jonathan placed his arm around her. *This is a superhuman DNA testing ground,* Jonathan thought but kept it to himself. "Is this a coffin?" she asked

Jonathan bent down to examine the stone lid more closely. Bewildered by its sheer weight, he said, "How are we going to lift this lid?"

"We're going to look inside the coffin?"

"Why not?" Jonathan replied. "We've come this far." Jonathan turned his eyes toward the wall behind the coffin looking for a lever. In a matter of a few seconds, Jonathan had found a moving piece of rock on the wall. He pressed, and the stone lid made a horrible grating sound and began to slide open. The noise thundered through the acoustics in the cave, and Kaira placed her hands over her ears.

Kaira expected to see another colossal skeleton and skull. But, to their bafflement, the inside of the coffin was dark and empty. The only contents appeared to be wisps of dust that swirled in the light of the flashlight.

"There's nothing here." Kaira declared.

Jonathan realized Victoria and Alex must have taken the contents to a lab for testing. He wondered if that was what Carmelo wanted. Brian said he was testing DNA of ancient bones in an attempt to create a weapon. Now observing the skeletons in the cave, Jonathan was beginning to believe anything was possible.

"Is this what the Order of the Serpent is looking for?" Kaira asked

"Brian said Carmelo is building a superhuman weapon out there in the desert," Jonathan said. "But, Victoria and Alex are the only two who have been here other than us. If there was a skeleton in the coffin, they've removed it."

"Where did these gigantic beings come from?"

"My guess is, they are pre-flood, which might place them 4000 to 6000 or more years before the flood."

"If that is true, why are they so close to the surface of the earth. I would think they'd be buried much deeper."

"Yes, but there's been upheaval from earthquakes and other natural catastrophe causing a shifting of the ground in this area."

"Incredible," Kaira said. "Alex said what he and Victoria discovered would change everything. What was his part in this?"

"I was thinking about that. The early Christians were familiar with teachings about the gates of heaven. The Maya theory describes past visits of a being they call Quetzalcoatl, the Feathered Serpent who can fly through wormhole stargates. There is a crazy prophecy made in 2012 that this serpent rope would emerge again from the center of the Milky Way, and Quetzalcoatl would return."

"It's difficult to take a prophecy like that seriously."

"Right, but now we realize that each culture tells a similar story using different names for the same gods they are describing. I think some believe beings did enter the world in 2012, but we can't see them."

"So, you think these skeletons might be visitors from another planet?" Kaira asked, bewildered.

Jonathan understood the logic but still couldn't imagine the task of proving that ET's were the answer to the equation.

"I think it's the greatest magic trick in the world. While everyone is looking one direction, something will come from another direction. Illusions."

***

At that moment, in the farmhouse with Guido, Giovanni sat transfixed, staring out the window toward the knoll, trying to make sense of what to do next. His friend Guido sat motionless in the chair across from him at the table.

With a surge of dread, he spoke.

"Guido?" Guido lifted his head to look at Giovanni. "What will you do to preserve your farm?"

Guido shrugged. "I will take it one day at a time." He replied with surprising courage. "And you? Your life was turned upside down."

Giovanni didn't know how to reply. He had always loathed the Roman Curia's control of his archeological finds. "I will be fine. I long to retire back to my home and enjoy the end of my days in peace." His uncharacteristic lack of passion for responding to the recent arrest surprised himself.

"It would be wonderful," Guido said, "to live in the presence of those you trust most in the world."

Giovanni shot an understanding glance at Guido and shook his head.

"I'm not sure what will happen regarding the reaction to your escape. I don't think the Curator wants to take responsibility for his actions at the Civico Museo." Guido said.

Chapter Sixty

The line was out the door at Local Steam Espresso. The patrons drank coffee and read the local newspaper. Catalina Sanchez sat in a corner with her laptop posting to BuzzFeed.

Local Police Investigate Gigantic Bones
Finding such skeletons is rare because gigantism itself is extremely rare. The unusual skeleton was found in Westonville after a hurricane hit the beaches along the east coast.

The colossal giant was found with artifacts. It has been suggested he was not included as part of the culture.

It was only during a later anthropological examination that the bones, too, were found to be not only gigantic but also unusual. Shortly after that, they were sent to a laboratory for further analysis.

Pirate Treasure…or Something Else?
One of the fascinating pirate stories is the legend of Captain Benjamin Munroe and his ship, the Southern Pacific. While the wreck of this legendary galley has recently been discovered, much of its treasure remains missing. Arthur G. Bell, the renowned treasure hunter who made the initial discovery of the Southern Pacific wreck, has been missing for fifteen years.

A Sect in Westonville
Why is the Vatican the most significant and longest owners of telescope Observatories? The Vatican also owns most of the early books of antiquity on astronomy, and they possess the most patents on celestial observatories. Strange for an organization that was adamant that the Sun, planets, and stars revolved around the earth.

Why would they set up the earliest observatories right at the end of the Dark Ages, that continues to this day some 500 years later, if they were so dead set on maintaining that the Earth was the center of the universe?

They allegedly crucified and burned at the stake heretics like Bruno and exiled Galileo for their trying to prove that the Sun was the center of our solar system, not the Earth. And the story goes that Copernicus waited until on his death-bed before publishing the work that changed everything we knew about our relation to the universe, *On the Revolutions of the Celestial Spheres*.

Chapter Sixty One

Father Murphy was in for another sleepless night. He had heard reports out of Castel Gandolfo of the kidnapping of Giovanni Fiorelli. A bold move by the Brotherhood. He had no intelligence on the ground in Albano Laziale, and he had been unable to investigate.

And still no word from his connection at the Pontifical Villas of Castel Gandolfo. The last message was exchanged twelve hours ago.

Father Murphy regretted not relating his suspicions to Jonathan and Kaira. But, they had only been suspicions. He needed time to finesse some further intelligence, and still, he wasn't satisfied. If he proceeded more boldly, Antonio the Curator would know of his allegiance. It would put Giovanni and others in further jeopardy. Father Murphy continued to work alone from his end.

A knock on his apartment door drew his eyes from the computer screen. He turned off his computer monitor and opened his door. A monk entered.

"They were seen at the pier. Jonathan, Kaira, and another man."

"Headed for Meadow Manor? Father Murphy asked.

The monk nodded. "About three hours ago."

"Why Meadow Manor and not the Abbey?" Father Murphy rubbed his tired eyes. "I haven't heard from Umberto or Jonathan in a while. Neither of them is answering their phone."

"I can confirm that a taxi dropped off two people at the manor."

"Only two?" Father Murphy straightened, frowning.

"I believe so. I can call and find out."

Father Murphy had to be careful from here. "No," he said. "That might raise alarm bells. Let's give them some space for now."

"Yes, Father. I also have requests from Castel Gandolfo. The Roman Curia has not heard anything and is getting anxious."

Father Murphy had to offer something, or the Roman Curia might react harshly. He considered carefully. It wouldn't take long for the Holy See to ascertain the relic's whereabouts.

"Cooperate," he finally said. "Let them know we have learned of the kidnapping, and we are investigating on this end. We'll pass on information as we learn more."

"Yes, Father."

Father Murphy stared at his computer screen. "Contact the Curia right away. I need to run an errand to Westonville Police Station."

The monk frowned.

"I've got to speak with Jackson Bennett." Father Murphy picked up a sealed letter in a manila envelope. "Don't let anyone know I'm going to the police station."

The monk's eyes narrowed quizzically, but he nodded.

"I'll be back for Mass." Father Murphy tucked the envelope in his robe. "Complete discretion."

"You have my word," the monk said firmly and closed the door on his way out of the apartment.

Reaching deep into the bottom drawer of his desk, Father Murphy took out a pistol and secured it beneath his clothing. He needed to be at Meadow Manor when Giovanni arrived.

***

Giovanni sat in the first-class cabin of the private jet. He had to give the Brotherhood credit. They knew how to travel. He glanced around the cabin. Eight seats, three passengers, and the pilot. Two men were bodyguards, there to keep him safe, he hoped. Giovanni would cooperate until instinct told him otherwise.

It was going to be a long flight. He drank two glasses of Piedmont's best red wine with his antipasto then fell asleep. A few hours later, he woke to feel refreshed. He turned to the window. The box should be in Father Murphy's hands by now. He pictured the older priest with graying hair. Influential, yet a heart as big and reliable as the large gold cross that hung around his neck. And Victoria. She had been an intriguing mixture of lace and steel. An intelligent and strong woman who knew what she wanted and often knew what others needed. She would be deeply missed. He ached and wondered how many others would suffer or die at the hands of the Order.

Below, the lights of New York glittered. The jet swept over a section of the airstrips and made a sharp turn then approached a private area nestled among some buildings on the outskirts. Moments later, they touched down and taxied to a hangar.

Giovanni waited for the bodyguards to exit before he gathered his carefully packed bag. Slinging it over his shoulder, he exited the cabin and searched for any signs of danger. A taxi took him to customs where he showed his false papers, had them stamped, and was on his way carrying one bag.

He strode across the airport to the arrivals area sensing rather than seeing the bodyguards. He shifted closer to a metal post and sat on a bench to wait for Umberto's call. He was grateful for his ally. Cut off from his home and University students, he felt vulnerable. He and Umberto would need to work closely together. Giovanni knew Umberto's cooperation with the Brotherhood was about his fury with the Order of the Serpent. It suited his desire to see the Order undermined. Though he wasn't a vengeful man, Umberto had a personal right to his anger.

After this was over, Giovanni would go home a free man, or he would die trying. His burner cell rang. He freed it from his bag.

"Umberto?" he asked, the tension evident in his voice.

"Welcome to New York, my old friend. "A black car will be picking you up in a few minutes. The guards will stay with you until you are safely in the car. The driver will be wearing a red Tam."

Just then, the car drove up, and a young man stepped out wearing a Scottish plaid tam.

"He's here."

"Good. I'm expecting you to be here in time for dinner. See you soon."

The line went dead. Giovanni found a garbage can next to the bench where he'd been instructed to toss the burner cell. With a curt nod, the young man opened the back door of the car and soon they were headed out into the New York traffic. It took two hours to get out of town. The driver made his way south on the coastal highway and out of the city.

It was another world. Nothing was intriguing in the high gray cement and metal buildings. Nothing compared to the beauty of his home in Albano Laziale, Italy. It was beginning to rain.

Chapter Sixty Two

Police Chief Jackson strode into the room, his dark hair combed neatly around his ears. He shot Brian a narrow-eyed look that indicated his loyalty lay elsewhere. Brian held still. Jackson looked tense though his uniform was crisp and clean as if he'd just showered and changed his clothes.

Brian gazed around the room at the other officers. They didn't meet his eyes. *Duh.* It hit him. Jackson had been trying to find his dad all these years hoping to impress Jonathan or maybe find the treasure. His throat was dry, knowing there was nothing he could say to get on the right side of Jackson.

He started the interview and asked for an outline of the past three days.

"When did you arrive in Westonville?" Jackson asked. His voice was level but with an edge.

"I came in on my sailboat three days ago, around ten in the morning."

"Was anyone with you?"

"No, sir."

"I knew your dad."

There was a huff of smothered snickers behind Brian. He wished Jackson would do the interview privately. He wanted to turn and glare at the officers. Jackson watched him carefully, knowledge burning in the depths of his eyes. Brian hated being the center of curiosity. He wanted to disappear through the floorboards. Unfortunately, it was time to face the music for his sake and Jonathan.

"On a normal day, you would have been out in the bay looking for treasure or digging up our cliffs. Why not this time?"

"I'm just going to tell you the truth."

"That's a good start," Jackson said sarcastically.

"I ended up in an Italian prison a few years back. I was there three years before a man named Carmelo bought my freedom."

"And why would he do that?"

"He thought I knew where my father hid the treasure."

"And do you?" He paused. "Do you know where your father hid treasure?"

Brian said nothing.

"Tell me about Carmelo."

"He's part of Order of the Serpent, a secret sect that does clandestine work for the Vatican."

"Do you have proof?"

"I know where their headquarters is located."

"Did you kill Alex?" asked Jackson

"No. Carmelo gave me a knockout drug. I was supposed to give it to Jonathan and create a diversion while I stole a map."

"A knockout drug?"

Crap. He'd lost the vials while escaping. He had no proof. Jackson's lips tightened.

"No. I didn't kill Alex. But, I can't prove it." Brian bit down on his frustration.

"We've had teams of people collecting DNA from Meadow Manor, and we'll enter the samples into CODIS. The work will continue until we identify exactly who the killer is." Jackson's knuckles whitened.

"Alex may have had information the killer didn't want anyone to find out. Know anything about that?"

Brian knew a lot about it but tried to think through what he should and shouldn't say without a lawyer.

"I only know that Carmelo wanted me to steal a map. He's looking for something in particular, and it has something to do with telling celestial time."

"Although there's no criminal prosecution yet, I need to make sure the scene at Meadow Manor is processed carefully so that we gain closure for Alex and his family and friends. We are treating this as a homicide now that we know Alex was poisoned."

Brian's looked at his hands. So far, they hadn't cuffed him. Something wasn't right. If they thought he'd killed Alex, they would have him in cuffs. He looked at one of the officers and thought he saw a look of concern, maybe confusion. He wasn't the only one with questions. Jackson was after something else.

"Why did you run?"

"When I saw Alex's face and the blood around his mouth, I knew something had gone horribly wrong. I don't know anything else."

Jackson leaned back in his chair and stared at Brian.

"What does Carmelo do for the Vatican?" Asked Jackson, and Brian heard another snicker from an officer across the room.

"It will sound crazy. You'll think I'm crazy, and you won't believe me."

"Try me." Said Jackson.

"Not with your officers in the room."

"Clear out," Jackson said, and the men left the two of them. Then he waited expectantly.

"Carmelo is working on a weapon. He's using DNA from ancient relics and bones to create a super humanoid robot. They are in a compound out in the Arizona desert."

"And, where did he get ancient DNA?"

"The Vatican and other private collectors and museums."

"Why are they creating this weapon?"

Explaining the phenomenon to Jackson left him empty. He could see the cold disbelief on his face.

"There's a planet that comes close to earth every few thousand years. It is approaching us at a fast pace. Carmelo and some at the Vatican believe there are aliens or fallen angels that will come to earth from that planet when it gets to a certain place in our galaxy."

"Yep. It sounds crazy, alright."

"They're spending billions of dollars on spaceships and militant robots that might be able to communicate with these ancient aliens." Brian knew it sounded lame. It didn't matter whether he believed in the aliens or angels. He just wanted someone to believe there was a compound in the middle of the Arizona desert with an unbelievable lab. He'd seen it with his own eyes."

"Too bad Father Murphy isn't here. He'd be interested in this story." He got up and filled his mug with coffee. The office outside the door was buzzing. Just then, Jackson looked through the office window. "Speak of the devil."

Father Murphy walked through the door and handed Jackson a brown envelope.

"Morning, Jackson. I have something I think you need to see."

"Father Murphy, meet Brian Bell." Jackson took the envelope and opened it.

"Brian." He said cautiously. "I haven't seen you since you and your brother played at the old Nike missile site behind the Abbey." Brian appreciated that he thought of him from that age instead of automatically tagging him as an obsessed treasure hunter.

"Holy sh…." Jackson held the photos in his hands. "Sorry, Father. Where the hell did you get these?"

Father Murphy didn't answer the question. Instead, he stated, "I think it is time this comes to the surface. I am sure it is the reason Alex was murdered."

"Alex knew?"

"Oh, yes. Alex and Victoria were planning to find a way to present it publicly through the Westonville Historical Society."

Brian wondered what was in the envelope. Jackson's gaze flashed uneasily to Brian. The silence lengthened to discomfort.

"Who knows, Father?" Jackson asked.

"Victoria, Alex, and Giovanni, an archeologist in Italy."

"Father, our community is unprepared for this kind of information. We cannot let this out." Jackson's eyes were wide, and Brian thought he saw fear. Scared kept people alive. Jackson held the photos so Brian couldn't see, but he made an educated guess what was in the envelope.

"One of the monks from the Abbey saw Jonathan and Kaira arrive at the Manor this morning." Father Murphy said. "We need to make sure they stay safe."

Jackson stood and shoved the photos back into the envelope. On top of finding the killer, he had to keep the community from freaking out. He looked at the packet full of volatile proof and locked it in a safe.

"Let's take a ride to Meadow Manor. Brian, you come with us." Jackson commanded. "We need to talk to Jonathan and Kaira, find out what they know and what the hell they've been up to."

Brian hid his reaction by looking at the floor. It wasn't what was in those photos that kept him awake at night. It was the wreckage from the covert sect groups that operated without empathy. He wondered if Father Murphy knew what went on behind closed doors. He seemed innocent. It was a matter of time.

Jackson gathered some things, suddenly in a hurry to get to Meadow Manor.

"There's something else." Jackson kept his voice low. I want no one to know where we are going, and no one else must know about this." He pointed at the safe and looked at Father Murphy. "Understand?"

Father Murphy frowned slightly. There was a bite to Jackson's tone he'd never heard before. He walked out of the office to his police vehicle, expecting Father Murphy and Brian to follow.

***

Crossing the cavern, both Jonathan and Kaira carefully avoided the huge bones scattered on the floor. They were a good ten feet from the opening in the wall when they heard voices. They were standing in an enormous room with no place to hide. "Quick, back behind the stone box," Jonathan whispered in her ear. Just as they turned, three men made their way out of the opening and into the cavern. Too late. Jonathan shined his flashlight in their direction.

"Jackson! Wow, I'm glad it's you." Jonathan felt relieved. Brian? What are you doing here?"

Somethings wrong, Kaira thought. Her instincts told her to stay close to Jonathan. Had she left the shelf open? She couldn't remember.

"Jonathan?" she whispered.

Father Murphy stepped in behind Brian.

"What are you doing down here?" Jackson asked.

"Isn't it incredible?" Jonathan ignored the question. His excitement was difficult to hide. "This is what Victoria and Alex were working on together. It's unbelievable. I wouldn't have believed it if I hadn't seen it with my own eyes."

The men at the door seemed stunned by the colossal skull embedded in the rock layer. Its giant jaw opened in a half scream and faced the cavern its vast empty eye sockets revealing darkness inside the head. Jonathan walked to the skeleton and stood beside it, grinning. The skeleton lay horizontal along the wall. Brian guessed the skull measured more than twelve inches. At least a foot and half wide from ear to ear. Unbelievable.

"Nephilim." Father Murphy said.

"Or aliens," Brian said.

"My grandmother told me these passages were here before they built Meadow Manor. They must be very old."

"They're ancient." Father Murphy corrected.

Chapter Sixty Three

Giovanni arrived at Meadow Minor at four in the afternoon. Earlier than he'd expected. He got out of the taxi and waved at Umberto in the distance. Umberto was hunched over examining some vines. The grapes were ripe and ready to harvest. The frost was precisely what the grape skins needed, and the sugar in the fruit was perfect. He didn't see Giovanni arrive.

Giovanni dubbed the taxi driver 'Tam' because of the Scottish cap he wore.

"Tam, we need to get inside quick."

Looking south across the Bay, a wall of clouds seemed to go up into endless space. A moment later, sprinkles of rain pinged on the roof of the car. Tam had parked next to the winery. The doors were open, and Giovanni went inside with Tam following close behind.

A huge clap of thunder rattled as the men stepped through the threshold.

"This is as good a place as any to wait for Umberto." Giovanni stared at the large casks of wine. He wandered down an aisle toward the end of the room, where he saw a door cracked open. Curiosity had the best of him, and Giovanni peeked through the slit. Seeing there was no one in the room, he opened the door further and gazed at the painting on the ceiling. The Scot followed, shoving through the door after the archeologist.

"What's that smell?" asked the Scot, wrinkling his nose.

Brought to his attention, Giovanni caught the familiar damp taint of earth and stale air. Within the room, Giovanni spotted the bookshelves and noticed they were slightly open. Why would Umberto leave the doors open? Someone else was in the winery apartment.

He glanced at Tam, who suddenly bore more intense interest in the bookshelves.

"You've been cave exploring, right?" He said. Tam nodded.

"Look," Giovanni said. He pushed the shelves, further revealing the winding stairs.

A sudden crash of lightning sent flashes through the stained-glass window. "You alright?" Giovanni asked, touching Tam's shoulder. "Someone is down here, and my guess is Umberto doesn't know."

"We should wait." Said Tam. "No good can come of it."

"It's okay. Umberto is a good friend; besides, he probably knows they're here." He patted Tam's arm and led the way down the steps. Halfway down, he stopped to give Tam a minute and pulled a flashlight out of his pocket. From the bottom, Giovanni could see it had to be at least fifty feet before the tunnel turned. The surprising strength of the tunnel walls suggested the builders may have known masonry secrets like those he'd seen in Italy. *But where did they all go?*

Breathing hard, Giovanni flapped his hand. "I'm fine." He moved aside as Tam made his way past. "Let's rest at the turn up ahead."

"If word gets out about this place, it'll be swamped and trampled," Tam said.

"Now's the best time to study it. These ruins have waited centuries to be explored. A little longer won't make a difference." Giovanni looked at Tam. "I appreciate your help. We'll be done here shortly and get back to dinner with Umberto."

"So, what do you make of all this?" Tam asked. Could it be a part of the antediluvian past? Pre-flood megalithic tunnels?"

"You mean the Noah's Flood of the bible?" He answered slowly. "Maybe. Hundreds of megalithic ruins have been found in the United States and all over the world. Many predate oral histories. No one has connected them until recently. The internet has changed everything." The mystery charged his blood.

"Have you made connections?"

"Who knows what answers may be found here. I know I've been brought here for a reason." He glanced at Tam. "There is only one way to find out."

Tam grinned. "If you say so."

The pair continued down the tunnel, staying close, Tam helping Giovanni over rough spots. The passage split, and Giovanni took the right shaft, which slanted downward.

A single monstrous slab crossed their path. It was cracked in half probably from seismic activity years ago.

"How did these ancient builders get the slab here?" Tam asked.

Giovanni nodded too focused to speak. He was stunned that such evidence lay only a few feet beneath the surface. Tam dogged his steps, viewing it from behind Giovanni's shoulder.

"Are you sure we should do this?" Tam asked as Giovanni pointed out a pair of slabs that had fallen against each other. Space lay between slabs, descending at a slant. "How stable are they?"

"Believe me; they are stable. The reason the slabs are still here after all these years is that they are so stable." Giovanni bent down to take a look at the slabs.

Giovanni snuggled through the space and wormed his way inside, using his fingers to find the edge of the rock on the other side of the slab. He had been caving and digging his entire life. This was no big deal. He was glad to be participating again instead of telling some students to explore for him.

He moved on. If he became stuck, he could always back out, plus Tam could pull him out if needed. There was no real danger. He was sure that Umberto would probably find them soon enough.

His body thrust forward. By now, his pulse pounded in his ears. His jaw ached from the tension of anticipation. He paused to crane his neck at the space which lay open before him. They had gone further down than he had anticipated. The cavern was vast, and the ceiling high. Something caught his eye on the far side of the expanse. It looked like an altar. That wasn't unusual. But, the large carved snake woven around it was sensational. A mane of feathers surrounded its fanged head, and red stones flicked from its eyes. Ignoring the luminous jewels, he moved his light.

He turned to the damp tunnel he'd just come through. Tam should see this. As he bent to make his way back through the space between the slabs, a sharp sound echoed in the small area followed by a scuffle and the sound of men walking. Giovanni tried to peer through the space without being seen.

"Tam!" Giovanni yelled. Another sound echoed from beyond the tunnel, muffled this time. He knelt on both knees, breathing hard. He should have stayed above ground. What was he thinking coming below? From the tunnel, Tam's face stared back at him. He was a bit thick around the chest.

"Help me. Pull me to you." He hissed. "Three men just walked down the other passage."

Giovanni dropped his flashlight and reached out to grasp Tam's wrists. Planting his feet, he pulled him through the narrow space. Panting and excited, Tam pulled away from Giovanni and leaned on the wall to catch his breath.

"What happened? Were they after you?"

"I don't know for sure. I couldn't see."

"I knew someone was in the tunnels."

"I guess I didn't realize there were others down here."

"I knew it because the doors in the apartment are open. And I hope they are friendly."

Tam nodded.

"Did they see you slip in here?"

"I'm not sure. I don't think so."

Already they could hear the men clambering through the tunnels, but the sound was distant. There was no way to crawl out and set up an ambush. Giovanni surveyed the area for another exit. They were trapped. All they had to defend themselves were flashlights.

Tam backed away from the opening. "What are we going to do?" He glanced at the snake-adorned altar, and his eyes widened. The sound of boots on stone approached, and voices grew louder again.

"We must not show ourselves yet."

Giovanni ducked to the side as a beam of light pierced their hiding place. He clutched his flashlight to his chest and flicked the switch off. The beam of light vanished, and the darkness reclaimed the chamber. Giovanni and Tam leaned against the damp rock wall. As long as they were still, they were safe. If anyone tried to crawl through the opening, they could quickly hit them on the head with their flashlights.

The best defense was to wait.

The men outside had grown quiet. Giovanni could hear scuffling and scraping but could not discern what they were doing. He bumped into Tam behind him. He saw Tam furiously tapping the tiny glowing screen of his phone.

"I'm trying to reach my contact." He said sternly, his responsibility as a part of the Brotherhood kicking in. "I can't get reception from down here."

"We must be beneath the vineyard. "Giovanni muttered while Tam continued looking for reception. The men were gone, but he didn't want to go out the way they came in if there was an exit passage.

"Look at the walls here. They are solid rock. It must have taken decades to carve out this chamber. It isn't a natural cave." Giovanni ran his hands along the smooth, glassy wall. Tam started to speak again, but Giovanni stopped him with an upraised hand. He pointed his flashlight overhead where bits of glittering quartz dotted the dome ceiling. A rainbow exploded from the crystals above as he shifted his light.

"My God."

A curled snake wound in and out of the crystals, strange icons and symbols which looked like crude hieroglyphics of ancient constellations and zodiac symbols. Squinting, he looked at the symbol in the middle of the ceiling. A man with shoulders and arms extended to grasp the head and tail of the snake.

"Ophiuchus!" Giovanni whispered.

"I don't understand."

"They must have been sacrificing to the serpent depicted in the Ophiuchus constellation." Giovanni shined his light on the altar.

"Why?"

"It represents the secret to immortality. Biblical text and other ancient texts tell us that before the flood of Noah, or the deluge, there were giants in the land. The *Book of Enoch* calls them the wicked fallen angels or Watchers who had transgressed God's law. Nephilwere the offspring of angels and human women."

"What does that have to do with the constellation?"

"They were fallen angels, previously from a star or planet in a particular constellation, possibly Ophiuchus. They had incredible knowledge and were immortal creatures. Confined to earth, the fallen rebellion displeased God, and he destroyed them with a flood."

"The hieroglyphics are pre-flood?"

"Right. The story is that the *Ben Eloha* or 'sons of God' numbered several hundred, and they descended to earth on Mt

Hermon in what we know as modern-day Syria. These Ben Elohim or 'fallen angels' were also known as the Watchers, the Grigori, and Irin. In Jewish mythology and the esoteric Luciferian tradition, they were originally a superior order of angels who dwelt in the highest heaven with God."

"Are you saying you believe the Watchers were here in this cave making sacrifices at one time?" Tam kept his voice low.

"I'm not so sure they were Watchers, but possibly the offspring of the Watchers. We call them Nephilim. Part human and part angel. Gigantic."

"Why here?"

"I'm not sure why here, but I do know that Enoch was the first among men to learn writing and knowledge of the signs in the heavens, the zodiac signs according to their months. The indication is that Enoch received information from extraterrestrial sources, the Watchers." He thought for a moment. "There must be a sacrificial graveyard nearby."

"Graveyard?" Tam looked confused.

Giovanni couldn't escape the feeling that more danger lay ahead. "Let's get back to the Manor. Umberto will be looking for us. We need to let him know someone is down here."

Tam sighed with shaky relief.

With a satisfied grin, Giovanni wiped the dirt and sweat from his damp forehead. "We'll come back more prepared next time. Do me a favor and go ahead of me, I'm going to take it slow. Find Umberto.

Tam shook his head. "I can't leave you here."

"Go. The men might come back. I'm a tired old man. Get Umberto."

Tam looked at him a moment, then grasped his shoulder. "Stay low while I find him."

Chapter Sixty Four

Giovanni followed the sounds and made his way toward the chamber, where he heard voices. Father Murphy, Brian, and Jackson stared at the enormous skeletons crushed between the layers of rock.

"Hello," he called, seeing Father Murphy in his robes.

"Giovanni? Is that you?"

"Buonasera, Father Murphy." Relief flooded his mind.

He entered the room and made his way toward the group.

"I knew there was a graveyard somewhere nearby," Giovanni said. Kaira wondered what he meant.

Jonathan turned to examine the skull. "I've never seen anything like it. But, when we get back, you can help us figure out where they came from." He smiled at Giovanni. "I'm Jonathan, by the way, and this is my brother Brian and Kaira Munroe. It seems you know Father Murphy. That's Jackson over there gawking at the skeletons.

"You won't find much information." Father Murphy said. All eyes were on him. "This is evidence of a fallen race of beings, possibly from another world. It is forbidden knowledge, and Victoria was the guard of the ancient sacrificial tomb."

"A secret sect called the Order of the Serpent was assigned to guard the megalithic ruins," Jackson said. Father Murphy gazed at Jackson, a quizzical look on his face.

"Was Victoria part of the Order of the Serpent?" Kaira asked, glancing at Father Murphy.

"No. It isn't possible. She wanted to reveal the truth." He answered.

"Look at the signs of the zodiac on the coffin lid." Kaira pointed in the dark. "They are the ancient Hebrew signs and names of certain stars in the constellation Ophiuchus." The group stepped closer to the coffin and shined the flashlight on the lid.

Jackson stood next to the wall and examined the skull.

"It seems my grandmother had plans to reveal that a planet would be passing close to the earth, and extraterrestrial beings or angels would visit from the planet. Now I understand why she believed it."

Jonathan nodded, feeling the first faint wisps of a new reality. Thus far, Victoria had proven herself a meticulous guard of antediluvian proof.

They were all gathered around the coffin staring at the lid when Jonathan realized Jackson wasn't there. He turned to see Jackson touch the skull with his hands. Odd. His face was calm but rueful.

He reached to his side and pulled out his firearm. "My friends." He said. "You've made it difficult to keep you out of harm's way. Your tenacity has finally brought us to this place."

He saw the expression of shock on Jonathan's face and was hopeful he'd understand the events that had guided them to this intersection.

"I have so much to tell you. We should make our way to the Manor. I'm sure Umberto would want to hear this too."

Kaira stood with her mouth open. Something in Father Murphy's eyes gave her courage. She should have trusted his loyalty, he had cared for her grandmother for so many years.

"Jackson?" Jonathan finally managed. "What the hell are you doing?"

Jonathan and Kaira couldn't seem to tear their stunned gaze from Jackson. Brian and Father Murphy didn't seem fazed a bit.

"I don't want to harm you. I want you to know I am not a killer. However, I have made a vow to the Order of the Serpent, and in my conscience, I cannot allow you to betray the Order." He looked at Father Murphy.

"When you walked into my office today, I hoped it wouldn't come to this. But all the loose ends are here together in one place. You discovered the terrible truth, and it is my job that the truth is never revealed to the world. Mass chaos…think of it."

Kaira drew her breath to protest, and Jonathan put his arm around her. She stopped.

"The Order of the Serpent is given a sacred charge to communicate with the fallen ones. The truth will be released when they arrive. For centuries, the Order has protected the secrets until

Victoria spoke with Alex and told him what was hidden beneath the winery."

"Alex, a member of the Order of the Serpents?" Father Murphy stated more than asked.

"He and Victoria had to be contained. But, we learned Alex had changed his mind, and he had to be contained as well."

"You murdered my grandmother?" Kaira declared her angry eyes drilled through Jackson.

"Your grandmother and Alex were traitors to a greater good, and now you are following in their footsteps."

Jonathan felt a fury rising deep within. Jackson's voice was arrogant and relentless.

"Father Murphy, you are sold out to the Abbey. It is obvious you do not understand the power you could have."

"I am sold out to God, not the church, and it is in his power I stand." Father Murphy's voice was persuasive. "You will fail."

Jackson laughed coldly. "Father, the church is riddled with the sins of the Vatican and secret societies."

"Do not make that accusation of all churches. Yes, some are corrupt, and you are the perfect example. A corrupt police chief does not mean the rest of the officers are corrupt. The same is true for the church."

Kaira was stunned and proud of Father Murphy.

"Here is the important thing for you to grasp," Jackson responded. "we will all meet in the winery until Umberto arrives. Then you will all be trapped in a fire." He paused as if to punctuate his next point. "The new millennium has arrived. Most of humanity will remain ignorant."

Jonathan and Brian glanced at each other. Only one thing mattered. Getting everyone out alive, especially Kaira. The brothers no longer felt guilt and anger at their strained relationship. Their rage had transferred to Jackson.

Jackson pulled Kaira from Jonathan's embrace and held the gun to her back. "Jonathan, Brian, get in front of Kaira." Father Murphy took Giovanni's elbow, and they stepped in behind the brother's, but Father Murphy kept his eyes alert.

Jackson's tone was smug as he continued to speak. "I knew Victoria was holding valuable information, yet I wasn't sure where or how to find it. But, with the arrival of Giovanni, I was sure you would all end up here at Meadow Manor. Father Murphy, you delivered evidence right into my hands, and I thank you."

With Kaira at gunpoint, Jonathan feared that revealing the celestial timepiece would be his only remaining hope for bartering. Forcing his mind to the task, he moved slowly up the passage with Brian behind. Without a sound, he reached into his coat pocket and wrapped his fingers around the round metal base, which held the crystal.

Back inside Victoria's apartment, Jackson demanded they all sit in the living area to wait for Umberto.

"I have the one thing the Order is clambering for." Said Jonathan allowing a knowing smile to cross his lips. He could see the dark resolve on Jackson's face and knew the moment was upon them. Once Jonathan revealed the celestial map, and Umberto showed up, Jackson would kill them. Now, waiting with the others like pawns, Jonathan pulled the crystal from his pocket.

Slowly he placed the crystal inside the round metal base and shined his flashlight through the bottom opening. Immediately the 3D image filled the room in stark detail, causing Jackson to catch his breath.

Jonathan gazed at Jackson's gun, which was now aimed directly at him instead of Kaira.

"A celestial map." Father Murphy exclaimed. Even in the severity of the moment, Brian had to smile.

"It's so much more than that." Eyes turned to Brian though Jackson kept the gun steady on Jonathan. Brian continued.

"It's the exact location in the stars where the planet will return. It was the exact alignment of more than 12,000 years ago when the planet Wormwood passed."

"Or Planet X, depending on whether you work for NASA, Wormwood, if you are a priest," Giovanni spoke excitedly. "Yes, this is what the stars would have looked like then. It is the constellation of Ophiuchus, and it shows the exact planetary alignment where the planet will once again be seen in the near future."

Jackson looked frustrated that he hadn't known about the celestial clock. Jonathan bent down as if to place the crystal and base on the floor. He caught Brian's eye and gave him a look, the kind that only one brother can give to another. As Jonathan's hand lowered, he suddenly sprung his arm up, launching the crystal and base behind Jackson.

In a split second, Jackson attempted to keep his eye on Jonathan and the crystal flying across the room. All his plans were crumbling. His gun exploded, just missing Jonathan by a fraction. Jackson heaved himself toward the object, stretching to grasp the tiny crystal. Brian was across the floor swift as a cat and flung himself at Jackson. The gun fired again, and Brian slumped to the floor.

"No!" Kaira screamed.

Jonathan propelled forward now with animal rage glaring from his face. Time seemed to freeze. Jackson backed toward the crystal, which had scattered in tiny chunks across the floor. The Order would be angry.

Panic gripped him. He didn't intend to kill Brian.

"He shouldn't have lunged at me," Jackson shouted. He was shaking uncontrollably. Jonathan rolled his brother over and checked his pulse.

In all the commotion, Father Murphy had silently made his way across the room toward Jackson. Giovanni and Kaira sat on the couch, breathless, waiting.

"Jonathan," Jackson stammered. "You have another map. Where is it?"

"No. I don't. There's nothing else. You cannot speak of the bones, as you said yourself. The Order will be furious when they realize the only star map they need so desperately is gone, crushed into tiny shards.

The sound of footsteps thundered outside the Apartment, and Jackson raised his gun once again. Father Murphy, now right beside Jackson, caught his arm as he attempted to aim at Jonathan and shoved it down hard. He maneuvered behind Jackson and pushed his pistol hard into Jackson's back and with his other arm, gripped him around the neck. Caught off guard, Jackson hadn't expected a priest to be carrying a firearm.

"Drop your gun. I'll shoot or break your neck. Whichever you prefer." Father Murphy said in a deadly tone. Jackson hesitated. "I said, drop it. Before I was a priest, I was in the military. Don't make the mistake of thinking I don't know how to use a gun."

The door burst open, and Umberto entered his eyes, scanning the group finding his target – Jackson Bennett. Exhaling, he turned to Kaira.

"Are you okay?" Two police officers entered on Umberto's heels and behind them a man in a red Tam cap.

"What are you doing?" Jackson screamed as one of his officers placed him in handcuffs. Umberto called for an ambulance and watched as the officers took Jackson out to his car and put him in the backseat.

Chapter Sixty Five

One Month Later

The chess piece slipped through his fingers, smooth from use. Giovanni saw him look up as he approached across the impeccably manicured garden.

"Giovanni, what a nice surprise."

"As if you would have scheduled a meeting."

Giovanni sat as the maid brought coffee for Antonio and Giovanni. As soon as the maid left, Antonio said, "Why did you do this? Destroy the relic?"

He continued to finger the chess piece in his hand.

"I will finish debriefing today with the Archbishop," Giovanni said. "He's going to want answers."

Antonio looked at Giovanni. "He already has answers."

"Excuse me?"

Antonio brought the coffee to his lips. "It was a simple choice. Carmelo has been disposed of, and the reputation of the Vatican spared."

It was a bright morning, the sky blue and cloudless. Giovanni wiped a bead of sweat from his lip. "What happened at the excavation after we left? Tell me now." He demanded.

Antonio clicked the chess piece against the cool marble board. When their eyes met, Giovanni saw the too familiar look that had always concerned him.

"Do you really want to know, Giovanni? Aren't some things better left buried? Literally?"

"Tell me."

The sun glinted off Antonio's smooth, greased hair. "Giovanni, you aren't the only one I was looking after all these years and not for the reasons you think."

"What are you saying?"

"I am Guido's lost brother." His voice was quiet. "It was difficult in the beginning. Physically at least. But, in time, I learned to obey and realized if I were to gain any freedom, it would be through loyalty and obedience. Of course, there is no proof, no paperwork."

Giovanni sat quietly, digesting the information. "You are playing both sides." He murmured.

"Secrecy is protection Giovanni, and you need to get used to that. Per il tuo bene."

Giovanni nodded. "In time, I may agree."

Chapter Sixty Six

The Westonville News had its offices in a small brick building across the square from the Local Steam Espresso and Deli. Brian sat at the front window, drinking coffee and reading the real estate section littered with photographs and descriptions of properties.

Under one headline "Great Investment," he saw what could only be the old Nike missile site up on Sugar Bush mountain behind the Abbey.

"$130,000 steals it," he read. *"Built in the '40s and abandoned since 1974, one broken and slanting shed, a bunker with oil heat. A piece of history on twenty acres."*

Brian smiled as he remembered the times he and Jonathan had explored the land 20 years ago. There was no reason to stay now, but something had changed inside Brian. He was ready to settle down. Maybe he'd have a family. Or not.

The thought of owning the old military missile site where he and his brother had played filled him with fond memories and nostalgia. He glanced out the window toward the cliff that held the Abbey. Who knew what lay beneath the old missile site?

He sipped the last of his coffee and stepped outside, slowly walking down the sidewalk to his car.

***

Kaira stuffed her hands in the pockets of her jacket and stood on the terrace overlooking the bare vines in the vineyard. The sun was setting, and she thought of her grandmother, who had been nearby and yet so far away for so many years. Kaira hoped she could forgive herself for not coming to her sooner.

She turned and started walking toward the winery wanting to sit in the cozy apartment Victoria had so generously left her.

The new President of the Westonville Historical Society had been doing a marvelous job, and Kaira was grateful. She had plenty to think about with the vineyard. Umberto was getting on in years, and she had much to learn.

Police Chief Jackson found a job in a new town. Somehow, he had managed to come out of the ordeal unscathed. Kaira thought she knew why. She was glad he no longer lived in Westonville.

Hard to cope with the fact that he fooled them all so thoroughly, she knew Jackson could have destroyed more lives if it wasn't for his own family and the threat of loss.

A light dusting of snow covered the ground. Kaira stepped through the winery door and made her way to the apartment. She still hadn't told him of her feelings, but they were entering new territory now. She was the heiress to much more than she had ever imagined. Alessandro's retreat, the yacht, and Meadow Manor. She wanted to navigate carefully. Her feelings for Jonathan went much deeper than she'd ever imagined possible.

Knowing he was ready to die for her was sobering. His passion for Kaira was bold, bright, and strong. She walked toward the apartment door. He was the only other one with a key.

She felt Jonathan's presence before she saw him as she entered the apartment, he grabbed her and twirled her around.

"We need to talk." His eyes crinkled at the edges. "There's something I need to tell you." He squeezed his eyes shut and pulled her close.

She gave a soft laugh and clung to him.

He drew back and looked her in the eye. "I have to leave in a few days. SSRL needs my help in the Caribbean."

Kaira touched his face. "First, we have to do something with those confounded bones in the basement."

He laughed. "The bones are undoubtedly creepy. However, I foresee a cruise in our future."

"Will the Ophiuchus do for you?" Kaira asked.

Jonathan kissed her.

"Absolutely. Your wealth does not threaten me."

She turned to the open bookshelf. "The Westonville Historical Society is still cataloging evidence and DNA. Notebooks that belonged to Victoria and Alex. But, they promised they'd finish soon, and we can lock it up for a very long time."

She wanted to read the journals and documents, but it wasn't possible until professionals had processed them.

Jonathan slid his arms around her, and she leaned back against him. Butterflies fluttered inside her. She smiled as a tear slipped from the corner of her eye.

"Just keep holding me, Jonathan." She whispered. He squeezed her tight, and his warm strength engulfed her. "I promise, I'll never let go, Kaira. Never."

***

"Much has happened in the past few days." Father Murphy said, standing in the dining area, speaking to a small crowd. Kaira and Jonathan were planning to remodel the glass atrium and banquet hall, turning it into a beautiful restaurant serving the best of Italian wine and food.

"We've lost some very great friends and comrades." He raised his glass in a toast. "To Victoria Munroe and her passion for preserving history." He glanced at Jonathan.

"Just as we've lost, we have also gained wonderful family and friends. Let's tip our glasses to the new owner of Meadow Manor and winery, Kaira Munroe. And, to my brother Brian Bell, the head chef."Jonathan said, smiling at his brother.

Brian looked different, clean-shaven, handsome. He favored his brother more than Kaira had realized. He bowed and waved to the crowd, obviously enjoying the moment.

Father Murphy stood next to an older man with gray hair and placed his hand on Giovanni's shoulder. "Last, we want to tell you about our good friend Giovanni. He will be a wonderful advisor in the remodeling process, helping us build a terrific menu. Giovanni's home is in Albano Laziale, Italy, close to Rome. He is an archeologist and a very close friend of the family. He will be guiding our Westonville Historical Society as we open a museum here at the Manor."

Giovanni bowed.

"We will open the museum this summer and plan to have a display with all the bones and treasures found along the beaches in Westonville. Hopefully, our legends now have a home." Jonathan said. "And there's one last thing…SSRL discovered a shipwreck in the Caribbean. We aren't sure what we'll be bringing up from the wreck, but we do know it belonged to Captain Benjamin Munroe."

"Here, here." Said one of the guests. He stood and raised his glass. "To the extraordinary future of Westonville."

***

The phone rang. Kaira picked up her cell phone, Jonathan, at her side. It was Father Murphy.

"There's something we must discuss. Giovanni gave me his original celestial precession mechanism, a clock. It is functioning. I think you'll want to see this."

Visit

Melissa Saulnier

At

www.justwritebusypen.com

Religion
Vatican Observatory on Mt. Graham
VOVATT.ORG
Vaticanobservatory.com

https://www.youtube.com/watch?v=FLW80SUBz-s
Jesuit Priest and Astronomer, Guy Consolmagno

http://khouse.org/articles/2013/1126
Exo-Vaticana The Vatican's Savior? By Thomas Horn

Mt. Graham and the L.U.C.I.F.E.R. Project
https://youtu.be/WFXhjS6_yFg
by Tom Horn and Cris Putnam

Megalithic
Hugh Newman
https://youtu.be/F61QHCIbiys
The Megalithic Giants – The Lost History of a Forgotten Race

Richard Cassaro
https://RichardCassaro.com/hidden-italy

Science
Crystals
Data Saved in Quartz Glass Might Last 300 Million Years
http://money.cnn.com/2016/02/17/technology/5d-data-storage-memory-crystals/index.html

Enormous crystal found in caves
https://news.nationalgeographic.com/2017/02/crystal-caves-mine-microbes-mexico-boston-aaas-aliens-science/

Made in the USA
Monee, IL
02 September 2021